QUEEN
OF CLOUDS

Also by Neil Williamson :

The Moon King (2014)
Secret Language (2016)
The Memoirist (2017)

QUEEN
OF CLOUDS

Neil Williamson

NewCon Press
England

First published in April 2022 by NewCon Press,
41 Wheatsheaf Road, Alconbury Weston, Cambs, PE28 4LF

NCP269 (limited edition hardback)
NCP270 (softback)

10 9 8 7 6 5 4 3 2 1

ISBN:

978-1-914953-10-1 (hardback)
978-1-914953-11-8 (softback)

Cover art by Reggie Oliver

Text edited by Ian Whates
Cover layout and interior typesetting by Ian Whates

ONE

Billy Braid reclined on the side porch, waiting for the five o'clock rain. It had been a sticky day and the residual heat lingered along with a familiar pang of shirker's guilt. But he was used enough to that. Billy sat with his shirt unbuttoned, impatient for the cleansing downpour, but the sky, deepening now with the onset of evening, remained empty. The rain was late again.

He spotted it at last to the North West, the supposedly punctual cloud array appearing like a cluster of sudden doves. It would take a full twenty minutes for those scuds to cross the intervening distance, growing fat on the moisture they sucked from the humid air as they traversed the fields, the wide Molde river, the forest itself. Billy reached around to pluck the gluey cotton from between his shoulders, spat on the ground and swore silently in the general direction of Karpentine. The distant city, identifiable by the circle of blue sky close to the horizon no matter the weather anywhere else, was a ripe target for curses for all occasions. The citizens there didn't have to wait for *their* rain, conveniently delivered at night while they slept, though it be bought and paid for by the same credits and kudos. They'd be quick enough to complain if the farmers of the valley were late delivering the harvest or the mountain woodsmen the lumber.

Billy sloshed the dregs of his beer around the bottle. After spending the day sawing and dressing pine lumber he'd figured he deserved a treat, but he'd idled so long that the beer was warm. The shirker's guilt itched. There remained chores to be done, but he'd get to them after his beer, after the rain. Soon. Sure, he could have taken a shower in the house. It would only have taken ten minutes of brisk effort to prime the pump, but this had become a matter of principle now.

He sipped from his bottle and stared off into the forest fringe, listening to the settling of the trees, the hollow coughing of birds. And, closer, the inexorable sloughing of plane and glasspaper from the workshop underpinned by Kim's semi-sung litanical murmurings. The end of summer was usually a good time of year for Billy because it was traditionally when many of the groves matured and the master shut himself away in the smaller workshop, bringing one sylvan at a time into

5

being. With the old man in there for weeks at a time Billy had more jobs to do, but at least he was free of the incessant carping when he didn't jump immediately to do them. Ah, that was unfair. The old man was decent enough, but the concept of taking a breather had become as distant to him as Karpentine was. The Law Of Man might commend everyone to daily labour, but there was such a thing as overdoing it. Billy often wondered whether everyone born in the city had such a thorn up their arse, or whether that trait belonged to Kim alone.

In truth, Billy admired his master's industry when the wood called, but a sylvan brought no money in – and this summer there had been an unprecedented number of them. Being left to his own devices was one thing, finding himself the household's sole source of income quite another. They'd have to have words. But... later.

Billy put his feet up and closed his eyes. Then he opened them again because a whisper of wind in leaves had echoed in his mind. The words he heard in it were: *Someone comes.*

Billy jumped up and turned and found himself looking into Chop's deeply grained face. The sun lent a golden glow to the old wood, a warm shine along the almond curve of the chin, a gentle lustre to the stream-shaped pebble eyes.

Billy groaned. "Blind me and cripple me, who?"

The mental impressions that Billy understood as the sylvan's voice stirred again. *A stranger. On the village road.*

"All right. I'll go down there now."

Better hurry.

Billy went down the flint path that connected the house to the road. When he reached the treeline, he looked back. Chop had taken his position on the porch bench, long timbered limbs folded up, head bowed. Billy might have viewed the exchange as a ruse, but sylvans didn't shirk. It wasn't in their nature.

When Billy reached the overgrown road he held his breath and listened. The birds had fallen silent, so it was easy to pick out the throaty rumble of something mechanical. The sound grew steadily louder then subsided. The vehicle must have stopped at the forest gate. He trotted down the weed-strewn track, relieved that the machine would not be bringing its cacophony any closer to disturbing the master's peace. Under his breath, he cursed again. Visitors from the villages were rare, but even those who politely announced themselves incurred the old man's ire if they disturbed him when he was with the wood. And Billy caught it double for failing to intercept them.

At the ridge, Billy looked down to where the road was collared by the forest and barred by the timber gate. Behind the gate sat some kind of a powered wagon. It wasn't dissimilar to the ones the foresters used to transport lumber to the wood mills, but this was no hard working leviathan built for strength and practicality. This was a gleaming piece of polished showoffery. It had six rubber-rimmed wheels, silver-bright trim and an open cabin, as well fitted out as any pleasure boat that ever tied up at Denit's Jetty. The wood was varnished a deep gold, the lines detailed in red paint. It all looked very impressive, but even out here they were not so far removed from civilised society to be taken in by appearances. This vehicle was a perfect example of what Kim called *a platform for conspicuous achievement.*

Billy's suspicion was confirmed on spotting the vehicle's owner, a red-faced man in an embroidered emerald coat wrestling with the gate's lock.

"Don't force it," Billy scolded the idiot as he trotted down the remaining stretch of road.

The stranger dropped the convoluted arrangement of hardened teak and the length of chain that bound the post and gate chattered guiltily. "Oh, I wasn't…"

"It only gets tighter if you force it," Billy said. "And it'll be the devil to undo next time we want to open the gate."

"Very well." The man removed his little leather hat to mop his brow with a lime coloured handkerchief, which he then used to dab at the most elaborate moustache Billy had ever seen. It began beneath the florid nose, a ginger thicket that blossomed to a tawny lustre as it spread along the upper lip before curling up into waxed dagger points.

The vehicle had been a strong indication, but the moustache clinched it. This oaf was from Karpentine. The fellow smiled. A wink of ivory below the golden moustache. "Perhaps you could see your way clear, sir, to unlocking –"

Billy interrupted him. "What do you want? We don't often get visitors from the city."

To his surprise the man laughed. "Well, if you'll forgive me for saying so, Master Kim, you aren't easy to find." He extended a petal-pink hand, its fingers encrusted with rings. If he observed how rough Billy's own bark-brown skin was when they shook hands, his smile didn't falter.

7

Billy relaxed. If he'd come all this way without knowing who he was coming to see, the man really was an idiot. "The master can't be disturbed," he said. "Do you want to leave a message?"

Now the smile did waver. Wrinkles creased the ruddy brow. A sigh hissed through the teeth like steam. "Well, now that's really too bad," the visitor said. "And after I came all the way here especially to see him. Say…" He brightened once more. "Do you like my charabanc?"

Billy glanced at the contraption. "I suppose it's impressive enough."

"Impressive, he says." A belly laugh. "Don't you know she won the red rosette at the Constructors' Fair? All made by my own fair hand, you know. How's that for an achievement?"

Billy had never heard of the Constructors' Fair, but he had to concede that the vehicle was a decent piece of craftsmanship. He kept to himself his dubiety about whether this buffoon possessed the necessary skills to have built it.

"Now, you mentioned a message." The visitor stroked his chin. "Well, I understand that Master Kim is a busy man, but as it happens I have exactly such a message on my person. You couldn't see your way clear to running up there with it right now could you? And tell him that Bullivant Smout awaits his answer… Oh, that's me by the way," he grinned. "Bullivant Smout, on behalf of the Family Crane of Karpentine. But you can call me Bully, er…?"

The pause in the man's babble took Billy by surprise and the arch of an eyebrow prompted a reluctant response. "Billy."

"Ha! Billy! Good to meet you." Smout reached across the gate again and clapped Billy on the shoulder. "Bully and Billy. Well, we're quite a pair are we not?"

There was probably no person in the valleys Billy might be less of a pair with, but saying so would only encourage this man to keep talking. He'd listened to enough of this nonsense. "I really can't," he repeated. "Now, if you don't mind –"

The visitor looked crestfallen but ignored Billy's attempt to end the conversation. "I know, son," he said in a low voice. "You don't want to fail in your duty. It's just… Well, it's more than *my* job's worth to return to the city without having achieved my objective. I'm sure you understand."

Somehow, a sheaf of crisp credits had appeared in Bullivant Smout's hand. It took Billy a moment to understand that this money was being offered to him. And that gave him pause to genuinely consider whether

8

it would be worth suffering the master's ire for that kind of money... but where might he spend it? There was nothing to buy in the villages that would cost so much, with the possible exception of an entire night with the energetic Michael, or the Levitt sisters, or even Miss Arlene herself, at the Well Earned Repose, and even then he'd be walking around bagged down by pockets full of brass kudos for weeks.

Still, it was surprisingly tempting.

"How much..." he began, but Smout's attention had shifted. The Karpentiner's eyes widened, his moustache twitched, and the money vanished as quickly as it had appeared.

Following his gaze, Billy saw Chop silhouetted on the ridge. The sylvan was coming this way, swinging a scythe over the surface of the road, tufts of grass flying with each stroke.

"What by the governor's lamp is that?"

"It's Chop, our sylvan." Billy raised his voice, annoyed. "It's *helping* me with the chores." If Chop heard, it gave no sign but continued down the track towards them. Swinging and cutting.

Smout shook his head in amazement. "What an *achievement*. Such balance, such grace... It does know how to stop, doesn't it?"

The Karpentiner had a point. As Chop strode towards them, the movements of the scythe became more erratic. Billy felt something pressed into his hand. Disappointingly, not a fistful of credits but a cream-coloured envelope. Smout was already back in his wagon and had begun manoeuvring the vehicle into a turn. "Make sure your master reads that letter," he called over his shoulder as he rumbled away.

Chop stopped at the gate. Its laughter, a playful rattle of twigs in Billy's mind, was not a thing Billy often heard. Then again, watching Bullivant Smout's fancy wagon jouncing down the uneven forest road was pretty funny. Laughing too, he put his hand on the sylvan's shoulder... and that punctured the mood. The wood was almost as weathered as the old porch bench. That crack below the neck joint was widening, he was sure, and there were a couple of twigs of stubborn new growth too. Billy made a promise to spend some time with Chop soon, prune it off, sand down its cankers, oil its grain. The master would chide him, tell him that he was only delaying the inevitable, that Nature would have her way in the end, but what mattered to Billy was that Chop did not repeat the master's arguments.

"You didn't have to do that," he told the sylvan.

Road needed clearing, came the reply. *And by doing it badly Kim will give credit to you.*

"I didn't mean that," Billy said. "I was talking about the Karpentiner."

We both know the rules about visitors.

Billy grinned, and then looked at the wax-sealed envelope he still held in his hand. The paper was silk-smooth, the master's name printed on it in a functional hand. There was no more to it than that, but Billy was suddenly consumed with curiosity as to what lay inside. "What do you reckon this is all about? Is trouble coming?"

Chop did not look at the envelope. *Only land knows,* it said. *Land and sky. They know all that is to be known.*

As Chop wandered off about its business, Billy stuffed the envelope into his pocket and climbed back up to the house. By the time he got there, true evening had closed in, stealthily like a conjuror's trick; the darkening of the blue above, the caramelised layer above the treeline like cooling bottle glass. After his encounter with Bullivant Smout, the faint but uninterrupted sounds of Kim in his workshop were reassuring and Billy allowed himself to relax. His thoughts turned to getting the dinner on, making sure the old man had something waiting for him on the stove at whatever hour the work released him.

Mounting the porch, however, he was puzzled to find the cabin door ajar. Lamplight from inside fanned the decking, glittered off the swinging wind chimes and edged the barrel of tools awaiting sharpening. Billy hadn't left the door open, Kim was still working, Chop had gone off in another direction and, even if Smout had halted his pathetic retreat and come back on foot, he could not have passed Billy on the path unnoticed. That meant they had another visitor. An accomplice, perhaps?

Billy eased a hoe from the barrel and peered into the house. Everything was as he'd left it. The lamp buzzed as its cranked power dwindled. The afternoon's laundry still lay heaped on the dayroom table. The doors to the kitchen and the bedrooms were firmly closed. The only difference was the marks on the floor, a trail of muddy deltas that led into the unlit rear of the house. He heard a noise – a stumbling, knocking sound, followed by something scoring against wood – and let out the breath he'd been holding. No intruder then, just some mooching animal. Not a fox after the chickens, though, the prints were wrong and a fox would never have come inside the house. More likely the bloody goat had got out again. He sighed and hoisted his hoe anyway, holding it out in front of him as he crept down the rear passage. It was dark, but he caught the yard door swinging shut before it latched and saw that he'd been half-right. The intruder was a buck deer, although with that silky black hide scored with those fine white stripes, like none he'd ever encountered before. The creature was beautiful, but there was something subtly wrong about it. It was in the exact symmetry of its facial flashes, the perfection of its white antlers mirrored down to the last nub and hook. It was in the soft black eyes when it turned its head and stared back at him.

Transfixed, Billy felt like he was being appraised.

The spell was only broken by a clatter from inside the workshop. The deer pricked, rolled its eyes and then bolted. The last Billy saw of it was a moon-white scut vanishing into the tree shadow.

Billy took Smout's envelope out his pocket and stood before the workshop door, listening. The tone of the master's efforts had changed. That circular swoosh of the sandpaper, that intoned breath of song: those were the sounds of finishing. Soon a new sylvan would emerge and go out into the world. This was always a cause for celebration, but there had been so many recently. The old man was wearing himself out. Billy could hear it in the crack of his voice on the long, low notes.

Billy turned the envelope over in his hands. There was only master's name, precisely lettered in blue-black ink. Nevertheless it conveyed importance. He hesitated, torn between disturbing the master or slitting the thing open himself, but he managed to rein in his curiosity. Returning to the house, he placed the envelope on the dayroom shelf and had the soup on the stove when the first drops of rain finally drummed on the roof.

TWO

In the morning, Billy tied a set of chairs onto the cart for taking down to the village later. He'd stained and varnished the furniture the day before, and hoped the newlyweds who had ordered them would be too blinded by love to notice the blobs and drips. In the kitchen he found a dirty dinner plate alongside a more recently used porridge bowl. He washed both, relieved at least that Kim was pausing to eat. Billy had stayed up with another unearned beer intending to tell the old man about both the envelope and the antelope, but had been asleep before he heard the master come in. Now, in the daylight, the visitations seemed more trivial than they had the night before. They could wait, as everything had to when the wood called.

He grabbed his things and headed down to the forest. The trees grew tight there, the trunks as close in places as stockade posts, but Billy slipped easily between them, enjoying the world under the canopy of the great trees: the softening of the earth beneath his boots, the diffusion of the light, the muting of sound. As a child he had meandered tirelessly among the lower reaches close to the village. His frustrated parents hadn't been able to keep him in the house. When he neglected his chores on the farm or skipped the classes his mother taught in the village school they had always known where to find him. Many had been the hours of punishment labour under his father's despairing eye. Countless, the readings of edifying passages from the Book of the Law with his furiously disappointed ma. He'd known it was wrong and felt guilty, but hadn't been able to help himself. The draw of the secretive, beautiful world beneath the trees had been too great. Nowhere else had he felt like he could be himself.

When the reclusive Benoit Kim had come down off the mountain to find an apprentice, the solution had suited everyone.

As a child, his arboreal adventures had felt illicit; and even now, though he had every right to stride between these craggy boles, he retained a sliver of that boyhood thrill. He crossed a rocky cascade, spume glittering like silica, and it was only a few minutes more until the pines gave way to a clearing. Of all his chores, Kim never needed to nag him into coming to the groves. This was the only work he had ever shown any natural aptitude for. He loved it here.

Billy squeezed his hand into the leather of his pruning glove as he circled the sylvan copse in the centre of the grove. He looked for indications of disease – leaf burn, frost cracks, fungal spores – and for general signs of divergence, overcrowding or bullying, but each of the young plants appeared in good health and more or less retained its intended proportion and placement in the grove. At second glance though, the ironwood in the centre of the group was perhaps getting too big for its boots, its boles reaching out towards the five other species that circled it. Its leaves were already close to touching those of the spindly silver birch that grew on its northern side and in a few weeks would be overhanging the black willow and the auric ash. Even the profuse copper beech and the bowlish canopy of the honey teak would be under threat. A little complementary shade was good, but you had to keep the ironwood in check. He'd need to bring the ladders down and nip it back. It was too much hassle to go home for them now, though. Tomorrow would be fine. He'd start early.

Billy entered the circle of trees, stepping carefully through the thicket of wirebush that caressed the trunks. For a minute he stood still, appreciating the atmosphere. The master had laboured this point during his apprenticeship and it had taken a long time to get the hang of it but, once he had, it turned out that he had a better sense for it even than Kim. There wasn't anything specific to look for, you just *knew* when a group of trees were at peace with each other and when there were troubles. Despite the ironwood's bullying, there was still harmony here.

The wirebush had become pretty unruly, though. The shrub trailed on the ground, thick like ivy with pearlescent leaves, but it had started curling a little too far up the trunks of the trees, caress verging on constriction. Billy *snicked* the thumb and index blades of his pruning glove as he bent to the task of cutting back the vine from the ash. The stem of the plant was tough, but a little effort made light work of it and soon the tree's lovely golden bark shone forth again. He tossed the extracted length of bush aside. It fell with a dry shiver. Involuntarily, Billy shivered too, and looked around as if expecting to see someone there, but there was no one.

Later, Billy pushed the teetering handcart down to the village of Sillip where the doctor and her new wife, as consumed as they might

13

otherwise have been with marital happiness, examined their purchases and missed none of the blemishes. They paid only two thirds of the agreed price and tipped him a solitary kudo. Billy spent most of the money on the provisions that they needed to supplement the milk, eggs and vegetables he and Kim provided for themselves.

Sitting on a doorstep in the village square to eat his meagre hunk of bread and cheese, he tried not to think of the sheaf of credits that had been offered to him the previous day. His and Kim's life wasn't defined by achievement. They had enough to live on, the privacy to do as they pleased, and the joy that was the company of sylvans. They needed nothing more.

It was rare to see sylvans in the villages, but there was one across the square right now helping unload hay bales from a wagon. The jowly farmer, with a deal of shouting and exaggerated mime, was trying to show it where to put the bales. The sylvan just got on with the job. Throughout this process, a small child with pigtails and a muddy face chattered happily to it. When the farmer wasn't looking the sylvan did a comic dance for the girl and she erupted into fits of giggles. Billy smiled to see that.

When he got home he toured the remaining groves. His route took him firstly up the mountain, then west across the slope and finally down again, following the gully lines that led back to the house. Mostly, things were in order. He pruned a little wirebush, made a note of cankers and spotted the early signs of sponge bracket among the groves along the sheltered south west ravine.

Instead of heading straight back to the house, he decided to check the trees on the northern side of the road too. That slope was more exposed, and the master rarely planted there though the pines grew well enough. Fungus was little respecter of species and Kim would want to know how far it had spread.

Billy encountered the first sylvan grove barely ten yards from the road, the second not long after that, and quickly counted a dozen collections of trees. When had he last checked over here? It couldn't have been *that* long could it? He sighed inwardly at the thought of so many. A new sylvan was always a happy thing, but the old man was going to kill himself at this rate. There were no signs, at least, of fungal growth on the trees. But that seemed hardly relevant next to the fact of their existence and the work they promised.

The last clearing he stumbled upon was of an altogether different sort. This was an old grove, choked with thorny, honey-scented gorse and waist-high emptyhead, the hollow seed cases *tocking* together as the grass stems swayed like springs. But the overgrowth didn't completely hide the hunched outlines of the sylvans who had come here to die. The shapes crouched among the grasses, heads bowed, could have been mistaken for rocks or logs. But if you looked closely they were recognisable, despite how weathered the wood had become, the once smooth grain split by the heat and the cold and the rain. Or that a face was obscured by a fur of emerald moss, an eczema of grey lichen, a caul of spiderweb. Or that rotted fingers had crumbled off. Or that the clenched wood had become a nest for beetles.

This grove was a private place. When Billy was young, the master had once discovered him in tears, trying to nurture the dead wood back to life and explained that it was nature's way to take the wood back into the land, but Billy hadn't wanted to hear it. From then on he had stayed clear of the old groves as much as he could. He still did. Now he thought about Chop again, the stiffness in the sylvan's joints, the condition of its wood.

Back at the house, he smelled cooking as soon as he mounted the porch. The newest crafting must be done then. Master Kim emerged from the kitchen wearing an apron and carrying two large bowls of mutton stew. He tossed Billy a glare, but his voice was gentle. "Wash your hands."

The old man looked... well, *old*. His arms and shoulders under his oily, sawdust-sprayed vest were pale and slack where once they had been nut-brown and tight as wire. Those shoulders trembled slightly as Kim returned to the kitchen for the greens. His hair, slicked into greasy tufts, resembled wild clouds more than ever. His eyes, rheumy holes in a face grizzled by salt and pepper stubble, made Billy think of knots in lichen-swept wood.

Billy went into the kitchen to scrub the forest grime from his hands. "You're working too hard."

The master, returning for the bread, blinked at him. "The wood is impatient," he said. "Come and eat."

Billy slipped into the chair that he'd sat in the first night he came to live with the old man and had used habitually ever since. The simple table had been old when he had first been apprenticed. The wood was smooth as marble, and Billy knew its faded grain as well as he knew the

15

eating irons, the chipped plates, his master's face. But there was something different tonight. At the centre of the table, in between the bread and the tureen of cabbage and peas, was an ugly vase. It was shaped like a lumpen onion and held briar blossoms.

Billy stared at the vase, fascinated and embarrassed in equal measure by the unexpected reminder of his earliest attempt at craftsmanship. "I thought that had been lost years ago."

The master grunted, "You wished!" and plugged a smile with a mouthful of bread and mutton.

"Perhaps I did." Billy was reminded again of the mess he'd made of the doctor's chairs.

They ate in silence, enjoying the herbed stew until their bowls were scraped clean. Billy cleared away the dishes and, when he returned, the master had produced a couple of brown beer bottles.

"It's finished?"

"Come out and see."

The master's workshop smelled of sweet oil and wood shavings. It had been swept clean and all the tools were back in their racks, allowing all of Billy's attention to fall upon the new creation.

Every sylvan was as different to the next as people were. No two the same, not even grove-siblings. Where Chop had always been square shouldered and thick in the thigh, and the one in the square earlier had been squat and trunkish, this new one was long-limbed and slender in a way that made Billy think of the village girls on laundry day. Its pose, seated on the floor with legs extended in front of it and supported by the struts of its arms, its delicate articulated fingers splayed as if there were grass and daises peeking up between them, reinforced this impression. Then again, the planes of the upper torso were sleek and angular, the head jutting like the proud lads who contested the athletics races at the fair.

"It's a beauty, this one," Billy said. The young woods that had grown together and had been pressed into its construction – ironwood for strength, willow for suppleness, birch for intelligence, beach for wisdom, ash for heart – had a greenish sheen of seasoning oil. The wirebush fibres that connected the joints glistened steel-bright. The stones of the sylvan's eyes were milky opalines that conveyed a wistfulness for all its leisurely dynamism.

"Ask it, then," Kim said.

On that first day, in the school yard, when the old carpenter had come offering work to the right lad or lass, he had held up a freshly cut elm branch and asked: *What would you do with this?*

Make a chair, make a broom, make a pencil.

Among all the stupid responses, Billy had been the only one to say: *plant it.* Kim had given the branch to him and told him to do so, to tend it and care for it however he saw fit and, when the old man had returned a month later, sure enough there had been a new twig sporting two vivid leaves. And that had been that. Even though it had quickly become obvious that Billy lacked artistic talent, his affinity with the wood had been deemed useful. Quite how deep that affinity was neither of them had known. It was two years before he admitted to the master that, while other people sometimes claimed to get faint impressions of the sylvans's intent, to him they had voices... and names. The old man had looked at him strangely and then nodded. *You're like a sylvan yourself, growing up with them,* he'd said. *The motes resonate in the earth and the air. Stands to reason that they should resonate in you too.* Even as a boy who paid little attention in school, Billy had known that motes were the inert particles left behind in the world after the Turners had turned away, but he preferred to think of the sylvans simply as a gift of nature. It made him feel less of a freak.

The young sylvan swivelled its head in their direction like a coquette to whom Billy had only now become of interest.

Billy cleared his throat. "Well, what do you call yourself?"

The voice came soft and sibilant like the breeze in the barley. It seemed to come from a long way away, but the meaning was clear. To Billy's mind it said: *Seldom.* The head swivelled from Billy to the old man as if looking for confirmation, then with more confidence it repeated itself.

"Its name is Seldom," Billy said.

The wooden creation drummed on the floorboards with long fingers. *Seldom,* it said again, this time excitedly. There was none of Chop's reserved grace here. Instead there was an endearing, puppy-like urgency.

The master shook his head. "If it says so," he said. The sylvan got to its feet with a clatter of limbs and the old man's eyes widened, having caught now a hint of its excitement. "Rest, rest," he told it. Then, as he locked the workshop and ushered Billy back towards the house, he said: "Didn't I say that wood was in a hurry?"

In the dayroom they sat down again and uncorked their refreshments. The beer was soft and gassy, and sweeter tonight because it was freely given, but Billy couldn't enjoy it. "You can't keep this up," he said.

The old man shushed him with a shake of the head. "Drink your beer, son." He tilted back his own bottle.

"I'm serious. Seldom's stain isn't dry yet and there are what, another four or five groves ready to fell?"

The eyes that gazed back at him were tired but defiant. "The wood calls, Billy. It is not to be denied."

"I know," Billy said. "But you've been working all summer and there are enough groves to keep you at it for months to come."

The master's face clouded, then he croaked a laugh. "How many times have I told you that the world is a poorer place without sylvans? It can never have enough." Then Kim's smile faded again as he produced Smout's envelope from his pocket. "So, tell me about our visitor."

The letter. In his concern for the old man, Billy had all but forgotten about that. He sighed, and recounted yesterday's odd meeting. He told it straight, or as straight as he could because in truth he didn't remember everything that gasbag, Smout, had said. While he told it, Kim fidgeted with the envelope, turning it in his hands, fingering the edges, the corners, the seal, and glancing at the writing as if the words were some great mystery, not merely his own name. He was burning to know, Billy realised, and the curiosity was contagious. He felt it too now, as he had when he'd held it himself last night. He rushed to finish his story.

When he was done, the old man snapped the seal, but still didn't open the envelope. "You're sure you don't remember which family this Smout claimed to represent?" His eyes were alight but his face was troubled.

Billy shook his head. "Does it make a difference?"

"It might do." The master licked his lips as if they had suddenly dried up, reluctant to speak what he was thinking. Something about the city, something about his past? Kim never talked about his past. *Nothing worth knowing,* he'd always said, and for the most part Billy had been happy to take him at his word. "The balance of influence in Karpentine is distributed, as it is everywhere else, according to achievement," Kim said now. "And highest achievement is awarded to those who provide most service. The Great Trades." Billy nodded. Everyone knew this. It was the reason you were paid in credits and kudos after all. "Well, in Karpentine the Trades have been monopolised for generations by certain bloodlines.

Families. For example, the Goughs who buy from the sawmills up here in the high valleys have been the lumber masters of Karpentine for generations. Of course, things can change. There are deals, alliances, usurpations, and the balance of power shifts a little this way and that but, for the most part, those in power don't easily relinquish it." Kim waved the letter at him. "Do you understand?"

Billy supposed he did. Up here people were, as commended by the Book of the Law, drawn to whatever work suited their own abilities. Skills were often hereditary, of course, passed on from parents to their children, but no one worried too much about keeping it in the family for the sake of it if the aptitude wasn't there. There was always something a pair of hands could do. What the old man was talking about was retaining renown, passing on not skills but achievement to those that had yet to earn it. From what little he knew of Karpentine, this news hardly surprised him. "Were you in one of these *families*?" he asked.

"Oh, all craftsmen are associated with the Artisans, and they've been under the Shankhills for as long as anyone can remember…" The old man's brow crinkled. "But I wasn't in the family itself. I was no one of importance. In fact, I was certain they'd forgotten all about me." He stared at the envelope again, musing to himself now, almost as if he'd forgotten Billy was there. "And this is not the Shankhills' handiwork. It's too plain." Humming nervously, he turned the letter over again. "It's not an official communication from the Judiciary either…" Then Kim looked up and Billy saw starkly the seesawing of curiosity and reluctance. "A letter like this? Delivered by a buffoon like that Smout fellow? Could be from anyone."

For the first time, Billy felt an itch of foreboding. When he was younger, he had been full of questions about what it was like living in Karpentine, and had been fobbed off with tall tales and admonishments to mind his own business, depending on the master's mood. Later Billy stopped asking because Kim had come to seem so much a part of the forest and the mountains that the idea of him ever having a life somewhere else seemed unreal. And now, the master's past was reaching out to him? What might it contain if Kim had hoped to have been forgotten? And if his second thought was to be glad the letter wasn't from the enforcers of the law? Curiosity be damned, they should burn Smout's letter and forget about it.

Before Billy could say this, however, Kim plucked the page from the envelope. "Well, whoever they are," the master said with surprising calm, "let's see what they have to say."

The old man read silently. As he did, his frown set, hardening into an unreadable expression that doubled Billy's unease. When Kim finished reading, he folded the page back into the envelope and immediately tossed both onto the fire. Billy gasped, but the master just sat watching the sealing wax bubble and the paper curl into embers, and while he did so he chugged his beer until his bottle was empty. Then he rose abruptly and disappeared into the kitchen, returning with two more beers. He placed one in front of Billy and popped open his own.

Billy ignored the gift. "Well?" he asked. "What did it say?"

"I always knew the day would come when the city caught up with me," the old man said after another long draught. "But even after all these years it seems too soon. And I never expected…" his gaze was drawn to the flames again, "…*that.*"

"What do you mean?" Billy asked, alarmed. He'd never seen the old man so melancholy.

"That man," Kim's voice ground like gravel. "That… egregious *Smout*. He's just the start of it." The bottle winked, the beer sloshed, gulped down greedily. The old man stifled a bout of wind. "That letter was an order for one sylvan, signed by Merit Crane, Chairman of the Guild of Constructors of the city of Karpentine. The *Constructors*, mind, not the Artisans."

"An order? We don't make sylvans to *order*," Billy snapped, dumbfounded and horrified equally. "What would they want a sylvan for in the city anyway? What work might there be for them there?"

"Hmm?" The master broke out of his introspection. "No work at all. I don't believe these people want a sylvan to tend their orchards for them. The Constructors' interest, I imagine, is in how our friends are made." The volume of his voice dipped. "The fee is twelve thousand credits."

"We can't agree to that." Billy said it even before he registered the sum. Selling a sylvan at any price was unthinkable.

"I know, Billy." The master's gaze drifted once again to the fire where a last scrap of paper blackened on the hearth. "But these city people have a way with pen and ink that is most persuasive. When I say they sent an *order*, that's what their request amounted to. And I have no choice but to obey it."

"But..." Billy didn't know what to say. Kim's will was stronger than the mountains. This feisty old man did not simply capitulate. Not to anyone.

"But nothing. It's settled. You will leave here at dawn and you will take young Seldom to Karpentine." The old man looked directly at him for the first time since he'd read the letter. His eyes glistened like marsh dew. "Don't look so miserable," he said. "It'll be an adventure for you."

Billy stared at Kim as if expecting his face to crack into his crooked old grin. For him to say *gotcha*, and laugh at his credulity. But it didn't come. The old man was absolutely serious. But he couldn't be. Billy couldn't go to the city. He had never been further than the villages down the valley. Eventually, he managed, "why me?"

"I'm old, Billy." And when Kim said it, again, he looked old. "And the sylvans need me here. What if I didn't come back?"

"I'm sorry," Billy said, shaking his head, unsure what he was even sorry for. For not turning Smout away or for his selfishness? *Why me?* It was the kind of thing a child would say.

"It's too late for apologies." The snap was an echo of the master he knew. "The matter is settled. Go and pack for the journey, and get a decent sleep. It's a long way to Karpentine."

Chop woke him, a brush of smooth wood against his cheek, a sound like breeze-stirred branches. Opening his eyes, Billy saw its face looking down at him, grey and ethereal in the dawn light, the eyes unfathomable. The gesture was so gentle that Billy felt the prickle of tears.

In the dayroom he found that his backpack had been lashed to a restive, canvas bundle. Seldom. The master sat at the table with pen and paper, scratching a list. At the beginning of each line he made a number, followed by a dot. Then the pen returned to a tiny pot of black ink, pausing to let all the drips find their way back into the bottle, before he completed the line.

Billy craned, trying to read, but the old man waved him away. "Eat! You'll need the energy."

The porridge was tepid. "We shouldn't be doing this," Billy said between mouthfuls. "It's an insult."

"Agreed." Kim didn't look up from his jottings.

"I mean, who do they think they are?" Billy reached for the milk. "Just because they have generations of achievement, doesn't mean they can command us to sell them something we don't want to."

21

"And we *don't.*" The old man's pen poised once more, dripping ink like blood from a pricked finger. "Unfortunately, we have no choice."

"Of course we have a choice. We can ignore their *order* and, when they send Smout back, we can tell them exactly why."

"No, Billy. We can't." Kim drew a line, blew carefully and folded the page emphatically. Then he picked up the tiny bottle. "Do you know what this is? It's Karpentiner Ink. Not the expensive stuff... although, stick and stone, this little supply of schoolbook Noteworth is bad enough and it pains my heart to be using it. This..." He shook the bottle. Its contents swirled darkly. "This is the stuff that makes children pay attention to their lessons. The ink the Cranes used on their order is much more powerful. It's *compelling.*" The old man's look reminded Billy of thawing ice over the rocks of the creek at the end of winter. "We have *no choice.*"

Billy shook his head at the craziness of all this. The day before yesterday everything had been normal but then there was Smout and this blasted letter, and now the master was capitulating without argument to people Billy had never even heard of, and sending a sylvan to have who knew what done to it in the city. He realised that his mouth was hanging open and nothing was coming out.

"You should have *told me.*" Kim's eruption was like the spring ice giving way under its own tension. "You should have told me, son. The *Constructors*? If I'd known who the letter was from I'd have destroyed it without so much as opening the damned thing." The fury died as quickly as it had come, the old man's shoulders sagging as he all but whispered the last few words.

Billy recognised the bitter resignation in those words and knew that there was nothing he could say to change Kim's mind. "It's my fault," he said with a sigh. "I should have burned it myself. I knew it couldn't be anything good."

"Not much of anything good comes from Karpentine, Billy. Not without a cost. But there it is." Kim furrowed his hair with worried fingers. "Son, I don't like the thought of you getting involved with those people, but..." The old man held his gaze as if he was going to say more but, seeming to lack the words, eventually he just shrugged. "Well, it's done now. You'd best be on your way. The day is dying already."

"Very well," Billy said. "As you say, it'll be an adventure." He put on what he hoped was a reassuring smile, though he scraped up the remains of his porridge and then laced his boots in a state of disbelief. He'd lived his entire life in these mountains, the majority of it in this house. He'd never wanted to be anywhere else. Then again, he recognised that he'd never wanted things here to change either and, like the weathering of the Chop's wood, he supposed it was inevitable that it would. Didn't everything?

When he reached for his coat on the peg behind the door it wasn't there.

"Here." Kim held out a different coat. It was old but well-preserved and when it was new it would have been a handsome garment; the brown leather, hard-wearing but stylishly tooled and solidly held together with stitches the colour of honey. "My old travelling coat." The old man's voice had become gruff. "Lots of pockets. Keep you dry too."

Billy shrugged the coat on. It was tight at the shoulders but otherwise wasn't uncomfortable, although all that leather made it heavy. He couldn't imagine the old man lugging this thing around... and that made him realise again how age had diminished Kim in recent years.

On the porch, Billy squeezed his cap over his wild curls and Kim helped him shoulder his burden. That too was heavier than it appeared, and it was an effort to manoeuvre from the house to the start of the road. The morning was cold, the sky like beaten metal. The world felt empty. Even Chop was absent.

Master Kim produced the note he had written, and slipped it between the pages of a slim book. Billy hadn't seen the volume for many years but he recognised the scuffed red boards, the gilt-edged pages, the embossed title. It was one of the few possessions he had brought from home: his old school copy of the Book of the Law. The old man tucked the book inside Billy's coat, then gave him a gentle shove. "Straight down through the forest, son, then follow the river till you meet the valley road at High Cross. Read the note then." There was a sad twitch to his mouth. "Please try and follow it to the letter."

THREE

Are we there yet?

The sylvan's enthusiasm hadn't waned one speck since they set off, but after twenty days on the road Billy was heartsick of its chatter. Especially now in this sodden moor mist that had reduced the world to a soft, grey nowhere. From the evenness under his boots, they were still on the road at least but they'd been on the road for what felt like forever. There shouldn't be long to go now. Another day or two at the most. The traveller he had camped with the other night had assured him he was almost there. He wished he could believe it.

Billy shifted the straps of his burden. Hard joints knuckled his spine. The impatience of budding blossom in his mind. *Let me see. I want to see!* Not for the first time, Billy considered throwing the bundle to the ground and walking away but the notion faded quickly, like numbing ice applied to a hammer-struck thumb.

He couldn't blame the sylvan. They had good legs and liked to walk. Being trussed up for so long must be frustrating. *You must be tired.* Seldom's wittering was like the chitter of sparrows outside his bedroom window heralding a particularly hungover dawn, but Billy *was* exhausted. His limbs were stiff as old wood, his muscles stretched and burning something fierce. He feared his back would be permanently bowed from the weight he carried.

We walk together, Seldom said. *We run. We race!*

"You'll break your feet to splinters before we even get there." Billy trudged on. A gust of wind made him shiver, a crow cried somewhere in the distance.

His grim mood wasn't because of the journey. Not really. With the old man's mind made up he'd had little choice but, to be honest, he'd agreed to do this willingly. And it *was* an adventure. He'd come to relish each rise and turn of the road as they unveiled new countries to him; plains, woods, rivers and all. No, what had narked was Kim's bloody instructions. Reading them under the signpost in the village of High Cross, they had seemed innocuous enough, hardly worth the fuss the old man had made, but the irritation had quickly grown and gnawed at him every step thereafter. He remembered them word for word, as if they had become etched into his mind:

1. Walk the entire road to Karpentine City, accepting neither aid nor transportation. That should be more than enough of an achievement to get you through the city gates.

2. Travel alone. Where you cannot avoid the company of others, discuss your reason for travel with no one. And do not unwrap the sylvan for any reason. No one can know what your load contains.

3. If anyone offers you a tip, don't accept a single kudo. Money is complicated in Karpentine. It's easier than you can imagine to become indebted.

4. When you get to the city, deliver your package to the Cranes at Radlett Hall. They may try to reduce the fee. Take whatever is offered.

5. As soon as your business is concluded come straight home.

Of course, Billy understood that the list was born out of concern, but the tone was so patronising it was hard not to be insulted. *No one can know…* Fine. He knew how to keep a secret. Doubly insulting was that Kim had seen fit to write the instructions in the ink of the schoolroom and Billy's mother's scolding voice: *sit up straight boy and pay attention.* Billy hadn't even known the old man possessed Karpentiner ink. He wished the old fool had used it to write back to these Constructors, telling them where to go rather than waste it on spelling out the bleeding obvious.

Mind you, he conceded, a lift for at least part of the journey might have been welcome, although that was immaterial because none had been offered. One of his ever-changing campfire companions – a cotton trader with a strong horse and a half empty cart – had patronised him for a solid hour on the subject of how strictly the people of Karpentine lived in accordance with The Law Of Man. "And you're walking all the way from the Mountains?" he'd said. "And your burden does look heavy, aye. Well that should see you through the gates in all likelihood."

Billy had heard similar stories throughout his journey. They didn't just let anyone into Karpentine. Only those of demonstrable achievement. "It shouldn't matter whether I've walked five miles or five hundred. I'm only making a delivery. I'll be gone in half a day."

The cart driver had shaken his head. "Well, sir, I'm not doubting you, but there's plenty would arrive at the gates of Karpentine with a similar story –"

"They *ordered* it." Billy's exclamation of exasperation had disturbed the other travellers who were attempting to settle to sleep. Heads turned his way, dim faces at the edge of the firelight, reminding him of Kim's instruction about discretion.

"Well, if you've an order," the trader said. "That could make all the difference. They like to see paperwork in Karpentine."

Paperwork? The last thing written at the bottom of the order had been the instruction to destroy it and the old man, apparently compelled by the ink the words were written in, had obliged. Billy fretted about the paperwork, and about what further surprises might await him when he arrived. Finally.

Still, not far to go. He trudged on, but in the fog he missed that the road bent. His next step found the softness of the verge, and the one after met a tangle of heather and he pitched forward, cracking both knees on a rock, his flailing arms unable to protect him from a smack on the temple too.

"Damn it!"

Even Seldom, for once, was silent.

Billy lay on the wet moss thinking that if the old man could've seen him, he would have cackled his balls off. He heard the crow again, more distinctly this time. A chattering call that, in fact, was not unlike laughter.

"I hope you choke." Billy rolled onto his side, shrugged himself out of the pack's straps. His knees throbbed and his palms stung too.

As if in response, the impudent bird swooped over, a wide-winged shadow dropping out of the mist. Billy barely ducked in time, and the bird was already climbing again as he scrabbled to his feet and cast a rock after it. "Oh, just *piss off.*"

Who's there? Seldom's voice was a tremulous skitter of gravel and sand. The bundle had come loose and a forearm stuck out, slender fingers groping across a lichenous rock.

"No one." Billy hurried to tuck the sylvan back in and secure the bundle. "No one's there. It's just a stupid crow."

Seldom wriggled in its wrappings. *I heard sylvan speech.*

Billy sighed. He was so weary. "No, mate." He laid his hand on the sylvan to still it. "There's only you here. There's not another of your kind for miles."

The wriggling redoubled. *I heard another!*

Billy reached down to hoist up the pack but, before he could grasp the straps, the crow returned, this time alighting clumsily on a thorny gorse branch. It looked directly at Billy, opened its beak and chattered at him.

26

What echoed across the moor were brash caws and clacks. What Billy also heard, with no little shock, in the same part of his mind that he heard the speech of the sylvans was: *Why in land and sky you resting? Why you not at city yet? Why you so slow, Billy Braid?.*

Up close, the crow resembled a real bird even less than sylvans resembled people. The old fool must have been in a hurry. The head was rudely fashioned, the eyes nuggets of amber, the mouth formed from overlapping steel hooks. The body was a lump of ironwood, the legs that supported it no more than crudely articulated cables of wirebush fibre. And the twitchy wings that stretched when the thing shifted weight from one foot to the other were an awkward arrangement of wire and canvas. The whole thing had been slathered in black paint, which added only a modicum of realism to the final effect. And yet, the creation still captured the essence of *crowness*, and that was all that was required. It was where the old man's skill lay, after all.

Billy got over his surprise quickly. "The old git!" He imagined the master pacing and muttering around the cabin. He wasn't good with things that were beyond his control.

The crow snapped its beak. *Master concerned about you.*

Billy laughed sadly. "Me or his precious delivery?"

The bird tilted its head, but didn't deny it. *Master Kim is obligated,* it said.

"I know, I know," Billy said, his smile fading. "Though he should have a little more faith. I can walk from one end of a road to another."

The bird looked around as if to make the painfully obvious point that he had in fact not yet achieved that simple task.

Billy sighed. "What's your name?"

The odd crow ducked its head for a moment as if in thought, then replied with a mental impression of pecking: *Tocka.*

"Well, Tocka, feel free to report back that all is well." He looked around and plucked a woody sprig of heather blossom. The moor was the first he had encountered along the road, so it would give Kim an idea of how far he'd got at least. The crow took the sprig in its beak, then extended its canvas wings and pulled itself aloft.

Billy scrambled back into Seldom's straps and got back on the road. It was only another hour or two before the road brought Billy down out of the mist. Meeting Tocka had lifted his spirits some. The crow's snappish concern, so like the master's, was almost enough for Billy to forgive Kim for the list, but as he went on, and during the cold night that

27

followed, he now brooded over the old man's obvious anxiety for Billy's welfare. It was touching but it felt a little extreme, and he couldn't decide whether he should be worrying now about the old man's state of mind or whether there was something he hadn't told Billy about the city of Karpentine.

Talk to no one. Don't take anyone's money. Deliver the sylvan and come straight home.

Could it be as bad as all that?

Whatever sense of adventure Billy had evaporated. He just wanted the job done now. Done and back home with the old man, getting on with their lives as if this had never happened. He made that the wish that would drive him forward, one weary step after the next, until the city was finally in sight.

The following afternoon they crested a rise and he spat out a curse. They still weren't there yet. Then he saw that the road looped around a hill on which a familiar silhouette rose against the shimmering backdrop of the sea.

"Ha, look!" Billy cried, his spirits lifting. Every child who had so much as glanced at their *Blackie's Illustrated Children's Histories* knew about The Tower Of Hands. The site where those that remained, after Those Who Turned Away had departed, had reached their famous accord of the primacy of human agency and drawn up the document that became known as The Law Of Man. Billy clearly recalled the illustration of the incredible edifice in all its colour and complexity. The italicised legend was burned indelibly into his memory. *The history of the Tower Of Hands is the history of our society. Through every disaster, our efforts by our hands persist. It is the embodiment of the Law Of Man.*

Even from afar, he was stunned by the grandeur of the tower. It was a strange agglomeration of design and organic growth, crenellations and minarets rising out of rough humps that resembled forest termite mounds but on a massive scale; slopes and hummocks overgrowing what had originally been walls. And the *colours*. The colours were fantastic, ranging from dull browns to bright patterns, soft pastels and rampant primaries, metallic glazes catching the sun. It was all exactly as his schoolbook had promised. What surprised him, were the crowds. People filled the tree-lined greensward that rose from the road. They streamed between the stalls, tents and cabins that were arrayed around the perimeter. And they swarmed leisurely around the structure itself. Billy had never seen so much activity. Still, it was on his road. It would do no harm to stop in for a few minutes so that he could say that he'd seen it.

What had started out as a fine day was now spoiling. An overcast of cloud drifted in from the sea, projecting drifting shadows over the tower and its hill as Billy left the road and mingled with the throng. Closer, the swarming activity was less like industry and more resembled a carnival. On both sides of the greensward there were stages on which musicians belted out tunes. A fiddle band with dancers on the one side, an energetic player sitting at jangly piano on the other. The stalls and tents sold food and drink. The beer and wine he recognised plainly enough, but they were also ladling out cups of something pink from a huge bowl. There were bits of fruit floating in it. The girl with the ladle mistook his suspicion for interest. "Handfast punch, sir?"

Billy moved on. He had no difficulty turning down the fancy drink, but food was another story. There were hot sausages with a choice of mustards and slabs of bread with slices of beef or pork between them that made his mouth water and his belly cramp. There were cakes too, miniature towers of sponge and cream, and pastries, and crumpets oozing jam. A finely dressed couple breezed past him carrying what appeared to be white fluffy clouds on sticks. The lady's blonde hair was as flyaway as the stuff on the stick, her teeth were whiter, and she laughed as she tried to trap the wisps.

Billy and Kim lived, for the most part, simply, although they were no stranger to fruit pies in the summer and soused puddings in the winter. The frugal fare that had fuelled Billy's journey had narrowed his culinary range even further, with dried fruits and withered tack supplementing what he was able to forage on the road. Now this confusion of cooking smells awakened a fearsome appetite in him. His purse had a few credits in it and so far he had managed to spend very little, but so close to his journey's end he reckoned he'd earned a reward. He decided to exchange a kudo or two for a steaming sausage, slathered in mustard and brown onions in a crusty bread roll, and was shocked to be charged instead a credit for the privilege. When he handed over the note, however, the stallholder appeared reluctant to take it from him. That whole credit lay folded in the man's open palm, as if *a whole credit* somehow still wasn't enough. It was only as Billy turned away that he realised the arsehole had been expecting a tip too.

The sausage tasted superb all the same. Billy gobbled it down as he wandered, watching the finely dressed people enjoying themselves in the glittering shadow of the historic structure. For the most part, though, their attention was on each other instead of the tower. Ostentation was very much the order of the day. The clothes of the richest were exquisitely tailored. Fashion came diluted to the mountains it seemed. Even at the harvest dance Billy had never seen such a display.

All of that paled, however, in comparison to the tower. From the road it had dwarfed the activities of the people around it, but from this perspective it was truly beggaring. He could see the pilasters and pillars, the battlements and buttresses, the cleverly approximated statuary, both realistic and abstract. In places only the knurled texture of knuckles reminded you that the entire thing was made from clay moulds of the hands of Karpentine's inhabitants, fingers gripping fingers, hand to hand to hand. Thousands upon thousands. A monument to the cooperation and manual effort that had enabled the orphaned rump of humanity to forge its own path all those centuries ago.

Billy couldn't quite believe that he was here. Even if this whole escapade was a monstrous imposition, standing here in the shadow of the Tower of Hands, he was quietly proud of himself. It had been a dog of a journey and his body ached all over, but he'd done it.

"First visit to lay on your hands, pilgrim?" The little man at Billy's side squinted up at him through brass-rimmed spectacles and nodded amiably. His thumbs were tucked into the waistcoat of a snug three piece suit cut from green and brown chequered cloth, and he rocked slightly on the heels of shiny boots. "Come a distance have you?"

"You could say that," Billy said. "I've walked all the way from the Molspur Mountains."

The little man's eyes widened in apparent appreciation. "Is that far?"

"Two weeks on the road." Aggrieved at his companion's ignorance, Billy couldn't help adding: "On foot. And with this great lump on my back the whole way." He stopped himself, remembering the master's list. Still, a little conversation felt good after so long with only Seldom and the occasional campfire acquaintance for company. Besides, now he was here, he was curious.

Appearing to notice Billy's burden for the first time, the man gave a low whistle. "The whole way? My word. And it's heavy, is it, this, er…?"

Billy limited his reply to one word. "Very." Then he changed the subject. "So this is where it all happens?" The couple he had seen earlier breezed by and headed for a stall that had comfortable chairs set out under a blue and white striped awning. As soon as they sat down someone came out to attend to them.

Nodding, the little man followed his gaze. "Weathermakers, son." A long tray was brought out and the couple rolled up their sleeves.

"What are they doing?" Billy asked. Of course, he knew that they were making their contribution to the Tower of Hands, as everyone did when they came here. But two at the same time?

"Sweetheart cast." The tone was dismissive. "It's just for show. The builders hate those things."

"Why?" The couple clasped hands and immersed them in the gloopy contents of the tray. Then they grinned stupidly at each other while the stall holder smoothed the clay with a spatula and set a brazier underneath.

"Because there's nothing to link to of course. No fingers." He spread his own and waggled them. "Come on, you clearly have no family, so you'll be wanting the general casters."

Seldom, who usually had enough sense to keep still when there were people around, chose that moment to wriggle. Billy made a show of shrugging in his straps as if the movement had been his own. His companion smiled patiently. Seldom quieted again, but Billy knew that the nudge had been a gentle reminder not to get distracted. "I should be getting along to Karpentine," he said, even though having his own hand cast was exactly what had been on his mind.

"Nonsense," exclaimed the little man. "You can't come all this way from... um..."

"The Molspur Mountains."

"From the... yes, the mountains, and pass up the chance to make your contribution, can you? Of course you can't! Leave your precious bundle with me for five minutes and go get your hand cast."

"Are you kidding? I don't even know you."

"Ralston Maundy!" A thin hand shot out of a worsted cuff, demanding to be shaken. "Freelance facilitator and all round friendly face." Billy shook the hand and was reminded of Bullivant Smout. Was everyone from the city so forthright? He scoured Maundy's face for the slyness of the courier who had brought the order that had started all this trouble. Maundy laughed at his hesitation. "You're right to be cautious, but look at me. Do you think I'd be as much as able to lift yon package there, let alone make off with it?"

31

The thought raised a smile. "Probably not," Billy said. Maundy had a warm likability and he would probably never get this opportunity again, but Kim's instructions had been explicit. "But still, no."

The little fellow pursed his lips shrewdly. "You're a credit to your employer, no mistaking that. I tell you what. Let's make it official. A service, if you will. I'll attend your bags while you pop inside there and do your bit." The tent he indicated was only yards away and in plain sight. "And when you come out, you can tip me a kudo." Maundy frowned then. "You *do* tip people for an honest service in your mountains, don't you?"

"Of course we do." It was an old tradition when someone did you a favour to tip them a coin on the understanding that they would pay it back to you at some point when you did something for them. "My kudo, my contract," Billy quoted from the Book of the Law.

"Precisely so." Maundy beamed. "Go on, be quick. I'm guessing you won't be back this way any time soon, will you?"

"Well, all right. If it won't take long." As Billy eased himself out of his harness he heard a stony skitter, felt fingers scrabble at his back through the canvas. He set Seldom down as gently as he could by way of reassurance.

"You'll be there and back in no time." The little man hunkered down on the grass, patted the bundle. "We'll be right here."

Billy retained misgivings, but this was too unique an opportunity and the process did seem to be a quick one, so he trotted over to the stall and ducked into the shade of the grey-green canopy.

"A cast, sir?" A sallow girl came straight to him even though there were others waiting. "Fisted or splayed?"

"What?"

She clenched then unclenched her hand, and Billy did the same before deciding on splayed. He held his fingers out like a star.

The girl shrugged. "Any extras?"

There was more to this than Billy had realised. He wished he hadn't bothered now. He glanced over at Maundy and was relieved to see the little man sitting on the grass and rolling himself a cigarette.

"Extras? What…?"

"Dull colours is standard. Bright colours is ten kudos extra. Metallics is fifty. Encrustation starts at a credit, but can get really pricey."

"Standard," Billy breathed. "Standard is fine. Look, how much is this going to cost?"

32

With an arching eyebrow, the girl launched into a well-practised litany. "For standard? All in, it's two twenty five. That's five kudos donation to the upkeep, fifty for the casting, fifty for firing and finishing, twenty for the standard paint, and a credit for guaranteed premium placement in the tower face for all your family and friends to see."

Over *two credits*. "I don't want a premium placement," Billy said.

"Where d'you want it then? Round the back somewhere?"

"Does it matter? I thought everyone's contribution was equally important."

The girl smiled at that. "Course it is," she said. "Tell you what. One of the masons is my brother. I can get him to stick it somewhere subtle but appealing and we'll call it one-fifty all in."

Billy sighed. "You couldn't make it any cheaper?"

That brought back the arched brows. "Wemyss is a fully affiliated Artisan Family, sir. Once removed from Lemuel Shankhill himself, on the distaff."

"All right then. One credit fifty." He counted the money out. It disappeared in a blink.

The casting itself didn't take long. The clay-like substance felt warm around his forearm and grew uncomfortably hot when she brought the brazier underneath it to harden it off. But she was gentle in extracting his encased arm from the tray, in rasping off the excess and then in slicing it open with a wet saw.

"Is that it?" The girl gave him a bowl of water and a rough cloth to clean up, then took up a fine paintbrush and began carefully numbering the two halves of his cast. He wasn't sure it'd come out as he thought it would. He'd intended to make a strong hand, open and supporting, but the shape in the halves looked like a grasping claw.

As he shrugged back into his coat, she rummaged under the table and pulled out a tile. It was segregated into coloured squares. "Pick a colour." She hadn't been joking about the dullness. Billy pointed out a green a shade or two off mountain moss, and she gave him a slip of paper on which she'd jotted the cast number. "People usually like to see where their hand has been placed," she said. "Come back in a few days and give the number to the masons, they'll show you." Then, correctly deeming him an unlikely source of a tip worth the name, she turned away to see to the next customer. Billy left a kudo on the table anyway out of gratitude.

Billy found Maundy and Seldom where he'd left them, the man's elbow propped against the canvas wrapping. He was staring distractedly up into the sky but his gaze dropped when he heard Billy return. For a moment there appeared to be something close to puzzled amusement in his expression, but then he jumped up and ground out the remains of his smoke.

"Easy as pie, eh?" He grinned, brushing grass from his trousers. "Just like I told you. And your cargo is safe and sound."

"Thanks," Billy replied, flipping a coin which Maundy caught and pocketed in an alarmingly fluid movement. "I feel like I've arrived in Karpentine now."

"Well, you've a short way to go yet, son, but dropping off at the Tower is a decent introduction to the ways of the old place."

If that meant pretention and over-pricing, Billy considered himself duly warned, but busying himself with tucking in a tail of canvas that had come loose from his bundle and shouldering the straps once more, he was glad he'd done it. After his brief break, the pack weighed even more than he remembered, but he consoled himself with the knowledge that this would be one of the last times he'd have to heft it. Although he tried not to think about what that meant for Seldom.

"Thanks, Ralston," he said.

The older man shook his hand and tipped him a salute. "Best of luck, Billy boy. Best of luck." His gaze strayed upwards again, and this time, fearing that Tocka might have chosen an awkward moment to make a return, Billy did the same but all he could see were clouds. When he looked down again, the little man was walking away, scratching his head.

Billy trudged down the greensward to the road. His burden may still have been heavy but his heart felt lighter. His journey was almost over and, despite Kim's dire warnings, he'd made it without incident. It was only then that it occurred to him that he couldn't remember telling Maundy his name.

FOUR

Beyond the Tower of Hands, the road veered inland once more, cutting between fields of long-eared barley. Above the fields, the clouds stretched like toffee, teasing apart as the air currents pulled them away to the south. Only a few belligerent scuds spoiled the promise of a pleasant evening. One plump little raincloud, blushed by the dipping sun, looked especially laden with evil weather. More importantly, however, the afternoon was wearing on.

"We'll need to get a march on," Billy said to his bundle as he leaned into the incline.

The sylvan inside made no response.

"Seldom?"

This time, the answer came as a sporadic series of clicks and cracks, like sharp stones being thrown against a wall. Billy had never heard sylvan petulance before.

"I'm sorry for leaving you alone."

Snick. Chack.

"It was only for a few minutes." He rounded a boulder-strewn corner and found himself among trees. Not proper trees such as they had at home, just a few westerwood apples, dry-leafed, niggardly of fruit and drab except for the bark facing where the sun would set, already beginning its fiery evening glow, but it felt good to be amongst wood again.

You left me, the sylvan said tersely, and after that it refused to speak again.

Somewhere among the trees, Billy felt the road start its decline. Then the boles thinned and at long last he set eyes on his destination. Beyond a final plain of fields and vineyards, under its renowned circle of uncluttered sky, stood the Sunshine City. Karpentine blazed with a hundred kinds of light. The burnished glow of metal and the airy brightness of glass, the glitter of minerals and the warmth of ceramics, every facet of the walls and the myriad ugly and elegant buildings that reached above them caught the diminishing daylight in a way that demanded attention. Even at this distance Billy could see how each building strove to out-do its neighbour. Ostentation piled upon ostentation. It was hideous. Nevertheless, it came as a relief after all the miles he had walked. He was nearly there, but not quite... and they closed the gates at dusk.

Quickening his pace, he was soon tramping between the vineyards. On both sides of the road, the vines grew tall and leafy and Billy glimpsed pendulous grapes. The sausage he'd eaten at the Tower of Hands already felt long ago and he found himself contemplating the chances of liberating a small bunch. Unlike the wild mountain fruit he knew, these technically belonged to someone, but there wasn't another soul visible on the road and the grapes were so plump. He looked once back in the direction that he had come, once in the direction he was going. No one would miss a single bunch of grapes.

"Hey, you. Yes, you with the bundle on your back."

Billy snatched his hand back as if the vines had burst into flame. Then there came a rustle of leaves, and a head appeared amid the foliage. Framed in a leather helmet from which a strap dangled was a pink face marred by grease smudges on the cheeks, brow and slightly pointed chin. The face had a firm mouth and insistent blue eyes. The owner of the face might have been attractive, if only she didn't insist on speaking.

"Hello? Are you deaf? Are you simple? I'm in need of help here."

Whatever it was she wanted help with, Billy felt disinclined to get involved. "Sorry, I have to get to the city gates," he nodded in that direction, "before –"

"Before sunset? Yes, well that's too bad. I'm afraid, my need is greater at the moment. Come on."

Almost laughing at her presumption, Billy stood his ground.

The woman's brow furrowed at his refusal. She emerged entirely from the vines, revealing a petite, boyish frame bulked out by a one-piece suit made of some sort of brown quilted material. When she put her hands on her hips she looked like a petulant child about to stamp her foot, but her voice was icy. "What are you?"

"My name is Billy Braid," he said.

"So, you *are* simple," she asserted. "I asked *what*. I don't care about your name." Now she spoke slowly, as if talking to an idiot. "What *family* are you?" She looked him up and down. "You're not a Ferguson by any chance? A Mechanic? Hmm? Yes?"

Understanding now, Billy shook his head. This was the conflation of trade and family that Kim had told him about. Regardless of their own efforts, everyone here got reflected achievement from just belonging to something.

"Damn. Are you sure? You have the hair of a mechanic. All springs you people, aren't you?"

"I don't *have* a family." Billy didn't know if he should feel insulted or not, but adjusted his hat to cover more of his curls anyway. "Where I come from, the only family you need us the one that houses and feeds you. Now, I'm delivering this package and I really need to arrive before dark."

"Oh, you're a *Porter!*" She clapped. "Well, that explains it. Sky knows why I was expecting more of you than that, but it can't be helped. Anyway, come on, Porter. I know you're an independent bunch, but didn't your family teach you that it's honourable to lend help to others when it's asked for?"

Now he did laugh at her presumption. "I've yet to hear anything resembling a request."

The woman's face pinched in a troutish way that only the stifled squawk of her own laughter indicated as one of amusement. "You're a cocky one for a Porter, Billy Braid…" She broke off, nostrils flaring as she reconsidered her approach. The smile that followed was almost convincing. "Very well, then… *please*. If it's not too much trouble, could you see your way clear to helping me fix my vehicle? It will only take five minutes – and in fact could have been accomplished already if you weren't so obstinate. In return I will not only be able, but *delighted*, to offer you transport for the remainder of your journey. Is that better?"

Billy's continued grin brought an answering scowl. "It certainly sounds more like a request," he said. "But I'm afraid I can't help. Even if I were so disposed, after walking all these days I'm not going to cheapen that achievement by accepting a ride."

The woman glared at him then, and for a second he thought she was actually going to utter the words: *Don't you know who I am?* She looked the sort who might.

To rub it in, as he adjusted his bundle, he added, more to needle her than because he meant it, "of course if there were a tip on offer I might have been able to spare a few minutes, but now I'm afraid I really have to be on my way."

"Oh, if you're going to be common about it, very well, I'll pay you."

"Ha! How much?"

She shrugged, obviously trying to work out what she could get away with. "Fifteen credits?" Billy felt his jaw drop open. "What? Don't they have money where you come from?"

Billy ignored that. For fifteen credits he could afford to. It would more than recoup what he'd spent at the Tower, and raised the possibility of a decent meal and soft bed for tonight, maybe even a bath. His knees went weak at the thought of soaking in hot water. "Five minutes?"

The woman beamed. "Ten at the most. Come on!"

He followed as she ploughed a trail through the profusion of leaves and fruit to reach the source of her troubles. When she had said the word *vehicle* he had imagined some sort of agricultural affair – perhaps a cart laden with baskets of grapes and a restless horse impatient to get home, or maybe something motorised along the lines of Bullivant Smout's charabanc, broken down and blowing smoke at the side of a farm track – but the reality turned out to be much stranger altogether. What he saw, in a flattened swathe, was a large inflated bag attached to a basket. Ropes were tied to cleats that had been hammered into the ground, and it strained against them. There was an engine in the basket, and a propeller protruded from the back of that. On the ground a variety of instrument cases had been neatly arrayed.

"This is your vehicle?" Billy couldn't keep the incredulity from his voice.

"Yes, it's a Weathermaker's field dirigible. I'm a Weathermaker, obviously." She set about yanking the basket upright and fiddling with the engine. "Had a bit of unexpected lightning trouble up there and I was just able to bring it down in one piece. Nothing broken, fortunately, but now the screw's a bit, well, screwy." The engine roared to life but with a straining, stuttering sound. The propeller turned unevenly. "See?"

Billy nodded as if he knew what he was looking at. Back in the mountains they stuck fairly strictly to the opening paragraph of the Book of the Law's treatise on manual work: *On The Beauty Of Labour.*

Do by the power of your hands. If your hands are insufficient, find another pair. Find a crowd of hands. The hands of man can accomplish all.

Only for the biggest jobs was machinery employed. He thought back to what the saw operators down at the huge lumber mills in the Molde valley said when their engines went wrong. "Could it be the governor?" he ventured.

That earned him a look of scorn. "No, you're certainly no mechanic, are you?" She turned the engine off.

"What do you want me to do then?"

"See this?" She indicated the oiled shaft that joined the propeller to the engine. Beneath a vicious scorch mark he could see that it was a little off true. "Hold it. Tight as you can."

Billy did as he was told. "What now…?"

The wrench whistled past his nose. Billy jumped aside as it resounded against the shaft. The propeller turned, blades knifing the air inches from his chest.

"I said hold it *tight*."

He regained his grip and, when the wrench came down again, managed to keep hold even though the vibration jarred up the length of his arms. The sound of metal on metal shivered through the vines until Billy's ears were ringing and his companion had worked a flush into her cheeks.

"That looks better, doesn't it?

The shaft did look straighter, although it was hard to tell due to all the scores and dings. When she gunned the motor, though, the blades spun with an even whirr.

"Congratulations," Billy said as the woman began to scurry around, loading up her instruments.

"Thank you," she smiled. "Hold the basket please."

"What?"

"The basket. Hold it down please. Put all your weight on it."

Billy did so, and watched her make ready for departure with remarkable economy. The ties came out of the ground with well-practised hoiks and the oval balloon in its rope harness immediately rose, jerking at the basket under Billy's hands. Then the woman swung herself in as well, yanking the last two cleats free as she did so and the whole contraption lifted.

"You can let go now," she said, easing his fingers from the canework and pressing something between them. The dirigible rose again, basket swaying then settling. It was well above the vines when the Weathermaker started the engine again and guided the vehicle around in an arc so that it pointed towards the city. Her face appeared over the rim of the basket one more time. She frowned. "By the way, it appears you've got a friend." She pointed upwards. "Troublesome blighter. Look out for yourself, Billy Braid."

39

Billy looked up, thinking perhaps that Tocka had returned, but was met only with the sight of the same little thunderous cloud that he'd noticed on leaving the Tower. The bloody thing seemed to be following him. Not that it mattered. He'd lived his life in the Molspurs. He could handle a little rain.

All the same, as if influenced by the cloud's presence, Billy's mood darkened too. The whole diversion had taken a lot longer than the promised five or ten minutes and the sky that the dirigible flew into was decidedly peach-coloured. It didn't improve either when he saw that what she had pressed into his hand was not fifteen credits but just a piece of paper.

On production of this Note, the printed text read. *The Family Loess will pay the sum of … on behalf of…*

In the first blank, the woman had scrawled *FIFTEEN CREDITS*; in the second, the most unlikely name he had ever seen: *Paraphernalia Loess*.

Well, he would much rather have had the cash in his pocket, but if this Paraphernalia Loess thought he wasn't going to collect on this paltry promise, she would be much mistaken.

Billy's mood remained piss poor for the rest of his journey. He resented the time he had wasted almost as much as he resented the Loess woman's presumption. With every step his pack felt heavier and all of Seldom's protrusions jounced against the soft parts of his already pummelled back. It was like carrying a sack of spanners. He would have tried talking to the sylvan again, but he was reluctant because he now had company on the road: people returning to the city from the Tower on foot and by bicycle, charabancs rumbling by too. Instead, Billy tried to enjoy the last of the evening sunshine, but that was a bust too because, although he had now entered the normally unspoiled circle that surrounded that city, the cloud continued to dog him. It cast the part of the road he walked on into shadow all the way out of the vineyards and through the fields of white-gold wheat that bordered Karpentine itself.

With every step, the shining city on the horizon grew larger, blazed more redly. Soon, the famous mosaics of the city walls towered, glittering over him, displaying the achievements of the Great Trades. Dull bronze and greening copper shouted some primal machine of Constructor design. Puffs of smoky glass represented a Weathermaker thunder cloud array. By the time he came to the fresco representing the Artisans – a wonderfully devised forest of trees constructed from a hundred different types of wood – Billy became aware of the beginnings of a makeshift village along the sides of the road. At first it was a few tents, their owners sorting their belongings or building cooking fires. Then, as the tents became more numerous, they were supplemented by canvas lean-tos, rudimentary huts, even some stouter looking cabins. Stalls too, Billy noticed, selling food and drink and other things, although most seemed to be in the process of closing up – presumably so their owners could get back into the city before the gates shut for the night.

As Billy gazed at the buildings, more permanent than in many villages back home, his heart sank. He had expected Karpentine to be difficult to get into but not to find a semi-permanent waiting area… He almost choked with relief when he saw, stretching back towards him from the gate, the actual queue. A line of people with no apparent connection to the tents. It moved. Slowly, but it moved. So what then was the purpose of this encampment? Then it dawned on him and his heart plummeted again. These must be the people who had been refused entry but had nowhere else to go.

For the first time, Billy considered the possibility that he might not be given the chance to fulfil his obligation. Karpentine, it seemed, had changed a great deal since the old man's day. Nervously, he edged forward to try and see what was happening.

"Oi!" A hairy arm thrust across his chest. It belonged to an even hairier individual with a handcart and a glowering female companion. It was the woman that had spoken. "End of the line," she said. "No one wants to spend the night out here, but those that's here first get in first. That's the rule." Neither of the couple looked like they were going to take his questioning of the rule kindly.

"All right!" Stung as much by his own frustration as their brusqueness, Billy shuffled into place behind them, biting his tongue to prevent himself adding the old man's favourite quote from *On The Sanctity Of The Law*. *The Law of Man is best obeyed with grace. It is no achievement to flout it.* "How long is this going to take?"

That earned him a longer appraisal from the shrew and her beast of burden. Both of them were dressed in finely made clothes and the cart held long bales of colourful cloth. He felt the stain of their scorn sink into him as their eyes lingered on his road-worn attire.

"A while. They inspect testimonials closely these days." This was the first thing the bear had uttered, and his voice had a syrupy quality belied by his appearance. "Making sure only those of demonstrated achievement can enter Karpentine." Ahead of them the line shuffled

41

forward. The couple did the same, the cart's wheels rolling barely a revolution before it was set down again. The pair in front elected not to resume the conversation but the brief exchange had fed the worm of worry in Billy's guts and the further forward the queue inched, the more hungrily it gnawed. He'd followed the old man's instructions and carried Seldom the length of the Karpentine road to make his delivery, but so what? He had no physical proof to present. What if they didn't believe his claim? Or, worse, even if they did, these were people whose idea of achievement was a gleaming charabanc or a flying machine. What if they laughed at him for being stupid enough to walk?

Behind the city, the sun began to set properly. The queue shuffled forward following the curve of the walls, and the guard post set up outside the city gates came into view. Billy saw another queue on the other side. Unbelievably, it was longer and the tent village it skirted looked to be ten times the size. Billy watched the applicants from both queues present themselves at the guard post, hoping for clues as to what might happen when his turn came. Some were admitted, but many were not. Particularly those coming from the other direction.

"What's the problem with them?" he asked.

The shrew in front of him rolled her eyes, but the bear deigned to offer him a response, although probably only because it allowed him to demonstrate his superiority again. "They're the reason this is all taking so long," he whined. "They say they're refugees from some famine in the east. I say that's their problem for choosing to live on the edge of the desert. They've been dribbling in along the Kinster road for weeks on end. Don't know what they expect to achieve by coming here." He sniffed. "Doesn't matter why, though, does it? If they haven't got the testimonials, they don't get in." This explanation did nothing to put Billy's mind at ease. He had no achievement to his name. Even in wearing his master's fine traveling coat he now felt like an imposter.

Time dragged by. The sun disappeared behind the city's rooftops. When the last of the charabancs from the Tower grumbled past, the guards heaved the gilded gates shut and Billy's horrified heart squeezed until he saw that the queue was not disbanding just yet. There was a smaller door set into the gates and it looked as if the guards would continue to process applications until true night had fallen.

Lanterns were lit, and in their glow Billy was close enough now to see the one thing that separated those applicants who slipped through the door from those who were turned away with bellows of rage, tears of frustration, was indeed the paperwork.

Billy fervently wished the old man hadn't destroyed the order letter. Kim had been compelled of course but, thinking about it now, he couldn't work out why. The Cranes must have known Billy would need something to get him through the gates, so why would they want him to destroy the one piece of paper that ensured he could do so? It didn't make sense. Unless, he supposed, their family was so replete with achievement that it had simply never occurred to them.

At least he still had Kim's instructions, although they could as easily have been written five minutes away as five hundred miles... There was a commotion somewhere behind him in the queue but Billy was fretting too much to pay it any heed. The silk merchants in front, although still at least ten minutes from the gate, had begun leafing through a sheaf of papers whose quantity would have impressed him, let alone the gilt lettering and the foiled imprimaturs.

The commotion grew nearer. He could make out words now. Curses and threats. *Away with you! I earn my way! Sod off, you leech.* When the noise reached Billy's shoulder he was finally compelled to look, surprised to see that he recognised the object of the crowd's ire.

It was Ralston Maundy.

"Billy Braid!" The little man beamed, although a fluster of sweat glistened along his sparse hairline. "I thought I might find you here." He dropped his voice. "That is, if I wasn't too late."

"What do you mean too late?"

"Well, before you got to the head of the queue, of course." Maundy spoke out of the corner of his mouth now. "And your unimpeachable achievements – your great journey from the mountains, not to mention all the rest which you were of course too modest to mention – were disregarded for want of a scant piece of evidence." The little man didn't say it, but it was in the otherwise careful blankness of his face.

"You're selling testim –?"

"Shh, son." The warning was unnecessary, because Maundy's iron grip on his fingers had already hushed him. "I'm no salesman. I told you before, I'm a facilitator." The squeeze became an affable handshake. "And, if there's anything I can do to facilitate your entry into the city, I'm only too happy to help."

Billy had paid enough visits to the Well Earned Repose to understand this kind of talk, even if the service being offered was markedly different.

"Fine," he said, although it wasn't fine, but what choice did he have. "I need to get into the city tonight."

"Then I might have something that will help you."

"Guaranteed to work?"

"Now, son, there are no *absolute* guarantees in life." Maundy's smile was impish. "But I'd stake my liberty on it."

The silk traders rolled their cart forward. Billy and Maundy filled in behind. They took more than a few steps this time because an entire extended family had just been dismissed from the other queue. They were gaunt. A red-faced baby was bawling.

"Very well," he whispered. "How much?"

"Twenty notes." Maundy's smile didn't waver. "Don't make a fuss about it," he went on, sensing Billy's outrage. "It's not negotiable. I know you have money, and that's what it'll cost to get you through that door."

"Then you've misjudged me," Billy said. "I started out with ten credits, and I spent much of that at the Tower."

The little man's smile evaporated. "Then maybe you'd better think about finding more from somewhere. After all, it's not just you, is it? There's your wooden man as well."

Billy froze with a mixture of fear and fury. "How do you know about that?"

Maundy grinned. "I peeked, of course."

Billy's anger bubbled. He didn't know what Maundy's interest in Seldom might be, but he was rapidly revealing himself to be the sort of person who could develop an unhealthy interest in anything. "I've got this," he said. From his pocket he unfolded the promissory note.

Maundy examined it, nodding as if the note were as impressive as any foil stamped testimonial. "It's not cash, but it'll do at a pinch. Now if you can stump up the balance, I believe we'll have a deal."

Billy counted out five notes. It left his purse light, but he could see no other option. A sheaf of papers was slipped into his hand in return. Dog-eared and creased, the paper was grey, almost furry, and the type faded, in places obscured by water damage and grease spots.

"What's this?" Billy's desperation boiled the exclamation so it came out like steam.

"Authenticity, son. Nothing more suspicious than newly minted papers. Especially on a backwards bumpkin like yourself. Oh, don't take offence. That's how this lot will see you, and your testaments have to match their expectations."

The lot in question, in their green uniforms and peaked caps, were close enough now that Billy could see that they lacked both humour and, at this time of the day, patience. The smallest excuse might be pretext enough to dismiss him. Assuming they saw him at all. It was near enough fully dark now. The lanterns swung in a chilling breeze. It was going to be a cold night out here and some of the guards had already begun to pack up. Billy watched one of the two tables outside the gate being folded away. His mouth went dry. He crossed his fingers and shuffled forward.

The silk merchants' impressive wad of papers passed muster without comment. They took their stamped chitty and, as the bear guided their handcart through the door, the wasp turned to deliver one last look of shrivelling dismissiveness. She was right. There was no way this was going to work. The civil guard seated at the table turned out to be a forbidding woman of middle years. One look in her eye confirmed that she would not be easily hoodwinked.

"So, what have you achieved?"

Billy could think of nothing that would impress this impassive face, nothing in his lazy life to date, not even his wasted epic slog to get here.

"Come on, we've not got all night." The guard's voice dripped disagreeableness. Billy thrust his hand out and Maundy's papers were snatched from it.

"Thank you." The guard flipped through the pages disinterestedly. When she got to the last one she snorted. Then she chuckled. "Look at this," she said to her remaining colleague. He peered at the sheet too, then looked at Billy and burst out laughing. "That's a lot of bacon," the first guard said. "Here you go."

Dumbfounded, Billy took his papers back. On the top was a stamped chitty. It read: *Karpentine Civil Guard. Permit Of Entry.*

"I can go in?"

The guard shook her head ruefully. "Well, there's not much to you, but at least you've given us a laugh. Better hurry up, though, unless you want to wait until morning."

Billy needed no further urging. Stowing his papers, and hefting Seldom one last time he stepped through the gate and entered Karpentine.

If Billy had found the crowds at the Tower Of Hands daunting, the queues and the camps outside the city walls bewildering, they were nothing to the riot of humanity that crowded the avenue beyond the gate. Everywhere there were faces, hands brandishing tools of various trades and voices shouting imprecations. And they all seemed to be directed at him.

"Work, sir?"

"Work for you, master?"

"Do anything for a kudo. You must have something I can do."

A gaudy piece of embroidery was shoved under his nose, a stitched circle of dyed threads representing perhaps a bird, though it was too ham-fisted to be recognisable. "Buy a favour, sir? Guaranteed to bring you fortune in the city."

Billy attempted to press on through the crowd, but they closed in on him.

"Fix your boots, no time at all. One clean credit. Just one."

"Don't be ripped off, sir. Resole your boots. Seventy kudos."

When he didn't react to either of the cobblers, an argument broke out between them, became a scuffle.

"Carry your pack for you, sir?" The speaker was a grubby waif. Billy guessed his age to be nine or ten, though he may just have been small for his age.

"What?"

"Your pack, sir?" The lad's eyes glittered, his cheeks glowed. "Been a long time on the road, I bet. Be glad to share the load for the last bit, I should imagine. No charge, just a few kudos so my sister and I can eat." The sister, hovering nearby, was older, but too pale, too thin. Her hands were filthy, and in them she cradled a basket of those embroidered favours. Both of them looked like they could use a meal, but Billy had nothing to spare.

"It's too heavy," he said.

To his credit, the boy puffed out his cheeks. "Is not," he said. "Let me try at least."

Billy just shook his head and pressed on, only to trip on something. He stumbled against the boy, who indeed fended him off with more strength than Billy would have given him credit for.

"Thank you," Billy said.

"Mind how you go." There was something in the lad's eye, but Billy didn't care. He just wanted out of there. As he walked away the crowd turned their attention to the next lucky entrant through the gates. They surged around Billy like he was a twig in a brook, buffeting him, tugging at his coat and his burden, but with a little persistence he was soon free.

"Billy." The shout came from Maundy who had somehow got ahead of him. "Over here."

When he reached the corner where Maundy waited he let out a relieved breath. He sagged against the silica-speckled wall, only for the colony of thumb-sized beetles that he'd mistaken under the lamplight for a metallic patina on the stonework to gyre into the air in a whirring, iridescent skein that spun away looking for a quieter spot to roost. Where they had been, the stone was freshly scarred and garish letters that had been painted there partially obliterated. There was enough left to understand that they had once said: *The Law For All*.

"My hands!" Billy shouted in surprise and frustration. "What now?"

Maundy smiled. "That was quite a scrum," he said. "Check your purse."

Billy dipped his hand inside his coat. Finding the pocket where he kept his purse empty, his heart hollowed. His hands fluttered quickly to pat his other pockets and he was marginally more astonished than relieved to discover the square of tooled leather in one of the outside ones. Opening it, he found his meagre savings intact and, along with them, there was a circle of bright embroidery. The rough linen scrap depicted a young tree, its branches crooked but its leaves vividly green. Where on earth had that come from? Who? He didn't know whether to feel violated or very, very lucky.

"Just as well there are a few honest people in the world, eh?" Maundy was looking over Billy's shoulder.

Billy turned to look. The lad had gone, but he spotted the pale sister. She watched him an instant longer before vanishing into the melee too.

FIVE

"Well? Are you going to tell me?"

Billy poked Maundy's newspaper. He had been reading the front page while the older man peered at the interior through a pair of tinted eyeglasses. The headline story was about the problem of the refugees from Kinster. Their lands lay at the very limit of Karpentine's aegis, the last inhabited place before the vast wasteland known as the Scour, and they'd had next to no rain for over a year though they paid for it like everyone else. The increasingly incompetent-seeming weather engineers were said to be working on the problem as a matter of urgency, of course, but there was also a question of defaulted payment, which the all-but-bankrupted region strenuously denied. It certainly put the occasional late shower up in Molspurs into perspective.

Maundy folded the newspaper. "So, what would it be that you wanted to know, Master King-Of-The-Pigs?"

"Very funny." Billy sipped his beer. Despite his determination to remain angry, he had started to relax. The inn was warm, the roomful of strangers already fading into the background and a good meal settled pleasantly in his stomach. In truth, he was very relieved to be here. Both despite Maundy and because of him. "I should punch you. Three Counties pig wrestling champion –"

"Five years running," Maundy chimed.

"Five years?"

"You started young."

"I must have." He remembered the guards' laughter. "But, man, couldn't you have made it something else?"

Maundy's eyes glittered with humour as he slugged from his own jar. "Does it matter? It got you in, didn't it?"

There was that. Then Billy remembered that this was Karpentine. "You used ink?"

Maundy laughed as he swallowed again, choking a little. "You're not so innocent to the ways of the city as you'd have us believe, are you? Even if you did manage to get dipped twice the minute you arrived."

"Twice?"

"Once for my nephew to take your wallet." Maundy raised a tufted eyebrown. "And once for his sister to return it. Bit of a ladies' man, are you?"

Those kids at the gate. Billy's mood cooled as he wondered again just how much of this had been a set-up. "Your nephew and niece. So criminality runs in the family, does it?"

Maundy shook his head amiably. "The boy's a scamp, but they're good honest kids who work hard and look after themselves. I'm only keeping an eye on them temporarily while their mother is... indisposed." He wiped his mouth, then dropped his voice. Maundy was all about the things you said aloud and the things you said quietly. "Believe it or not, the city gate is the last place you'd get away with the tricks of the Inksmith. Although, perhaps if one knew one's business, a tiny but judicious application of assurant might not go amiss."

Assurant? Inks that compelled obedience? There was a lot more to the ink business than Billy could ever have guessed.

"But, I'm hurt," Maundy went on. "Any fool with the right tools can knock up a plausible looking testimonial document. The skill is in the psychology of the content."

"So...?"

"So?"

"Are you going to tell me?"

"Tell you what, Bill?"

"Tell me how you just happened to have documents on your person that would help me – *specifically me* – get into the city. You already knew who I was when you met me at the Tower of Hands."

Maundy gave him a measuring look, then reached into his jacket and extracted a pack of cards. "Let's have a friendly game of Monument."

"You're kidding." The man was shameless. "You've already got enough of my money."

Maundy shrugged. "Not for money then, just for show. Some conversations look suspicious without some other activity."

Billy sighed. "All right then." It appeared to be the only way he was going to get answers.

Maundy slid the cards around the table with hypnotic ease. One to Billy, one to himself, two to the monument.

"You've played this before," Billy said. When he had first encountered the man, he had seemed inconsequential. That had been an act. Now he was clearly in his element.

"You were wise not to play me for money," Maundy said, placing the last card. "I'll be honest with you Billy, because I like you." His voice had assumed that private cadence again. "I have an arrangement with Thomas, the inn keeper here. I regularly play cards with new arrivals. Usually I win."

"Usually?" Billy spread his hand. The cards were fancier than the deck he and Kim played with, but the seventeen suits were the same. He started sorting them, judging his position.

"Almost always." Maundy grinned. "At least enough to make a living from it. Thomas takes a slice, of course, and in return he extends certain hospitalities. Which is why you have a room to spend the night in rather than hunkering down outside Radlett Hall waiting for the gates to open."

"I'm grateful," Billy said, although he preferred to consider that the reason that he was too poor to pay for his own room was because Maundy had cleaned him out. A fact about which the little man seemed entirely unrepentant.

"You to start, son."

Billy considered his first move. He was strong in the oversuit of insight, and in the undersuits of provender, clocks, and music, but weak in all the other oversuits, with a sporadic assortment of undercards completing his hand. Specialisation was always a high risk strategy, but he had no choice than to attempt to build his monument on insight and hope that the cards came up. He placed a foundation card in front of him.

Maundy's own move was to discard. "You'll understand, though, that there's only so high a standard of living to be made by scamming a few credits from travellers," he said. "I make most of my money from information. Titbits passed on over a few beers and a game of cards. Usually there's someone will pay a few notes for a bit of inter-family gossip. Occasionally, there's something of real interest." Maundy held his gaze. There was humour there, and respect. "Your arrival has been hotly anticipated, Billy Braid."

Billy returned the man's gaze until uncertainty overcame defiance again. He looked at his cards instead. He couldn't discard, nor could he add to his foundation, so he was forced to pick up Maundy's cast off: a clock. "I can't imagine Bullivant Smout coming here to play cards after he got back from our mountains," he said eventually, reckoning that he might as well see how much Maundy knew.

Maundy laughed as he discarded again. "Indeed he did not. But I personally saw him driving his ridiculous vehicle through the gates and straight on up towards the factories. And I had it on good authority that he went directly to Merit Crane."

Billy picked up the discard again. Another clock. He began to doubt his strategy, but it was early in the game yet. "And this good authority is the same that told you the reason behind Smout's journey? The same that spilled the nature of my cargo? My name?" The words sounded a good deal cooler than Billy felt. None of this was what he had expected. *Deliver the sylvan and come straight home.* That was what Kim had written and the entire length of his journey he had spoken barely a breath about his mission. Now he'd arrived, it turned out that everyone knew all about it all along.

Cards came and went in a flurry. A run of insight cards finally allowed Billy to start building his monument, but Maundy seemed content to continue discarding as if he didn't care. The game was just for show, after all. Then Maundy raised an eyebrow. "You're catching on," he said, laying down a *trompet*, a back-up move that awarded points in the event that no one's monument was complete by the end of the game. It seemed that Billy wasn't doing so badly after all.

"So, why?"

"Why?"

Billy shrugged. "Why the hospitality? Tomorrow, I'll deliver the sylvan and after that you'll get your fifteen credits. If you'll pardon me saying so, you're a crook. And the Book tells us: *kindness born of dishonesty is no kindness at all.* What more can you possibly make from me?"

"Never had you pegged for a pious man, son."

"I'm not especially." Billy glared. Those had just been the words that had sprung to mind. His mother's schoolroom lessons had always sunk in deeper than he liked to admit.

His companion didn't bother denying the lingering accusation. "I suppose if I'm being frank with you I should expect the same in return," he said. "The answer is, because the Constructors paid me to make sure you entered the city without a hitch, to keep you safe and sound until the morning and then escort you to make your delivery in one piece. I'm doing a job, nothing more."

"So," Billy gaped. "You've been paid *twice* for those testimonials?"

Maundy smirked. "Would you have trusted me if I'd just handed them to you? Besides, I have two waifs to feed, remember." He glanced at his cards, swapped the places of two in the fan. "Billy, I've already told you that I like you. You're a refreshingly straightforward fellow. You say what you think, even when you shouldn't, and that's a rare thing in this city, believe me. See, I'm being perfectly honest. Even though I've already made credit off you, I'm now currying favour with you so that if an opportunity arises that doesn't affect your business transaction or further disadvantage you while you are here, then you won't begrudge my taking further advantage from it." With that he drew a final card, lifted his *trompet*, and reassembled the whole lot into a neat stack on the table in front of him. "I believe that's Monument," he said.

Billy dropped his own cards onto the table.

"You play well, by the way." Maundy swept the cards together, shuffled them. "Considering the hand you were dealt. And you ignored the clocks. I like that. Single minded."

"What kind of opportunity?"

"See? A perfect example. Unshakable." Maundy squared the pack with three neat taps, then looked over Billy's shoulder. "I have no idea," he said. "But your arrival in Karpentine brings a wind of change, I feel. I'm just waiting under the trees to see what gets shaken down."

Turning, Billy saw that two men had entered the bar room. They were as close to identical as any two people could be. Both were as tall and slender as willows, and their skin too had the same olive lustre as that tree's bark. It contrasted pleasantly with their cream-coloured suits. They had burgundy bands on their wide-brimmed hats, matching handkerchiefs in their pockets. They scanned the room until they spotted Maundy, then they smiled broadly, causing their moustaches to arch like black gulls.

"Who are they?" Billy said when Maundy tipped the men a greeting. The twins waved, then went to the bar.

"Men of disparate talents in the current employ of the Weathermakers. Don't trust them an inch, Billy boy," Maundy said. "You think I'm mercenary in chiselling out an advantage. I'm nothing compared to Innocent and Erudite Bello."

"Ralston, my friend." The men came over and each set a pair of glasses on the table. "Wherever have you been hiding yourself?"

"Maundy, *compadre*." Two chairs were brought over. "Keeping busy, we hope?"

Their voices were sonorous and the men operated with a liquid interchangeability.

"Always busy, always." Maundy spread his hands. "Please join us."

"Who's your companion?" When the men switched their attention to Billy, he immediately felt sweat prickle on his neck.

Maundy smiled. "Billy Braid," he said. "Meet the Bello brothers. Never ever play cards with them."

"Pleased to meet you," Billy said, although he felt inclined to heed Maundy's words on this occasion. Instinctively, he suspected playing cards was just one of a long list of things it would be unwise to do with these men.

"Likewise," said the one on the left, who he thought was Innocent.

"We've heard a lot about you," said the other, who must therefore be Erudite.

"Nothing interesting, I'm sure," Billy said. The feeling that everyone here knew his business was becoming unbearable.

Maundy fanned the cards, snapped them back into the deck. "So, am I going to take money from the pair of you or not?"

When the brothers' scrutiny lifted from him, Billy felt released. They unbuttoned their jackets and removed their hats, revealing heads as smooth as cascade stones. Billy had thought they had bought themselves two drinks each, but they passed the glasses around the table. Three of them held pale whisky. The one they pushed towards him was colourless except for a trail of milky pearlesence around the ice.

"What's this?" Billy swirled the tumbler.

"Local delicacy." Innocent raised his own glass.

"A token of welcome to the city," Erudite did likewise. "Before we get started. Always interesting to pit wits against an unknown commodity." Billy knew he wasn't imagining the slight emphasis on the last word but he didn't reply. Instead he sipped his drink.

Before he'd swirled his glass the contents had been odourless but the agitation turned the liquid opaque, releasing a complex of sweet odours. He took a mouthful. It was hard to say what the liquid tasted of because it had a numbing effect on his mouth. It wasn't entirely unpleasant.

"You're out of luck, gentlemen," Maundy said. "The lad's already played and lost all that he can afford."

The men all laughed, but Innocent's dark eyes sparkled. "That's not what we heard. Not everything."

"Mr Bello, I'm ashamed," Maundy spun the cards across the table top, "that you'd suggest that a hard-working, loyal fellow, an obedient student of the Book, should even contemplate betting with merchandise promised for delivery to a customer. It's beneath you even to joke about it."

"Of course." There was no heart in Innocent's laugh. "A joke. Just that." Erudite, examining his cards, did not laugh, and he scowled when his brother went on. "Still we are intrigued as to the nature of this merchandise. This wooden manikin is the talk of the Exchange." He leaned towards Billy, and his voice got softer. "Perhaps Billy can be persuaded to play with a stake of morsels. Perhaps even a peek at the artefact itself?"

Billy's lips were paper-dry. "I can't," he said.

"You're amongst friends," said Erudite.

Innocent's teeth were bright as stars. "Who would know?"

"You don't understand," Billy said, thinking of something that might curtail their interest. "It's not loyalty. I'm compelled to keep my counsel until my delivery is complete. My master wrote my instructions in ink."

Innocent cottoned on immediately. "Ah, well. If you are compelled, it can't be helped." His fingers riffled through his cards, then paused as if something had occurred to him, and the smile that returned to his lips as the card game began was an unpleasant one.

Billy watched the game take shape. All three of the players affected a casual attitude, hardly looking at the cards they scooped up and tossed away, but Billy could tell they were playing the game seriously. No one had mentioned the stakes, but Innocent's gaze drifted his way too often for his liking.

To quell his nervousness, Billy drank. He quickly got a taste for the milky stuff, and when he'd drained his glass another appeared beside him.

"You must be exhausted," Erudite murmured to him at one point, "after such a long journey."

Billy realised that it was true. His concentration was slipping, his head buzzed and his limbs heavy, but he didn't want to sleep yet. It felt too much like admitting weakness. He sat up straighter in his chair, shook his head to clear it and concentrated on the game where the monuments of cards grew and shrank. It wasn't a fair match-up. The two brothers were sharing barely disguised tells, working together against their opponent. If Billy could see that then Maundy must as well, but the little man didn't seem to care and was managing to hold his own. The advantage rolled around the table like the river tide.

When Billy got up to piss, none of them appeared to notice. The cooler air in the bathroom came as a welcome shock. It restored his alertness a little and he resolved to take the next drink slower.

Karpentine's toilets it seemed were no different to conveniences anywhere else. They had the same smell, the same standard of cleanliness, the same quality of humour in the graffiti. Next to a small window that was wedged ajar, someone had scrawled *The Law For All*, but someone else had scored out *Law* and written *Cock* instead, with *Send a Messenger for Indiscriminate Anthony* added below. The rest of the artwork was of the usual boastful kind, including the customary height chart above the trough. People could turn anything into competition.

Billy wasn't particularly impressed by what he'd seen of Karpentine so far. Once you were inside those decorous walls, once the sun set on the shining towers, there didn't seem to be a whole lot to justify the hype. There were plenty back home who had no special achievement to their name other than getting up every day of their life and working until the sun went down, than making sure there was food on the table and shoes on their family's feet. If he was truthful with himself, even those achievements were beyond what Billy had so far managed in his life, and yet those same people would have been turned away at the gates. Of course, Billy had only made it this far himself because he had been helped. It seemed that all you had to do to get into Karpentine was cheat. It spoke highly – if *highly* was the right word – of Maundy's reputation if the Cranes had entrusted Billy's entry to the city to his forgery skills instead of their own paperwork. It said even more about their wish to be able to deny any connection with the delivery of a sylvan. He wondered why.

As he buttoned up, Billy realised that fatigue really was catching up on him. Even out here his eyes were drooping shut. A sound directed his attention to the window, something like a tap and a snuffle, and in the darkness beyond the frame he thought he saw a black snout, striped with symmetrical white. Above it, two black, unblinking eyes. Billy shook his dizzy head. When he looked again the animal was gone, and he honestly could not say whether he had really seen it or whether he had finally succumbed to a combination of paranoia, exhaustion and alcohol.

He felt the weariness of his journey burning in every muscle now so, instead of returning to the bar, he climbed the narrow stairs to the third floor, then the even tinier flight that led his and Maundy's rooms. He had been nervous about leaving Seldom alone up here but he had been assured that the key he held was the only one and, while he had little faith in such promises, Maundy and Thomas had been most sincere. He regretted his trust now, so it came as a relief to find the door still locked.

In Billy's mind as he turned the key, he heard a welcome shiver of leaves. He ducked inside, locking the door behind him. Then, remembering the interest of the Bello brothers, he wedged a chair under the handle.

He flicked the light switch, impressed despite himself with the simple ease of not having to wind a charging handle. Clearly the achievement of getting into Karpentine was sufficient to obviate expending effort for such mundanities as light. Seldom stood in the corner by the window, and the light made its limbs gleam. *You came back*, it said.

"I told you I would." On arrival, Billy had checked the sylvan for transit damage and found none. Now, despite his tiredness, he did it again. His fingers slid the length of Seldom's limbs, across its chest, around the articulated angles of its joints; lingering, relishing both the natural texture of the wood and the old man's skill. Running his thumb around the shoulder joint, he felt a slight irregularity. It was nothing, for now; but in time it would raise, splinter out. It didn't need immediate attention, but it was something for him to do. Even as he opened his tool kit and unfolded a small shave, he understood that he was really only doing this out of guilt. Over the years he had watched many sylvans leave Kim's workshop and stride off to find use in the forest or the fields as they chose, happy because they were happy. Because they had exercised their own choice. This, though, he detested. From the first meeting with Smout, through Kim's impotent anger and the journey to get here, he had spent the entire time trying not to imagine what would happen at the end of the journey. But with so much time on his hands, it had been impossible not to. None of his imaginings had been pleasant ones, and none of his encounters since his arrival had done anything to dispel their plausibility in his mind. He had never before felt such misgivings for a sylvan and, from the uneasy creaking of boughs that sounded in Billy's mind, Seldom shared his apprehension.

The sylvan sat patiently while Billy chamfered the blemish away. He may not have possessed a hundredth of the old man's aptitude with tools, but he had a certain touch of his own and when he smoothed the raw wood down with a calloused thumb he felt it knit together – *like magic*, Kim would have said with a half-easy laugh. It wasn't magic. It was just that he had a feel for the way wood worked. A skill. Maybe slightly more than a skill.

When he was younger there had once been a village girl who'd been keen on him and knew her own mind enough to dismiss his reputation for oddness. One spring, they'd gone for a walk in the low forest. Held hands beside the ladder pools and everything. To please her, he'd coaxed the twigs of a budding elm branch to grow into a heart-shaped wreath as she watched. She fled and he never set eyes on her again.

"There you are." Billy closed his tool box. "Now you're perfect."

Seldom let itself clatter to the floor in a manner that was half way between a child in a strop and a puppet with its strings cut. Billy should have chastised it for being careless with itself before its new owners even saw it, but he didn't. Not when he saw the way it rolled into the corner and curled up facing the wall.

Billy knew how it felt. His eyes were so heavy now, and the room seemed airless. He tried to open the window but the complicated latch defeated him. He sat on the bed to kick his boots off and the last thing he saw before passing out was the embroidered coverlet; a folksy scene of forests and mountains that had been rendered by someone who had never seen either. His last waking thought was that he'd soon be on the road back to his own mountains, with all of this awful business behind him.

SIX

The light, strained through the curtains, was as grey as a good Molde valley mist. It turned the tiny glass beads woven into the gauze to drops of glistening dew. The throbbing in Billy's head and the taste in his mouth were like the results of a night-long binge. Sure, he'd been exhausted from the journey, but to pass out fully clothed after just a couple of drinks? Then he remembered: they had been special drinks, hadn't they? And they had been bought for him by those brothers. The Bellos.

The curtain fluttered. The draught made him shiver. Surely he hadn't left the window open all night?

Then came a repeat of the sound that had woken him. A rapid tapping against the glass. Billy got up and pulled the curtain back to find Tocka hopping on the sill.

"I wondered if you'd put in an appearance again." Billy scratched himself. "Aren't you coming in? It's cold."

No sky, agitated the ersatz bird, the conveyance of its thoughts like an uproar in an entire rookery. *Don't like no sky. Come outside.*

Billy was distracted by his first view in daylight of the interior of the city. It was an impossible jumble of roofs and crenellations, crows steps and chimney breasts. Family flags fluttered and slates of every colour and design bullied for space in a pit fight of abutments and overhangs. "What a midden," he said.

The crow snapped its scissor beak. *Come outside!*

"All in good time," Billy said. It was still early after all and he was determined to have that bath before he did anything else. He stretched. "How's the old man? Was he pleased when you told him –?"

No time. Tocka snapped again. *Come now. Seldom is gone.*

Billy looked to where the sylvan had curled up the night before and saw that it was true. Stupidly, he searched the rest of the room, but there was nowhere else for it to be. And the door remained locked and barricaded. And the window was open. And now that he looked properly, there were signs: skid marks on the mossy pantiles outside, a footprint on the sill. A golden splinter snagged in a tear in the curtain.

Billy scrambled for his coat. "Where did it go? Did you see?" He forced himself to stop. He wasn't thinking straight. Seldom may have been despondent but there was no way the sylvan would have opened the window, climbed down to street level and run away. He looked at the print again. And it didn't wear point-toed boots either.

Billy thrust the chair aside and unlocked the door. The distance between his room and the one opposite was two strides. He crashed his palm against the wood. "Maundy?" He thumped harder, not caring if he woke the whole pub. "Maundy! Open up. We're going to those Weathermakers."

The vision of Maundy that opened the door was decidedly un-dapper. "What's going?" The fraudster scratched his chin above the collar of his threadbare pyjamas. "What are you shouting about? What time is it?"

"Get dressed," Billy pushed him back into the room, threw a shirt at him. "We're going to the Weathermakers."

Maundy caught it but made no move to put it on. "At this time in the morning? Don't be daft. No one will be up. Wait until after breakfast at least... Anyway, don't you want to deliver your package first?"

"Your two friends changed that plan when they slipped me a mickey and stole my merchandise." Billy picked up a shoe. "So I'm going to their employers to put things right."

Denial ghosted across Maundy's features, but wasn't voiced. It was clear that even if there was no proof, even if it was only Billy's suspicion, Maundy knew those twins were certainly capable of this. His grim nod was as good as acknowledgement.

"Good." Billy tossed the shoe at the man. "I can't do anything about the money promised to you by the Cranes but, if you want to collect your fifteen credits from me, I suggest you hurry." Then something else occurred to him, something in the continued corner-of-the eye regard that Innocent and Erudite had cast upon him. "Who won the game, Ralston?"

"Eh?" The older man was struggling into his trousers.

"Who won first crack at me?" Realisation flushed across the little fraud's face. "Never mind, I already know?"

"No, son, it wasn't like that. I swear." But Billy was already bounding for the stairs.

Outside, he found Tocka waiting on the scrolled stanchion of a lamp post. The street was otherwise deserted. The cobbles were slick with the evaporating mist and in the space framed between the buildings either side of the narrow street a blue sky promised a pleasant day.

"Which way?"

Maundy, arriving breathless, mumbled, "High Town, of course," but his eyes were fixed on Tocka. With a flourish of distaste the sylvan crow *whumphed* into the air, leading the way. The street that took them uphill quickly opened out onto Prospect Avenue, a thoroughfare so broad it was used here as a market square. Stall holders were already erecting their gaily coloured stands and laying out their wares.

Billy no longer needed to ask for directions. "If you want to find a Weathermaker, look for a cloud," he muttered. At the high heart of the city where the grandest, brightest edifices jostled for prominence there was a mirrored tower, and above that tower hung a single black cloud. He recognised it immediately. Only it wasn't so little any more, and it threatened much more than rain.

Striding towards the tower and the cloud above it, Billy decided that he really didn't like these Weathermakers. First it was the snotty woman in her dirigible, then the deceitful brothers, and now this. "If people spent more time getting the rain right for the people that needed it," he said, "and less time making clouds to follow innocent people around, this would be a better world."

"What? Clouds don't follow people, son." Maundy was out of breath trying to keep up. "They're just... *water*. It's a coincidence, that's all. Oh, will you slow down for a second?"

Billy didn't answer, didn't slow down, didn't check to see if Maundy was keeping up. Of course it was a coincidence. He hadn't meant *follow* literally, but that cloud had dogged him from the Tower of Hands right into the heart of this supposed Sunshine City and, even though he knew it to be a ridiculous notion, he realised it really did feel like being followed. And he didn't like that. Billy wasn't used to being worthy of attention. The villagers in the mountains viewed him and the old man as outsiders, at best ignoring them unless they had money to spend. At worst telling them to get lost in no uncertain terms. The *sylvans* were more welcome in the villages than they were, but that suited both of them fine. Since the night Smout had come to the house, however, the quiet life had deserted them. People had taken an interest. No, Billy didn't like that at all.

As he climbed through the city, the avenue got busier. Porters heaved handcarts ornately decorated with family emblems, long legged Couriers powered by with the mail and workers of all types converged on their ways to earn a day's kudo. The street corners were initially congested with urchins like those who had crowded him at the gate, selling favours and seeking any sort of menial employment, but their numbers dwindled as the surroundings became more affluent. The buildings themselves got taller, wider, grander. The frontages became more elaborate. Pillared porches and porticos replaced mere doors. Simple sashes gave way to mullioned dormers that were in turn eschewed for huge picture windows. Bricks became granite blocks became whitewash became coloured tiles became sheeted copper or storeys-high picture mosaics or walls of glass. At every turn, every junction, Billy looked for the cloud and soon enough, near the top of the hill, among all the other buildings and compounds and complexes, he arrived at the gates of the Weathermakers' headquarters. The lower storeys of the mirrored tower reflected the architectural chaos that surrounded it, but higher up its walls were pictures of wide sky.

A small crowd had gathered in the courtyard. They stood near some barn-sized buildings, gazing upwards at the vicious thunderhead that practically touched the apex of the tower. The air smelled of ozone and Billy's skin tingled.

"Protocol…" Maundy had managed to keep up after all, although he was purple in the face. "Ring the bell and wait."

"Hey!" Billy shouted at the crowd in the courtyard but they ignored him. "Hey!" He started to clamber up the gates.

"Ah, now don't do that, son."

Billy ignored the little man and continued to climb because he had spied a familiar face. He couldn't tell which one it was and he was less flamboyantly dressed than last night, but Billy still recognised him… and the shape that lay under a sack inside a nearby shed. "Seldom!" he yelled as he crested the ironwork and jumped down. Some of the crowd looked his way now and uniformed guards had appeared, but Billy continued unchecked. He marched right up to the Bello brother who first attempted to close the garage doors and then, realising it was too late, came to meet Billy instead.

"Young hand Braid," the brother began. Erudite, Billy felt sure. "You have no rights here. Please leave."

"I have every right to reclaim my master's property."

He was met by a white-bright smile. "The ownership of the property is in dispute. The…" The smile vanished. "The *device* was discovered on

61

Weathermaker property this morning, having apparently come here of its own volition."

"Own volition?" Billy found that he was boiling with rage. "No, Seldom was stolen. As you well know!"

Erudite's response was infuriatingly smooth: "I really don't know what you're talking about..." But then the crowd chose to involve itself in the conversation. At the apex of the delegation was a slender woman who walked with a cane. From the elegantly restrained greying-blonde hair and the severe set of her face, Billy judged her to be in her late middle years. And she was very clearly in charge.

"What in all the wide sky is going on here?" She pointed a cane made of some sort of gleaming metal. The hand that held it looked grey and wasted, all skin and skeleton. "You. Explain."

Only when Erudite cleared his throat did Billy realise that she was talking to the Bello brother instead of him. The Bellos had acquitted themselves in grand style the previous evening but now Erudite sketched a nervous bow. "Yes, Maestra," he said. "This man," he indicated Billy, "is responsible for the anomalous event." His eyes strayed meaningfully upwards to where the cloud churned above the tower.

"Well?" The woman turned on Billy. "Is this true?"

Anomalous event? Billy stared at the cloud, at Erudite, at this accusing woman. They couldn't actually be suggesting that he had done something to make the cloud follow him?

"What have you to say, man?" She did something with her stick then that caused lightning to sizzle from the end, blasting a cobble out of the ground between Billy's feet.

Billy jumped away from the smoking stone.

"Well? Speak up."

"No, it's not true," Billy said. "What do I know about the weather? I came to Karpentine to deliver goods, that's all." He glared at Erudite. "And I came here this morning because this man and his brother stole those goods –"

"Requisitioned under emergency laws, Maestra," Erudite cut in, smoothly changing his lie to suit the audience. "We believed that the goods in question were the cause of the anomalous nimbus and, since all such materials are liable to Weathermaker custodial jurisdiction pending investigation..."

The maestra looked thoughtfully up at the cloud and, following her gaze, Billy now spotted figures on the roof of the tower. They were brandishing what looked like longer versions of her weaponised walking stick. The air around them was blinding with stutter bursts of intense light.

She snapped back to Erudite. "That is so," she said. "Your expediency is an achievement worthy of note, Courier." She glanced at a decrepit man hanging at her shoulder. "Be sure that this is recorded should any consideration for promotion arise." Both the attending secretary and Erudite nodded. One in assent, the other in fawning gratitude. "Very well, let us examine this dangerous merchandise," the woman said.

"It's not dangerous," Billy protested. "It's just a sylvan."

The woman's eyes widened. "You would do well to speak only when you are addressed," she told him. "The civil guard will be summoned, but before they arrive you shall have a chance to explain yourself. Should you do so satisfactorily, it will go better for you."

Erudite went into the garage and peeled back the sacking. Seldom was curled into an awkward knot.

The woman peered. "So *this* is a sylvan? It looks like a pile of sticks to me. What does it do?"

Billy took a couple of steps closer to the shed. "Seldom?" he whispered. "Seldom, please stand up and let these people see you." The sylvan was silent, and at first it did not seem inclined to do as it had been asked, but then the wood rocked and unfolded, drawing gasps from the crowd. Billy gasped too, although in his case out of shock at the condition the sylvan was in. There were dents in its face and a raw gouge across its torso. Clearly it had put up a fight.

Billy rounded on Erudite. "You could at least have taken care. Do you know how long it took to make?"

"It's certainly a work of artisanship." The maestra circled the sylvan now, running the fingers of her good hand along the grain of its shoulder. "A pretty puppet to be sure. But what's it for? How does it work?"

Billy sighed. "They enjoy working on the land. Taking care of trees, that sort of thing. You can ask them to do something, and if they feel like it they'll lend a hand."

"If they feel like it?"

"They're very helpful —"

Neil Williamson

"So it's true? It has a mind? It thinks?" A grimace of revulsion. Her hand clawed over the dome of Seldom's head. "There's intelligence in there? Can there be any greater affront to the Law Of Man?"

"No," Billy rushed. "It's not a machine."

"Well, what else under the wide sky is it?" She turned back to Billy. "If it's not a machine?"

"I told you," he said, realising it was hopeless to try and explain this. Occasionally back home they came up against humanist die-hards with that kind of talk; who refused to accept that the Law, which had been written to counter the myriad Turners' machines that had sidelined humanity in every imaginable way, should not be applied to the sylvans. Sylvans didn't replace people. They coexisted with them, for the most part quite happily. Back home, at least, they'd had plenty of time to get used to the concept. Here it was a different story, and now Billy was really beginning to understand his master's dismay. "It's a sylvan," he said. "That's all it is."

"I must correct you there, Billy, my boy." Everyone turned then to meet the latest additions to their growing group. Flanked by two guardsmen, standing out against their grey uniforms with his lime-coloured coat and huge tawny moustache and grinning like a cat, stood the man who had begun all this trouble. "It is *our* sylvan," said Bullivant Smout. "I'm afraid, Lady Loess, that the Constructors have a prior claim on this. Bought and paid for, though not, as yet, delivered."

"Technically," Billy felt disinclined to let the criticism slide, "not paid for either."

Smout laughed. Behind him Billy saw that Innocent Bello had also appeared from somewhere. Maundy too was standing at the back, his frown no doubt caused by the effort of trying to work out how to make a kudo from the increasingly complex situation at the same time as wondering if Smout was about to usurp his duty of delivering Seldom to the Constructors.

"No one in this city would consider an order from Mr Crane anything less than surety of payment," Smout said.

"As an ignorant mountain peasant," Billy snarled back, "I have no such faith."

"Enough." Billy was satisfied to see Smout chastised by the reprimand from the woman he had addressed as Lady Loess. "Mister Smout, there are clearly matters of prior claim to be arbitrated. The device will stay on Weathermaker property until the Judiciary has considered the matter."

Still grinning, Smout shook his head. "I'm afraid that is not acceptable –"

Loess cut across him. "It is not negotiable. If the puppet is indeed the reason for this cloud's behaviour, it is our responsibility to contain and neutralise it."

At that moment there were distant shouts and everyone looked up. The efforts of those on top of the tower appeared to have failed because the cloud, seething and boiling, had begun to drift down towards the courtyard. When half way down the height of the tower, the gathering was pelted suddenly with stinging hail. The crowd scattered, seeking the shelter of the tower entrance on one side or the sheds on the other.

"Seldom," Billy shouted as the light diminished and the hail pounded heavier. "Come with me. We need to get inside."

The sylvan stood, rooted and abject.

"Seldom." Billy felt the charge building in his hair and skin. "Please."

The sylvan stayed where it was, but at least turned its head in Billy's direction. And there was a sound in Billy's mind, a soft, ticking crackle, that could have been frost or fire or the jaws of insects, but what it conveyed was clear: absolute fear.

At last Seldom reached its arm out, beautiful fingers extended. Billy reached his own hand out to grasp it, and then the world exploded in light and cold heat and he was blown off his feet. He tried to get up again but he couldn't work out which way that was. He smelled charred wood. There were tears in his eyes, but he made himself look.

Seldom sat on the ground, arms supporting itself, legs outstretched in a manner not at all dissimilar to the first time Billy had seen it. Elegant and coquettish like the village girls, strong and athletic like the boys. But it would never be beautiful again. The chest was cracked through and ablaze. The head had been blasted clean off, who knew where. The fingers drummed, as if still impatient, on the cobbles.

The second strike of lightning reduced the remains to blazing pieces and left an after-image seared into Billy's mind. But that wasn't all. Beneath the rattling of the hail and sizzle of the lightning, there was a roar of inchoate rage.

SEVEN

Something smelled burnt and it took Billy a moment to realise that the source of the odour was himself. Sitting up made him cough until his chest hurt, as if the lightning had cracked his ribs instead of poor Seldom's. The blood in his head pulsed, his ears rang. His mouth was parched and filled with a taste that he doubted even the old man's homemade strosh would sluice away. He'd been placed on a leather couch in an office, judging by the row of oak cabinets and the desk with its prim stack of paper and rack of pens and tiny inkpots. The map on the wall, covered in arcane symbols representing the weather, told him he hadn't been moved all that far. The view from the window across the rooftops of the city confirmed it, a vista of wide sky. He walked over, braced his hands against the frame and noticed that someone had left the window ajar. The intention to allow some fresh air in might have been a considerate one, but it reminded him of the moment he had discovered Seldom's disappearance. A sound behind him made him turn. Something familiar.

"Come out," he said, absurdly glad. "It's safe enough."

A rattle of nervous beak. *They come soon.* Tocka waddled out from under the desk. *They not be pleased to find me.*

Billy nodded agreement. "You saw what happened to Seldom?"

The bird waggled its head, hopped around in a jittery circle. *Do not like it. Want to go home.*

"That's a good idea. The master needs to know." He grabbed some paper and scribbled a note informing Kim what had happened to Seldom, and that he should not send another sylvan to the city no matter how any such further request might be written. He wadded the paper and squeezed it into the bird's leather body.

Tocka hopped up onto the sill. *I go.*

"As the crow flies." Billy realised he had become fond of the odd creation.

As the crow flies, Billy Braid.

Hearing footsteps approaching, Billy scooped Tocka onto the sill. "Quickly." The bird squeezed its head and body through the gap then launched into the air. He watched it weave through a maze of industrial chimneys, heading for the city wall and the lands beyond.

The sound of a key turning told Billy he'd not just been put in this room for the good of his health. Someone wanted to hold him to account for something, and he had a good idea what it was. He braced himself for an argument. Seldom deserved that at least. When the door opened, however, he was confronted not by Lady Loess or Bullivant Smout or even the Bello brothers, but by the woman he had met in the vineyards. He gaped with surprise before he remembered her name: Paraphernalia Loess. Of course. She'd said she was a Weathermaker, but not that she was a member of the ruling dynasty. He should have guessed, though. She looked different out of her flying gear, but that smug curl to her mouth, the spark in those blue eyes: they spoke unmistakably of entitlement. She hadn't come alone, either. In the hallway behind her Billy caught sight of a charcoal uniform, polished leather, the handle of a pistol.

"It's good to see you back on your feet, Porter." She placed a plate of sandwiches on the desk. "Though don't you look a sight? Mind you I told them it would take more than a little lightning to keep you down." Her tone was friendly, almost sympathetic, but then she made the mistake of smiling.

"Do you find this amusing?" Billy injected his tone with every ounce of his anger at what had happened to Seldom, his fury with the people that supposedly controlled the weather. All the same, he wasn't too proud to ignore the sandwiches. He bit into one. The bread was fresh, the ham thick and salty. It was worth the flare of pain caused by even the simple act of reaching.

Loess perched on the corner of the desk, hooked one leg over the knee of the other in a motion that, constricted by the buttoned jacket of her suit, was not as elegant as she intended it to be. "Not amusing in the slightest. Do you know that four engineers, myself included, risked their lives trying to get your little cloud under control?"

Billy choked on a crust, spat crumbs. "Why do people keep calling it *my* cloud. What has it to do with me?" In truth, he wanted to know. The existence of a connection of *some* sort seemed undeniable now.

She folded her arms. "'It's no achievement to accept responsibility where it is due. And much less to shirk it.'" She imbued the quote from *On The Precepts of Duty* with exactly the right hectoring tone. "'The cloud went awry because of your machine. Since you were the nominal custodian of said device, the responsibility is yours. It's inarguable."

Billy took a second sandwich. "Seldom did not interfere with that cloud," he said slowly. Whatever had happened, the one thing he knew for certain was that the sylvan was blameless.

"Yes, it did."

"No. It didn't."

"It's really the only possible explanation. It was a normal little cumulus until you showed up. Next thing we know it's peeled off from its array and turned nasty. It practically blew me out of the sky when I went up to try and bring it back in line, you know. And who just happened to be toddling by when I came crashing down in the vineyards? You and your sylvan."

Billy however remained adamant. Whatever she thought she knew, she was wrong. "Fine, then it's me. But it has nothing to do with Seldom."

She glared at him as if he were arguing that white was black just to spite her. Which, right at that moment, he would gladly have done. Then she nodded at the sandwiches. "Are those good? I'm starving."

"Help yourself."

She needed no second invitation, tearing into the food as if she hadn't eaten in a week.

"Why are you here?" he asked her. "Don't tell me. Playing with the weather is your hobby and you're really a kitchen servant?"

She grinned, swallowed, wiped her mouth with the back of her hand before replying. "I find you interesting."

"Me or Seldom?"

"Both, actually. Of course, everyone's been curious about your wooden machines for months."

Every time someone new mentioned how hotly anticipated Seldom's arrival had been, it got worse. "It's *months* now, is it?"

"Oh, at least." She rolled her eyes. "When it got around the higher levels of the Exchange that someone had been building intelligent machines, the Artisans saw it as yet another straw to grasp at and of course the Constructors simply *had* to get the jump on them…"

"Wait a minute. These Artisans wanted a sylvan too?"

"Well, of course. Stands to reason. But knowing old Shanks, they'd have gone about it in a typically roundabout fashion. The Cranes are so much more direct. Anyway, simply everyone wanted to know how these oddities worked, and if it was true that someone had broken the first law."

"Broken the –?"

"Do you want this?" The sandwich was gone before Billy finished shaking his head. "The first law," she said. "'No machine shall be given intelligence capable of thinking, reasoning, computing or interpolating of its own volition. The reasoning of Man shall be paramount'."

"I know what it is," he snapped. "But no one has broken it. The sylvans' intelligence is not *given* to them. The wood grows, they're made and it's just there." If the old man had been here, he'd have grumbled some convoluted explanation about motes. *Resonant harmonies*, he'd have said, something like that. Billy could never remember half of that stuff.

"Hmm?" She raised thin, auburn eyebrows. "Well, perhaps. I daresay all of this will come out at your hearing."

"My... *hearing*?" He heard the tremor of alarm in his own voice. He'd expected a confrontation, but this sounded worryingly official. "Why? I've haven't done anything."

"Well, that's for them to decide." She slid down off the desk, retrieved the empty plate and went to the door. "Oh, don't worry, I'm sure it'll be fine."

"Wait," he called after her. When she turned, the sculpted wave in her copper hair bounced. "Will I see you again?" Self-satisfaction widened her eyes. He gave her a second to enjoy it then drew a piece of paper from his pocket. "Because you still owe me fifteen credits."

Her eyes narrowed, but only for a second. "I'm afraid that'll have to wait," she said. "I couldn't possibly give you money now because in the eyes of the court it would complicate our relationship."

"What relationship?"

She smiled broadly, slipping out of the room with the final word. "Precisely."

Billy wasn't given the opportunity to vent his aggravation any further because Paraphernalia Loess's place in the doorway was immediately taken by three large guardsmen.

"We'd like to inspect your papers, please," said the burliest of the three. He had shiny pips on his lapel. Still confounded by the news of this hearing, his brain scrabbling to judge exactly what sort of trouble he was in – could they *really* think to charge him with breaking the first law? – Billy hardly hesitated to hand over the sheaf that Maundy had given him. If the Cranes had trusted the grubby documents to appease the guards at the gate, they would surely fool this lot. If they didn't, they were the least of his worries.

"Thank you." The jowly man pocketed the papers without glancing at them. "Now, if you'd come with us?"

"Where to?"

"The Judiciary," the guard captain growled. "Now, move."

Disbelievingly, Billy allowed the three guardsmen to march him out of the room, down a long flight of stairs every step of which awoke some new pain in his body and out into the courtyard, but he stopped when he saw the Bello twins. They were scrubbing the cobbles at the blackened spot where Seldom had met its end. A grubby, lumpy sack nearby could only be the poor sylvan's remains. A snake of cold fury uncoiled in Billy's chest to see them smirking as they worked. Over what? A joke, a triviality. As if this task were of no more significance than cleaning up after horses. He started towards them, intending to claim the sack, to wipe the smiles off their faces, but the guard captain's hand clamped down on his shoulder.

"Do you know how prisoners demonstrate their willingness to submit to the judicial process in Karpentine?" The captain oriented Billy towards the compound's gate. Billy shook his head and the three guards laughed. Looking over, the twins laughed too. "Donkey ride. Eh, lads?"

The other two guards nodded. "Donkey ride."

"Bend down."

"What? Piss off." Billy shrugged out of the captain's grip, but was kicked in the back of the leg and he buckled. Before he could rise again the guard captain had clambered onto his back. Billy grunted in pain.

"Oh no, mister donkey." The man's hot breath stank of rollmop. "We're not going to be stubborn, are we?" Stubbornness was precisely what Billy had in mind now, but the other officers stepped into view, their hands resting on hardwood truncheons. The captain took Billy's silence for capitulation. "Off we go, then," he crowed. "All the way to The Scales."

Another kick from behind made Billy stagger forward, and once he was in motion he had to keep going to prevent himself falling over.

"Gaahn, donkey. Giddyup!"

The captain was heavier than a whole lumber pile, but Billy managed to stagger out onto the street. Heads turned and cat calls rang out, but he ignored them, just as he ignored that the captain's subordinates now both swung their truncheons on their leather straps in case he might be tempted to shy off his cargo. And he *was* tempted. He wanted to stop and explain himself make them understand that this was all a mistake, but he could tell from their leisurely attentiveness that they were just waiting for that opportunity. So, he kept walking. What else could he do?

So, this was how things were done in Karpentine?

Billy loathed this place, but he wasn't going to give them the satisfaction of seeing it – not the cat callers, not the guards. He recalled a passage from the Book about silence being the best wall within which to keep your dignity, so he kept his mouth shut and placed one foot in front of the other. He put from his mind the question of how, in a blink, he had apparently gone from eagerly awaited visitor to prisoner. He refused to dwell on what awaited him at the end of this journey. He forced himself to ignore the city entirely. He pretended instead that the street was the mountain road and that his burden was Seldom, and that every vicious dig and jostle was simply the young sylvan shifting in its dreams.

He wished he'd heeded the old man's list more closely. *Talk to no one. Don't take anyone's money. Finish with the business and get the hell out.* Sound advice. Well, what's done was done, and Billy was well and truly done with Karpentine. He would get through whatever this hearing entailed and then leave this place and never come back.

The guard captain dismounted where the avenue opened out on a vast plaza, and not a moment too soon. Billy crumpled to the ground, simultaneously trying to get breath back into his aching lungs and trying not to throw up on the intricate patterns of coloured bricks.

He vaguely recognised the plaza from the journey up. In the centre was a mismatched assortment of interconnected buildings. The central, and presumably original, component had been a circular structure with a green coppered dome, but the years had seen it all but buried beneath towers and steeples, external stairways and buttressed wings. There were as many doors to the place as there were styles of construction. Wanting now just to get this over with, Billy heaved himself up and started towards the one with the longest, sorriest looking queue, but one of the guards grabbed him. "Not there you clot, that's the Labour Exchange." The hand turned him around to face a grander-looking terrace. "That's the courts in there."

Inside, they passed Billy on to a grey-faced clerk. "Another one for the Scales." The Captain shoved him forward. "Never a moment's rest for you lot these days is there?" Billy growled when the clerk attempted

71

to take his details, but was met only with resigned civility. The fellow knew nothing of Billy's troubles, cared less. He was a waste of Billy's anger.

The cell they put Billy in was warm and airless, and they kept him there for hours. He tried to stoke his anger but, unable to decide on a focus, he felt it wane. Any number of people had taken advantage of him since this escapade began but, pricks though all of them were, could he really blame them? Not when presented with someone who made the kind of mistakes he had: getting involved with first Maundy, then the Loess woman, delaying his delivery overnight on the promise of a soft bed and being hijacked by the Bello twins. He was a gift for the likes of these people. As his fire leaked away, tepid self-pity seeped in. He groaned through clenched teeth at how this had all come to pass. He'd not expected his time in Karpentine to be a holiday by any means, but he'd never imagined that events would turn out as badly as this either. Kim had tried to warn him, he supposed, with his instructions, but the old man was out of touch. The Karpentine he left many years ago could not have been as mercenary as this one. And, while Billy appreciated the concern, even with its special ink it hadn't been enough. He wished Kim said it to his face instead of relying on that scrap of paper. He wished even more that the master had resisted the order altogether.

Billy slumped onto the cot bed, back scraping unyielding brick, and pulled the old man's coat around him because despite the stuffiness he had goose pimples. Something jabbed at his ribs, a hard corner. He'd forgotten about the Book. He reached into his inner pocket and extracted it.

The Book of the Law was a slender volume because it was not a directory of the legal strictures of the land, rather the founding humanist aphorisms upon which they were based. And there were only so many ways you could phrase 'work hard and be nice to each other'. Editions of the Book came in a variety of guises, from the large, utilitarian tomes displayed for public reference in the civic halls of most towns to the more ornate and expensive editions displayed ostentatiously in the homes of some of the more rewarded families. The version most people were familiar with, however, was Blackie's Scholastic edition. That one of the batters of Billy's copy was faded, the other the original dark red, told a story: when he had come to live at Kim's house the book had been placed on a high shelf facing the window and never touched again. Even during his childhood, he'd opened it only when his mother considered that his wayward behaviour required remedial work. He brushed the cover with his fingertips, traced the title, remembering the contents even now as if he'd last opened the book ten minutes ago instead of ten years. He recalled the iconic illustrations: the happy, healthy men and women, driving a plough and chopping lumber, building a brick house and constructing a chair and baking a high crusted loaf of bread, tending to one sick child and consoling an unhappy one, making music on a violin and giving birth. He also recalled the crisp, thin paper, edged with gold to connote how precious the words were. But it was the words that he remembered most clearly. Not just the content of individual passages, but the serious typeface, the large, bold initial capital letter that began each of the laws. Even the exact position of each word in each line on each page.

Most people in the villages lived their lives by the Book. His mother read from it every night before sleep and again on waking in the morning. She sought guidance in it, drew comfort from it and had used it to decide how to punish him for neglecting his duties. When Billy read the Book it had been like a conversation in which he was offered a collection of rules, most of which were common sense, even obvious. He'd taken most on board, although some he privately chose to reinterpret. His mother's experience had always appeared to be much more unquestioning.

He opened the book now and found everything exactly as he remembered it. The paper, the pictures, the typeface, the words. The ink glistening exactly as it had during his schooling, making him think that the words had only just been laid down, the idea they encapsulated newly formulated and conveyed with import. Always fresh in his mind.

Karpentiner ink. He shut the book with a snap.

The valuable supply of Noteworth, Kim had used to pen his list *should* have been enough to make Billy keep his instructions in mind too. And yet, somehow, he had managed to disobey most of them. No, that was taking self-pity too far. He'd made mistakes but it wasn't all his fault. And sure, he resented Kim for the ease of his capitulation, but the master wasn't wholly to blame either. It was these Karpentiners. The sylvans had become of interest to the families and that had started them scheming. It appeared to be dumb luck that these Cranes had got in first, but to Billy's mind every one of these bastards was equally guilty.

Two guards came and escorted him silently from the cells to a sparse ante-room a number of storeys above. There he was met by a bored-looking woman who introduced herself as his defender, Imelda Spence.

"Defender?" His heart fluttered, but he made himself sound unconcerned. "What do I need a defender for? I only went up there to retrieve my master's property."

"The court is ready for you, Mister Braid," Spence said. She sounded bored. "Let's get this over with, shall we?"

They went through a connecting door into another equally unremarkable room. Three people sat on one side of a long table. A man fiddled with a typewriter at one end. The guardsmen took up position in the corners.

"Is this it?" Billy grunted, finding that his anger hadn't flickered out entirely after all.

"You were expecting what?" Spence indicated that they were to take the remaining seats.

"Of your great city's courthouse?" He couldn't help the sarcasm. "Something, I don't know... more impressive?"

The central of the three figures opposite looked up and hinged an unruly wirebush eyebrow. "Panoply feeds the notion among the criminally disposed that notoriety is a kind of achievement." The man peered at the top page of the stack in front of him. "That is not a notion to be encouraged. Your name is Billy Braid?"

Reluctantly, Billy nodded.

"Say 'yes'," murmured Spence, barely audible above the sound of the typewriter.

"Yes," said Billy.

"Very well. My name is Magistrate Hleb of the Family Schillmann." The lead official indicated the woman on his left and the man on his right. "This is Magistrate Kigho and Magistrate Noone. What are the charges?"

His male colleague passed him a typescript with a worrying amount of text on it. Seeing right through Billy's defiance, the female magistrate who had soft, cloud-like hair and a faded complexion twinkled at him.

Magistrate Hleb read for a minute or so, then returned his attention to Billy. "Now, suppose you tell us how it all happened."

"Aren't you going to tell me what the charges are first?"

"No fair peeking!" squeaked Magistrate Kigho.

"All in good time," said the other one.

"Just tell your story," Spence said. "Start at the beginning and answer any direct questions."

Realising there was no option but to go through with this, Billy related the story of the last couple of weeks. It proved an uneven telling because he annotated his narrative with liberal accusations, and because the magistrates too interrupted frequently.

"We have a deposition from Bullivant Smout?" This came just after Billy had begun. A sheet of paper was located in the pile. "Ah, yes. A witness of good family." Magistrate Hleb scanned the statement before him. "You say the order was written in a compellant ink?"

Billy nodded curtly. The old man hadn't used that precise word, but it described exactly the effect it'd had.

"That is a serious allegation of business malpractice against Mr Smout's employers. Why is this order not presented in evidence?"

Spence leant forward. "Because he didn't bring it with him." She could not have laden the sentence with more disdain. Nevertheless, Billy attempted to outdo her.

"Because my master destroyed it," he said, "in accordance with the final instruction on the order."

Hleb raised his overburdened brows again. "That is unfortunate. Proceed."

Billy described his journey, taking care to detail what had occurred at the Tower of Hands, hoping that his obeisance to tradition there would be looked upon favourably. He made special mention of Maundy's role too. Neither fact appeared to register with the magistrates.

"Go on," said Hleb.

So, Billy told them about the last leg of the journey. About giving up his time to help the arrogant Weathermaker. "And she still owes me for my services." He brandished the now crumpled promissory note.

"We also have a deposition from Paraphernalia Loess," murmured Noone. He passed this over. Both of his colleagues read it. Hleb almost managed to suppress his smile but Kigho tittered.

"Very well," Hleb said. "And when you arrived at the city?"

Billy hesitated, then told them how Maundy had convinced him to purchase the letters of testimonial.

"But you walked all the way from the Molspurs." Kigho's voice was a saccharine whisper. "Was that not achievement enough?"

Billy honestly did not know whether it would have been or not. Certainly, the journey no longer seemed so worthy of praise to him now.

75

More like a horrid waste of time. "My master was very particular that I should do so," he said. "He also wrote my instructions in your ink."

Kigho's face collapsed into a purse of disappointment. Hleb leaned forward. "And were these instructions destroyed too?"

"No, they are here." Billy produced the list.

Hleb examined it, showed it to Kigho, who then passed it to Noone who extracted an eye glass and scrutinised the page before passing it back. "This is not compellant," he said. "It's a fine, if rather aged, noteworth. But there is nothing here that would lessen the achievement of your journey."

Billy felt his anger curdle once more at the patronising tone. "I know that…" he snarled, but Spence put a hand on his arm.

"You'll just make it worse for yourself," she muttered, not looking like she cared whether he did or not.

"So, you arrived at the city…" Kigho prompted somewhat impatiently.

Billy composed himself and completed the story in short order.

"You stayed the night at the Brickface Inn?" Hleb said. "As Ralston Maundy's guest?"

Billy knew how that sounded. "It was late and I had no money. My options were limited."

"And this sculpture… device…"

"Sylvan."

"This *sylvan* was left unattended in your room for how long?"

Billy sighed at the inevitable line the questioning was taking. "A few hours," he said, "but it was still there when I went up to bed."

"How much had you to drink?"

From then on, the conversation dwelt on the time he'd spent with Maundy and the Bello twins, to the drinking and gambling. When he protested that he'd not played cards with the brothers, they merely tapped their papers to indicate that they had someone's word that it looked very much like he had. They paid close attention to his account of the theft, although they referred to it as *appropriation*, but they glossed over the end of things when the cloud had destroyed Seldom. They had a stack of testimonies about that part of the story.

The magistrates each consulted the sheet on which his charges were written. Magistrate Kigho patronised him once more with her kindly smile before Hleb turned to address him.

"I think we've heard all we need," he said. "Here is the judgement. On the first charge, of possessing untrue testimonials, we find you guilty."

Billy opened his mouth to protest but Spence touched his arm. "You admitted it."

"On the second charge, of using those testimonials to enter the city, we find you guilty." This time the magistrate himself forestalled Billy's interruption. "This is irrefutable. On the third charge, of interfering with the weather without authority or proper licence, we find you not guilty. Whatever link between that cloud and your device might exist, it is clear you are not intelligent enough to understand it. And on the final charge, of possessing technology heinous to mankind under the Law Of Man, we find not proven. This charge will remain open on your record until sufficient evidence indicates either guilt or innocence in the matter. Your sentence is twelve months in the Institute of Improvement." The magistrates gathered their papers and stood. "Good day, Mister Braid." They filed out of the room.

"Wait!" The word exploded out of him, more with desperation now than rage. "What do you mean?" he asked the door that closed behind the departing officials. He turned to Spence and repeated his question.

"We take the Law of Man very seriously in this city, Mister Braid." There wasn't a scrap of pity in her eyes. "I don't know how things are done in your part of the country, but if I had a kudo for every bumpkin who tried to waltz through the gates I'd live in the highest part of High Town." As she slipped into her jacket, Billy caught sight of a golden wristwatch that suggested that more than enough of those bumpkins had come her way. "The Institute isn't so bad," she said as the guards came over. "Spend the time attending to your own efforts and it might just turn out to be a worthwhile experience."

The ride to the Institute of Improvement was short but the road through the district they referred to as the lowtown – a winding thoroughfare, rather patronisingly, named Diligence Way – was choked by traffic. The four bull-necked Porters employed to pull the Judiciary carriage shuffled and cursed every time they were forced to halt. The official who rode on the other side of Billy's bars tapped her leg and craned ahead, looking past the wagons bearing crates stamped in foreign scripts, the carts piled with boxes brimming with ice and silvergold fish, the trolleys, the rickshaws and the bicycles, to see what the hold-up might be this time.

77

Then she glanced nervously in at him to make sure he wasn't going to try and kick the door open like he had the last three times they'd stopped.

Billy huddled inside Kim's old coat and stared resentfully out of his cage. A year of his life. *A whole year.* He kicked his boot heel at the lock anyway. It held but the carriage shuddered, making the official tut and the porters curse. Scant compensation for the year he was about to lose thanks to the infernal curiosity of Karpentine. Not to mention Kim's capitulation to their bloody ink, hapless and helpless though it might have been.

Billy had no idea what to expect of this Institute of Improvement. In the mountains, criminal punishments were meted out in days of unrewarded labour in the Canza stockade, but he'd bet his life this place was nowhere near so straightforward. He would find out soon, he supposed. At least it would be a break from the crowds. Billy rubbed his eyes as if to make the noisy throng vanish. What he wouldn't give for the stillness of trees right now. For the scent of pine and autumnal bonfires instead of soot and the harbour tang that had been growing stronger as they inched along this road. For the simplicity of the open sky instead of all the weirdly fussy, often dilapidated lowtown architecture.

As they waited to turn off the harbour road onto a street that nudged up towards the city's seaward wall, Billy found himself staring at a truly freakish building. The faded signboard read: *Wilson Simcock & Sons, Tallower and Candlemaker*, but Billy would have guessed the nature of the business from the three storey structure alone: a cylindrical tower whose walls had been enhanced with bulbousnesses that housed the windows and not coincidentally resembled long drips of wax. The walls, though now leprously flaked, had once been assiduously whitewashed. The chimney stack was even sculpted to resemble a wick. The stupidity of the structure was compounded by the fact that it had long since fallen into disuse. As he watched, a chunk of lintel that had probably only been held on by the paint, fell, causing passers-by to jump aside with yells of alarm and showering them in a rain of dust.

Even his jailer turned to look.

"Why don't they demolish that?" Billy asked. "Why don't they raze this whole place?"

The woman scratched her nose. "Legacy," she said in a bored voice. "Simcocks was once *the* candlemaker in Karpentine, but the last of the Sons died twenty years ago and, since the business was foundering anyway, it has been allowed to die. The building is all that's left."

78

Someone heaved the larger pieces of rubble to the side so the traffic on the pavement could resume. "In the meantime, as long as the place stands, anyone with the name Simcock gets a little reflected recognition."

Billy snorted. *These people.*

The Institute of Improvement, when they finally arrived at the compound on the seaward side of the city, was a disappointment too. Billy had expected a fortified stockade like the jail in Canza but, while there was a wall around the compound for matters of delineation, it was neither particularly high nor topped by rolls of splintered wirebush. Decorative, was the word that came to mind. Even the detention blocks were painted a not unpleasant shade of beige.

"Read this." The official slipped a folded paper through the bars. The page was officiously creased and sealed with black wax.

Billy shook his head. "I'm not reading anything you people give me."

"Take it. It's your sentence. It's your duty to read it." A cluster of guards had emerged from a building just inside the wall. When he still hesitated, she touched his arm kindly. "Honestly. It makes it easier. They'll force you otherwise."

She was right. Furious as he might be about his situation, nothing he'd been accused of at the hearing had in the end been unfair or untrue. Whatever his reasons for doing so, he'd broken the law and it was his duty to take his punishment. How bad could it be?

Billy snapped the wax and unfolded the paper. There was a single handwritten line and he had read it before he could change his mind.

Afterwards he would only remember the rough gist of the sentence, confirming the judgement against him and his term of confinement, and expressing the city's thanks in advance for serving it in an exemplary manner, but the words themselves were lost to him.

Of course, it wasn't the words that were important.

It was the solid, rectilinear pen strokes that formed the letters into passive blocks, and most of all the black, black ink.

When he had read it, Billy no longer cared how long he would be away from the mountains. He read it again as the cart passed through the compound's gate and the institution's wall became a safe, cosseting boundary. He read it one more time while being helped out of the cart and found that he already felt at home. The paper was taken from his hand, and the official carefully put it to the match.

EIGHT

Billy was given two sets of clothes and a bed at the end of a long dormitory room. He was told that the other inmates would be returning soon, but if he hadn't been he wouldn't have known there were any. There were no signs of habitation, no personal effects of any sort. Billy thought that seemed perfectly natural.

He watched the sea from the window until his dorm-mates came back. When he saw Ralston Maundy among them he was neither surprised nor unsurprised, except that he noticed the degree to which the normally ebullient man was now subdued. In the blue institutional suit he looked aged and any remaining vague enmity that Billy harboured for him trickled away.

"I'm sorry you're here," Billy said.

"It's not your fault," Maundy's voice was soft, like he'd forgotten how to use it. "You told your story truthfully without coercion. Which is why you only got a light stint. What, eighteen months?"

Billy knew he should have considered his sentence harsh for what he had done, let alone the enforcement of it using ink. He should be appalled and raging, but none of it really seemed to matter. "A year," he replied.

"There you are then." A watery smile. "It'll pass in no time. Me? Well, they had rather a longer list of charges waiting for me, so your contribution was hardly anything at all." A bell went somewhere in the building. "That's lunch time. Look sharp." That should have been funny – neither of them were capable of looking anything of the sort – but Billy didn't feel like smiling. They joined the slow flow filing downstairs. As they shuffled outside, Billy noticed the other blocks. There were more of them than he had at first supposed and they were split into men's accommodation on this side of a landscaped garden and women's on the other side. There was room for a lot of people in this Institute, but judging by a half-constructed building they passed, apparently still not room enough. Billy's queue meandered through the garden. There were trees and sculpted shrubs, and it was quite a pleasant place to stroll. They shuffled into a refectory where each person waited patiently to be served a meal.

Chewing on his food, Billy's thoughts returned to the length of his sentence. "A year is a long time for me, Ralston." He wanted to shout it, to rage, but couldn't. "I was only meant to be in Karpentine for a day."

The fraudster poked at his sloppy potatoes. "Just keep that in mind, then, son. That way you'll come out of here improved like they want or embittered. Either is fine. They both mean you're unlikely to be back. Keep it in mind and the time will pass before you know it. For some here a day is a blink, a year a yawn, a life…" Maundy dried up. His thoughts were elsewhere.

Billy put food in his mouth. It was warm, filling, easy to chew. If it had a flavour, he couldn't say what it was.

"It's the kids, you know?" Maundy said.

"What?" Billy's attention had drifted. What had they been talking about?

"The little 'uns," Maundy said. "My sister, their mam, is already in here, see? I was supposed to be looking out for them."

The brother and sister at the gate. They'd seemed pretty capable as children went. "I'm sure they'll be all right."

"More than likely." Maundy's face creased in a grimace. "It's not as if I ever did much for them anyway. Ah, well there's worse crimes. You see him?" Gravy glooped off Maundy's fork as he pointed across the refectory at a large bald man with the same placid air as everyone else. Billy nodded. "That's Carlton Herring. Murdered his family," Maundy said. "And her?" The fork swung to the woman sitting opposite the murderer. Her hair was gathered into a pineapple atop her head and she had soft eyes. "Ruthine Boothby. Ink thief. Stole several very rare concoctions from the arch-Inksmith herself, Moraine Otterbree's own vault. Caught blue handed." At the table where Billy and Ralston's dorm-mates sat, there was a sallow skinned man with a hooked nose. Maundy saw Billy's interest. "Finlay Giteau," he said. "Small-time seditionist. Got put in here for distributing leaflets about the so-called mistreatment of the lowtowners."

That snagged a memory. "'The Law for All'?" Billy said.

"That's the one." Maundy nodded. "As if anyone believes that people should be equal. What's achievement without advantage, hmm?"

"Who are they, then?" Billy lost interest in Giteau and looked towards the end of the dining hall where the tables were populated by emaciated men and women. Their skins were ashen, hair listless, spines curved like old willow boughs. There were soup bowls in front of them and glasses of water, but few of them made the effort to eat or drink.

"Them?" Maundy's voice was hollow. "They're institutionalised. Unimprovable."

"What do you mean?"

"It's a horrible way to live, is this," Maundy said. "A punishment, right enough. But some get a taste for it. The continual pressure to achieve out there is too great and they become serial offenders, getting themselves slung straight back in here as soon as their time is up. They're addicted to this life. They're going to die here."

Billy couldn't imagine a life spent like this. Without passion, without engagement. He might feel like this now, because of the sentence, because of the ink, but he would always be aware of the emotions that had been stolen from him, would always want them back. "It must have taken a long time to get to that stage," he said.

Maundy shook his head. "It can be very alluring," he murmured. "Once you've had your first taste of it… your second…" He put his fork back on his plate with a snap. He even managed something like a smile. "But that's not for you to worry about, son. Your year will be up before you know it."

"What about you?" Billy asked as they carried their trays to the hatch.

Maundy didn't look at him. "Well, you know how it is, Billy." He fumbled passing his tray through. "Things mount up." A mug teetered, fell to the floor. Maundy stared at the pieces for a second then turned away and walked out.

In the afternoon, Billy's crew got on a truck and were taken to a factory building where they were set to work degreasing machine parts. It was filthy, nauseating and physically hard work, but each man in his team followed the supervisor's instructions without complaint. It was dark when they returned to the Institute. Wordlessly, they showered away the grime and the aches in their backs and arms and fingers. When they went to bed, Billy discovered that his neighbours included one of the men Maundy had pointed out to him. What had he been? A pornographer? A writer? He paid him no further mind, and when the lights went out, fell immediately asleep.

The watchword of the Institute of Improvement was *routine*. There were dawns and there were sunsets. There were meals and periods of work and periods of rest punctuated by the bell that rang when one activity ended and the next one began. A never-ending loop of sleeping, eating and working. The work itself was tiring but simple labour. It changed daily. In the morning they could be boiling laundry and in the afternoon they'd be hauling lumber, without much awareness of where these activities took place. Most of the labour would have been considered unpleasant. One location in particular Billy associated with sufficient foulness to leave a mark; he understood it to be the premises of the Inksmiths. There his crew delivered factory soot and slaughterhouse bones, or leaned for hours over stinking vats, inhaling acrid fumes as they mixed the contents. Later, they had to scrub their skins raw to remove the stain of that place.

Few specific events lingered long in memory. The days smeared from one to the other, like a light bulb continually being wound to brightness and then dimming. The only other occurrence that snagged in his memory was a remarkably vivid dream. In the dream, a sense of presence had tugged him awake. The dormitory was in darkness, the only sounds the rhythmic breathing of sleepers and the distant shuffle of a work party returning to another part of the complex. By some meagre light, Billy could see his neighbour's brow. There were beads of sweat on it, damp strands of hair and his eyes were open. The rest of the man, and the source of the light, were obscured by the outline of a cloaked figure – a woman, he thought, from the glimpsed profile – who crouched at his bedside, and who whispered in his ear while she pulled back the sheet to reveal the upper part of his chest. Then the visitor produced a little bottle and something like a pen. His neighbour's eyes tracked the visitor disinterestedly while they placed the bottle on the nightstand, opened it and dipped the glinting sharp tip of the pen into it. He showed no alarm when the pen pricked his skin. Billy watched the intruder casually wipe aside a weal of blood, and then return the pen to what could only have been ink. She worked quickly, rhythmically, the stippled design becoming almost recognisable, perhaps an animal of some sort, but Billy fell asleep before it was finished.

In the morning, the dream of tattooing – no doubt brought on by the numerous trips to the Inksmiths' factory – had faded but, curiously, the bed next to him stood empty and the guards that escorted the detail to the refectory were uncommonly edgy. By the time breakfast was over, of course, Billy had almost entirely forgotten the incident. That night there was someone new in the bed, and the next day proceeded exactly like all the rest.

Time passed. Then one morning, the guards came for him. Of all the inmates, Maundy was the only one who reacted, but even then only to look up and blink sheepishly. Then he went back to his porridge and Billy was escorted to the administration offices.

"Billy Braid?" This Judiciary officer was short and overweight. She handed him a pile of clothes.

"What are these for?"

"These are your clothes. Please put them on."

"Why?"

"You're being released, Mister Braid."

"Am I innocent?"

That brought a sorry shake of the head.

His old clothes felt stiff and unfamiliar after the thin Institute uniform. His coat, heavy and unyielding as sheet steel, his boots like buckets weighted with stones.

The official brought him to the gate. It stood, as always, wide open, but since Billy had been here it had never once occurred to him to walk out of it. Now he was about to be prompted to do so and he could not imagine how he was going to obey.

The official handed him a piece of paper, folded and sealed in an identical manner to the one he had been given when he had arrived. Billy cracked the seal, unfolded the paper and read what was written inside.

Then he walked out through the gate and straight towards a glossy black car. It reminded him of Bullivant Smout's garish contraption, but only in general terms: this car was still conspicuous, any self-powered vehicle would be, even in Karpentine, but it was also relatively understated. The engine growled patiently, a door swung open. The driver was a woman in a cloud white suit. She had auburn hair and blue eyes and quite a nice smile.

"Get in, Porter," she said. "You're mine now."

The second he closed the door, Paraphernalia Loess gunned the engine and pulled away from the Institute Of Improvement. Billy found the interior stifling and the smells, hot engine and resinous leather, overwhelming. He slumped, his forehead contacting the cool window. His eyelids drooped.

"Well, Simcock's candle melted at last," Loess said, conversationally. "And about bloody time."

Billy opened his eyes in time to see that they had paused at the junction with the harbour road, and true enough, the derelict candlemaker's building had collapsed entirely. There were people amid the rubble, put to the hard labour of clearing the stones, loading them into carts, and no doubt also looking for salvageable scraps that they could sell for a few kudos. A tousle-headed tyke stopped what he was doing long enough to stare at their car. He shouted something to the older girl labouring next to him who turned to stare also.

"Gives some a job of work at least," Paraphernalia Loess muttered as she urged the car into motion once more. The children may have watched until they were out of sight. Billy was asleep long before then.

NINE

The shivers lasted for hours. Helping him out of the car, Paraphernalia had told him it wasn't uncommon when people came out of the Institute. Inmates nearing the end of their sentence usually went through a staged release, but Billy had been awarded no such consideration. When he paced, the movement of the air irritated his skin. When he sat still the upholstery rubbed against his arms. The shaking was uncontrollable. Gradually, though, the hypersensitivity wore off and the memories of what had led him here began to return. And with the memories, the anger. *These people.* The sharpest image was of the Bellos smirking over the sack that contained the dead sylvan. They'd had no right.

"Call me Para." His benefactor had left him to suffer alone for several hours, although she hadn't been quite so careless of his welfare as to have conveniently left the door unlocked. Now she reclined in a chair and bit into an apple. The sweet-sharp smell made Billy's stomach flip. "My late mother believed in a long name." She crunched into the apple again. "Builds character, apparently. Something to live up to. Personally," she said through the mouthful of fruit, "my preference is for directness in all things."

Billy glanced at the room's single small window. It offered an uninspiring view of rooftops belonging to some workaday part of the Loess mansion. He'd already gauged that he should be able to squeeze through the frame and perhaps find a way from there onto one of the adjoining roofs. Had he felt that he might be able to achieve that without falling over, probably to his death, he would already have done so.

Anyway, all of that was irrelevant for now. She'd returned and he could just tell her to her face that he was done with this place and as soon as he was able intended to obey the master's final instruction and leave. "Look," he said. "Thank you for your hospitality but I need to be getting home."

"Well, I'm sorry," she said, "but you can't."

"What?" Billy gripped his hair. His skin was hot. "Why?"

"Because there was a bidding war, and we won it. You're far more valuable out here than in there." She tapped her skull. "You know things that we think will help us, Billy."

"What are you talking about?" The woman made no sense. "I don't know anything. And I'm bloody going home."

"Sorry, no. You'll work for us until the end of your sentence."

"I've served my sentence."

"Not for another eleven months and four days."

Billy gaped at her while the arithmetic clunked its way through his throbbing head. He'd only been in the Institute of Improvement a month? It had felt like a lifetime.

"But I'll explain all of that later." Para tossed the apple core across the room where it rimmed into the bin. "First we need to get you some new clothes. My aunt is throwing a Grand Ball tonight, and you are to be my escort." She sprang to her feet. "And while I would relish the effect of your turning up in your travelling clothes – their odour alone would cause a pleasing amount of comment – in the long run it would be more trouble than it's worth. Come on." Billy disdained the hands she offered to help him up. Whatever she claimed, he considered that he'd paid for his mistakes and owed nothing to anyone. Her hands went to her hips instead. "I'm afraid you have to, Porter. You're indentured to us for the duration of your improvement. *Work first for your creditors*, and all that. Come on, it's only a quick trip to the shops."

He lifted his head at that. She wanted to take him out into the city? That was a different matter. An *opportunity*. Certainly a more appealing one than taking his chance with the rooftops. Shakily, Billy heaved himself up. "Fine, then," he groaned to disguise his nervous anticipation. "Whatever you say."

"Excellent." Para went to the door and opened it. A young man in pale blue livery who had been waiting in the hallway shuffled to attention. "This is Kingsley," she said by way of introduction. "He's one of our drivers. I don't normally use a chauffeur, but I'm afraid my aunt insisted." She met Billy's gaze with a meaningful glance. She wasn't stupid then, but it didn't matter. It just meant he'd have to choose his moment carefully.

"Oh, and before I forget." Para pulled out a leather purse and extracted a fold of credit bills.

"What's this?" he said.

"Pocket money, just in case anything takes your fancy."

87

Billy counted the notes. There were fifteen of them.

*

The people of the mountains bought clothes only when their old ones wore out, and when they needed new togs they went to the seamsters in High Cross or the tailor of Canza. Or they waited until one of the travelling fairs came around bearing exotic garments reputedly from all parts. Kim held a dim view of the sorts of people who bought the impractical clothes sold at the fairs, but Billy had never seen anything wrong with a little colour, especially as a gift on the rare occasions when he'd tried to impress a lad or a lass. Not that such gestures ever bore fruit, but he'd persisted until he was old enough to get the message that very few wanted a tumble with a strange boy from the mountains, whatever gifts he may bring. He'd long since stopped bothering.

Here, shopping for clothes appeared to be a competitive pastime. Judging by the number of dressmakers, milliners, cobblers, tailors and general outfitters in the affluent High Town streets, the citizens here must have many more clothes than they could possibly wear. For years Billy had listened to the old man banging on about the evils of conspicuous achievement, but now he really understood what he meant. When a Grand Ball was announced, it seemed simply everyone needed to have a suit in the season's new style and made sure everyone else knew it.

"I'm not wearing white," he said, making a pretence of caring about a suit he had no intention of wearing while eyeing Kingsley positioned stoically at the shop doorway.

The tailor, kneeling in front of him with his tape measure, stiffened. "The shade of the moment is ivory, sir, not *white*," he said through a mouthful of pins, and his next application of the tape was not gentle.

"What's this colour?" Billy fingered a bale of material. It was the shade of a cockscomb and the feel of it sent an electric tingle across his still-sensitive skin.

"That is carmine, sir," said the tailor. "For your accents. The hoi polloi are sporting scarlet and crimson in their hat bands and handkerchiefs, but carmine is very much the shade for the gentleman of taste. So much more earthy, more passionate –"

"I want the suit in this colour." Pins pattered satisfyingly to the floor. "With the accents in white."

88

The bewildered tradesman looked to Billy's escort for help but Para merely shrugged. "I have no objection," she said. "He'll certainly be harder to lose in the crowd."

Obtaining a promise that the suit would be delivered to the Loess house by the close of business, Para then proceeded to drag Billy around the rest of the sunwashed mercantile neighbourhood. The emporia were numberless and she seemed determined to visit them all. She tried on hats, she looked at soft leather gloves, she hummed and hawed over pairs of boots, although none of this with any genuine enthusiasm. Billy could at least empathise with that. Despite having more cash in his pocket than he'd ever possessed, he saw nothing that he could imagine wanting to own for himself either. He wanted nothing to do with this place at all.

As the first hour rolled into a second, Billy became increasingly fretful that the chance to run wouldn't present itself after all. Everywhere they went the dutiful Kingsley was never more than three discreet paces behind. The driver was hefty but by no means a mountain. Under normal circumstances, Billy might have been able to knock him down and outrun him, but even though the post-sentence sensitivity had largely worn off the weakness lingered. He gritted his teeth, and bided his time. He *would* have a chance, and when it came he'd make it count. With every new fancy parade or ornamented colonnade they entered he found himself memorising the positions of sidestreets, blind corners, doorways and other places to hide.

One benefit of this excursion, Billy realised, was getting to stretch his limbs in the sunshine and breathe the clear High Town air into his lungs. As the last of the muzzy caul of the Institute slipped away he felt a little sharper, if not that much stronger. This trip couldn't last for ever, though. He would soon run out of opportunities. A change of tack was required.

"Hey, I'm tired," Billy said as they entered the umpteenth arcade. "Any chance of a rest before your party?"

"Well, that's nice." Para turned on her heel outside a shop whose window, unusually, was dark and empty. "I'm just trying to show you around after cooping you up all day. But you're right. We should be getting back to the car."

Closing his eyes, Billy allowed his knees to buckle, bracing himself against the glass. He hoped it didn't look too melodramatic. He'd never been much of an actor. "Sorry," he said. "I don't know if I can."

Billy heard Para sigh and, as he'd hoped, made complacent by his obedience so far, murmur to Kinglsey to fetch the car. He heard the chauffeur's footsteps echo down the arcade and, when he opened his eyes again, he and Para were alone. He tensed, ready to sprint now, but something caught his attention. Behind the smoked window glass, a large brown eye had appeared. It blinked slowly and regarded him with a calm and certain vigilance. "What is this place?" he said, shocked by the familiarity of that gaze.

"It's an animeaux emporium," Para said. "You know, pets?"

The eye blinked again, and this time the animal that it belonged to turned and Billy caught a glimpse of a brindled hide, a swish of tail.

"You mean animals?"

"*Animeaux*," she repeated. "Crafted creatures?" She sighed. "Come and see, country boy."

Crafted creatures? Billy felt torn. He had to take this chance of escape, but… there had been something similarly, strangely watchful about the buck that had visited the cabin, and he *hadn't* imagined its reappearance at the Brickface Inn. As he thought about that, he experienced that crawling feeling of being under scrutiny all over again. He almost laughed aloud at his next thought… that the Cranes had sent a second spy along with Smout. One that had kept tabs on Billy's progress all the way back to the city. It was ridiculous. It was stupid. Animals couldn't be *spies*… but he couldn't shake the feeling that this was exactly what had happened. Yes, he needed to get out of here, but if they could craft animals what was to stop them sending more after him. What if it were wolves or bears next time? He needed to go… but he also needed to know.

Reluctantly, he followed her inside. A soft bell chimed and from the interior there came a ruffle of feathers, a stutter of hooves which settled quickly into quietude again. "Why is it so dark?" Billy peered into the brown gloom, already regretting this and wondering, as a contingency, about the possibility of a rear exit. There must be one, mustn't there? For the feed and the shit and everything?

"It's for the animeaux. If they think it's night they're less active. Most of them anyway."

With a leisurely rap of claws on varnished boards, a majestic wolf emerged from the darkness. Billy recognised its eye as the one that had regarded them from the window. The wolf was followed by the shopkeeper.

"Hello, hello, yes." The shadowy gentleman's voice was a croak. When he struck a handheld lamp Billy saw that his clothes were covered in hairs and specks of down. As the proprietor raised the lamp, all manner of animals were revealed on either side of the shop's central aisle. Cats and dogs and softskin hogs all lying beside each other, raptors on perches improbably ignoring a veritable carpet of rodents. A rainbow of finches fluttered through the lamplight before disappearing into the gloom. "What's your pleasure?" The shopkeeper ruffled the wolf between the ears in a manner that Billy, who was familiar with wolves in the wild, considered unwise. Placid as it seemed right now, he wouldn't fancy coming across it out in the far groves after dusk. Except that this one wasn't wild, it had been crafted. "Lady, gentleman? You want a good dog, yes?"

"We're not buying anything," Para said quickly. "My friend's new to the city. He's never seen animeaux before." The shopkeeper cast Billy a disdainful look before snapping his lamp off again.

That was enough for Billy. He ran.

The clap of his boots on the floor flustered the menagerie, aiding his escape amid a cacophony of alarm. In seconds he was through the door and out on the narrow street. He didn't know Para's reaction, he didn't waste time checking. When he reached the street's end, he charged on, barely breaking stride. They'd come from the road to the right, so he chose the one that curved left and down. Down he hoped would take him eventually to the city gate. He barrelled on. The new street was wider and busier with shoppers who shouted abuse as he barged through them. He started to tire but didn't slow, using the slope to keep his pace up even though his legs already felt like jelly. Make it to the gate, was all he could think. Make it *through* the gate and they couldn't touch him. Once he was back out in the world he could leave this whole sorry mess behind. It irked that it meant letting them get away with their actions, but there was nothing he could do about that. The road dogged left again, narrowed, and became a set of stone steps. He careened down them, leaping the last few and rushing headlong through an archway. Two, three seconds of darkness and then he was out into disorientating daylight again, only becoming aware of the grand avenue he emerged onto – and of the black car waiting on it – a fraction of a second before he sprawled, heaving for breath across the vehicle's bonnet.

Someone helped Billy back to his feet. Hands framed by sky blue cuffs. Wordlessly, the redoubtable Kinglsey guided him back into the car. Billy tried to shake him off but could barely manage a shrug now.

"And you were doing so well," Para said as Billy crumpled in beside her. "I blame myself, of course. You're hardly more than a few hours out of that place. Your poor brains must be scrambled."

Still panting, Billy stared at her, looking for sarcasm or duplicity, but she actually appeared to be sincere. The car executed a swift manoeuvre that nauseated his stomach. He closed his eyes. The Institute sickness had affected him more deeply than he'd thought. He probably wouldn't even have made it as far as the gate anyway, even if he hadn't been so easily out-thought.

"I suppose you only have natural animals in the mountains?" Para said as the car nosed through the High Town streets. "Ones that breed and kill and shit wherever they please, and all the other things that get in the way of them making good pets."

Billy had breath now but didn't reply. He wasn't sure which aggrieved him more: that Para was so dismissive of his bid for freedom as to deem it unworthy of mention or that these people, who'd the effrontery to look at Seldom and accuse Billy and the old man of breaking their most precious law, apparently thought *crafted animals* perfectly acceptable. The thought of Seldom dumped somewhere, broken and burned – or worse sold off to line the pockets of the Bellos – brought a renewed flush of anger and also a tinge of shame that he'd been ready to leave this place without taking the sylvan's remains back to the mountains where they belonged.

"And I suppose," Para went on, "that you're going to give me a lecture about nature. Well thank you, but I know my Book. I've read *The Husbandry Of the Wild* at least as many times as you have –"

"I've seen one of those before," Billy said at last, keeping his voice level. "Something like them anyway. Except more so. The one I saw was intelligent."

They were back on the main boulevard, climbing towards the Loess mansion. "Intelligent?" Para scoffed. "What utter rot. Animeaux aren't intelligent. They're selectively bred to have a rapport with their owners, that's all." To prove her wrong Billy started to tell her about the buck. How it had appeared at the house on the same day as Bullivant Smout, and had followed him from the Molspurs and sought him out at the Brickface Inn. When he got to the part about it standing on its hind legs to peer through the toilet window, she cut him off. "Oh, please. You're making a fool of yourself now." And, when he began another retort, "Billy, I won't hear another word." He would have argued on, but there was something in the look she flicked at the back of Kingsley's head that stayed him. They passed the remainder of the journey in a discomfiting silence.

After they left the car in the mansion garages, Kingsley helped Billy into the house with a firm grip. He protested that he didn't need help, but of course Para knew that. His short-lived bid for freedom had been noted after all and she was making her displeasure evident. Not that anyone would have known from her breezy hellos and how-are-yous to the household staff.

Once they were in his room, however, she dropped the façade. "Tell me about the deer," she said seriously. "From the beginning."

Wrong-footed by her switch in demeanour, he did as she asked, although she interrupted with constant questions. Was he sure? When he said *intelligent*, how did he know? Why hadn't he mentioned this at his hearing? Billy did his best to answer, but he had no reply for the last question other than he hadn't wanted to make matters worse for himself by coming across as a fantasist. And, after all, it was Smout's visit, not the buck's, which had led to all the trouble. Although if the Cranes *had* sent both emissaries…

Para smiled at that. "Oh no, Merit Crane wouldn't form an alliance with the Artificers Animeaux in a million years. It must be someone else."

"Why would it have to be an alliance?" Billy asked, although he realised as he spoke that even these Artificers were the dominant force in the pet trade, that hardly made them big shots in the city-wide scheme of things.

"Breaking the First Law? The Artificers would never be bold enough to attempt something like that." Dropping her usual high-handed attitude, Para's tone was thoughtful. Her eyes brimmed with curiosity at his story. It was almost like talking to a real human being. "No," she said. "Someone put them up to it. This feels like Lem Shankhill's style. Sneaky."

The Shankhills bossed the guild of Artisans, Billy remembered from the old man's lecture on Karpentine's trades and families.

Para scratched her chin. "Only to be trumped by Merit Crane's usual gauche directness, of course," she went on, "but that's why the

93

Constructors remain a strong family, and the Artisans lag perpetually behind."

"They do?"

She nodded vigorously. "The days of the Handmade Dynasty are long behind us, but Shankhill keeps trying, bless him. If there's an alliance between the Artisans and the Artificers Animeaux, that's interesting. But *intelligence*...?"

"I told you what I saw."

"And I believe you. I just have difficulty believing that it's *possible*. Let alone that they managed to succeed in creating a thinking animax without even the slenderest rumour slipping out." Para stared at Billy as she contemplated this preposterous thing, as if he might provide an answer. Then, realising who she was talking to, she shook it off. "Well anyway, the question of how they managed it aside, if it's true it proves that Shankhill is getting really desperate now. See? You're earning your keep already, Porter."

"You people." Billy didn't disguise his distaste at the amount of scheming and duplicity that appeared to be the norm in Karpentine. "You're all poke and whisper, aren't you?"

Para's answering smile was weary. "Oh, natural wisdom too? Well, you'll have the chance to judge for yourself tonight. Pretty much all of them will be at the party. And they'll all want to be introduced to you."

Billy had forgotten about the ball. He sighed. "What kind of party is this, anyway?"

"Oh, the usual sort of thing," Para replied. "A perfectly dull, overly lavish affair that will involve various members of various families and coalitions playing a complicated game of one-upmanship for no one's benefit in particular. The Loess family will benefit in newspaper coverage of the attendance of the *noms-du-jour*. Like yourself." She grinned at his snort of discomfort. "Well it's true, and the members of the other families will make sure they are conspicuously visible in your presence. Everyone achieves a little more." She grimaced. "And you're right. It's also an opportunity for poke and whisper, as you call it; deals to be done, alliances to be made, and sundry other tiresome pieces of business. Anyway..." Para stood. "Time marches on and I haven't even decided what I'm going wear yet. Your suit should arrive soon. Kingsley will come for you when the ball is underway."

She took a few paces towards the door, but then turned back to him. "Billy, I know this is hard for you," she said, "but we do have your best interests at heart."

It had been a welcome surprise to learn that underneath those aristocratic airs Para concealed a sense of fairness and a willingness to listen to him instead of the blithe dismissal he'd received everywhere else. But *best interests*? Was she taking the piss? Had she been laughing at him all along? The Loesses hadn't bought out his indentureship out of pity. "Of course you do." He couldn't hold in the hollow laugh. "Just as long as my interests and your family's interests align."

The corners of her mouth tightened. "I know it doesn't seem like it," she said. "Keeping you locked up here with Kingsley outside the door and the guards down in the courtyard." With that tidbit, Billy's heart sank a measure further. "But if it hadn't been us, it would have been someone else. And they might not have been so accommodating towards your comfort." Her gaze travelled round the plain little room – his cell in anything but name. Then, as if realising exactly that, it dropped to the carpet for a second before she met his eyes again. "As I said before, I'm sorry that we can't just let you go. We're bound by the Judiciary to ensure that you see out the remainder of your sentence. But working for us here has to be better than whatever they had you doing in the Institute, hasn't it?"

Billy could only remember a handful of moments from his time in the Institute now – some effect of the sentence they used to release him from the habitual daze he'd been in during his time there, no doubt – but even the mention of the place gave him gooseflesh. Nevertheless he'd have been quite prepared to tell her what he could remember if the look in her eye hadn't said that, surprisingly, she already had some knowledge of what inmates were subjected to in the name of improvement. So, he nodded. Certainly, he couldn't imagine anything they could have him do out here that would make him feel as disconnected as he had in there. He never wanted to feel that again.

"So, within reason," she said, "is there anything we can do for you as a gesture of good faith?"

Billy was taken aback. If they weren't prepared to let him go, what could he ask for? His first thought was to ask her to contact the old man for him, but Tocka had already conveyed the news of Seldom's demise. He'd be spitting mad at that. To follow that up with the news that Billy had been arrested and sentenced and now was supposed to serve the

Weathermakers… Who knew how he would react? Besides, one way or another, he still intended to get himself home before the old man even got wind of his predicament.

So, if not that then…? Ah, yes… "Can you find out what happened to Seldom?"

Para stared blankly before the penny dropped. "Oh, the –"

"The sylvan. Its name was Seldom and it never deserved the treatment it received in Karpentine. I need to know what happened to it."

"I'm sorry," Para said. "There was nothing salvageable. My aunt commanded it disposed of. Burnt to ash." With a last apologetic shrug, she left.

So much for good intentions, Billy thought.

Once the key had turned again in the lock, Billy went to peer out of the window. What little he could see of the courtyards below the nest of roof ridges were in late afternoon shadow and he saw no sign of the guards that Para had mentioned so apologetically, but that didn't mean they weren't there. It looked like he was going to the ball after all.

He took the bath he'd been craving since his arrival in Karpentine, steaming his aching bones and distracting himself with the evening edition of the newspaper that someone had left in the room while he was out. They didn't half like their news here. Three editions a day, each a thick sheaf of pages crammed with tiny print. The narrow columns were only broken up by shouty headlines, the occasional artist's rendering and advertisements for must-have devices that guaranteed to do ordinary household chores better than doing them by hand, but promised to take at least as much manual labour. Back home, Billy was occasionally happy enough to read both sides of the weekly sheet from Canza. Here, he'd never get through a single edition before the next was published.

Still, as you dipped through the pages the stories drew you in, in their own fashion. Well, they would, wouldn't they. If the Book of the Law were written in some degree of Karpentiner Ink, sure as the sky the newspaper would be too. As he read, he tried to keep that in mind.

As Para had predicted, the Weathermaker's ball featured prominently. He recognised the picture accompanying the story as that of the despicable woman whose intervention had sent him to the Institute. It bore the caption *Jelena Loess, Queen Of Clouds*, and the nickname was sprinkled affectionately throughout the piece. The journalist even went as far as to hope that the ball wouldn't be marred by the continuing fuss over the drought refugees.

Much of the rest of the paper was devoted to the reporting of achievement stocks. Page after page of complicated figures. Billy managed to puzzle them out sufficiently to understand that in the table of primary stocks, the Weathermakers' value had slumped overnight, continuing a recent downward trend. There was a sidebar table on the same page. It was titled: Persons Of Note. It came as no surprise to find the precocious Miss Loess's name on it, but that she sat only third amused him no end. He was still smiling to himself when a knock announced Kingsley dropping off his suit with a promise to return shortly to escort him to the ballroom.

As soon as he unwrapped the tailor's package he regretted his rebellious impulse in the shop. He had never seen so much red in one garment. Nervously, he put it on. The tailor had done an expert job, but when Billy looked at himself in the mirror he realised straight away that the vague notion he had begun to harbour of perhaps hiding at the back of the room was never going to work. The shiny material would have screamed *red* from a mile away. Even the stiff, creamy shirt wasn't going to prevent him standing out, literally like a sore thumb.

Again, he considered the window, but Kingsley had taken his own clothes away to be laundered. Any guards waiting for him down there would hardly have difficulty spotting him. And then another knock announced the driver's return anyway. When the door opened, however, it wasn't Kingsley. It was one of the Bello twins. He wore a fashionable ivory suit, with a carmine pocket square and band in his hat, and he made it look good too.

"Well, I see you dressed for the occasion." Erudite, Billy thought. He remembered that one's voice as being a fraction deeper. His face a mite more punchable, although it was a close run thing.

"What are you doing here?" Billy grunted. "Where's the driver?"

The question seemed to amuse the Courier. "Oh, our friend, Mr Kingsley, has more pressing duties. Fortunately, I was available to shepherd you to the festivities. I happen to be going that way myself."

Billy scowled at the glib lie. "What duties?"

Erudite rolled his eyes. "Sundry ones," he repeated airily. "But very important and quite unavoidable, I assure you."

Billy folded his arms. He might as well have asked: *how much did you bribe him?* "What do you want from me, Bello?"

The grin vanished. "I've already told you, Braid," he said. "To take you to the ball. Now, are you coming or not?"

Billy would have loved to have smacked the Courier one right then. Growing up no stranger to a scrap, he'd learned how to steer clear of someone who seriously knew how to look after themselves, even if he hadn't always heeded that instinct. A dandy as he might be, Erudite was one of those that Billy would happily make an exception for, whatever it cost him later. But not right now, because this unexpected encounter presented another opportunity. He jammed his hands in his carmine pockets and followed the man out.

The servants' wing was a maze of turns and junctions, but Erudite navigated it confidently and soon they emerged into the public area of the mansion. Plaster and paint gave way to marble and crystal, ironwork to gilt. Passages became mirrored halls. Servants bustled by them continually. Some even managed not to stare, but all were watchful. Should Billy have clouted his guide and made a run for it he wouldn't have got far.

When Billy and Erudite passed through a pair of painted doors, emerging onto the upper balcony of a cavernous vestibule, muffled music reverberated and a terracing of gleaming stairs to'ed and fro'ed downwards towards a tessellated floor. "I know what you're thinking." Erudite's voice echoed as he skipped down the stairs. "You're thinking: what kind of Couriers get invited to a Grand Ball, aren't you?" Billy didn't deny it had crossed his mind. "The answer is clever ones. Useful ones." The corner of a smile. "Perhaps, just by way of example, ones who have recently returned from a long and fruitless trip to a certain forsaken mountain region." They were approaching an enormous set of doors flanked with guardsmen now but, before they reached them, Erudite drew him aside. "Listen, I'm telling you this for your own benefit. You are going to be engaged in conversation by a lot of charming people, all of whom will attempt to persuade you to favour them with tales of your crazy master and his quaint little toys. Do yourself a favour and don't indulge them for a second."

The impertinent bastard. "Wouldn't dream of it," Billy said.

Erudite flashed his sharp smile again. "Of course not." He dropped his voice. "All I'm saying is, if you were to be persuaded *at all*, the way to play it is to hold out. Keep your options open and you'll walk all the way back to those benighted mountains of yours a richer man."

The Courier turned to open the door. That was it? No sordid offer? No kid-gloved coercion? The man was just going to walk away having given him free advice? As Erudite raised his hand to push the doors, Billy caught his arm. "Wait. Did you talk to him?"

A sigh and a roll of the eyes. "Yes."

"How is he?"

"Awkward."

That one word at least brought a little warmth to Billy's heart. "Tell me one more thing," he said, as Erudite reached again for the door.

"What?"

"What did you and your brother do with Seldom? Who did you sell it to?" Because if there was one thing Billy had learned about the people of Karpentine, they didn't turn down an opportunity to make advantage.

Erudite blinked, then grinned. The grin became a laugh. "Who's to say there was value in that bag of old sticks?"

"*Who to?*"

But the Courier had already pushed the door open. "The highest bidder, of course."

TEN

Billy had been in villages that were smaller than the Loess mansion's ballroom. The ornate, vaulted cavern was impossible to take in all at once, and his first impression was of echoing, buzzing space created within more tiles and plaster and glass than he had ever set eyes on. At one end was a small orchestra outfitted in the family colours of sky blue and white. Their music was sweeping, airy and expansive. At the other end, a troupe of acrobats towered and tumbled to the beat of pipe, squeeze box and shivery tambourine. Entering from the middle, Billy could barely hear either of them over the raucous seethe of people. The room teemed like a fry pool in spawning season. Erudite Bello had melted into the throng, so Billy looked for Para himself, but it was impossible. Everyone wore the same fashionable ivory, with only a few individualists clearly attempting to make an impact by going against the flow, although none as conspicuously as himself.

All of it made Billy dizzy. The crush of colour. The wafts of alcohol and spiced meat from the trays carried by circulating staff. The churning surf of music and conversation. For a moment he had the impression of a plaintive moan all but lost in the storm of bonhomie, but put it down to his imagination. For all he knew he might have made it himself.

Every instinct still told him to flee. Get away from these horrendous people, out of this awful house and – under sentence or not – find a way back home. But there were guards outside the room, guards out in the courtyard. He'd already tried and failed to escape once. Who knew another attempt would see him slung back in the brain-rotting banality of the Institute. He didn't think he could take that. Besides, he now had an additional coal smouldering in his heart. He wasn't leaving Karpentine without Seldom.

Seeking respite, he looked up and saw a great ceiling that swept upwards and gathered above the assembly like nothing so much as the marquee tent in which the aerialists and horsemasters performed their shows in at the Canza fair, but with glass instead of canvas, slender white-painted metal in place of guy ropes and timber. Beyond the glass, the sky. Wide and blue, freckled with drifting scuds of cloud that were pinking at the edges as the sun took its leave for the evening. Billy watched a skein of geese arrow across the vault, tracked them to where the roof abutted the wall, and then realised that it was all wrong. The fringes of this marvellous view should have been spoiled by the city's surrounding towers and chimneys, but there was just sky, even if it was more populated by clouds than the Weathermakers were reputed to allow above the Sunshine City. Then he realised another thing. The clouds were not in the sky. They were inside the room, gathering under the ceiling glass like party balloons.

"Rather clever, isn't it?" The speaker was a fat gentleman in a dove grey suit who stood beside a settee occupied by a matron and a younger man who presented, to Billy's eyes, a schoolroom tableau.

"You know I'm proud," he heard the dame say to the younger man, "if a little surprised given your current position, that you have achieved an invitation, so don't do anything to spoil it, darling." Billy would have rolled his eyes but the fellow merely ducked his head obediently.

"They do it with projections and mirrors, I understand," the first man went on. "Not the clouds of course – that's *their* thing after all – the view, I mean." The fat man sipped fizzing wine, then dabbed with a silken handkerchief at his florid neck. "A neat trick, but there's no real art in it, is there?"

Billy's heart sank. Though Erudite Bello had warned him that all sorts of people would be keen to make his acquaintance, he hadn't expected the ordeal to start right away. He had no knowledge of art but, if he had to converse with these people, he did not want to have cross words with them straight away. "I suppose," he said, "that depends on what you mean by art." He pretended to gaze around the vast room, but watched him out of the corner of his eye.

The man dabbed again, this time at his mouth, but failed to hide his prissy smile. "Well now," he said once he had mastered his mirth. "That is indeed the most pertinent question. What do we mean by *art?*" He turned to the people on the settee. The woman, dressed in blue and wearing an iridescent mantle printed with a pattern of butterflies, was still haranguing her companion.

"Cecily," the fat man said.

The woman, interrupting her lecture with visible displeasure, turned to greet her hailer. Doing so disturbed the mantle and the butterflies rose from her shoulders and circled above her head. It was like a momentarily disturbed flight of the insects that had been basking on sun-warmed bark in one of the groves, and Billy felt a fresh needle of homesickness.

"What is it?"

The florid man ignored her sour disposition. "The infamous Mister Braid here was just raising the question of what we call art," he said. "What do you think of that, eh?"

The woman's smile was no more pleasant than the pursed lips it replaced. "I think we'd be honoured to hear your opinions, Mr Braid," she simpered. The butterflies had begun to settle on her shoulders once again. "On the subjects of, oh say, the articulated human form. Now I think we can all agree that there is art in that, can we not? It is one of the very foundation pillars. Killick, no. You'll get sugar on your clothes."

The young man was reaching for a pastry. "Sorrow, Auntie," he murmured, though there was a flinty displeasure in the look he cast her.

"I suppose so," Billy said, even more cautious now on learning they knew who he was. Although perhaps that shouldn't have been so much of a surprise. Para had called him a *nom-du-jour* after all. He looked again in vain among the milling throng for her, then decided that for now avoidance was the best tactic. "Those are beautiful butterflies."

The woman pressed her lips into the meagrest of acceptances.

"Lady Roach is the Grande Dame of the Artificers Animeaux," said the florid man. "Such adornments are her stock in trade."

Ah. So *these* were the people responsible for those unnatural animals, for possibly colluding with the Artisans if Para was to be believed. Billy realised it was no coincidence that these should be the very first people he met on arriving here in the ballroom and wondered how much Erudite Bello had been paid for the service. Well, he didn't like being set up. "We don't often have the opportunity to see such fine things in the mountains," he replied casually, "but I have had occasion to admire your family's work. A beautiful buck, and do you know, it had real intelligence in its eyes."

"Watch your words." Lady Roach's eyes narrowed. "Some might take that for an accusation."

"And what if it is?"

"Careful, son."

Billy knew who the fat man was too. "And you must be Grandhandmaster Shankhill."

The man mopped himself again. "How very astute," he said. "I am the head of a great family. I imagine you've heard my name even out in your mountains."

Billy enjoyed the discomfiture. "My master has mentioned it from time to time."

"And how is Handmaster Kim?" Shankhill inquired. "Is he still doing our family proud?"

Now it was Billy's turn to be surprised. "Handmaster?" Kim had claimed an association with the Artisans, nothing more. *No one of importance*, he'd said.

"You didn't know your master was fully incorporated?" Shankhill tapped his lips. "I wonder why he omitted to tell you that. Given his skills it should have been obvious, after all."

Billy's confidence was short-lived, with the advantage wrested away from him as quickly as he had attained it. He felt that the next thing he said might get the old man into proper trouble.

"There you are!" Every head turned as a vision in red descended on them like a carmine hawk. Paraphernalia was wearing a suit that, save for the tailoring, was identical to Billy's. "I've been looking for you everywhere, Billy Braid. Kingsley had instructions to bring you directly to me but I see you've allowed yourself to be distracted. Really, though, I thought you had better manners than to leave me standing around like a…"

She wore no shirt beneath the suit jacket and a curl of fiery orange glass hung between her lapels. "A plum?" he suggested, the humour springing more out of relief than any real levity.

Para laughed. "Exactly so. Like a *plum*." She spread her arms in a look-at-me gesture. "And a lonely one at that. Well, it's good to see that you're no wallflower at any rate." She nodded to the rest of the group in turn. "Grandhandmaster. Grande Dame."

"Hello, Paraphernalia." The young man's attempt at a smile made him look like a donkey hungry for a carrot.

Para slipped her arm around Billy's before she answered. "Hello, Killick." It was a friendly greeting, but no more than that.

"What on earth have you done with your hair, girl?" Cecily Roach's lips smacked with distaste.

Para bounced her new red curls with her fingers and grinned. "Oh, it's just a bit of fun in honour of our new friend. I think it's rather natty. I might keep it like this."

Roach glared in response.

Para tugged Billy's arm. "Come on, mountain man," she said. "There are simply loads more people for you to meet."

Shankhill cleared his throat. "I hope we'll have the opportunity to talk further, Mister Braid." The look in his eyes was that of a fisherman letting his catch swim free, for the moment at least. "Our conversation had just become interesting."

"Of course, Uncle Lem," Para smiled. "There'll be plenty of him to go around. First of all, Billy, let's get you a drink."

Para wheeled him away from the trio. When they were far enough away, she said: "Well that was very cosy, wasn't it? The Artificers and the Artisans together like that. How very brazen of the Grandhandmaster. What did you tell him?"

"Nothing."

"You don't pass the time of day with Lem Shankhill on the subject of nothing, Billy. Red or white?" They had arrived at a freestanding pedestal. It held a shallow steel bowl with a drain. Para reached underneath for glasses. "Wine? Red or white?"

Billy looked for bottles but saw none. "Well, red seems fitting, I suppose."

Ignoring his joke, Para placed the glasses in the bowl and then pressed a button. "You might want to stand back a bit," she said. "So? What did you talk about?"

Billy watched a small cloud detach itself from the cluster under the roof and begin to descend. "He asked my opinions on the subject of art." Recent experience with the Weathermakers' clouds made him take Para's advice in stepping away from the bowl. "But I know nothing about stuff like that, so there was nothing to tell." As the cloud descended, it grew darker, purpling underneath like a livid bruise.

"You have to watch what you say around people like Shankhill and Roach. They're very good at making advantage out of the smallest crumb. Even agreeing with an innocuous suggestion, even just a nod to be polite, can be used against you."

Thinking back, Billy realised he might have agreed or nodded. "Well..."

Para flashed him a look. "What was Kingsley thinking, bringing you close to them, anyway?"

"It wasn't Kingsley that came to escort me," he said not caring overmuch if it got the driver into trouble. Best she know how easily bought her staff were. "It was Erudite Bello." The anger was more than a flash this time and it took her a moment to master it. *"Be loyal and you shall never want for reward?"* he added. It was the quote that his mother had somewhat desperately inscribed in his copy of the Book when he had left home. It was petty to do so, but he took a little pleasure from repeating it now.

Para ignored the barb. "So, what did our friend, Bello say?"

"Nothing much. He did deliver something of a warning about talking out of turn but I think his main purpose was to bring me to the ballroom exactly where Shankhill was waiting."

"Well of course he did," Para said glumly. "He's an Artisan spy after all."

The cloud had become thunderously swollen and now huge drops of ruby liquid began to fall from it spattering the steel. The glasses filled and overflowed, the spillage draining away along with the rest of the excess rain.

"Why do you employ him, if you know he's a spy?"

Para managed something of a smile. "Oh we've all got spies, Billy. It's all part of the game. Poke and whisper, remember?"

The cloud rained itself out and Para's expression as it began to break apart into wisps appeared momentarily sad. She wiped the stems of the glasses with a napkin, then handed one to Billy. "These things are so messy. But they do make an impression, don't you think?"

Billy found the wine heavy, a bit sour. He'd rather have had beer. "Shankhill said something about Kim, too," he said. "He said that he had once been a Handmaster of the Artisans. Is that true?"

Para sipped from her own glass. "You didn't know?"

"He rarely mentions the city, unless it's to curse."

"And you were never interested enough to ask?"

Billy shrugged. Karpentiners evidently thought of their city as the centre of the world and it was inconceivable to them that those from outside didn't share their self-absorption. Growing up, when the old man told him there was nothing interesting to tell about his time living in the city – that it was a noisy, smelly place that paid little more than lip service to the Law – Billy had been happy to take him at his word. He realised now how naïve he had been. Perhaps after all there had been more to Kim's departure than simply having the good sense to walk away from this place.

"Then it's probably just Uncle Lem looking for some connection that he can use to gain a claim to you." She might have been trying to put his mind at ease, but she looked pensive.

"Just like you Weathermakers?" he said, and found that he regretted doing so. She was trying to be nice.

"We bought and paid for your services fair and square," Para replied stiffly. "Now come on and meet the rest of the guests before Aunt Jelena sends out a search party."

"Para…" Billy put a hand on her arm and she turned.

"What?"

"You look all right in red," he said. "Thanks for not making me the only plum at the ball."

She grinned and linked arms with him again. "One is an idiot," she said. "Two is a statement. Next week it'll be a revolution."

The evening turned out to be less of a pain than Billy had feared. He got a taste for the wine, and he relaxed once he understood that, while Para introduced him to this person and that person, she controlled each conversation, allowing each interlocutor to struggle to frame their questions, then restricting Billy's replies to pleasantries before whirling him on to the next encounter. It was like a game. Almost fun.

Everyone wanted to know about the sylvans.

Is it true that they play chess better than a man? This was a burly Provisioner called Langstrom.

Is it true they will attack humans without provocation? An elderly Actuary who hid his obvious terror behind his haughtiness.

Is it true that they are made with astonishing anatomical accuracy? A gaggle of scandalised, tittering teenagers.

Each time Billy regarded the amused, scornful, suspicious faces and pretended to ponder. "Well…" he said and counted the seconds before Para interjected once more.

"What will happen when they learn to carve their own kind?" This came from a woman with copper-coloured tresses bound by cream ribbons into a tail that draped around her neck. Her stare while she awaited his answer was unnerving.

"Why would they want to do that?" had been his response before Para spun him away once more.

"I think that's enough small talk," she said. "Time for the main event." It was only then that Billy realised their circuit of the room had all along been a trajectory towards Para's aunt. The disappointment he felt surprised him.

"You're proving quite a hit with my guests, Mister Braid." The Queen of Clouds shone in brilliant white, but the delicacy of her gown did not

106

soften her. It merely streamlined the woman's severity, from the silver band woven into her hair to that deadly cane, planted on the tiled floor as if it connected her to the core of the earth.

"I'm happy to be providing amusement," he replied, unable to keep the annoyance out of his voice. "Thank you for inviting me."

She did something with her lips, the ghost of smiling for one who no longer has to bother with such niceties. "I didn't." She turned to her niece. "Paraphernalia, I believe you promised Mister Roach a dance this evening."

The fellow in question was standing at the hostesses' shoulder. "Sorrow," he said, although it wasn't clear what he was apologising for.

"Of course," she said brightly through a somewhat fixed smile. "I'm so sorry Killick. It's all been such a whirl."

"Oh, it has," Roach agreed as they went off in the direction of the orchestra. "It really has."

"Now you've been separated from your minder there is someone *I* would like you to meet," Jelena Loess said to Billy. "Since it is my ball, I don't suppose you have any objections? Good, now take my arm. This cane isn't just an offensive weapon, you know."

Billy did as he was told, and was surprised to find the woman's flesh soft. He had imagined that she was made of steel.

"You should know that I instructed my niece that in the interests of protecting our commercial property you were not to attend this event."

Billy groaned inwardly. Not back to this again. "The sylvan was not your property –"

"I'm not talking about your toy," she snapped back. "I'm talking about you. In any case," she went on, "I'm relieved to see that her disobedience has not been a huge disaster, and the fact that you have proved yourself little more than a boorish ignoramus with criminal tendencies might even lessen the interest in you from our competitors."

It seemed that Para, for all her faults, was the exception to the rule that the high ups of Karpentine were grasping, entitled bastards. After being steered away from Shankhill and Roach, Billy had almost begun to believe he'd misjudged the folk here. Privately, he thanked this so-called Queen of Clouds for reminding him of the truth. Publicly, for now, he kept his mouth shut.

On one side of the room was a long table laden with food. Guests jostled for access to the elaborate pastries that held honey-coloured suns and powdered sugar clouds. Billy hoped optimistically that he and his

107

companion were heading there too, but it became apparent that their real destination was a secluded ring of chairs beyond. "I don't understand," he said as they negotiated around the grazers. "I thought the Loess family *were* the Weathermakers. Who are your competitors?"

"And there precisely you prove my point," said Jelena Loess. "In Karpentine, all families are competitors. Especially the people you are about to meet. I don't like this, but I accept that I would not have been able to prevent them contacting you at some point, and at least this way I can control what is being said." The circled chairs had high backs and encompassing wings, and Billy now saw the tops of heads showing above two of them. Loess stopped before they reached them. Her stormy grey eyes were absolutely serious. "Not one word."

The heads in the chairs belonged to men, both dressed in suits that were smart while pointedly eschewing any claim to fashion. One was perhaps in his fifties, with greying temples and a moustache that rode his upper lip like the line of a draughtsman's pencil. His companion was a younger replica, but paler and stiffer. They could only be father and son.

The two men were clearly who Loess had intended Billy to meet, but there was a third member to the group who had not been visible from behind the chairs. And the Queen of Clouds was surprised by their presence. She recovered quickly, but she was plainly annoyed. "Billy Braid, may I introduce you to Merit Crane, Governor of the Guild of Constructors, and his son, Stillworth Crane, Karpentine's brightest engineering mind." Both men inclined their heads in greeting. "And Lady Moraine Otterbree of the Inksmiths, of course." The tiny lady with the bobbed black hair could have been any age. She smiled sweetly and regarded Billy with arresting indigo eyes. Unbidden, a tang of remembered smell assaulted him. The cloying stink of the ink vats where he'd laboured during his incarceration. He felt his gorge rise and did his best to keep his expression neutral until it subsided. To distract himself he nodded at the two men. He already knew the name Crane, and despised it.

"Mister Braid." The elder Crane refocused Billy's attention. He was swirling a thimbleful of golden liquid in a squat glass. "I believe you owe us a sylvan." It would have been a small pleasure to hear someone using the correct term for once if the man's tone had not been exactly as condescending as Billy had expected. This was a man, he thought, who paid attention to the details and was the head of a powerful family because of it. *Direct*, Para had called him. Well, that suited Billy fine.

"Seldom would have been delivered as requested," he said, "if that cloud hadn't –"

"Seldom?"

"That was its name."

Merit Crane leaned forward. "You give your machines names?"

"Mister Braid," the hostess butted in, "will remember, I'm sure, that he promised not to discuss matters that are still under judicial review. Especially since his own liability in the affair remains unresolved."

The threat was imprecise. Jelena Loess must have known that the magistrates had found Billy innocent of causing the cloud's behaviour. It was the matter of Seldom's intelligence that remained unresolved. Nonetheless, Billy chose his next sentence carefully. "It doesn't matter anyway, does it? Seldom is gone. You'll have to go back to the master if you want another one."

Crane ran his finger around the rim of his glass. It vibrated unpleasantly. "And would he accept our request, do you think?"

"He wouldn't even open the letter."

The Otterbree woman had been twirling her own wine glass with fingers sheathed in gloves of exquisite black lace while she watched the exchange, but now she smiled. "Oh, Merit, you weren't so gauche, surely?"

Crane glanced at the woman whose expertise lay in producing the product she was chiding him about. "It was expedient. And it would have achieved the desired results." He turned his attention to his hostess. "If it hadn't been for an inconvenient little accident with the weather."

"Of course it was an *accident*," Jelena Loess snapped.

"Precisely," Crane interrupted. "It's shoddy, is what it is. If one of my manufactories malfunctioned like that there would be public uproar."

The two family heads were clearly skirmishing around a long standing argument. If Billy hadn't been the subject of it he might even have found it entertaining. Moraine Otterbree was certainly enjoying the show. Her lips were pursed in a crimp of satisfaction, but it melted away as two more people joined the exclusive gathering. The man was older, balding with unkempt grey-gold tufts of hair around his ears and air an about him that Billy could only describe as vacant. The woman shared enough of her companion's features to be his daughter, and Billy recognised her as one of his interlocutors from earlier. The one with the copper hair and the unwavering stare.

Otterbree murmured the slightest of introductions. "My husband, Augustin Creasey, Mr Braid, and his daughter, Alicia."

Merit Crane, into his stride now, ignored the newcomers. "You see, Stillworth," he said to his son. "It's these new families with their half-baked, unproven technologies and no respect for tradition."

His son, however, wasn't listening. With obvious effort, he levered himself to his feet. "I'm going to get a drink," he said.

"I'll come with you." As far as Billy was concerned, having met Crane his duty to Loess was discharged. And he really did not want to get into another round of questions. Stillworth barely glanced at him, but he did not object. Jelena Loess possibly did, but said nothing, perhaps judging it safer after all to keep himself and Merit apart. Her stare as he slipped past her chair was enough of a reminder: *not a word.*

It wasn't far to the bar and buffet tables but Stillworth walked as if every step caused him pain. It wasn't visible on his implacable face, but his gait was agonisingly slow.

"Are you all right?" Billy asked him.

"Whisky." The liveried server reached for an ornate decanter whose contents were the colour of rich caramel. When Stillworth took the offered glass the cuff of his suit rode up exposing leather and steel strapping. He tossed the drink back. "Again." He took longer with the second one, his calm eyes turning at last to observe Billy. "I was born with a congenital weakness," he said. "It's been long documented and not worthy of note now, but it's not something I can easily disguise."

Though the engineer was clearly not playing for sympathy, Billy did feel some. Back home, people who were unable to carry their share were considered sorry cases. "Wasn't there anything the doctors could do?"

Stillworth's countenance was gnomic. "There might have been," he said. "But my father refused them."

"Why?"

Stillworth's gaze drifted away to pass over the heads of the dancers on the sunken dance floor. The orchestra was playing a sweeping, lyrical tune. Like a corn dance, but with more frills. Everything here had more frills. The aromas from the buffet table roused Billy's appetite. He selected a hemispherical dome of blanched pastry in a foil tray. The server handed him a napkin, which Billy considered pretty insulting until he bit into it and a puff of fine sugar escaped. Some of it sprayed his face, and he was still wondering how they made it cold like that when he saw that the rest of it had formed a cloud and was now falling like gentle snow onto his suit. He wiped at his face and then at his red lapels.

"My father believes that early obstacles seed great lives." If Crane noticed the mess, he chose to ignore it. "I believe he is correct."

Below them the dance finished, the partners bowed politely and a new, more sprightly tune was struck up. There was a flash of red in the centre of the crush, which Billy realised must be Para. When she came round again he glimpsed faces: Killick Roach not disguising his pleasure, Para's smile so fixed it had become a grimace.

Stillworth saw them too. "Don't you think you'd better do the gallant thing?"

"What do you mean?"

Stillworth flicked a disparaging glance at Billy's suit. "She's your partner for the evening, is she not? This will be the poor girl's fourth dance with Baby Cock." He laughed. "I beg your pardon, Killick – some childhood names have a tendency to stick, don't they?"

Baby Cock Roach? That was cruel, even for children.

"Look at her," Stillworth continued. "Witness the misery. Even if they're matched, I'd say that's more than enough punishment for anyone."

"They're betrothed?" Billy was surprised. "By Matchmakers?"

"Didn't she tell you?" Stillworth's expression might have been a smirk, but it was hard to read. "I'm not surprised. It's not exactly official yet and it hardly reflects well, but Jelena does so want ink in the bloodline. However diluted it may be."

Billy watched as the dancers whirled round again. Para had dropped all pretence of having a good time but Roach was in his element. He did feel some sympathy for her. She'd treated him unexpectedly decently, after all. "I thought Killick's family were the pet makers."

Stillworth snorted. "Like most of us, he had *two* parents. The mother was a minor Inksmith. Of course neither lineage did him any good...until now."

They watched the couple perform another circuit. Even half-hearted, Para's nimbleness almost made up for Roach's clumsy enthusiasm, but not quite. The next time they stumbled Roach used it as an opportunity to attempt a move so obvious that back home it would have earned him a hot handprint on his cheek. Stillworth was right. With a sigh, Billy waded into the throng. When he reached the pair he didn't even have to ask to cut in. Para dropped her partner like a steamhouse coal.

111

"Mister Braid." There was scold in her voice, but she was beaming. "It's simply not the done thing for one's partner to loiter all night with the boys without dancing at least once." Clearly she had not been unobservant while stuck in the round. "Killick, darling, you don't mind if I teach our uneducated friend here the error of his ways, do you?"

Roach evidently minded a great deal, but he seemed to know better than to make a boorish fuss. Instead he bowed. "It's been a pleasure," he said stiffly.

Billy watched Roach depart. "When you said a ball, I didn't think I'd be required to dance." He meant it as a gentle joke, but it was born of a yawning self-consciousness. At the mountain fairs, dancing was more of an enthusiastic ruck that everybody joined in with. Here it was a much more refined pastime. Judging from those whirling around them, a performance. He had no clue what he was doing, and everybody was watching.

"Oh, don't be such a child." She took his hands. "We all have to do things we don't want to sometimes. Just do what I do and you'll be fine."

"Because you own me and can tell me what to do?" The barb came more from nervousness than because he felt she shared her aunt's mercenary opinions.

She rolled her eyes. "If you like. Just try not to make a fool of yourself."

Para kept things simple, making it easy for him. While they danced, the other dancers glanced their way often but no one stared and he relaxed enough to enjoy it. At least out here with her he was free from interrogation.

In hardly any time at all, however, the dance changed to a slow waltz. "Maybe we should sit this one out?" Billy started to walk away, but Para pulled him back in.

"We have to," she said. "Otherwise Alicia Creasey will get you." She whirled them around and Billy saw the woman with the copper hair at the edge of the dance floor toying a wineglass against her lips and regarding them intently. Behind her, perhaps more surprisingly, the aloof Stillworth Crane was doing the same.

Billy was relieved when Para spun him round the other way again. "Who is she?"

Para shrugged. "Augustin's daughter. No one of note, though you do seem to have caught her eye. But, more importantly," she continued, "if we leave the floor now it will look as if you staged a rescue, and poor

Killick will look bad." She stepped in close, slipped her arm up to his shoulder. "Don't worry, it'll be over soon."

"I didn't mean…" But they had begun to move again, close and fluid, to the sway of the violins.

"I know." She lifted her head so that he could look into her eyes. They were impossible to read.

They didn't speak for the rest of dance. With her arm around him and his around her waist, with her head now resting on his shoulder, he had to admit that it wasn't such a bad way to spend the time. After that one ended, Para kept him on the floor for another dance, which again passed in silence. When the fourth tune began Billy said: "He's not that bad, is he?"

Her eyes were bright now. "Would you marry him?"

"Fair point." It was another full revolution before he thought of something else to say. "Certainly not if there's any truth in his nickname."

Para laughed then. It was a snotty sound. She held up her pinkie finger and wiggled it. "It's true," she said.

Billy was mildly surprised. "You mean you've already…?"

"We've known each other since we were children." She slid her arm around him again, her fingers gentle against his spine through his jacket. "And kids judge achievement in all sorts of funny ways. You know: conquests, dares."

Billy did know. He'd always suspected that his own rare teenage fumblings had been the result of dares. "You all know each other pretty well then," he ventured. "You, Killick, Stillworth, Alicia?"

Para nodded, then said. "Though, not Alicia. She's always been a bit strange."

"Well, in Killick's case, you must have made a lasting impression."

"Billy…?"

This time when he looked into her eyes there was no mistaking what was behind them.

Para's apartments were more modest than Billy had expected. Just a couple of public rooms, a small private kitchen and a short passage leading he assumed to a bathroom and bedroom. The walls and drapes were a pretty enough pattern, but somewhat long in the tooth. There were clothes everywhere. Billy guessed that the red outfit hadn't been an automatic choice after all. He searched for somewhere to sit while Para rooted around in the kitchen's cold store. She came back with a bottle and a couple of grubby glasses.

The contents of the bottle were clear and a little oily. Billy accepted a glass, inhaled a familiar herbed scent. "Is this *strosh?*"

"Guilty," she said. "I may have all the advantages of class and good breeding, but deep down I have the basest of tastes." She knew how to drink it too, taking the entire glassful into her mouth to get the full flavour of meadow grass and lilac then gulping it down, doing well not to retch. Billy followed suit. It froze his mouth and burned his throat.

Her lips were cold too, her tongue hot and liquid. The kiss lasted an age, during which all Billy could think of was that this was the very last way he had imagined the evening turning out.

They were almost entirely naked by the time they reached her bed. Then she was sitting astride him, and he was inside her, and she was looking down at him with challenge in her eyes. Then she began to bounce and grind with such vigour that it resembled more a session of physical exercise than lovemaking. He'd never had the like, not with the few village girls who had given him the time of day, who liked as energetic a tumble as anyone, and not even with the working lads and lasses at the Well Earned Repose, who were of course paid for their industry.

Billy grabbed her thighs to hold her still. "Steady," he said. "It's not a competition."

"No?" Para leant down to kiss him again. "Everything is a competition."

And if it was, she won. But afterwards she held him tight. Less like a prize, more like something needful. And that was an unfamiliar experience for him.

ELEVEN

"Get up, lazy bones." Something thudded into Billy's pillow. He smelled citrus.

"You weren't calling me lazy last night." He still couldn't quite believe how the previous evening had played out. Truly, Karpentine was a place of surprises. He certainly had no complaints.

"Shut up and get up."

He couldn't see her in the dark. "What time is it?"

"Time to go to work and get some value out of our new commodity."

The light came on. Framed in the bedroom doorway he saw Para had dressed already, and she was holding a large orange in each hand.

"What about last night? Wasn't that value enough?" He meant it as a joke, and perhaps to test what their lovemaking had meant, but even in silhouette her indignation was clear.

"My aunt did not," the remaining oranges flew, one forcing him to duck, the other hitting him in the belly, "I repeat, *did not* buy out your improvement indenture to provide me with a gigolo. Now, get back to your room, get changed into something appropriate for work – because sure as the sky's blue I am not going to be seen out with a carnival clown today – and meet me up at the Weathermakers' Tower before the sun has cleared the horizon."

Well, that was clear then. Billy had borne enough morning regrets to see that she was genuinely angry. Pissed at herself, maybe out of sense of duty to her match with Killick Roach but more likely because she'd let her standards slip. Well, fine. At least he wasn't going to have to worry about emotionally attachments. He'd just been starting to like her too.

Billy got out of bed, started searching for his clothes. "What about breakfast?" he said.

"I just threw it at you."

Billy found his way back to his own quarters largely by trial and error. The mansion was quiet. Not even a servant haunted the halls, not even a guard, and he hadn't seen Kingsley since the previous day. After such close attention it felt weird to be allowed to wander around on his own. What he couldn't work out was whether it was due to an assumption that

Billy would toe the line… or, equally unexpectedly, to *trust*. Either would be foolish. What was to stop him just walking right out of here right now, brazen as his scarlet suit?

The answer to that, he told himself, was his promise to Seldom now that he knew the sylvan's pieces were not after all destroyed. He had to stick around until he found out who Erudite's buyer was. Until then, he may as well play along with whatever the Weathermakers wanted of him.

Someone had laundered his clothes, and beside them was a pile of quilted flying gear. It didn't take much guesswork to figure out what this morning had in store for him, and the idea of *playing along* suddenly had less appeal. The thought of going up in that contraption of hers made his knees weak. He went for a hot shower that would have would have cost him half an hour of pump-priming at home, and stood too long under it while he convinced himself that it wasn't going to be as bad as he feared – Para flew in these things all the time after all – but it did little good. By the time he left the Loess mansion and started up towards the Weathermaker's tower he was jittery as a barkfly. Worse still, the sun had got there ahead of him.

"You're late." Para's dirigible had been dragged out of the sheds. There was hardly a trace of scorching on the cobbles now. Even the stone that Jelena Loess had blasted out of the ground had been replaced. All evidence that Seldom had ever been here erased.

The combination of her brusqueness and his nerves made him defensive. "What of it?"

"Billy –"

"Who did your Couriers sell Seldom's remains to?"

He didn't know which of them was more surprised at him blurting out the question. But why not? He was entitled to know.

Barely even pausing in her preparations, Para muttered, "Some help, please?" And when Billy didn't move, she unbent enough to explain. "This work is time critical. We need to get up there before the drift starts. Now will you help me load up, please?"

Billy relented. He could wait for a better opportunity. And, if it didn't arise, he could always press Erudite for that information instead.

The cargo stacked nearby comprised leather instrument cases and wooden boxes, their contents identified on brass plaques. Para climbed into the basket and asked him to hand the items over. It didn't take long. "If that's all you wanted me for, I can go, right?" It slipped out as he passed the last box over. Another nervous, half-meant joke that wasn't remotely funny.

She rolled her eyes. "Just get in."

The first lurch when the tethers were loosed was the worst. A sideways bounce as the balloon found the breeze and then was dragged upwards in the opposite direction. Billy's fingers whitened on the turned wicker edge, but Para deftly started the engine and steered the craft up and over the city.

As soon as they were aloft, her demeanour changed and a glimmer of a smile appeared below her goggles. The dirigible climbed into a sky losing its blush and revealing itself to be, once again, wide and blue. In the mountains, this would have been a rare start to the day. What the old man liked to call a big empty kind of morning, waiting to be filled with achievement. With a pang, Billy wondered what Kim might say if he could see him now? Call him a fool of all the seasons, no doubt.

"At least we have a nice day for it," Billy muttered through clenched teeth.

"It's always a nice day in the Sunshine City." There was a note of discomfort in her tone. "A blue sky in the morning is the number one way to keep the stockholders happy." Billy remembered the Weathermakers' plummeting performance in the newspaper's tables of achievement. It had seemed abstract at the time, but up here in the clear air he understood properly why the cloud that killed Seldom had caused so much fuss.

The dirigible rose and the rooftops of Karpentine spread out below. The colourful panoply of family flags and corporate banners. The towers and basilicas, the minarets and masts, spires and steeples, all striving to be an inch taller than their neighbours. From this vantage, all rendered equally inconsequential. Certainly, all were equally capable of killing him should the bag burst or the propeller shaft shear. Billy swallowed drily and gripped the canework even harder, but he made himself continue looking in the hope that he would eventually get used to doing what he was quite certain that only birds should ever do. That there was no admonishment against flying in the Book of the Law was an incredible oversight.

They passed over the northern quarter of the lowtown where the rare simplicity of the Institute of Improvement sat in shadow, as yet unaware of the beautiful sunrise now warming the tiles and chimneys of the other side of the hill. Of course, when the sun did touch that part of the town, the inmates would be oblivious. Billy thought of Ralston Maundy. Despite everything, he had liked the mischievous fraud and hoped that the rays found his face even if he was unable to enjoy them. He hoped too that his nephew and niece managed to scrape a kudo or two today to keep spirit and bones together. But nowhere near as much as he hoped to have his boots back on solid earth again soon.

The dirigible climbed and the cliffs passed below them too, and then to Billy's relief there was only the sea. Like the sky, it was blue and it was wide, and the higher they climbed the bluer and wider it got. His first thought was that it would probably provide a better landing should something go wrong with their vehicle. His second that this was probably entirely wrong and, even if they survived the fall, they would be too far from shore to swim to safety, but the cheerful winking of the sun on the waves helped him cling to his first notion. The calming beauty relaxed him enough to finally let go of the basket edge and think of things other than his imminent death. "Where are we going?" he asked.

Para had a chart in one hand, her other lazy on the rudder. He recognised the look on her face. He felt the same when he was among the trees. She was at home here. "Seeding grounds," she said.

"Okay." Looking down again he saw that their course followed a straight-line shadow beneath the waves. "What's that down there?"

Para looked to where he indicated. "Cables from a collector station." She pointed ahead. "See?" In the middle distance now was an island. It was octagonal, forested with metal constructions. "The islands are how Karpentine gets its power. The Weathermakers' achievement doesn't come just from selling rain. We grow thunderclouds out here in the seeding grounds and collect their discharges." As the dirigible approached, Billy stared at the cluster of angular treelike structures. Some were shiny, some blackened, some missing limbs. He groaned inwardly as he finally comprehended their destination. "Don't you want to know why we're going to the seeding grounds?" she asked.

"To 'get some value out of your new commodity'?" His half-hearted sarcasm didn't nearly cover the tremor in his voice but it was a better response than *to get us both blown to tiny pieces?*

Para tucked the chart under her arm and operated a complicated device resembling a compass. "Sort of." She stowed the device and leant on the rudder and Billy felt the vehicle veer away from the artificial island. "Believe it or not there are restrictions on what work indentures can be put to. You can't use them as slaves, for example, and they're not supposed to be forced to do dangerous jobs against their will. So, before we do this, I owe you an apology." She offered a smile of contrition, but there was an edge of something else too. "Because we're breaking quite a few rules here." She was excited.

"Your aunt doesn't know about this?"

Para widened her eyes. "She'd be horrified. We only bought your indentureship for information about your charming sylvans."

"Then why…?" He didn't know if he should be relieved that she was going against her aunt's wishes or even more terrified.

"I need to check a few things. Don't worry, you'll be perfectly safe." She said it so sincerely that he almost believed her.

Billy still couldn't work Para out. So much of the time she was as high handed as you'd expect of anyone of her station, but every now and then she let the mask slip and displayed that softer centre. The trouble was he never knew which he was going to get. She was as capricious as the wind itself.

"How did you know the manikin's remains had been sold by the Bellos?"

"Erudite told me." Surprised by the switch in subject, Billy replied immediately and then wondered if he would regret that. He might have to pursue the matter with the Courier himself and, whether he got what he wanted through finesse or force, he was sure she wouldn't approve. Well, perhaps he wouldn't have to. "What I want to know is who to?"

"Drop it, Billy." Para was serious, as if she could read his intentions. "You'll never stand a chance against those people."

He might have known. Every time this woman gave him hope, the next moment she snatched it away. "What people?" he said, frustrated.

"Any of them." And when he refused to drop his gaze, she added: "I don't know for certain, but my best guess would be the Inksmiths."

"The Inksmiths? That Otterbree woman?" The stink of the vats came back to him again over the fresh zing of ozone. It was almost all he could recall from the Institute now. Even in his padded suit, he shivered. "Why them?"

Para cocked her head as if gauging something, then she looped her arm around the dirigible's tiller. "You know how ink is made? It's made from water and shellac and carbon… which comes from burnt things. Most ink carbon is a mixture of lampblack from the Constructors' manufactories, boneblack from the abattoirs on the Meadows and, of course, carbonblack – wood ash, burnt trees… imported from your own precious forests for all I know. But inks have many varied properties and, while the secrets of the Inksmiths' ancient craft are jealously guarded, everyone knows that sometimes there's a little something special added to the mix. Trust me, if it did end up in their nest under the Exchange, whatever remained of Seldom will be in a labelled canister on a special shelf in Otterbree's laboratory. I'm sorry." Para attempted a reassuring smile that, this time, was anything but. Then she changed the subject again, using her High Town voice now. "Your interrogation with my aunt is scheduled for this afternoon, by the way. There will be a cream tea. I advise you to skip lunch."

"Well, that's something to look forward to," Billy said glumly as Para returned her attention to flying the craft. It was getting cold and the dirigible had now risen so high above the sea that the water looked as flat and hard as iron. "So, this classifies as dangerous work, does it?" he asked.

"Just don't start jumping about and you'll be fine." She nodded ahead and Billy saw that they had ventured beyond the city's clear-sky zone and were heading directly towards a churning bank of clouds. "This is where we make the weather."

Billy stayed silent as the dirigible climbed towards the thunderheads. There were winds up here that seemed to delight in tugging and buffeting the balloon. The motion upset the oranges in his stomach and he reached for the rolled canework again. The light shifted, now silver-dark and unsettling. Billy began to shiver, his skin simultaneously slick with moisture and tingling with electricity. But worst of all was the noise in his mind. He heard it in a similar way to sylvan speech, except there were no impressions that formed into words, just sounds and emotions. Beneath the bellowing winds and thunderous discharges was what could only be described as... *wailing*. Not just one voice, but many. Loud and petty and dissatisfied. And he knew that the hissing rage he had heard when Seldom met its end had been exactly what it sounded like, a fit of pique from the cloud that had struck the deadly blows. The noise became unbearable.

Para eased back on the throttle, locking the rudder out so that the dirigible began to describe a wide circle that passed through the misty lower reaches of the clouds. Glancing at Billy, she observed his distress and offered him another nod of reassurance as she opened one of the wooden cases. It contained a selection of glasswear. She mixed two liquids together in a flask and then screwed on a cap like that of a perfume bottle and pumped the mixture into the clouds in a fine green spray. Immediately it began to rain, and as drops splashed her face and flattened her hair she collected some of the precipitation in a tube. She corked it, scrawled something on the label and placed it in her case. She did this five or six more times on their slow circuit of the clouds but Billy was only peripherally aware of her industry. As they circled, the winds became fiercer, the voices got louder, brasher, more needy. Shaking, he clapped his hands over his ears but it made no difference. There was no escape.

Para's next task involved a long metal rod. He thought he heard her say: *So this is the dangerous bit*, as she held it by a rubber handle and pointed it out into the clouds. *Just a tickle and no more.* But it was impossible to be sure over the racket going on in his head. Sizzling white whipcracked from the end of the rod.

The effect was instantaneous. Lightning discharged in chain reactions throughout the cloud mass and the tone of the voices changed to one of outrage.

"Shut up." He couldn't hear his own voice over theirs. "Just shut up."

And for a shocking moment, they did. The lightning ceased, the thundery grumble stilled. Only the sound of the dirigible's motor and the creaking of the basket intruded on the questioning silence which stretched on as if the owners of the voices themselves were astonished to have been spoken to.

Para's eyes were wide.

"I think…" Billy's voice came out hoarse. The longer the silence stretched, the more uneasy he got about what would replace it. "We should consider getting back." Para was already nosing the dirigible down, away from the clouds. *"Quickly."*

The howls resumed as a gust of wind slewed across them, battering the balloon with stone-sharp hail, and there was a palpable build-up of energy behind it that frizzled in Billy's hair, tingled his skin, filled his nose with the smell of ionised air. Without needing to ask, Billy knew they were both remembering what had happened to Seldom.

Para's express was deadly earnest as she throttled the engine for all it was worth but there was nothing she could have done to escape the skull-shaking boom and blinding bolt that barrelled Billy off his feet. His vision blurred and his ears rang. He smelled smoke. His only thought was relief that he could still feel floor underneath him. As he waited for the next blow to come the voices resolved into one voice.

"Don't move. Stay where you are." The even purr of the engine, the creak of canework.

Billy opened his eyes. He was on the opposite side of the basket from Para and between them there was a large ring of charred wicker and a clear view of the sea.

"Are you all right?"

She was ashen, but nodded.

"And the balloon?"

Her laugh was shaky. "Sky knows how."

Billy thought that the sky very likely did, but he didn't say so. The people of Karpentine had been pretty damning when they discovered that sylvans were conscious. He didn't want to cop the blame when they found out that the weather was too.

They shared a swig of strosh in the dirigible sheds. The drink settled Billy's nerves some but not quite enough to stop his legs from shaking, grateful though they were to be braced on good ground again.

She stared at him as she poured them both another. The flush of fear in her cheeks became one of exhilaration as she choked down her second shot through a smile. Billy had no interest right then in asking what she found so funny. Shaking his head, he knocked back his own drink.

Para's humour was extinguished by the arrival of a servant who whispered something serious that lit her up like a firework. "We need to get to The Exchange," she said. "Aunt Jelena's being grilled in the Trades Hall."

Ten minutes later they had changed and were driving into the great mosaicked plaza. Even without the morning's drama, Billy's nerves might have jangled when he set eyes on the extraordinary administrative complex for the first time since they'd sent him from here for improvement. He breathed a little easier though when they veered away from Judiciary wing and towards the copper-domed central edifice. Para nosed the car through the milling throng and left it with a handful of others in a quiet compound around the side. From there she led the way into the building and down a curving corridor which was partitioned by a series of ornate doors. Billy could tell that the oak had once been spectacular but its grain had been lost to decades of varnish.

"This place has seen some times," he muttered.

"Trades is one of the oldest parts of The Exchange," Para said, barging ahead. "It goes all the way back to when people judged merit according to talent and the Artisans were in power." She banged the next door off the wall. "It's practically prehistoric."

The final set of doors brought them into a foyer at one end of which stood a much grander entrance flanked by two green uniformed guardsmen. Para ignored it, electing instead for a side door above which hung a sign: *Viewing Gallery*. Entering, they climbed a flight of stairs to a raked gallery packed with a jostling crowd. Para immediately backed out. "Not good." She took the next flight two at a time. "Not good at all."

"What's not good?" Billy had to run to catch her up.

The upper tier was more lightly populated. Para chose a position a couple of rows from the balustrade on the far side of a pillar. "Family meetings are the dullest things you can imagine." She hunched forward, peered down at the huge central table on the floor of the hall. "The only time they draw a crowd is when word gets around that someone's going to get a carpeting or when people are worried about the value of their achievement stocks." She shot him a worried look. "Or both."

Billy peered down at the people seated around the great table, working out that these must be the ones with greatest stockpiles of achievement, the elite few that governed the city of Karpentine. He recognised some of them. There was the ramrod figure of Merit Crane, his son at his side. They were backed up by a cohort of administrators who sat between the table and a secondary circle, along with representatives of lower ranking trades, and who exchanged missives with black-garbed Couriers who buzzed around the business of the meeting like flies. Between the Cranes and the Artisans, Billy also recognised two men. Both had been taciturn at the previous night's party but he knew they were the most influential of the Materialists: Henson, the Ore Master on one side, Gough, the Lumber Master on the other. Lem Shankhill had turned around in order to converse with Cecily Roach, whose Artificers Animeaux were relegated to the second circle. After the Artisans, Billy recognised representatives of the Cooks and Caterers, and one of the last places at the table was taken by Moraine Otterbree. At that moment she was barely paying attention to the ongoing shouting match centred around Jelena Loess, distracted apparently by something she had spotted beyond the gathered representatives. She passed a folded paper to a Courier and nodded imperceptibly towards the far end of the room. Next to her, with apparently equal status, was her husband. That was a surprise because, from their first meeting, Billy wouldn't have thought he'd have the wits for this. Augustin Creasey's spooky daughter sat behind her father and step-mother, apparently doodling, uncaring of the drama unfolding around her.

"Why's that old dodderer involved?" Billy asked.

Para scowled, she'd been trying to catch what her aunt was saying. "Creasey? He's the patron of the Papermakers. It's his right to be here."

The old man didn't seem to be following the vitriol now flying at Jelena Loess from several directions at once. In fact he looked on the verge of falling asleep.

"He doesn't look like he's adding much to the proceedings."

"Don't they teach you anything in your village schools? The Papermakers and the Inksmiths attend all the meetings. They're the ancient crafts that the Law was founded on. Of course, papermaking has been pretty much left behind compared to the modern industries, but it's part of our tradition. *Paper and ink are the twin safeguards of integrity.*" She indicated the corner of the hall where a clerk tapped intently on a typewriter, the stutter of keystrokes underpinning the tension of the exchanges as he attempted to capture them. "Ring a bell, no?" Exasperated, she went back to trying to male out what was happening.

If that line was in the Book, it had been one his mother had not felt it necessary to belabour. "He must be powerful, then," Billy mused.

Para sighed and this time followed his gaze towards the old man. "Well, his workshops haven't produced any innovations in years." There was tinge of sadness in her voice. "And with the loss of his faculties, Otterbree has taken over his family business as well as her own, but he used to be influential. Immensely."

"...*immensely*, not only disappointing, but frustrating for ordinary, hard-working Karpentiners to have one of their senior families falling down on the job with such unfortunate consistency." Merit Crane's words carried with perfect clarity. The rest of the complainants ceded the floor to him, leaving Jelena Loess to face him as he reeled off the Weathermakers' perceived deficiencies.

"If it wasn't bad enough, Lady Loess, that what looks to be the population of an entire state is now encamped outside our walls due to an inability to resolve what you have been assuring us to be a simple technical issue for almost a year now. Or that the electricity supply provided by your offshore stations is in some districts less stable these days than a one-legged man on a bicycle. Or even that those blue skies our citizens pay you good money to guarantee, seldom are these days. Now we have psychotic clouds destroying valuable property with abandon?" Crane spread his arms. "Really, madam, your father, Mackie, performed a worthy service to this city in taking that old kook, Tatsuko Oshi's mad notions and gleaning from them something approaching a practical application. The proper understanding of motes is certainly a goal that will reap great future achievement, but we are not there yet. It's becoming abundantly clear that your family's understanding of the technology which holds such sway over our lives is not up to the task." His smile was vulpine. "If you require aid, the engineers of the guild of Constructors are only too happy to share our own meagre knowledge of motal behaviour."

Loess faced him along the length of the table, her cane planted on the tiles. "The Weathermakers," she spoke deliberately, "do not require help. As we have established many times in this chamber, the situation in the lands bordering the Scour is at the limit of our influence but we are working around the clock to rectify the problem. The electricity supplied to our customers may fluctuate, but it remains more plentiful and cheaper to produce than that from any other source, even Radlett Hall's turbines, sir. And that errant cloud was a one-off aberration." She cracked her cane to punctuate that last assertion and sparks scorched the tiles beside her chair. "Governor Crane, far from *consistent failure*, this has simply been a confluence of unfortunately timed issues of the sort that any major Karpentinian organisation has to deal with from time to time. Even your own, sir. I'm sure no one here needs to be reminded of the pumping fault that caused fatalities among the lowtown sewer workers last year? Or the continued preposterousness of your looming machines, that not only rob skilled weavers of their chance of honest work but actually endanger the lives of those few still employed by the textile industry." She paused, making sure that everyone heard the clacking of the typewriter as the words were committed to the record.

Crane's moustache didn't even twitch. "The concerns of the citizens have been amply conveyed," he said. "I'm afraid to say that the situation has become grave enough for the Constructors to request a formal show of hands." This was casually spoken, but it brought audible gasps from not only the audience but the assembled representatives too. Only

Augustin Creasey appeared unmoved and if his daughter, hunched over her page, cared, she didn't show it.

Para hissed through her teeth. "That's unfair, Merit," she murmured.

"You don't show hands to express a vote here?" Billy said.

Para scowled. "Of course we do. But our problems aren't serious enough for that. He's trying to destabilise us."

"Very well." This was Gough, the Lumber Master. "A show of hands has been called. The subject is: does the assembly consider the Weathermakers incompetent to resolve their ongoing failures? Please vote now."

The hall felt still as breaths were caught. Even Jelena Loess appeared frozen as one by one the representatives around the table raised or did not raise their hands. Less than half of them did, the Shankhills and Cranes principal among them, but there were more supporters in the secondary circle.

"Those against the motion?"

The count was close, but the Loesses had it by a margin. In the mountains that would have been all that mattered, so Billy was surprised to see absolute fury on Jelena's face as she turned and strode from the chamber. The rest of the assembly, taking her exit as a sign that events had come to a conclusion, broke into a flurry of chatter and his and Para's erstwhile companions on the upper balcony ambled out deep in conversation. As Billy prepared to join them, a smartly attired, dark-skinned man approached the table.

"If it pleases the assembly," the speaker's voice was laced with nervous humour. "Now that the mundanities of family politics have been dispensed with," this earned a surprised titter from the remaining audience, "perhaps we can turn our attention to an issue of genuine concern. The parlous decline of the dispensation of justice in this city."

The expressions of the trades' representatives ranged from annoyance to surprise to interest, but it was Moraine Otterbree who leaned forward. "I regret, Master Golspie, that we've run out of time for this extraordinary meeting. If you'd like to table your concerns for discussion at the monthly Law and Order sessions, you will have all the time —"

"I'm sorry, Madame Otterbree, but I've done so on several occasions and not one of the people in this august gathering has ever showed up to hear me speak. Well, you will hear me now."

Otterbree tried to interrupt again, but Golspie merely shouted over her. "Why are our courts so busy? Why are so many being summarily sent for long stretches of improvement? Families are being torn apart on the flimsiest of pretexts and they demand answers. The Institute of Improvement is not fit for purpose. The system needs to be overhauled entirely."

As Golspie became more worked up, there were shouts of support from the audience. Otterbree, however, disengaged from the conversation, sitting back with a tight smile as the tirade went on.

"I have court records." Golspie waved a fistful of papers. "Case histories. Take this one…" As he glanced at the top sheet, he trailed off. "I… uh…"

"You're overtired, Master Golspie. Your hard work in caring for our citizens does you credit, but it has taken its toll." Otterbree had risen from her chair. "Go home."

Golspie's head nodded like a log on a spring. Without another word he turned and left the chamber.

Brow furrowing at this unexpected exchange, Para touched Billy's arm. "We need to go."

Billy rose to join her, but his attention was snagged again. This time by something under the seats.

"Billy, come on."

"Right with you."

He ducked and peered but saw nothing, and was on the verge of giving it up as imagination when he saw it again. Two yellow-green eyes in a bony face. The eyes blinked, then the face emerged fully and revealed that it belonged to a cat. It was a sickly looking animal. Hairless down to its twitching wand of a tail and, worse, there were patterns on its naked hide. Wings had been inked in blue on the grey-pink skin in incredible detail. The tattooed cat arched in an insouciant stretch.

"Billy." Para was waiting at the door. "We've a meeting with Aunt Jelena, remember? Trust me, we don't want to be late."

Billy turned around for a last look at the cat but it had gone. He was still looking for it when a missile came over the balcony ledge, a fluttering thing that swooped towards him with a soft whirr and struck him in the centre of the forehead. "Ow," he said even as the ingenious paper helicopter dropped into his open hands. He stared at it stupidly, wondering what it could be…

"Porter! Move your lazy arse."

He stuffed the paper into a pocket and ran to catch her up.

Para hadn't exaggerated the tea. The spread covered an entire table in the panelled office suite. Billy hadn't had much time to think about food since their experience in the clouds and everything that followed. Now, he couldn't take his eyes off the array of cakes and scones, the crystal pots of silken cream and jewel-like jams. Annoyingly, neither Para nor her aunt displayed any interest but, while a server poured tea, Billy helped himself to a currant bun. He felt he was owed that much for the day's trials.

"Well, Mister Braid." Jelena Loess reached for her china cup. The nails of her wasted fingers were painted a stormy silver. "Paraphernalia tells me you had a close thing this morning. Something of an accident?" She spoke casually but, looking at her hand again, Billy realised that she was talking from experience.

"It wasn't an accident," Para said.

The matriarch opened her mouth to reply, then thought the better and, instead, addressed the server: "That will be all." The boy bowed and left.

"Mister Braid, at some point during this encounter my niece and I are bound to play out an old argument. For no one's benefit, I might add, not even yours. I don't imagine that I shall need to tell you more than this once that anything you might learn here is commercially sensitive. To be perfectly clear: if you so much as breathe a word to another person you will find yourself back on the slow climb to improvement before you've finished digesting that bun. Do I make myself plain?"

Snarling inwardly, Billy stared stonily back at her. He swallowed and nodded.

"Very well then. Now, tell me about these sylvans of yours. In detail if you please – leave nothing out."

Billy hesitated. If he was going to stick around long enough to locate Seldom's remains, he'd have to satisfy at least some of their curiosity but he disliked the proprietary gleam that came into everyone's eyes whenever the sylvans were mentioned and he wanted to be careful not to say anything that might increase their interest. So, he told Loess the minimum of what he knew – which wasn't much anyway – trying to make it sound commonplace and uninteresting. He told her which trees were used and how they were planted and nurtured, and how the master then shaped and assembled them. And, when she probed, he told her that once completed the sylvans went out among the farmers and foresters to make themselves useful. There were no secrets there. Anyone could have learned as much merely by visiting.

"So, it's true, that they have intelligence?" Loess had an inquiring mind and, despite Billy's guardedness, her questioning revealed genuine interest and the tone of their discourse shifted from interrogation into conversation. "But you omitted to say how your master manages this."

"He doesn't," Billy said. "If the trees are grown the proper way, the intelligence comes from the wood itself. It's something to do with motal resonance."

"Is it now?" Jelena sipped her tea thoughtfully. "Your Kim sounds like a unique man. How did he discover all this?"

"I don't know. He left Karpentine before I was born. He never discusses the past."

"You've never thought it curious that an undistinguished Artisan should absent himself to a lonely craggy peak in the back of beyond to create wonders?"

Billy ignored her insults. "Grandhandmaster Shankhill said at your party that the master had once been aligned with the Artisans," he said. "But I honestly know no more about his past than that."

"I see." She paused in thought again. "And Benoit Kim is the only person who knows the secret of their construction?"

Billy smiled wistfully. "He tried to teach me but I don't have his skill. I'm okay at repairs, but I've never crafted a complete sylvan myself. Just a few arms and legs. The ones who carry my handiwork all say it doesn't matter, but you can tell that they think of themselves as inferior to those that are solely the master's work."

"*They say?* They can speak?"

"I mean…" Billy tried to cover for his slip. "I *imagine* that they speak. It's in their body language."

Para gave him a deep look then got up to top up their tea cups.

"Why do you need to know all this?" Billy asked. "They're just sylvans. They're not harming anyone."

"Our family," said Madame Loess, "is a relatively young one. We have risen to prominence by inventing a technology and a new set of skills to go with it. By pioneering the science of weather engineering. My father ruffled feathers among the meteorologists when he discovered how to not only predict when it was going to rain, but also persuade it to do so. Since then we have come far and fast in Karpentine society and we hold this preeminent position because our work is of more practical

129

benefit to more people than a hundred labour-saving machines or a thousand works of so-called *art.*"

Her lips were pressed thin, her eyes shining.

"Only..." It was Para who punctured her flow.

Lady Loess nodded acknowledgement. "Only," she said. "As you heard upstairs, recently something has gone wrong. We have stuck to the techniques that were the foundation of our success, but where precision and control for so long were guaranteed, now it is no longer so." She glared at him as if it were his fault. "Cloud arrays are late, Mister Braid. Or they don't manifest at all. Our reputation is being eroded. It's in the newspapers. Constantly."

"I'm sorry. I still don't see what this has to do with me." That wasn't true. He knew exactly where this was heading. Merit Crane had given her the clue in the Trades Hall. She was looking for the link between the sylvans and the clouds.

"A moment ago you mentioned motes," Loess said. "Some property of resonance that imbues your sylvans with animation."

"So what?" Billy said warily, wondering now if even the little he had told her had been too much.

"It has been many centuries since the Turning Away, since true humanity took its stand and the Law Of Man was written. The Law states that all men must undertake to live according to their own efforts and the resources nature puts at their disposal. Since it is beyond the skill of humanity to unmake the motes or separate them from the world, we have long since accepted, for good or ill, that they must be considered to constitute part of the natural world. And, over the years, people have occasionally found a use for their limited properties. Do you understand what I'm saying?"

Billy scowled at her patronising tone. "You use motes too, in the clouds."

"Precisely. My father found a way to make use of the motes in the atmosphere, but then he was something of a genius. However, people continue to dedicate their lives to motal study and some of them have very outlandish ideas."

There it was. "You think the old man knew this person... *Oshi*, was it? I never heard him mention the name."

"You're not as slow as you appear." Loess's smile was like a razor. "That's exactly who I was thinking of. You're sure?"

"Yes," he sighed. "And, as I told you before, all Kim does is plant and craft the sylvans. Their ability to walk, to manipulate tools, their intelligence... all of that is just a natural result of that process."

Loess frowned again, dissatisfied. "I'm sorry but that's just not possible."

Billy's frustration spilled over. "I said so, didn't I? Isn't it the same with your clouds?"

"Our business may be predicated on direct motal manipulation," she said. "But it doesn't result in *intelligence*..."

Para had been silent throughout the conversation, but now she chose to interject. "Except that there is clear evidence for just that."

"Paraphernalia, I was not serious about conducting this argument again."

But Para wasn't going to be deflected so easily. "Why won't you even consider the possibility?"

"It is *not* a possibility."

"Then how do you explain this behaviour? It's not predictable, but it is wilful and petty and... and... *histrionic*. Honestly, it's like working with a two year old child. In fact," Para's eyes widened as the idea took hold, "that's exactly it. Dealing with the weather lately is like trying to control a fractious toddler."

"Anthropomorphising the situation will only obscure judgement," Jelena said stiffly.

"No, it's true. What happened today, when we sparked a lightning chain was a temper tantrum. And it's not the first time that's happened. And unless I'm very much mistaken the cloud that followed Billy on his way to the city and then destroyed his sylvan did so out of jealousy." She was looking at Billy now, her scrutiny intense. "That's right, isn't it?"

Billy remembered the thunderstruck courtyard, the hissing roar in his mind. "Yes," he said. He also remembered her look of triumph when they were coming down in the dirigible. She had known, but how? "That's exactly true."

Lady Loess scowled. "Don't be ridiculous."

Billy stared back at Para. Somehow... she'd suspected the clouds had a sylvan-type intelligence and that Billy would be able to hear it. She'd taken him up there to confirm her suspicions. And now, to prove something to her aunt, she wanted him to admit it. She was asking for his help.

Billy took a deep breath. "Look, I didn't tell you the truth earlier. Sylvans *can* speak. Not out loud but I can hear them in my mind." He watched the disbelief crawl over the older woman's features, before adding the rest: "And I heard voices in your clouds too."

He didn't begrudge Para her smile of satisfaction. "I knew it. When I saw you talking to Seldom down in the courtyard it looked like half a conversation. But I had to get you up in the dirigible to be sure. Auntie, he screamed at the clouds to shut up. *And they did.*"

Jelena Loess looked from Para to Billy and back again. "I still don't believe it."

"But think about it. It makes sense," Para said. "If the weather system out at the seeding grounds has developed a rudimentary awareness, it would start off like an infant, wouldn't it?"

Billy nodded slow agreement. "What I heard was more like wailing than clear thought, but there were strong emotions behind it. Rage, want, curiosity. Very like the nature of a young child."

"You see?" Para continued. "It's in their *nature*. Billy's sylvans have a more mature personality when they are assembled because their wood has been growing for years, but the intelligences in the clouds are created right there in the seeding grounds. Like newborns."

Jelena Loess took a deep breath. "I shall need to consider this before I decide what to do next." She stood up then and nodded to Billy. "Thank you for your contribution, Mister Braid."

When she had left the room Para grinned at him. "Well done, Porter. I think Aunt Jelena might even be persuaded to keep you around if you continue to prove so useful."

Billy grunted, uncomfortable with suddenly becoming someone with an opinion people wanted to hear. "Unless she decides that you seduced me into making all that up to support your story."

Para stretched. "Don't be an idiot, she doesn't credit you with that much imagination."

"Thanks." Billy got to his feet too. "What have you got in store for me next? Any tigers need fighting?"

"Well, I don't know about you," Para started to pile cakes onto a plate, "but I'm starving."

Grabbing a plate of his own, Billy cleared his throat. Since he'd done her a turn, this might be a good opportunity to try for some answers of his own. "Why all this sudden interest in sylvans? I mean, not just the

Weathermakers, but the Artisans, the Artificers Animeaux, the Constructors?"

"Well it's obvious, isn't it?" She chewed while she spoke. "Machines that do the work of men?"

"Would be against the Law…" That much was obvious. It was why this Oshi was held in such dim regard and why Kim had hidden away in the mountains. So why the interest?

Para laughed brightly. "Screw the Law. Your sylvans are a commercial threat to the likes of the Constructors and the Porters unless they can monopolise them for themselves. And not only would such a monopoly unsettle the balance in the city, there are enough people desperate to earn a kudo as it is without bringing in yet another thing that will take a job they could do. It's bad enough that we use improvees for cheap labour."

Billy was surprised enough at that to lower the éclair he was about to bite into. "You're a philanthropist?"

The levity fell from her like beech leaves in autumn. "Would that be such a surprise?"

"It'd be the first indication of caring for your fellow man I've seen since I came to this city."

He meant that with respect, but Para stared at him hotly and put down her plate. "Oh, fuck off, Billy." She slammed the door as she left.

While Billy tried and failed to work out what exactly he'd said to cause offence, a blob of cream dripped slowly onto his plate. Belatedly he realised he ought to go after her. It took him several minutes of blundering around corridors to locate an exit from the Exchange and, when he did, it was the wrong one. He found himself in a choked concourse between the central building and one of its neighbours. From the second he emerged, people clutched at him, thrust papers and sketches in his face, beseeched him.

Can you help me find my mother? My brother, my neighbour, my child? The complaint was universal. *They've been sent to the Institute.*

Looking back along the alley, Billy saw how long the queue was. People closer to the corner around which it snaked, becoming aware of the fuss his appearance was causing, craned to look, faces etched with an indecision balanced between the hope that someone had come into their midst with news and the fear of losing their place in the queue. One face in particular caught his eye. Pale, framed by wisps of blonde hair. A face with only the ghost of hope left in it. Maundy's niece. Poor sod. She and her brother certainly didn't have their troubles to seek.

The crowd surged around Billy and the beseeching redoubled. Muttering apologies, he pushed through until he reached the corner, and there he spotted Para again. She was talking to the unfortunate Golspie as the dazed man was led away by a friend. Her face was washed with concern but she hid it when she saw Billy approach.

They drove back to the mansion in a frosty silence.

TWELVE

Billy breakfasted in the servants' mess. Cast adrift by Para the previous evening, he'd explored the mansion for a bit and ended up here, eating with the mansion servants in the hope of learning where he might locate Erudite. Most dried up at the mention of the Bello name, but he did manage to prise a nugget from one of the footmen. A pub where the Bellos liked to take lunch, the lad said in return for a kudo or two. Famous for its pies. Billy had chewed over that morsel as he finished his meal, and then the fatigue of the day set in and he went to bed.

So today's question was going to be whether he could manage to evade the Weathermakers' whims for a few hours in order to pay a visit to a certain lowtown hostelry. He guessed he'd find out soon enough.

A copy of the morning newspaper had been left on the long trestle. Grease spots and congealed egg partially obscured the lead story, but the sketch of some grand building under the one-word headline: *Disgrace!* was clear. The picture was drawn accurately enough for Billy to make out that giant letters had been chiselled out of the marble façade. He recognised the slogan: *The Law For All.* He'd seen it all over the lowtown when he arrived but he also had a nagging feeling that someone had told him what the phrase meant at some point. His inability to recall any more than that made him suspect the Institute amnesia. He'd probably never know.

Still, it was an impressive feat. The letters were crudely cut but, from Billy's own experience with hammer and chisel, that this had happened overnight was astounding. The article, however, glossed over the mystery of how it could have been achieved in favour of directing scorn at the perpetrators – whom they called the Refacers – and their naively expressed political aims. The persecutory tone of the story annoyed him initially, but the more he read of the report the more he began to sympathise with the owners of the property. Who would vandalise such a beautiful building, even one so long disused? That was someone's achievement that was being marred.

Billy flicked on until he came upon a sketch of himself and Para. As she'd predicted, their attendance at the Loess ball had garnered some notice in the society pages. In the sketch, they were in their red suits and the artist had given Para's caricature an air of gloating self-importance. It was in the bounce of her carmine hair, the cock of her hand on her hip and the uptilted thorn of her nose. Billy, they had treated even less kindly. He was drawn no bigger than a child, his own suit grossly too large. His hair was drawn as wild as wirebush and his eyes were like saucers. Worst of all, there was a collar around his neck and Para led him by a chain. Faint and diminished, around them were a variety of other men and women. A string of putative suitors, he guessed. The ones who stood out were the goofy face of Killick Roach and poker-stiff one of Stillworth Crane.

Billy was surprised at the clawing humiliation he felt. Even in the mountain villages, it was hardly unusual for a young man or woman to set up suitors in competition to each other. It wasn't even the first time he'd been used as a barb to provoke jealousy. Certainly, the unfortunate Roach would not need much provoking. Billy was annoyed with Para. He might be indentured to her family, but he was pretty sure that didn't entitle her to use him to taunt her suitors. Hell, he was pretty sure he could take any of them in a fight, but he didn't see why he should...

Billy folded the newspaper and pushed it away. He breathed out, slowly and deliberately. He should be annoyed at himself. He'd been in Karpentine long enough to be wary of what he read in the newspaper. It was owned by Moraine Otterbree, after all. He was pretty sure that even a woman that powerful couldn't get away with anything absolutely blatant, but given what he had come to learn about Karpentine inks, he wouldn't put it past her editors to subtly influence their readers' opinions here and there. These Refacers were not to gain support, and Paraphernalia Loess needed taking down a peg or two.

Otterbree's disapproval was definitely a count in favour of his sponsor, but Para still confounded him. She'd been excited, not scornful, about his ability to talk to her clouds. She'd professed philanthropy, but guardedly. He kept seeing glimpses of sincerity, only for them to be covered up again. As if kindness were a secret she wasn't sure she could trust him with. And as for sleeping with him... she'd had her own reasons for that. If you believed the paper it was to antagonise others... Ah, there he went again. *If you believed the newspaper.*

As Billy swirled the dregs in his mug, someone coughed discreetly at his shoulder. "My bones," he barked to cover his surprise. "How long have you been there?"

Tactfully ignoring his fluster, the servant proffered an envelope with Billy's name on it. "From Miss Loess, sir."

"Thank you." Fearing the worst for his plan of a lunchtime excursion, Billy extracted the contents: a neat list of addresses, a sketched map of the city and a clipped sheaf of credits. Confused, he looked up again as the servant placed a tooled leather satchel on the table. It contained more envelopes. "Shouldn't you be giving this to one of the Bellos?"

The servant shook her head and smiled. "Miss Loess was quite specific in her instructions."

Then, glancing at the map again, he realised: it was perfect. This little lot would take him all over. He'd have plenty of opportunity for a detour.

When the servant lingered, he asked: "Is there something else?"

The servant ducked her head so that her next words were delivered with discretion. "Miss Loess asked me to convey, sir, to put little store in what you read in the newspaper today."

Billy came out through the garages. A team of valets were working their way along the ranks of sweeping bonnets and fenders, washing and waxing each vehicle to a gleam. Outside, the sky had a sulky look, an overcast of sullen steel. Billy nodded to a pair of mechanics at the doors. "Nice day."

This earned him grimaces. "Haven't you got eyes?" One of the mechanics inclined her head upwards. "The stocks are tumbling as we speak."

"It'll mean lay-offs for sure," her companion supplied. "Far off climes is one thing, but this is sloppy."

The mechanics turned back to their conversation in disgust.

The work Billy had been set was a simple enough task of delivering messages around the High Town. Any Courier could have done this, of course. It was obviously busy work, Para finding things to keep him occupied while her aunt deliberated over what they'd told her. And perhaps to keep him at arms' length for a while. Whatever the reason, he intended to turn it to his advantage.

Then Billy read the first address and his stomach flipped. The headquarters of the Inksmiths. He told himself that he only had to deliver his envelope and go. It would be fine. He realised however that, for all his lingering loathing for that place, he remembered so little that he didn't know where in the city it was. At a guess, he'd have imagined it at the heart of some lowtown slum, but following the map down the winding length of Prospect Avenue led him right to the Exchange. And circling the complex, he discovered an archway decorated with twin colophons, one representing a dripping pen, the other a scroll of parchment. The Inksmiths and the Papermakers shared premises directly beneath the Trades Hall. For a second, fancying that he smelled the acrid whiff of hot ink again, his feet froze. He had to talk himself into motion again. However bad it had been, his labour for the Institute was done. And if there was a chance to find out more about Seldom, surely this was it.

Descending a spiral ramp, Billy came upon teams of Porters hefting bundles of newspapers, pallets of books and huge rolls of paper onto outgoing carts, while more unloaded incoming supplies: lumber, bags of factory soot and the unpleasant, lumpy sacks from the abattoirs. It was fine, though. He could handle it. When he saw among them a shuffling, slack-faced work detail from the Institute, however, a visceral memory flashed: the stench of burning pine resin, the crust of soot on his sweaty face, the backbreaking effort of loading the furnace with logs, good wood being turned into ash to make ink. He thought about Seldom, similarly roasted to soft grey flakes and felt physically sick. He blew out, breathed again until the nausea passed and all he could smell was the stale underground air.

The Inksmiths' reception office was soberly furnished, and the receptionist and the guard that blocked the door leading into the interior offices were equally serious. Para's warning that he'd never stand a chance against these people came back to him, and any thoughts Billy might have entertained of blagging his way inside vanished. Besides, he didn't know for sure that this was where Seldom was. He made his delivery and fled back up to the open air. There he gasped in several good lungsful and moved on to his next assignment.

And that was when it all went wrong.

The map was difficult to follow for a start. The Exchange had been easy because Karpentine's central artery led directly there. Beyond that, to a newcomer at least, the city was a maze. Finding the wine merchant's on Pride Row should have been a simple matter of a few streets along and one down, but on the map there were too many, too close together to work out which one exactly it was. With half the lanes lacking signage, his search became an exercise of trial and error. In desperation he chose one and immediately got himself lost in a nest of brickfaced alleys. The boutiques in these winding thoroughfares were less salubrious than the ones he and Para had visited in the arcades. Many of them looked closed.

As Billy stumped around with increasing frustration, the sounds of city life dwindled and he was left only with his own huffing breath and the flat echoes of his boots shimmering off the walls. He'd been trying to find a way back to the main road for several minutes when he stumbled into a courtyard so small and so deep in shadow that it was almost in darkness. Walls towered above him, featureless but for drainpipes and a few high windows. It was more like a chimney than a square. Billy groaned with frustration, causing a colony of beetles to lift, glittering, from the wall, twisting into a rising gyre that rose, seeking out the tiny square of sky.

"Well, thanks a bunch." Just as he'd not seen the beetles in the dim light, neither had he noticed the boy, frozen in a crouch, mesh net in one hand, sack in the other. "That's our lunch you just scared off." His face was pugnacious, and familiar. It was Maundy's nephew.

"I'm sorry," Billy said. "Are times so hard that you're reduced to eating insects?" He meant it kindly, and the last thing he expected the lad to do was burst out laughing.

"Oh, things are hard, mister. Not only our mam's banged up, but our uncle now too. Only he's not that much of an uncle, to be honest. We look out for ourselves mostly, but even we don't *eat* glories. We sells them for their shells. Look!" The boy uncinched the knot around the neck of his sack, held it open for Billy to peer inside and see the crawling mass of beetles he'd already collected, their gold-green carapaces winking like treasure. "Glories, see? There's good kudos to be had from the inkers for a bag of glories."

Billy remembered Para saying that one of the components in ink was shellac, a substance which he sometimes found on the trees back home, excreted by insects. "Are you hungry?" he asked the boy. "Show me how to get out of here and I'll replace your lunch."

It took the lad, whose name Billy learned was Vern, all of a minute to guide him back to habitation again. They found a bakery and Billy bought him a meat pie. Vern nudged his elbow. "One for my sister too." So, Billy ordered a second and they left the shop and sat on a bench outside.

The pie looked delicious, the crust ornately fashioned and the smell of beef and gravy inside savoury. Vern talked as he ate. "Our mam's a Tailor, see. It's a respectable trade, but Tailors don't get the same

139

business these days 'cos of Governor Crane's manufactories. So it's bin hard but, me and Clymie, we get by."

"Why was your mother sent to the Institute?" Billy swept the boy's crumbs from his coat.

"Don't know, boss. All we know is one day she never came home from work. Every spare hour we have, Clymie stands in line at the Exchange to find out why, on account of she's the one in our family that can read proper, but the queues is too long, in't they?"

Billy remembered Golspie's plea at the Trades Hall. It seemed it was a tough time to commit even a minor infraction of the Law. It was no reason though for kids like this to be left to fend for themselves. "Don't you go to school?" he asked.

The boy's grin was all teeth and pie. "Uncle Ralston says not everyone has the luxury of schooling."

"My mother always said that literacy is lawfulness," Billy replied, though saying it now, it sounded trite. "But she lives in the mountains where things are simpler."

"Mm, perfick." Finishing his pie, Vern wiped his mouth on the back of his hand. "So, what are you boss? A Courier?"

Billy smiled. "Trying to be. But I'm not doing so well. I don't know where anything is."

"I can show you." The boy's eyes were wide with eagerness. "For a kudo or two."

"Oh, I don't know." Billy got out his list but hesitated. It felt like shirking. "It's supposed to be my job..."

"You can trust me. I'm a Messenger."

Billy smiled again at his enthusiasm. "You mean a Courier?"

"No, boss. Couriers is who delivers letters and stuff. Messengers is the most trustworthy in the whole city. You tells us a thing and we remembers, word perfick. We're good at remembering on account of none of us is that good at reading, see?"

Oh, why not? If he didn't get help, this job was going to take him hours. Para might have wanted to keep him busy but she wouldn't want him still to be at it when it got dark. "You know the city well, do you?"

"Like me own hands, boss."

"All right then. Help me find this wine merchant and we'll go from there."

The itinerary turned out to be a proper tour around the grand establishments of High Town. From the mercantile mansions that preened along the boulevards to the walled private residences. From the gilt-gauded emporia of the colonnades to the discreet upstairs boutiques, and from there on to the academies and the concert halls and the gin palaces. With Vern's help, within an hour he had a reasonable map of the upper part of the city fixed in his mind. Not the upper *half*, however. On the occasions when the route afforded him a view of the rest of the city spread out below – and such occasions were rare because the High had clearly taken architectural pains to put the low from their minds – he surmised that the lowtown was three times the size at least.

At each stop, Vern waited patiently while Billy made the delivery. After the mercantile deliveries their next port of call was the Lodge, the seat of power of the Guild of Artisans located on the metropolis's south-eastern side, at the end of an avenue that wound down and around the hill. It seemed that each building along the road attempted to outdo its neighbour, as if in an exercise in competitive aesthetics. The styles varied wildly from one to the next, from the restrained to the overwrought and – even by Karpentiner standards – to the outright weird.

The Artisans' Lodge itself, however, was the epitome of craftsmanship. As soon as he stepped into the entrance hall, Billy gasped. The mosaic floor he stood on was dazzling. The intricate and precise placement of tiny pieces that extended across the room as well as up the risers of a dozen staircases and the entire height of the slender pillars that braced the roof like jewelled trees, created not one but a series of thematically linked patterns that appeared to coexist in the same space. It was as if several mosaics had been layered on top of each other. It reminded Billy of the plaza around the Exchange, no doubt laid down as a display of proprietary hubris when the Handmade Dynasty had been at its peak. And as if the floor wasn't amazing enough, the plasterwork ceiling, supported by pillars that rose up into delicate shadowed arches constructed from layer upon layer of geometric shapes, was impossible to believe. Kim was ham-fisted compared to the artists who had built this place. Billy could have marvelled at it all day.

"Master Braid." Lemuel Shankhill had appeared at the top of the largest staircase, the Grandhandmaster's florid skin clashing with his pale suit. As he descended the stairs, he said: "Come to bestow your wisdom on the nature of art at last, have we?"

There was no way Billy was going to do any such thing in a place like this. Instead he held up an envelope. "I've a letter for you from Miss Loess."

Shankhill's face fell into an exaggerated moue of disappointment. "Leave it there on the table, then."

Billy did as he was asked. The table near the door was beautifully crafted, if ridiculously overdesigned for its function, carved from honey teak and festooned with dookets and tiers and drawers and hinged things whose function he couldn't even begin to fathom.

"Another time, then." Shankhill stopped him as he reached for the door handle. "For our chat. There will, most certainly, be another time."

Billy hurried out and didn't slow down. All the way up the Artisans' avenue he kicked himself. Shankhill had links with Erudite. That could have been his chance but he'd allowed himself to be awed by his surroundings, like the bumpkin they all thought he was. Allowed himself to be cowed by the High Town superiority too. By the time he and Vern were back in the heart of High Town, he was angry at himself.

There was one more delivery to make. To Radlett Hall, the place he had been meant to deliver Seldom to when he first arrived in Karpentine. He anticipated anything but an easy time from the Constructors, but it couldn't be as unpleasant as the Inksmiths and he wasn't going to let himself by intimidated as he had been at the Lodge.

Billy knew they were approaching the right place from the pall of rising smoke. Then, closer, the muffled din of metal on metal. Then, closer still, the acrid stench of cinders and oil. The reek of industry.

Vern had brought him right to the entrance. "Reckon you can find your way from here, boss?" he grinned.

Billy ruffled his hair and paid him a pocketful of kudos. "Thank you," he said.

"Happy to be of service, guv. Beats actually working in that place." The coins disappeared like a conjuring trick. "If'n you need any more help, find a street corner and ask a Messenger for Vern."

In a better mood for the time spent in the lad's company, Billy turned his attention to the Hall's massive gate. It was a complex device constructed from black iron. The central part was a ring of interlocking hands and it was clear from the exposed gearworks and the sheen of grease that the contraption was designed to do something significantly more flamboyant than simply swing inwards. Two of the hands were inscribed. *By your hand move ten*, read the first. *By your design move the world*, proclaimed the other. Billy looked for a handle or a knocker.

"Lowtown gate, mate." The disembodied voice had a tinny ring to it, but nevertheless sounded as if the speaker was right next to him.

"What?" Billy asked the gate.

"For deliveries. All the way round to the low for." The voice didn't speak again.

It took another twenty minutes to discover the other entrance to the Hall. The lowtown gate was a much less ostentatious affair than its uphill counterpart and stood wide open, admitting an incessant stream of workers. Billy joined them unchallenged.

The Constructors' complex constituted a cluster of cavernous buildings, each with a forest of belching chimneys to prove their industry. Originally, the buildings had been separate but over the years they had become encrusted with connecting ladders and gantries and growth-like annexes. A crew of workers Billy had followed in trudged towards one of the dim, smoky caverns, their faces red-lit by furnace glow as they passed inside.

The open yard swarmed with purposeful activity. Sweating Porters making materials deliveries, sooty foundrymen toting hammers. The air rang with the shouts of teamsters and the clash of iron, and reeked of oil. A chain of wagons rolled around a corner then climbed a rising rail to be swallowed by the dark maw of a loft. Billy suspected he must have been here in his Institute days because the rattle of those wheels was chillingly familiar.

The beating mechanical heart at the centre of all of this industry could only be Radlett Hall. The chimney-crowned, ironclad building had an exterior of gears, pistons, cams and all sorts of other mechanical gubbins. And it was never still. With the workings constantly chugging or ticking or rippling, the building gave all appearance of breathing.

Billy gazed at the Hall, mesmerised. Then his attention was snagged by two people standing in its lee. Stillworth Crane and, surely surprisingly given their supposed rivalry, Killick Roach. Well, this ought to be easier than that pompous Shankhill. He thought of winding them up for a bit of fun but, disappointingly, the two men ended their conversation as Billy approached. Roach made a show of initiating a handshake that Stillworth reciprocated without enthusiasm, but Billy did not miss the goofy fellow slipping a brown envelope into his coat pocket at the same time.

"Good morning, gentlemen." Crane nodded in response to his cheerfulness but Roach stalked off without acknowledging him. "Something I said?"

"Who can say, Mister Braid." Stillworth's demeanour gave nothing away. "Killick's always been an odd fish. But I'm sure you didn't come to Radlett Hall to banter."

Billy produced the last letter. "Para asked me to give this to your father." If there was any truth that Stillworth had a thing for Para he showed no annoyance at Billy's familiarity. Perhaps the newspaper had employed more than just Billy to make a point at her expense. Behind the unperturbed Constructor, there was a purring rattle as a sequence of switches flip-flopped across the kinetic skin of the hall. "In there is he?" Billy asked.

"Just give it to me." When Stillworth held out his palm there were red abrasions beneath the leather strapping. Again, Billy felt sorry for the man, although he was certain Stillworth wouldn't welcome his sympathy. If he were a little less cold he might almost be likeable. The envelope was plucked from his fingers. Pocketing it, Stillworth turned away. "Tell your maestra that she can send you back tomorrow."

His maestra? Billy changed his mind about that likability.

Although the deliveries had taken a good portion of the morning, it was still a while before lunchtime. Nevertheless, Billy's appetite had been grumbling since he'd bought Vern his pie, and he knew just where to get one of his own.

He left the Constructors' complex by the lowtown gate again. The pub he was looking for was called The Pinnacle and, if his informant was to be trusted, it was to be found in one of the lanes off Helpmeet Street, in the warehouse district not far from here.

Sure enough, he located the place in short order. The side street contained two pubs whose smeary upper storey windows faced off like the belligerents that no doubt stumbled out of their doors at closing time. The Pinnacle was recognisable by the ham-fisted mountain on its sign.

As Billy hesitated outside and wondered if this really was such a good idea, a hand reached past him and gave the door a push. It had neat nails, elegant fingers and protruded from an ivory cuff. "After you, mountain boy," said a Bello's mocking voice. Through the door, Erudite was perched on a bar stool as if he'd been waiting. Which Billy realised now, he had. The footman's information had been cheaply bought, and worth less than the paltry sum he'd paid. Innocent gave Billy a gentle nudge from behind.

"What do you want?" he said, reluctantly crossing the threshold. As far as he could tell in the dimness, the three of them were alone.

"Me?" Erudite mugged a look of surprise. "Surely it was you who came looking for me? But since you're here, I believe, by sheer coincidence, there is someone else here who would appreciate a discreet word."

Cheeks burning, Billy felt like a fool. All he could do now was try not to compound his error.

"Fine, I do want to talk to you," he said. "But no one else. The Weathermakers would prefer to protect their investment, but I'm sure you know that."

Erudite exchanged a look with his brother. "This is not a business discussion," he said patronisingly, indicating one of the shadowy nooks along the back wall. "Besides, you might even benefit from it."

Curiosity prevented Billy from turning around and walking out like he should have. If this had nothing to do with the sylvans or the weather then what else could it be? If he ended up having to tell Para about this, she would certainly want to know. He peered into the booth, but could discern no more than the booze-softened planking of the table top and the scuffed leather of the banquettes. All else was shadow. Then the occupant leaned forward and revealed his face. It was Killick Roach.

Billy actually laughed. Out of relief and because the situation was so absurd. To see the fellow at the Constructors' had been a surprise, but not unimaginable. This was something else entirely. "What on earth does he want with me?"

Innocent gave him a shove. "Why don't you go over and ask him?"

When Billy neared the table, Roach pulled dramatically back into the shadow, but not quickly enough to disguise his discomfort. "Sorrow, Mister Braid," he said. "But please sit. It's not good for me to be seen in your company."

"Likewise," Billy muttered, but he sat down anyway. The banquette was lumpy. "The Loesses will tan my hide if they get wind of this." He glanced at the Bellos. They were perched on bar stools with their backs to the booth, but he knew they were listening.

Roach shifted uncomfortably. "It is on the subject of Paraphernalia that I wish to engage your assistance."

Billy choked back another laugh. So that's what this was about. He should have guessed. "*My* help?"

Roach's face ghosted forward again. It reminded Billy incongruously of an owl in the forest. "You need context. Very well, bluntly, Paraphernalia Loess of the Weathermakers and Killick Roach of the Civil Service are matched."

"Matched?" Simultaneously, Billy tried to sound like this was news to him and not to be insulted that Roach thought him so ignorant.

"By the Matchmakers. An arrangement between families to the mutual benefit of both, do you understand?"

He really did think Billy was stupid. "You're *engaged?*" He put affected surprise into his whisper.

The toothy smile was genuine. "Yes."

Billy almost felt sorry for Roach then. He was infatuated with her. And more than that, he was confident that the arrangement was going to go through. Billy knew Para to be far less enamoured by the prospect, but did she have any actual choice in the matter? He wondered again about the other night. About the caricature in today's newspaper. Had he just been a convenient way for her to give the finger to them all? Or had she been trying to convince herself that she could still do what she wanted?

But still, *matched*. To *this* oaf.

The work of the matchmakers was respected even in the mountain villages. Many were the marriages that hung on their perceptive appraisal of prospective suitors and the wielding of arcane formulae, carefully balancing credits and deficits across many spheres of achievement so that neither family lost or gained too much. Even allowing for the peculiar ways of the city, the idea that matchmakers had sanctioned Para's betrothal to Killick Roach felt unlikely. Para was highly connected in the Weathermakers, while the man sitting here was, as far as Billy knew, merely a paper shuffler. The Weathermakers must really be desperate for this alliance to the Inksmiths, no matter how tenuous.

"Well, if that's the arrangement," Billy ventured, "then it's surely all settled. I'm really not sure where I come into it. You can't think I've any influence over her."

"Oh, sorrow," Roach wheezed. "I've not made myself clear. Yes, the families have agreed it. It's done. What I want from you, Mister Braid, is a guarantee not to *muddy the waters*. If you agree, I shall pay you five hundred credits. If, however, you have the effrontery to as much as touch Paraphernalia again I shall ensure that every part of you that does the touching is unsympathetically removed."

146

Billy was at a loss for how to respond to this puffed up tirade. He couldn't take either the threat or the bribe seriously.

"Can I take your silence as an indication that you'll at least consider my offer?" Roach said. "We won't meet again. You can let Mister Erudite Bello know of your decision. And, sorrow, it goes without saying that this conversation must remain confidential."

"That's it?" Billy was relieved to be able to walk away without having to dignify the proposition. "I can go?"

"Please do," came the reply. "And think carefully about what I've said."

Billy slipped out of the nook. There was no sign of the Bello twins, although the bar had gathered a handful of real customers.

Juggling annoyance and bemusement, he left the pub and started along the lane towards the main thoroughfare but something caught his eye. A flutter of paper against the still grey sky, white but dense with a familiar etching of the Tower Of Hands. It was the colour of the ink that he didn't recognise, a red that was almost as rich as the suit he had worn to the ball. Fifty credits in one note. He whistled to himself.

The note fluttered again then jumped into the air and danced in front of his face. The illusion only lasted for a second or two, but that was long enough. Billy saw the gossamer thread. Sensed someone at his shoulder. Smelled astringent herbs. Cried out as rough cloth was placed over his nose and mouth.

He awoke on the floor with a headache and a vile taste in his mouth.

"The beauty awakes." A familiar voice. Erudite or Innocent.

"Get up, Braid." The other one, much closer. "We require a conversation of our own."

Billy dragged himself into a sitting position, rubbed his eyes. Too slow. Someone gripped his collar and hauled him to his feet. He blinked into Innocent's appraising brown eyes.

"He's all right," the Courier said to his brother.

"Bring him over then and let's get this done."

They dragged Billy to a table. On it sat a ticking rotary lamp. Its glow pooled across two envelopes.

"We have been instructed by separate employers," said Erudite. "To offer you a substantial incentive to share whatever information that you've provided to your owners about those sylvans of yours."

147

"Oh, and a practical demonstration would be nice too," Innocent added.

This was a more serious game than Killick Roach's charade. He felt no special loyalty to the Weathermakers and already regretted telling Jelena Loess as much as he had about the sylvans. True, her focus had been on the clouds, but she had been awfully interested. To raise the interest of other families would hardly improve their position. Then again, Erudite did have something he wanted. "I thought your employers and mine were the same," he said to give himself time to think.

Innocent leaned in from behind. "You're a clever lad, Billy," he whispered. "Act like it and we'll be done with this in a quick and civil manner."

"Or maybe you're both really working for the Inksmiths?" he chanced. "What did they want with Seldom's remains?"

Innocent didn't deny it. "Who knows? It was all burnt up, and they have a penchant for burned up things. We don't actually care, and Madame Otterbree has nothing to do with this." In many ways Billy had been hoping Para's guess had been wrong, but at least he knew for sure now. And perhaps there was a way after all he could turn this to his benefit.

Erudite looked bored. "For the sake of clarity," he said. "My brother and I represent individual interests that are contrary to those of Jelena Loess."

"The Constructors and the Artisans, then," Billy ventured. It didn't take a genius to guess that. "But your paymasters are competitors too. Do they know you work jointly like this?"

Innocent's laugh echoed flatly in the low-ceilinged room. "I knew you were smart," he said. "The answer is: up to a point. They even use our relationship to conduct certain delicate types of negotiation that might otherwise take forever. But in this instance, no."

"But of course my brother and I both knew that the other would be asked to approach you, so in the event it's more convenient for everyone, is it not, that we present our offers like this?" Erudite indicated the envelopes. They were both sealed. "Neither of us knows the detail of the other's offer. All we ask you to do is read them both and choose the one that pleases you. The rest will follow on from that."

Billy looked from one brother to the other but did not reach for the envelopes. "Money? What do you think I want with money?"

Innocent snorted. "Look at the offers. You'll change your mind."

Billy stood his ground. Shook his head. "Get me Seldom," he said. "Then we'll talk."

Erudite and Innocent exchanged one of their looks, then creased up laughing. "Break in to Otterbree's lab?" Innocent said. "Not even remotely worth the risk. And the risk would be considerable."

Erudite tapped the table, his smile slipping away. "It's the money or nothing," he growled. "And this is the last time we're going to ask nicely."

Billy refused to back down, but there seemed no alternative. "I'm not reading anything you people put in front of me," he seethed.

Erudite nodded grudgingly and reached inside his coat. "You're learning," he said, unfolding spectacles of a familiar design. Billy had thought Maundy needed aid for his eyesight when he read the newspaper, but apparently they did considerably more than that. And these eyeglasses were more complicated than Maundy's, with brass rims and an array of tinted lenses on hinges. Erudite chose three and pushed them into place in front of the eye pieces. "These filters will negate the effects of most compellants. I will tell you that my own is written only in standard correspondence ink, and I'm sure my brother will say the same." Innocent nodded, but he was amused. "But to ease your fears I advise you to give each only a glance and then look away. In your place, I would do the same."

The glasses were heavy. "And if I refuse to look?"

Neither brother answered. It was threat enough. Billy put the glasses on and opened the envelope on the left. A glance through the murky lenses at what was written proved enough, and he did not feel any effects. He looked at the second one and then closed that too. He handed the glasses back to Erudite and then, just to get it over with, pushed the first envelope into the centre of the table. "This one." They hadn't exaggerated the sum. Both figures dwarfed the amount that Roach had offered him, and the first outweighed its neighbour by a margin.

Erudite snatched a glance of his own then passed the envelope to Innocent. The brothers exchanged a look and then Erudite said: "Wait here." They took the envelopes and left.

Billy didn't even think about hanging around. He was out of there as soon as the coast was clear.

"Where have you been?" Para had caught up with him in one of the Loess mansion corridors and dragged him into the nearest room, which turned out to be a book-lined reading room. Now she paced the cramped space as if by keeping in motion she could wear out her anger. She knew something had occurred. Perhaps not the details, but *something* was bad enough.

Billy was distracted by the silvery ticking of the room's fussy mantle clock. A stupidly overwrought artefact with all sorts of moving, spinning, whirring things surrounding a tiny face. "After I finished your list? I went for a walk." It wasn't enough to fill the ticking space. "And I talked to some people." The arch of her eyebrow demanded the full explanation and, yes, she was right to be angry. So he told her of his two encounters with Killick Roach, then of his run-in with the Bellos. He didn't quite tell her everything, but he told her enough. Para managed to still herself long enough to hear him out, but her face was stony.

"Aunt Jelena laughed when I told her I'd given you a job to do," she said when he finished. "*Laughed*, Billy. I convinced her that you could be trusted."

"Everyone on your list got their delivery," he protested. He disliked the petulance he heard in his own voice, but ever since Smout's letter, people had been treating him like a child. He had the sense not to mention that he'd had to enlist Vern's help.

"It should have been obvious that you were supposed to come back after that. Did you think that was your work done for the day?"

Billy bit back a further retort and took a deep breath. "Look. If someone employs me to do something, I do my best to do it. My kudo is —"

"Your contract?" She threw her hands up. "Really? So what were you doing out there today? Sharing your good will with *all* of your new friends?"

"It wasn't like they gave me a choice."

"Oh, of course, they threatened you with oodles of money, didn't they?"

They glared at each other. "I wasn't going to take their money. I just agreed so I could get out of there."

"You really are more stupid than I gave you credit for, aren't you?" Para continued to glare at him while the awful clock continued to tick, but her front wavered, just a chink. There was the thinnest edge in her voice that betrayed to him how much he'd let her down. How much she'd hoped he could prove himself, even if it had only been busy work. Billy felt surprisingly chastened. She may be thorny, but those thorns really did protect a decent heart. He wished her needles didn't provoke him to say things he regretted.

Just when he thought he was going to have to say something *else* he was going to regret, if only to block out the clock's tinny ticks, Para sighed resignedly. "Come on then," she said. "The Queen's been screaming for you."

She took him to the ballroom. Empty, it felt like a cavern. The only remnants from the party, a few scuds of purple-bellied wine cloud that lingered near the apex of the roof like forgotten party balloons.

"Lock the door, girl." The Queen of Clouds had sat down while she waited but now levered herself up. "You, man, come here and prove your usefulness." Her cane swung upwards to point at the clouds. "Show me what you can do."

Billy bridled at the demanding tone. The implied expectation for him to perform like dog doing a trick. "With those?" he scoffed.

Loess was in no mood to brook prevarication. "They're as real as any other cloud. Just modified for a different purpose. If you can talk to those in the seeding grounds, you can talk to these."

He folded his arms. "Well, maybe I don't *want* to talk to them?"

Jelena Loess's face darkened, but it was her niece who answered. "Billy," she said, her thorns retracted for now and he could see how weary she was of all this. "Have you forgotten the accusations that Merit Crane levelled at us at the meeting? We wouldn't ask you to do this merely to boost the fortunes of the Weathermakers but those refugees outside the city gates are there because of us. People are going thirsty in their homelands, and we're out of solutions."

Jelena smiled, approving what she probably assumed to be a clever ploy from her niece, but the plea hit the mark. Playing along wasn't an option when lives were at stake.

He appraised the little clouds again and this time he listened too. And heard them. The voices were tiny, the emotions vague ones of dissatisfaction and maltreatment. Such quiet voices wouldn't have been discernible amid the hubbub of the ball, except now he remembered that he thought he *had* heard their sadness, just for a moment. "Oh, you poor little sods," he breathed. He got no answer, but one of the purple clouds bobbed lower before drifting back towards its fellows. "Aye, you hear me, don't you?" he said. Again, the cloud dropped a foot, and this time it hovered there timidly. "You don't have much reason to do favours for these people." From the corner of his eye, Billy looked for Loess's moue of displeasure and was rewarded. "But if you would do one simple thing for me, I think we might be able to return you to the sky."

"Do not promise what you cannot deliver," Loess admonished, but the clouds were agitated now and her interest was well and truly engaged. Para too looked impressed, but also pensive.

Billy spoke again to the captive clouds. "Come down to me now," he said. "Come down and I'll lead you to the sky."

The clouds came. The first, hesitantly, then the others following until they were no more than six feet above his head. With them they brought their overcast of despair, but now it was threaded with weak breezes of something like hope. Incontinent claret dripped across the tiles.

"Open the door," Billy said. "We're going out –"

"I've seen enough." The Queen of Clouds pressed the button on one of the fountains and whatever it was they had done to these sorry clouds forced them to be drawn to it. The voices whispered resigned fear.

"No!" Billy shouted. "I promised them."

"They're only clouds, Mister Braid." The first of them had reached the dish and began raining itself into the bowl, shrinking to nothing as they watched. "They don't require sentiment. Paraphernalia?"

"Aunt Jelena?" There a genuine nervousness in Para's voice.

"This would appear after all to be a useful skill. Take him to the Sisters."

THIRTEEN

Para left Billy at the garage gates while she retrieved her vehicle. It had become colder and drops of gelid rain fell from the sullen sky. Billy snugged his coat collar around his neck while he waited. The mechanics and garage hands worked in pensive silence, pausing only to cast resentful looks his way. He was grateful when the beetle-black car finally pulled up on the courtyard cobbles.

The automobile jounced out of the gate and down the hill. The sudden sleet had emptied the streets, which was just as well because Para drove the vehicle at speed, peering through the downpour as she guided them towards their destination. Who these Sisters were she refused to disclose. On leaving her aunt she'd walked out onto the street and approached a group of children loitering at the corner. Billy had watched from across the road, unsettled at not knowing what was going on. He'd seen Para in a variety of moods, but rarely as tight-lipped and jittery as this. From the way the kids had listened intently to her and then dashed off, he guessed them to be Messengers. He hadn't twigged when Vern mentioned them that they were a guild of children. Well, everyone had to make a kudo somehow. The pig-tailed tyke who was first to return snatched the proffered credit from Para's fingers and in return gave up a sweet, toothless grin and a name that Billy soon learned to be Belleview Park.

Whoever these Sisters were, they made themselves hard to find. And, from the way Para kept doubling back in an effort to confound anyone who might think to follow them, someone you didn't want anyone to know you had visited either. Sure, everywhere had folk whose company was poison to one's reputation, but how disreputable could they be to warrant this level of caution? Billy's unease was spreading deep roots long before Para finally brought the car to a halt close to a hedge-bounded public garden.

The garden was artfully designed, a beautiful spot for High Towers to idle away an hour or so. It decorated a promontory jutting from the hillside and, in better weather, would have offered spectacular views of the countryside beyond the city. Billy guessed you would have to lean quite far out to be reminded that the lowtown below existed at all from here.

"Come on," Para muttered, reaching into the back of the car to retrieve a pair of items which Billy would not have expected anyone in the Sunshine City to own. Umbrellas. She handed him one and extended the other and then led the way into the garden. Many of the trees and shrubs here were shaped into bowers, and Billy was musing that perhaps they were intended to afford privacy to romancing couples when Para yanked his arm and pulled him into one. She shushed him and peered out at the cinder path they'd just left.

The reason quickly became evident. Two men strode past their hiding place from the direction in which they'd been heading. Neither looked happy and both walked stiffly. The older one because that was his nature, the younger because that was all his body allowed. Merit and Stillworth Crane.

Billy and Para watched from the arbour until the Cranes were gone and then resumed their own journey. "You think those two had business with these Sisters of yours too?" Billy ventured.

"Well they didn't come here for a tryst, did they?" Despite the half-hearted snark, he could see that she was bemused to see them here, and his misgivings about where they were going multiplied. Whatever was happening now went well beyond the remit of simply *playing along* with the Weathermakers' requests. Despite Para's impassioned plea back in the ballroom, he had reservations about what he was getting himself into, and why. And he didn't want to admit the answer to that. Not even to himself.

Deep among the hedges they came to another gate, this one paint-scabbed and rusted, and beyond it they found a staircase whose steps were slimy with moss and crumbling from neglect. The sleet came on harder as they climbed. Billy pulled his collar up again but failed to prevent the ice from finding a way in. At the top of the steps they found a forgotten street. The rubble-strewn stretch of road, choked with weeds and bordered by aged tenement blocks in such a state of disrepair it was a wonder that they still stood, had at some point been blocked off by the back of another thoroughfare. A high wall of dirty, windowless brick at the far end, sealing it off from the city and leaving it to the drifting skeins of green-gold beetles that gyred and sparkled through the freezing rain. Vern would have been in his element in this place.

"You're kidding me," Billy said. "Surely no one lives here?"

Para's disquiet was undisguised now. "Look, I don't like this," she said, "but we have to take whatever opportunities remain open to us. No matter how unlikely." She touched his temple with surprising gentleness. "What's in here," she said. "What you can do. We need to be able to do that too."

Billy's mouth went dry. "You mean hear the clouds? Talk to them?"

"And control them, if we can."

"I'm really not sure —"

"Neither am I," Para said. "But the Queen has finally acknowledged that the clouds' intelligence is the root of our problem. So, we have to try." She licked her lips nervously. "And, Billy, this is important. No one must ever know about what we're about to do. If anyone finds out, it'll be the end of the family. The absolute end."

It struck him as commendable that her priority remained her family, even though doing this upset her so much. "It's that serious?"

She took a shuddery breath. "This goes so against the Law that I can't believe we've been asked it. But it's for the good of the family, do you understand?" Billy had the impression that she was trying to convince herself as much as him. "And before we go any further, I want to ask your permission. If you'll do this for the family. For me."

For the Weathermakers, no. For her? Billy shrugged, as if that disguised his readiness to agree to this. Whatever *this* might be. "It's the Queen's command, isn't it?"

She served him another sad look but took his reply for assent. "Come on," she said.

Under the glowering clouds, the street looked desolate. Billy had never seen a habitation so neglected. The windows were dull eyes. Short flights of stairs lolled from gaping doorways like the tongues of the dead. Para counted along and chose one, climbing the steps and entering the dark hallway. They left their umbrellas by the door.

"What is this place?" His words bounced off tiles, coming back to him harsh and amplified. Para produced a lamp from her pocket, wound it briskly. It cast an insipid glow, just enough to see their way to the stairs at the end of the passage. The steps had once been mosaicked, but there were so many missing pieces the design was lost to the ages. There had been a banister too but little of that remained.

Ascending, Billy and Para smelled the rancid candles on the next floor before they saw their light. They were smoky and misshapen, one every few stairs, and odd shadows dogged the climbers until they stood

155

before the door on the very top floor. Para pocketed her lantern and looked to Billy. Her mouth was puckered into a dry cinch, her eyes wavering with uncertainty. She took a breath and pushed open the door and immediately Billy wished he was somewhere else. There were signs that this place might have once been a respectable, even nice, family home, but that had been long ago. Now it was a ruin. The trail of candles continued down a short hall, illuminating wallpaper heavily inked over with obscene drawings. The carpet was a hodge-podge of stitched together materials, the clashing textures and designs further obscured by a fur of grime. At the end of the passage, another door. This one enough ajar that light threaded the jamb. This light was harsher than the candles and it pulsed arrhythmically like an old man's heartbeat.

A pale shadow slid past them then. An animal, mottled flanks tattooed with a plumage of blue feathers. It nevertheless attempted to carry itself with the haughty grace of all its kind, its bald tail waving behind it like an imperious finger. At the door, the cat from the viewing gallery turned and delicately dropped the thing it had been carrying. A starling with glossy feathers and a broken neck. The beast regarded them for a second, then Billy heard it speak, not in his head like the sylvans but aloud. Its voice was a pleasant baritone.

"Which sister, Sin or Skin?"

Para licked her lips, then said: "Sin. Sister Sin."

"Follow then." The cat picked up the dead bird and led them into a long room strung with slow-pulsing bulbs. From the suspended cables dangled sheets of fabric, a maze of muslin that grew near-opaque in the centre. Around the walls were propped age-scratched mirrors from a hundred different boudoirs and hallways and bathrooms, and these echoed the pulsing lights.

The lighting cables were attached to an odd contraption placed between two boarded up windows. A generator, hooked up to a pyramid of ribbed wheels. Inside the wheels were more of the tattooed cats and the light ebbed and flowed as the animals sped up or slowed, leapt lithely from one wheel to the next or dismounted altogether. The other cats watched as Billy and Para followed the first cat down the side of the room. Underfoot, the dank carpet was replaced by rough boards littered with odd things. A granite mortar bowl sparkled with fragments of beetle shell, a row of oil lamps that had left sooty scorches on the muslin, a neat row of bottles and a pot that contained a fist of scrimshawed implements, needle tips lashed to bone handles. Something about these sparked recognition but Billy couldn't recall of what. The path was littered too with clawed feet and skeletal wing fans and desiccated bird heads, and when the cat led them nimbly around a small furnace Billy's boot snapped a piece of debris.

"Who is it?" The voice was a scratchy mezzo. "Is it canvas? Nice clean canvas for Sister Skin?" There was a rustle from the hanging sheets and a tall, skinny silhouette appeared. "Bastipol! Bring it here for Skin." If the cat was Bastipol, it chose not to obey. Instead it scampered the remaining distance to the end of the room, where there stood another door. This one had scratch marks at the bottom, and the cat added to them with a noisy display. Para took the hint and pushed.

This room was more intimate than the first. The occupant, who Billy deduced to be Sister Sin, watched their entry from a decayed couch. In the slow pulse of the room's only bulb, he saw that she was young, but wore a weariness that made her appear older. Her black hair scraped back and threaded into cornrows, her body tiny inside those baggy cotton pyjamas, a general air of exhaustion. "Thank you Bastipol," she said to the cat as the door swung shut. Then to Billy and Para she indicated a second couch. "Please sit, and pay no mind to my sister. She gets jealous that my services are more popular than hers."

"Why?" Para whispered. Billy had never seen her so discomfited.

"Because my gifts are invisible, Weathermaker. Skin's proclaim themselves." Billy thought she was making some sort of joke, but there wasn't even a hint of a smile. "Now to the point of things. You're not some silly little girl wanting to forget an indiscretion, and you've achievements enough not to require a lie laid so deep inside you that you'd believe it yourself. So, come on..." As she said this her gaze alighted on Billy for the first time. "What is this curious thing you bring me?"

"This... is Billy Braid." Para shot him a beseeching glance. Asking his permission again. At the mention of his name Sister Sin's red-rimmed eyes came alive. "He has a *skill* that we are anxious to learn," Para continued. "He can talk to clouds."

"Can he now?" If Sin was surprised she did not show it. "So get him to teach you."

"I don't even know how I do it myself," Billy said warily. "I was just born with the ability to understand our sylvans."

"*Sylvans.*" Sister Sin perked still further at mention of the word, tried it again experimentally on her lips, which curled into a cat-like smile

157

afterwards. Then she nodded to Billy. "Come here then." She patted the damask.

Para nudged him. "Please, Billy."

Billy perched at the edge of the couch, stiffening when he felt the woman get to her knees behind him. She was warm and smelled a little sour, like milk on the turn.

"Relax." Sister Sin's fingers burrowed into his hair. Her touch was light as feathers. "It's very easy."

Para chewed her lip. "Too easy," she muttered.

The fingers slid across his scalp, caressed the contours of his skull. He felt Sin lean close. "Are you sure you want to do this for them?" she murmured in his ear. "A unique gift is a valuable commodity." The couch unsettled as she shifted to the other side. "My sister and I were born with unique gifts too," she whispered. "We turned them into something we could profit from." Then she released him. "Yes, he is awakened and, oh, he's a wild one. What you ask is possible, if he is willing and you have a suitable receiver in mind."

Awakened? Billy wanted to ask what she meant, but Para spoke first. "Me." Her voice trembled.

Sin's hand shot out and grasped her wrist. A second later she nodded. "You too, Weathermaker? Aren't you full of surprises?" Her lips crinkled. "Very well then. What will you offer?"

Para mastered herself and became business-like again. "I am authorised to offer you a maximum of sixty-five thousand credits," she said. "I don't see any reason to bargain."

"What would we want with *money?*" The sister grimaced as she echoed what Billy had told the Bellos, but this was no bravado. "Money is for tiresome braggarts who accumulate piles of it to prove their worth to each other. We can get most of what we want without money."

Para managed not to look chastened. "Ink then."

Sister Sin clapped her hands. "Ah, Weathermaker. You know the real currency of Karpentine."

Para nodded stiffly. "The family has a private collection of some very specialist inks. Purely historical, of course. What specifically do you want? Compellants? Allurants?"

Sister Sin shook her head slowly with a tutting sound. "No, no, no," she said. "None of that manufactured stuff. Where's the craft in them? We mix our own here. We manage to make quality lampblack and boneblack in our little rooms, shellac for binding too. But what we'd

158

really like is something unique in the carbonblack line." The woman looked at Billy when she said this, and he knew exactly what she was referring to. *Seldom*. He felt his heart tugged in opposite directions with the acknowledgment that while something did remain of the sylvan in the city, yet another party was eager to use make use of it.

Para must have worked it out too, but she had she didn't let on. "We can only go to the charcoal makers like everyone else."

"Well, that's a shame," the sister said, clearly not fooled. "Perhaps you should ask Moraine Otterbree for some ideas. Get gone now, and return when you have our fee." Her gaze burned Billy one more time. "Failing that, bring this one back. We can always try roasting his bones instead."

When they had left Sin's room, Billy whispered furiously to Para. "Who are these people? How can they even exist?" He wasn't sure if his outrage came from the bewildering invasiveness of what had happened to him or for the casual bargaining over Seldom's remains as if they were any old sticks. Either way, he silently renewed his vow that they would *have* to make do with his bones. They'd have nothing of any sylvan if he had any say in it.

"Shh." Para let out a breath. "Very few people know about the Sisters but those who do find them more than useful enough to be tolerated."

"Oh, yes, we are popular with your sort. Your families, who amass credit while always keeping your faces clean and honourable." The other sister, the one called Skin, was waiting for them. She squatted in front of a mirror. A dark outline, a darker reflection. Glittering eyes watching them from the glass. "Your sort know us well."

The second sister levered herself to her feet, unfolding her long limbs like an insect. Her hair was tufted, her eyes huge. But it was her naked skin that captivated the attention. Its natural tone had been a sugar soft brown like her sister's, but it had been overlaid repeatedly with tattoos. The density of the designs made it impossible at first to pick individual images out of the whole, but the more Billy stared the more he began to see patterns and shapes. Mostly, they were shining black but there were patches of vibrant colour too. On her upper arm, the wing of a yellow bird. Low on her belly, a red flower.

"You like me?" Sister Skin came closer. The light flowed over her like waves of water. Billy realised he was staring at her breasts, nipples the centres of black roses. He dragged his attention to her face. "It is all right," she said. "You can look." That rasp in her voice had become a

159

sensual purr. "If you like what you see," she altered her pose and the light flowed again, making the designs appear to move, "maybe you let me draw on you, huh?"

That was it. That was what the implements in the pot were. While almost everything else had faded, he'd remembered his Institute neighbour's tattooing as a dream, a spike driven into his subconscious perhaps by the amount of time he'd spent at the Inksmiths. But the scrimshawed pen-things, the cats and now this woman with these living illustrations on her skin told him it had been anything but.

Billy expected Para to intervene with her customary brusqueness, but she was even more dumbstruck than he. She stared at the red flower on the pillow of the woman's belly. It looked larger now, a deeper, more velvety shade of red. The sister put her hands on her hips, rotated them. The light pulsed again and the designs rippled, flowed up the outside of her thighs, around her buttocks. On the next pulse, the ones on the insides of her legs writhed, the dense intricacies inked around her slender mons, too, but Billy and Para were most captivated by the flower. Its petals peeled back as the sister danced and Billy got painfully hard. The light pulsed, and the flower exhaled. And Para half-breathed, half-whimpered, and Billy's own breath was trapped behind his teeth. And the light pulsed. And the petals of the red flower spread wide.

"Well." Sister Skin was grinning. "You two have a good day." She turned away, went back to her muslin nest.

They kissed each other hard up against the stairwell wall in the rancid candlelight. A brutal devouring that could have led to anything if Para had not pushed herself away and, panting, warded him off with one hand while holding on to the broken bannister with the other until the passion subsided. Then she sorted her clothes and ran down the stairs.

When Billy caught up with her outside, the sleety rain had settled into a steady downpour that shivered the weeds and made rivers spew from the rusted drainpipes. Para's wince could have been one of physical pain but, for the moment, the failures of the Weathermakers were the least of Billy's concerns. "What *was* that?" he asked.

She shot him a look venomed with disdain, but her cheeks and neck were still flushed. "*That* shouldn't have happened." Her teeth fretted her lip. "I didn't want it to happen."

"Neither did I." That earned him another glare. "But that's the point, isn't it? Those women can manipulate people…" He replayed the events in the tenement and something clunked into place. Sin had said *awakened.*

She could only be referring to what Kim had always referred to, when attempting to explain Billy's connection to the sylvans, as motal resonance. The property that he claimed was responsible for the sylvans in the first place and which, whether Jelena Loess believed it or not, may also have accidentally resulted in the weather's sentience. *Awakened* was a good word for it. And if motes could be awakened in the wood and the clouds and himself, why not elsewhere...? He peered carefully at Para, who had *somehow* known that he could talk to the clouds. "Sin said that you –?"

"And all this time you thought you were unique?" Para turned her fury away from him, back to the sky and the rain.

"Para..."

"We need to go." Para stalked off into the downpour.

Following, Billy sensed it'd do no good to push the matter. If she didn't want to discuss the fact that she could hear the clouds too that was fine, but they'd have to talk about it soon.

It was only when they reached the park end of the deserted road that he realised they'd forgotten the umbrellas, but Para showed no sign of caring so they pressed on. When they reached the car they were both soaked, although Billy's coat had protected him from the worst. Para started the engine and allowed its heat to dry them out a little. The rain coursed down the windscreen like a stream in spate.

"Listen." He touched her shoulder. She flinched away. "No, it's not that. There's something else you need to know. Something I only just realised when I was in there. I saw her, Sister Skin. At the Institute. One night I woke up and she was there right beside my bed. She was tattooing another inmate with one of those pen things." He could picture the man's face now, but could not remember his name.

The look she gave him attempted derision but was undermined by the way she nervously finger-combed her hair. "You didn't see that. It's not possible. No one remembers their time in the Institute."

"I do," Billy replied. "Snippets anyway. Smells, tastes. Places they made me work. Bits of conversations, faces. And I definitely remember that man being tattooed." He could almost see the sister hunched as she worked, inking his neighbour's chest. And suddenly he recalled the design too. An odd sketchy thing, a winged cat.

Para's expression was hard to decipher. "I'm not calling you a liar, Billy, but I've never heard of such a thing," she said. "Although, you have woken motes, according to Sister Sin. So maybe... I don't know..."

161

She put the car into gear and rolled it out into the road. They had negotiated several streets before she spoke again. "But it doesn't make sense. What would the Sisters gain from tattooing people in the Institute?" As they entered the Exchange plaza a thought appeared to occur to her, but then she shook it away.

As they trundled down the ramp that led to the Inksmiths' premises, Billy asked her: "What do you hear?"

He didn't think she was going to answer, but then she said: "In the clouds? It's not like you, not words or anything..."

"More like feelings?"

She nodded. "Vague ones. Before you arrived with your sylvan it was anger, frustration, a reluctance to do what they're told. It varied, but the overriding emotion was of being trapped. Of wanting to be free. I felt sorry for them more than anything."

Billy knew how they felt.

Visiting the Inksmiths for a second time that day wasn't a treat Billy relished, but he'd been presented with a gift. If Para intended to talk to Moraine Otterbree about buying whatever remained of Seldom, he'd suffer the experience if there were any chance of her succeeding. The difficult bit was going to be persuading her not to pass on her purchase to the Sisters. It might be easier just to steal the sylvan's ashes and run.

Para parked the car behind a lumber wagon. The place was even busier than it had been earlier. "That woman, Otterbree, has a lot going on," Billy said.

Para looked around, as if noticing all the industry for the first time. "If the Exchange is the beating heart of our city," she muttered, "then ink is the black blood that flows round it. Technically, she only owns half of this. Augustin Creasey owns the paper half, but she's had him in her pocket since their marriage. Which was, as you may guess, very much one of expedience. Me and Baby Cock are lovebirds by comparison." Now she lowered her voice until it was barely audible. "They don't call Moraine Otterbree the spider for nothing. She's made a web out of the Exchange, and sits at the centre of it, turning every little thing to her profit. Be sure and smile when we meet her."

Para breezed through the Inksmiths' dispatch offices with the air of one who had every right to be there. When they approached a door at which a black liveried sentry stood straight and serious, however, there was a fractional hitch in her step. It was tiny, but it was enough to remind Billy how much of Para's confidence was front.

"...which is why Madame Otterbree," she said as if continuing a conversation and pitching it for the guard's notice, "is keen for you to tour the production facilities before she meets you. I'm sure you'll find it interesting." The sentry barely blinked as Para strode past him and through the door. "And here," she continued as the door swung shut behind them, "are the furnaces."

Billy remembered the furnaces, but now he *really* remembered them. He and Para were on an iron gantry that ran the length of the enormous room, most of which was below them. The air smelled of smoke and the heat was stifling. Billy watched the sweat-slicked workers below stacking logs carefully inside one of a row of conical burners and now recalled that heat fierce on his own face, parching his own lungs with every breath he sucked in. "There is much demand for paper and ink in Karpentine," Para said, going on with her pretend tour. Billy had to force himself to follow her. Through the heat haze he saw more workers opening up the next burner along and carefully extracting wood ash into a steel hopper. "Everyday inks are mostly based on carbonblack," Para said, moving along the gantry. "But they also add amounts of lampblack and boneblack, depending on the application." Now the furnaces below were larger than the wood burners, the heat even fiercer. These, the workers were feeding with stinking animal bones that glared glistening white in the flames.

Billy whispered silent thanks when they reached the end of the gantry and another door. The next room was much cooler but Billy froze, blanching as the first whiff of boiling ink reached his nostrils, certain he was going to vomit.

"The mixing vats." Para didn't appear to notice his difficulties, although she held her own nose. Keeping Seldom in mind, he took a deep breath through his mouth and made himself step inside. From beneath the new gantry came a rhythmic grinding and quiet liquid slop from the open tuns, their contents glittering like black water as the huge paddles were pushed slowly around by straining workers on a circular track level with the top of each vat. More workers in ink-stained cotton masks took periodic samples with long spoons and drew quantities off into jars. The familiar stench was so acrid that Billy staggered and grasped the walkway rail.

"Are you all right?"

He shook his head. "How can they force people to work here?"

"You'd be surprised what people in this city will do to earn a little honest achievement. Employment is in increasingly short supply."

"Wouldn't it be more plentiful if people like Otterbree and Crane didn't use improvees?"

She regarded him curiously. "You remember working here when you were in the Institute?"

"Often, I think. We were a convenient and uncomplaining workforce."

"Marcus Golspie and his friends would agree with you." She wrinkled her nose even though she was still holding it. "Come on, this really is awful." They'd come to a spiral staircase and she started down it. "This way."

Beyond the mixing room was a bottling area at the back of which they found a steel door guarded by two blackcoats with side arms. Figures moved indistinctly behind the glass of a long window.

"Inksmithing was traditionally a craft," Para whispered, "but they have laboratories now. We're going to have to come clean here, I'm afraid." With that she took out an elegant notebook and a reservoir pen. She scribbled a quick message in the book, blew on it to dry the ink and then ripped the page out, creasing it once. "Deliver this to Madame Otterbree immediately," she told one of the sentries. He took the paper and disappeared inside.

Billy felt his palms prickle. He didn't know what he was going to do when they got in there. He hadn't formulated a plan as such but until this moment he'd vaguely expected he was going to let Para do her stuff and then perhaps try and persuade her to substitute the ash of Seldom for something else, but he knew in his heart that would never fool the Sisters. Even if Para could be persuaded to agree. Too much was riding on this for her family. He could go back on his promise, withhold his skills, but where would that get any of them? The only alternative action that he could see resulting in the removal of the sylvan from this nest of avarice would be just to grab Seldom and run. The question was whether to do it now or later, perhaps when they were in the car and Para was occupied by driving. But after all this time, he really didn't know if he could wait that long.

There was a long delay before a face appeared at the window. Moraine Otterbree's unblinking eyes scanned quickly from Para to Billy and back again, then she was gone. The guard reappeared moments later.

"You can go in, Miss Loess," he said with minimal respect. "But just you, I'm afraid."

Para's glance at Billy conveyed her frustration. "Stay out of trouble," she said. "I'll only be a short while."

"No chance, I'm going in too." He started forward but the guards stepped into his path.

"*Billy.*" Para hissed, her hand on his shoulder. "I know what you want, but that is not the way to get it. Trust me." She held his gaze. "The Sisters only need to get a little bit."

After the door closed behind her, the sentries fixed Billy with a gaze of such intense disinterest that he was compelled to walk away. *The Sisters only needed a little bit?* He didn't want them to have even that. Frustrated, he wandered among the bottling racks and then he spotted someone skulking in the shadow of a line of trollies laden with Prussian blue jars. It was Vern. He found himself absurdly glad to see the lad. "Getting good money for those glories?" he said.

The boy spun, fists balled, ready to fight. When he recognised Billy, he relaxed only a fraction. "Piss off, will you?" he hissed. "You'll get us lifted by the spider's boys and you don't want that. They say she bathes in the blackest ink; they'll do *anything* she says."

Billy held his hands up to placate the boy's imaginative fears, but nevertheless crouched and lowered his voice. "I'm guessing you're not meant to be here. What's the matter?"

The boy's gaze flicked to the sack at his feet. He shrugged. "Mister Bartholemew pays us for glories out the front. But I needs to be in here because –" Vern stopped talking, grabbing Billy's coat and tugging him deeper into the shadows. Billy's exclamation of surprise was cut off by the approaching rattle of another trolley. Metal clashed and the trolley was still, and Billy waited for the sound of retreating footsteps to let him know that it was safe to talk again. It didn't come, but in its place, a whisper: "Are you there?"

Billy widened his eyes at the boy, but his companion smiled when he replied: "Back here." There was a movement among the trolleys, a chinking of glass, before the newcomer found them. In the bluish light, the lad's sister was even paler, the white-blonde wisps that were not trapped beneath her worker's scarf, leached to translucent grey. If she spent her days working among these fumes, it was hardly any wonder she always looked so sickly. On seeing him, the girl wiped at the indigo smudges on her cheeks.

"Mister Braid," beamed Vern. "Let me formally introduce you to my sister, Clymie."

The blush that came to the teenage girl's face was the first colour Billy had seen in it. Then she smiled. "You still got the luck I gave you?"

Luck wasn't a concept Billy could think of without hearing his mother's voice calling it *shirker's work*. He took out his wallet and withdrew the scrap of embroidery. "This? It hasn't brought me much fortune to be honest."

Clymie's smile faltered. "I don't know what life is like where you come from, Mister Braid, but by the lights of most folks you've landed on your feet." She looked down at her stained hands. "Here you can work harder than you'd ever think possible and have nothing for it. Most of us get our luck handed to us when we're born, and it ain't never good."

Billy nodded, chastened by the girl's simply delivered truth and unable to think of a worthy reply. Thankfully he heard his name being called, although Para's tone edged between impatience and anger. That was fine, it matched his own mood, now stoked by Clymie's gentle rebuke.

"You better go before you get a row," Vern said. "We'll see you again."

"You will?"

The boy, who Billy thought now might be older than his stunted stature suggested, laughed. "We're the downtrodden underclass, ain't we? You can't escape us."

"Wait," Clymie stopped Billy as he was turning away. "You could help us."

"Help you, how?"

"Find out what happened to our mam," she said as Para called for him again. "You know people. *People of influence.*"

"I promise, I would if I could but I'm afraid *I'm* not a person of influence. None of them listen to me." Billy turned away from their disappointed faces wishing he could have helped them. They might have been Ralston Maundy's kin but they were nice kids and, like many lowtowners it seemed, they were prepared to toil hard at whatever scraps of work they could get. Then he remembered something and turned back to them. "Vern, you want to know where there's a *huge* colony of glories?" As he gave directions to the Sisters' street, Vern's face lit up. Clymie's remained sad, but there was nothing he could do about that.

166

Billy found Para where he'd last seen her, and he knew immediately that her encounter with the head of the Inksmiths had not gone well. "I thought I told you not to muck about." She strode for the exit.

"What happened?"

"That woman..." Para seethed. "That *woman* is not only an evil spider witch. She's a bastard to bargain with too."

"What happened with Seldom?"

"Seldom?" Para shot him a pointed look. "Indeed I saw Seldom. Moraine was very obliging on that score –"

"You didn't get it," Billy interrupted. "Did you?"

Para shook her head. "Otterbree showed me the samples of carbonblack her technicians had already made from it and, although she was careful not to say why, they were all very smug about something. Billy, I'm sorry but she turned me down flat."

So quickly were his hopes snatched away that Billy felt winded. "What? How much did you offer her?"

"A lot. Way more than I was authorised to. It didn't make any difference. I don't know what she wants it for but she's keeping your sylvan for herself."

When they got back to the car, Billy sat in brooding silence, barely listing to Para's continuing rant while she guide it up out of the bowels of the Exchange. He only looked up when she slammed on the brakes. They both looked up through the rain-flecked windscreen and saw that an impossible column of black cloud towered above the city. The base of it, all but touching the Weathermakers' tower.

FOURTEEN

The tower roof was crowded with scurrying weather engineers, their efforts hampered by the swirling rain and the shuttering light. Para was drawn immediately into an urgent discussion with her aunt and several other high ranking members of the clan, leaving Billy to his own devices. Their urgency was advisable because in his head the wind-shaped emotions of the belligerent cloudmass were ones of crowing and catcalls, exultant childish glee. He could tell from Para's repeated upward glances that she felt them too.

The roof was cluttered with instruments. Bright brass, the glint of lenses, the worried murmur of technicians. Billy buttoned his coat, jammed his hands into the pockets and watched an engineer fiddle with her telescope, all the while scowling balefully at the clouds. "What are you trying to achieve?" he said. She ignored him and he tried again. "Can I look?"

The engineer threw up her arms in frustration. "Oh, knock yourself out."

Billy bent to the device. It was a lot larger than the spyglass the master watched the road with back home, but the principle was the same. The base of the clouds wasn't as close to the tower as it had appeared from the ground, but through the lens he found himself staring deep into the heart of the churn. He watched the mass of vapour boil, a chaotic, giddy, jeering riot that was dizzy to watch. After a bit of experimentation, he found the knob that gave him a wider view and twisted it all the way. "Ha," he said. "There you are." Almost immediately there came an answering rumble. It sounded like a challenge.

"Mister Braid. A word if you please." Billy looked up from the eyepiece and saw from Jelena Loess's face that, whatever word she had in mind, he wasn't going to like it. "Our family has paid an exorbitant amount to secure your abilities," she said. "Now is the time to demonstrate that it was worth it."

Her proprietary tone would have annoyed him anyway, but he realised there was more to it. By asking him – a nobody; worse, a *criminal* – for help, her family were gambling their increasingly scant reputation.

By asking him to do what she wanted him to do, she risked making them a laughing stock. Now he understood why they had approached the Sisters. It would have been much more palatable if it were Para doing this, not him. "What?" he said, taking his time in straightening up. "In public? Are you sure?"

Loess's face darkened nearly to the shade of the cloud above her. The words spat out of her like steaming summer rain. "Our family's standing is dropping faster than a seaman's barometer. The rain is bad enough, but every minute this monstrosity demonstrates to every person with eyes in their head that the Weathermakers cannot control their own weather, the worse the situation becomes and I will not stand for it. So, let me make this perfectly clear." She jabbed her stick at him to punctuate her next words. *"Get that thing out of my sky."*

All of them were staring at Billy now and, disinclined as he was to obey the Queen's commanding tone, he had promised Para that he would help. If not for the Weathermakers' sake, then at least for that of the Kinster refugees and others whose livelihoods and lives depended on something as simple as predictable rainfall. And, Billy realised, if he *was* able to do this, perhaps the Weathermakers would have a better bargaining position over Seldom's ash. The engineer he had talked to watched him with resentful expectancy. Whatever she might be expecting him to do about the problem, it wasn't to try and reason with it.

Billy raised his head to the sky and shouted. "Do you think this is funny?" Instantly, the whirling glee in Billy's mind intensified to a deafening level and he suddenly wasn't confident that he could do this after all. Conversing with a sylvan was a proper conversation. Those few pathetic wine clouds had possessed barely any personality and had been easily persuaded. But this? This had the finger-pointing, name-calling mob-mentality of a class at early school, as vicious in establishing its will and as quick to lash out when challenged. He remembered the tone of his mother's voice on the numerous times she'd discovered him cornered by such a mob.

"Well, do you?"

Someone tittered and that started others laughing, but Billy ignored them. Amongst the insolent squalls there was one dissenting rumble, in his ears and in his head and vibrating through his boots too, and in it he was sure he could now make out words.

Go... away.

169

The sulky rumble came again, louder. And again. Each time louder and more defiant.

Go away! Go away! GO AWAY!

The assembly sensed the change in the mood. The laughter stopped.

"I'm not going away," Billy scolded. "And neither are these people. They only want you to take your rain where it is needed as is natural for you. They're not interested in forcing you to do something against your wishes." He couldn't banish the thought of the pathetic wine clouds fast enough. "So, why don't –"

A concussion of thunder shook the tower. Weather engineers leapt to catch toppling equipment.

"*Others.*" The clouds bellowed. "*Don't like. Others likeusnotlikeus.*"

Billy was puzzled. "What do you mean others?" And then he realised. They were talking about similar entities, ones with voice thoughts. They were talking about poor Seldom.

"There's no others here," he shouted. "Not any more."

"*Others. Othersothersothers.*" The gale in his mind whipped itself into a frenzy. "*Others come!*" At that, the winds rose from bluster to gale and the column of cloud began to lift. It spiralled up and out and moved rapidly away towards the south and west. The gyring blast skittled people and instruments alike. Regaining their feet, the engineers watched the departing formation. There were a few sighs of relief, and a small ripple of applause. Someone clapped Billy on the back, but they were celebrating prematurely. The cloud stream had already begun to descend again outside the city's southern wall. Above the gate, and the road.

Others come.

The first engineer he had spoken to was checking her telescope for damage. Pushing her aside, Billy wrenched the instrument around in its mount. There was the city gate. There was the queue of petitioners, the crowded refugee camp, everyone running for cover now under a vicious assault of rain. There was the road through the vineyards, and in the distance the ungainly monument of the Tower Of Hands. He focused the glass, magnified and focused again. And sure enough there on the road was an ostentatious vehicle. The resplendent figure driving it could only be Bullivant Smout. Beside him was the austere shape of an old man, and in the back of the gaudy charabanc, a canvas bulk. They were driving directly for the city, and they were going to have to pass under this fury of cloud to get here.

"Oh, no." Billy backed away from the telescope and made for the stairs.

"Where are you going?" Para caught up with him.

"The old man is coming," Billy said. "He's bringing another sylvan with him. And your weather knows. Remember what happened to Seldom?"

Para managed to look aghast and furious at the same time. "Bringing a sylvan for whom? We offered him half the sky… What?" She saw Billy's surprise. "The moment you arrived in Karpentine with your cursed manikin every family of standing sent someone up there with offers, threats, you name it. Don't look at me like that. We didn't have to ask your permission."

"So he refused you too?"

Para rolled her eyes. "He was as intransigent as the mountains themselves. Which makes it all the more annoying that he seems to have changed his mind. Who is he with?"

"Smout." Billy puffed his cheeks, blew a sigh out on the wind. "Benoit Kim is a man of honour. All Smout would have had to do was point out that I failed to complete the contract that he originally agreed to."

"No one would hold him to that," Para said. "He was *compelled*."

"As far as he's concerned, he still is." Although, the old man had really been a confederate of this Oshi person, why was being so stupid as to return here in person?

Billy was interrupted by another sequence of aerial disturbances. This time the boom of thunder was accompanied by a crackling sheet of lightning. Even this far from the city wall he heard the voices.

Go away! Go away! GO AWAY!

"I have to stop them before they get here." He broke away from her grasp.

"Billy…"

"What?"

"You'll never make it on foot."

She drove in her usual style and, with the streets full of sky-gazing citizens, they came close to disaster more than once. When they came in sight of the gate, the guards were dragging it shut but a furious blaring on the vehicle's horn stalled them just long enough for the car to shoot through. Entering the wall of rain was like plunging into a waterfall. They drove blind, water streaming in opaque sheets down the windows as they

171

careened through the campsite, only Para's familiarity with the road keeping them true. Billy glimpsed petitioners scattering, refugees struggling to keep their tents from washing away in the muddy torrents. From somewhere he smelled burning. And then, as suddenly as they had found themselves in the midst of the petulant rain, they were through the other side.

Para slewed the car to a halt across the road. When the windows cleared, trundling towards them in the sunshine, they saw Smout's ridiculous jalopy.

Billy got out and waved the approaching vehicle down.

"Why, if it isn't young Mister Braid! What a coincidence." Smout's teeth gleamed beneath the flagrant moustache. Beside him, the old man looked as if he might actually be asleep. "And Miss Loess too. You mustn't be too disappointed, my dear."

"Why would I be disappointed, Mister Smout?" Para's tone frothed with sarcasm.

The Constructors' flunky smiled his self-satisfied smile but Billy wasn't going to let him boast about his success. "I'm sorry, Master," he said to Kim, rounding the vehicle. The old man had no coat. In fact, dressed in his workshirt and a thin jerkin, he looked just like he did when he dozed in front of the fire. And what Billy would have given for him to be there right now rather than entering the city to face whatever consequences his past had in store for him. That he had completed the journey here without a coat brought an additional guilty lump to Billy's throat. "You must not go any further."

The shrewd eyes opened and took everything in. "I think we might brave a little rain," Kim said.

"It's not that simple." Billy leaned into the charabanc because what he had to say next was for the old man's ears only. Smout's smile became fixed. Billy knew that Kim already knew what had happened to Seldom, but when he told him why the old man's eyes narrowed.

"Are you really determined to make this delivery?" Billy asked him.

"It is an obligation," the old man replied.

"Damn right it is." Bully Smout had got out of the car and begun wrestling a canary yellow hood into place over the cabin. "And if you don't mind, I'd like to make sure it is fulfilled as soon as possible."

"If you want to have a sylvan at all, I advise you to turn back," Billy said. "Otherwise it'll end up in the same condition as the last one." Out of the corner of his eye he thought he saw the sacking in the back twitch.

"Actually, I think it may be too late for that." Para had been watching the weather and the crackling, booming cloud mass was now reaching towards them.

GOAWAYGOAWAYGOAWAYGOAWAY!

"Give me the sylvan." When the master hesitated and the Constructor stammered the beginnings of an indignant rebuke, Billy added, "Smout, unless you want your chances of studying my master's craft to go up in smoke for a second time, this is the only way."

Kim gave him one last appraising look, then began unbuckling the strapping around the bundle. Reaching in to help, Billy heard a questioning, leaf-shiver voice. The sylvan that was revealed when the canvas was removed was slender and nervous. Billy suspected that several days bouncing around in the back of Smout's vehicle had contributed largely to this state of mind.

"It's all right," he said as he helped it unfold its thin limbs and climb out of the charabanc. "What do you call yourself?"

The sylvan tottered a distance from the vehicle as if it were scared of being bundled back inside, then it ducked its head and turned its riverglass eyes to the ground. Its answer was a sniff and a snuffle. *Rabbit.* An appropriate name, as always.

"Can you run as fast as a rabbit?"

Do not know.

"Well, I hope you'll have plenty of opportunity to find out. For now you'll just have to be able to run faster than the clouds. I'm sure you can do that, can't you?"

I'll try.

"Billy?" Para had been observing the exchange with a look of concentration, but now she pointed at the approaching bludgeon of cloud. It had almost closed the distance and Billy hoped it wouldn't be necessary to find out how fast Rabbit really could run.

"Para, take the master in your car and meet me inside the gates."

"No!" He could see that she guessed what he was going to do. "They'll destroy you."

"I think I can talk my way through it," he reassured her. "But this sylvan it seems is not a fan of motor cars. If we try to drive it through there…" He didn't need to finish, Para understood.

"Talk?" Smout had found his voice. "With whom?"

Para ignored him. "Just be bloody careful then," she said to Billy and helped Kim into her own vehicle.

"Wait!" Smout raised his voice. "That's my creditor!" When he was ignored again he lunged for the old man, but Billy pulled him back.

"You can settle your claim once we're inside," Billy said. "But for now, my advice to you is to take your outrageous machine as far away as possible and wait until this is all over." Smout looked fit to answer back, but a well-timed sizzle of energy from within the downpour ahead of them made him reconsider.

Billy turned to the sylvan again. "Are you ready?" The head ducked in what he took to be agreement, so Billy led it forwards. "Don't say anything," he said, watching the black vehicle pass them and enter the pounding curtain of rain. "And if I tell you to run, run straight for the gates as fast as you can. Paraphernalia will take care of you when you get there." The sylvan's lack of reply, Billy took once more as a sign that it understood. There was no time to explain further. Within the darkness between here and the city gates, he could see the stricken tents of the refugee camp. A gritty pall of smoke coiled close to the ground. The rain itself smelled charged and sparky. Its hiss, like a nest of rock adders that grew angrier still at their approach.

Billy took a deep breath and spoke up: "What's all this shouting about? Why all the violence?"

The thunder responded with an ear splitting crack.

Not like. The weather said. *NOT WANT.*

"What can you possible object to about my friend Rabbit here? Look at it. It's tiny. Smaller than a man even. What harm is it going to do to you?"

Not like voicethoughts.

"If I promise you that Rabbit won't make any voice thoughts, will you let us pass?" Rabbit had the good sense to say nothing at all. "See?" he said to the weather. "Rabbit will be silent. No voice thoughts, I promise."

The clouds above the road roiled, then reluctantly withdrew. Billy led Rabbit into the gap. The road was sodden and muddy, and runnels streamed off to either side. The camp was destroyed, reduced to small lakes of brown water choked with canvas and clothes, and other things mostly submerged that Billy did not want to look at, but recognised anyway as fish-white hands and hair-plastered faces. The majority of the refugees had found shelter beneath the city's picture walls, and their stares as they followed Billy and Rabbit's progress were ones of hostile disbelief. The connection between these two and this sudden destruction could not be clearer. Billy and Rabbit measured their paces evenly and with every yard they gained the weather relented a little more.

It was only when the barrier of storm clouds severed completely and they had clear sight of the open gates that timid Rabbit's nervousness finally overcame its obedience. It wasn't an important utterance. It didn't even form a recognisable word. It was just the sylvan equivalent of a whimper of relief. With the noise of the rain still thundering down on either side, Billy himself hardly noticed it, but the clouds reacted instantly, closing over the road again, thunder roaring like a pack of beasts. In seconds Billy was drenched, but he was already pushing Rabbit and shouting: "Run!"

The sylvan took off like a hare, and Billy, whose reactions were seconds slower, was the one who took the brunt of the first bolt. He felt the power and the heat of the blast at his back as he pumped his legs and followed. There were two more strikes before he gained the gate, but somehow both he and Rabbit escaped destruction. Para's car waited with the doors open and a crowd had gathered. Billy bundled Rabbit inside and dived in after it. "Get us out of here," he shouted at Para. "As fast as you can."

The vehicle leapt forward. The clouds followed, boiling over the city once again, but Para's car was faster, racing the length of Prospect Avenue towards the peak of the hill. When they reached the Weathermaker compound, she drove them straight into one of the sheds. Outside, the weather vented its fury in wordless violence. The stinging rain doubled and then trebled in intensity. Thunder and lightning raged above the courtyard and a hammer-fisted gale gripped the shed and shook it as if to rattle its contents out.

FIFTEEN

"Are we safe in here?" Kim had been grimly silent throughout the chase to High Town, but he'd found his voice since getting out of the car and had been using it mainly to complain.

"Yes, I should think so." Para replied, but her tone was far from reassuring. "All these buildings have lightning courses at least."

The old man sniffed and peered out into the courtyard. The rain kicked up off the cobbles and nearby discharges bounced unsettling shadows off the walls. "And the next part of your plan is?" He had a point. They may be safe inside this barn, but they were effectively trapped.

"We wait it out." Billy said it without any clue as to how long that might take, but almost to the instant the wind and rain abated. He thought he might even be able to detect the faint glow of sunshine behind the overarching grey. "Well, that's suspicious." Billy ventured out into the courtyard. "What're they doing now?"

"I'm not sure they know themselves," Para said. "It's not like they're just one voice, one mind. Mostly they're confused by their own thoughts as much as anything. This is the first time that something has had them all in agreement, at least as far as I can tell."

"That something being the sylvans," Billy said. "They don't understand where these different voices come from."

"Whatever the reason," Kim said irritably, "I suggest we make use of the opportunity and finally fulfil this damnable obligation." The master flexed his old limbs. His clothes were still sodden from the downpour.

"I wish you wouldn't," Billy said. "It's bad enough that the Inksmiths have what's left of Seldom without another of the high ups getting –" The look in the old man's eye stopped him. Billy knew that look. It told him the decision had been made and nothing would change it. "Here, then," he sighed, unbuttoning his coat. "You should take this back. It's served me well, but it really belongs to you."

Kim laid a gentle hand on his shoulder. "That old thing? It was a gift, son. A hand-me-down. I don't want it back." Then he turned his attention from Billy to Rabbit. "You, climb on my back. Your feet are dirty enough as it is."

The sylvan understood the half crouch and did as instructed. Slight as it was, its weight bent the old man double and a hiss of breath expressed between his teeth as he settled his burden.

"You're not going to carry it all the way to Radlett Hall," Para said. She tactfully didn't add *at your age*.

"Why not?" Kim took a couple of experimental steps across the courtyard, then made ponderously for the street. "That Smout might prefer you to believe that he portered me all the way from the Molspurs but the truth is he puttered along at my heels the entire journey, begging me to get into his vehicle. It was only when we stopped at the Tower Of Hands – and let me say what a flagrant pile of steaming shit that place has become, laying your hands *meant* something in my day – that I allowed it, and then only in the interests of disambiguation."

"Wait..." Billy said. He couldn't let him do this. It wasn't just the sylvan.

"Nothing's done by waiting." The old man slogged on out into the middle of the road where pedestrians, venturing out once more after the storm, had to step out of his way.

"The Judiciary has a long memory," Billy said. "They're not just going to let you go home again."

"True enough, boy." The driver of a delivery wagon, trying to find room to pass the burdened old man had begun to berate him loudly but Kim changed neither course nor speed. "But I shouldn't have sent you in the first place. If I committed any crimes, they were mine and there was always a reckoning to be faced."

"What crimes? What did you *do?*"

Kim just kept walking.

Para intervened. "At least let us drive you. If you like we can let you out at the gate so that the thing is seen to be done properly."

The master stopped, eliciting a fresh volley of curses from the wagon driver. Then he lowered Rabbit to the ground and stepped to the side of the road. He wiped his leathery brow. "Thank you."

The journey to the Constructors' complex was not a long one and, as promised, Para pulled over to allow the old man to carry the sylvan the remaining distance. At the High Town gate, Kim received no challenge. Instead, there was a quiet *clunk* and the rattle of a running chain and then the clasped hands separated, pulling cleverly away from each other to form an arch.

Kim wended through the purposeful chaos of the Constructors' yard, making directly for Radlett Hall. The building looked much the same from this angle as from the lowtown side and the exterior of the edifice was even busier than it had been earlier. As they approached, a rose of geared dials aligned, and in a cascading flurry of motion several columns of shutters flipped their faces from black to white or white to black with a noise that, to Billy's ears, was the harsh clatter of lumbermen's mattocks. A group who had been waiting for the new configuration took eager notes.

"How do we get in?" Billy had seen no sign of an entrance to the Hall.

The old man peered at the wall, shuffled along a dozen steps, then back again. Then he strode forward and vanished. It was only when Billy reached the spot himself that he saw how subtly the entrance was concealed.

By the time they caught up with him, the old man was introducing himself to a sharply uniformed official seated at a gleaming steel desk. He spoke with barely disguised disdain. "Handmaster Benoit Kim, formerly of the family Leung of the Artisans, now of the Moslpur Mountains. I have a personal delivery for Merit Crane."

The man at the desk matched Kim's disdain. "You're late." He rose and opened a door, revealing a long corridor beyond. "This way please, Handmaster."

"Wait here," the old man told Billy. "You don't need to be involved in this." With that, bowed now almost to a crouch under the sylvan's weight, he followed the doorkeeper out of the vestibule.

When they were alone, Para said: "He's going to be arrested."

"I know."

"Do you always do what he says?"

"Almost never." They slipped through the doors just before they closed.

The floors of the hallways inside the Constructor's headquarters were straight grey ribbons, but the walls and ceilings were all part of the same interconnected machinery as the exterior of the building. Fly wheels spun, gears meshed and rotated, cams and pistons pumped with purpose, but if outside it had been a noisy, kinetic carnival, inside the whole thing moved with quiet dynamism.

"What is all of this for?" Billy whispered. They were a distance behind the master, but he didn't want to risk being overheard. "Are they just showing off or what?"

"Well obviously they're showing off," Para whispered back, "but the Hall is functional. It's a machine, of course."

"All of this is *one* machine? What does it do?"

"It performs calculations."

Billy stopped her. A large cog wheel was ratcheting around, each turn shifting the positions of a dozen smaller cogs, their rotations affecting a myriad more whose further connections spread up and down and along, and vanished into the walls. "This? It *thinks?*"

Para shushed him with a finger to her lips. "Billy, we don't have time for this."

"If it saves a sylvan's life, I say we do. Remember the fuss you people made over Seldom. And it wasn't even a machine. This…"

"Doesn't think," Para hissed. "It's all mechanical. A glorified abacus. It's an incredible achievement, really. A testament to Stillworth's genius. He makes it perform highly complicated calculations, a service for which people pay very handsomely. That's why you saw Killick here this morning."

It took Billy a moment to catch on. "And why you sent me here. With that letter."

She nodded. "And I'll be sending you back for the results tomorrow. The Weathermakers prefer to be independent where possible, of course, but the cloud behaviour… we thought that we must have made a mistake. The Hall never does."

They reached a junction in the corridors that threaded through the inconceivable mass of machinery, peering around the corner to make sure the old man and his escort were still ahead of them before following. "How does it work?" Billy asked.

Para's brow crinkled at his persistence but answered. "I used to play here with Stillworth when we were kids. I remember asking him that once, and do you know what he said?"

Billy shook his head.

"He said *magic*. He was a sarcastic bastard even then."

"No, but really?"

"Ingenuity and hard physical labour." When she saw the disbelief on his face, she said: "You'll see. Come on, we need to catch up with your old man."

"Very well," Billy said. "But even if it is just a machine. Isn't it depriving a lot of people who are good at adding up of the chance to earn a kudo?"

"That," Para said, "is the eternal argument with the Constructors."

The machinery in the walls became denser as they ventured deeper into the building. And the thicker the layers of interconnected mechanisms got, the busier they were. By the time Billy and Para turned around one final corner everything about them was awhirr.

Kim and his minder were waiting for them. "You may as well come in, if you've come this far." The old man's voice sagged under his lack of surprise. "But for the love of nature, keep your mouths shut from now on."

They entered an enormous space whose walls, ceiling and floor dazzled with gleaming industry. The space was traversed by gantries and stairways up, down and along which the polished heels of Constructor shoes clipped with purpose. Grey suited operators were everywhere, reading gauges and adjusting wheels and feeding ribbons of paper into parts of the Hall. And if Billy had wondered about what powered the Hall, that was answered here too. At various levels there were colossal horizontal wheels whose bases were attached by crankshafts to the Hall's largest cogs. Each of these wheels had a hundred spars, and each of those had enough room for five people abreast, straining to rotate the enormous gearings. And, even giving their whole effort, every one of those people had the listless passivity of the inmates of the Institute of Improvement.

"Billy." Para's whisper brought his attention back.

Across a walkway to a central dais, a delegation waited. Billy recognised Merit Crane and his invalid son. Smout was there too; even at this distance the smugness unmistakable. There were others on the platform as well, suited in Constructors' grey, but their business was with the meters and dials that surrounded them.

Master Kim cast Billy one last warning glance and then crossed to the centre. Rabbit followed meekly. Its feet rapped a lonely tattoo on the walkway plating. The artfulness of its lines, the lustre of its wood glowed with natural beauty against the backdrop of all this metal.

Billy and Para followed, but stood back while Kim and Rabbit went meet the Governor.

"So this is our *sylvan* at long last," Merit Crane said. "I must say it doesn't look like much. What do you say, Still?" His son, however, wasn't paying attention to Rabbit. Stillworth Crane was staring at Billy and Para, and on noticing this a nasty smile crossed Merit's lips.

Smout however lost no time in filling the vacuum. "It's just as I told you, sir." He stroked his moustache as looked Rabbit up and down. "They're just simple puppets."

"And yet there is a motive grace about them." Crane's counter wiped the smile from Smout's face. "That balance cannot be easily achieved, that dexterity." He approached Rabbit then, peered at its joints, stroked its limbs and tapped its skull. "And where does it get this infamous –" He glanced at the old man. "Let us not court controversy for the Handmaster's sake, let us call it *volition*. In fact, while we have the Artisan himself in our presence, we should take the advantage, should we not? Well, Handmaster, suppose you let us into your secrets? We will discover them anyway, in the end, but you could save us the effort if you were so minded."

"There are no secrets," Kim said slowly. "Only good planting and patience."

"Huh." Crane appeared amused. "Well, if that's all it is, what exactly is your involvement?"

"I honour the wood."

"Ha, well. No one is doubting your skill, certainly." Crane lifted Rabbit's arm, dropped it. Even some yards distant Billy could hear its shivering fear. It was a wonder the sylvan's joints weren't knocking. "But I cannot help but wonder if the image of a man was necessarily the appropriate form for such machines."

The master ducked his head. "I will confess to that flaw," he said. "I do not know if the human form is the one the sylvans would wish to have, but it is the one I am best equipped to give them."

Crane nodded thoughtfully, still amused. "It occurs to me even so whether there might not be improvements to be made. See here." He bent Rabbit's arm. If you added motors at the joints you could increase the strength tenfold. All you'd have to do is connect them up to the power source. Which is where by the way?"

"There is no power source."

"Well then, what moves them?"

"The same as any other wood. The sun, the earth, the rain."

"Huh. Really?" Crane's expression was extremely sceptical.

Kim nodded.

"Well, this little fellow gets more intriguing by the second, doesn't he? And please, indulge my insatiable curiosity a moment longer, but how does the machine know what you want it to do."

This time it was Kim's turn to laugh. "Oh, it doesn't take orders from me. I might chunter to it, but it really does what it wants."

"Yes, but how does it —" Crane gripped Rabbit's skull again, wrenched it around to look into its glassy eyes. "How does it *understand* you?"

"I told you, I don't think it listens to me. If it does understand me... I don't know how."

Crane boggled. "You don't know?" he repeated. "Do you expect me to believe that, what, you knock these pieces of wood together in your backwoods hovel and they just stand up ready to do your bidding?"

"I don't care whether you believe me, Governor Crane. It is the truth. Except, as I've said more than once now, they awake ready to do *their own* bidding."

Merit Crane thrust Rabbit aside. The sylvan's feet skittered on the plate deck, then it tumbled with a clatter. "You cared what people thought of you once. Enough to flee Karpentine like a skelped dog."

Kim met the Governor's gaze evenly but said nothing.

Crane sighed. "Very well, Captain," he said. "I'm finished with him now. He is yours to dispense with as the Law dictates."

Billy heard the sound of boots on metal and saw guardsmen striding towards the platform. Kim however held up his hand. "One moment. Our business is not yet completed."

Crane frowned. "Oh?"

"There is the matter of remuneration."

"You are unlikely to have much requirement for money in the foreseeable future, Handmaster Kim. Why don't we hold on to your fee for now and release it to you when you are at liberty to use it?"

"That was not the contract." For the first time in the conversation, Kim acknowledged Billy's presence. "Give it to the lad."

Crane pursed his lips. "Very well, the family Crane did not build its reputation on bad faith. Smout, see that Braid is paid according to the terms of the contract for this sylvan."

"Turners return, no!" exclaimed Billy, alarmed at the old man's air of resignation. It was as if he didn't expect ever to have need of currency again. Billy suddenly had shocking, vivid image of him in the Institute refectory, thin and still and staring at something beyond his untouched meal.

"'Turner's return'," Merit Crane bellowed a laugh. "There's a phrase I've not heard in years. Do they still say that out in the wilds? Don't they know that the Turners can't return? We destroyed their machines centuries ago."

"It's just a phrase," Billy bristled, then took a breath and brushed the slight aside. "Look, we can work something else out. I'll tell you everything you need to know. I told your man, Bello, I would, and I will. I don't care about the money."

Crane's look was steely. "I'm sure I have no idea what you mean."

The captain chose that moment to lay hands on the old man. The master offered no resistance. "Benoit Kim of the Family Leung," he began, but Billy knocked the meaty paw off the old man's shoulder. The guardsman aimed a rigid finger at him. "Try that again, son, and you'll end up afore the beaks and all." A slow grin spread across his face. "And that wouldn't exactly be a novel experience for you now, would it? Didn't your improvement sink in the first time?"

Billy took the warning. He let his hand drop.

"Good man." The captain returned his attention to the master. "Now, Handmaster, you are to be detained to answer to the following longstanding charges. Um…" He patted at his uniform pockets. "I've got a list somewhere…"

"Just take me to the courts, Captain," the master sighed. "We can sort out the details when we get there."

Looking relieved, the guardsman gave the old man a shove in the direction of the walkway. "Not entirely sure you'll make it that far, old fella. Here lads, have we ever killed a donkey en route before?" The laughter of the departing guardsmen echoed down the hallway.

"Well, Mister Braid." Merit Crane regained Billy's attention with a resounding clap of his hands. "We have our sylvan. Smout will give you your money. I believe our business is concluded."

"You set him up," Billy spat, shaking with anger.

"We acceded to a request from the Judiciary," Crane said, unperturbed. "That is all. There is no escaping the Law, Braid. Your master had the good sense to understand that. You should follow his example. Now…" He gazed with no little scorn at the sylvan. "Still, my boy, I would like this specimen appraised and analysed down to its primary constituents and I would like your preliminary report by the end

183

of the day." When his son did not reply immediately, Crane and Billy both looked for him. He was engaged in some deep debate with Para. "*Stillworth*, I'm talking to you." Both of them started. The normally aloof Stillworth Crane was flustered. The face of Paraphernalia Loess was carefully neutral.

In the background, two overalled women were failing to coax Rabbit to climb a precipitous stairway because the sylvan was rooted with a branch-knocking fear that Billy could hear from the other side of the platform. They changed tack and carried it bodily up the stairs instead.

The Governor opened his mouth to repeat his instructions to his son, but he was interrupted by the clamour of a high-pitched bell. He walked over to a console and lifted some sort of handset. He listened and, with each passing second, his face grew more still. "Say that again," Crane said quietly. When the person he was speaking to had done so he replaced the device in its cradle.

Merit Crane approached Billy and gave a chilling laugh. "I have to say," he said too calmly, "that I had expected your master to display more resistance than he did, but not... *this*. What is he up to?"

"I don't know what –" Billy began but the Governor smacked him across the cheek.

"Don't bother." Crane's eyes glittered. "In fact don't open your lying mouth again." With that the Governor stalked from the room.

"What was that all about?" Para said. Stillworth was still hanging by her shoulder.

Billy rubbed his jaw. "I think we should find out." They crossed the walkway into the mechanised halls where an atmosphere of urgency had replaced the idling calm. Liveried Constructors passed them at a run. Billy glared at Stillworth. "Do you want to find out what's happening in your own back yard or shall I?"

Stillworth accosted the next group that came along. His demand of an explanation was more like his normal self.

"What's wrong with him?" Billy said to Para while the employee mumbled a response that they couldn't hear. Para's attempt at an innocent shrug was completely unconvincing.

Stillworth returned. "It appears there are more of your puppets in the city," he said. "And the weather has gone completely crazy."

The three of them raced for the exit. Outside, they found the sky entirely black as a storm raged across the lower part of the city. Not caring if the other two followed, Billy ran for the lowtown gate. The streets beyond were dense with panicked citizens, their cries of alarm almost lost amid the howling of the wind and an unending barrage of sleety rain. Billy navigated the treacherous gradients, the slick stairs, always heading downhill, towards the centre of the storm. Because he knew that the heart of the disturbance was where he would find the sylvans.

Even Kim's coat did not protect him from a drenching by the time he reached the city gate end of Prospect Avenue. There were huge holes in the cobbles here, and a crowd fighting to douse the flames of a burning building. Billy ran, following the trail of similar evidence through the streets. It led towards the port area of the city. Towards the Institute of Improvement.

It wasn't long before he began to hear the cacophonous voices of the weather screaming HATEHATEHATEHATE, and as he neared the Institute the volume both inside and outside of his head grew overwhelming. Thunder crashed. Lightning blasted down in blinding sheets. Billy's lungs and heart were bursting as he rounded the final corner. He skidded to a shocked halt. Gasped drenched air.

The square outside the Institute was filled with sylvans. Hundreds of them, kneeling in groups around boles of ironwood that had been uprooted from the Institute's perimeter and driven into the earth. When the lightning struck, it found one of these, and was conducted away into the blackened ground.

Standing defiantly at their centre of it all was Chop.

Billy tried to reach his friend but as soon as he took a step towards the Institute he was seized by foreboding. He tried again, but it was no use. The dread clamped his limbs like a bear trap. Then he remembered the last time he had been in this square: the paper that released him from his sentence had included a promise not to return. They did not encourage reoffenders in Karpentine.

Holding fast to a lamppost, he concentrated and realised that within the howling of the weather he could now also hear the sylvans' voice sounds... shouts, *taunts,* like volleys of stones being tossed into branches. Each round of abuse brought a lightning bolt retort.

"Chop!" If Billy's voice carried to the centre of the square, the sylvan ignored it. "What are you doing?" Then he remembered what his friend had said on the day the letter had come: that whatever trouble might have been in store only land and sky alone knew its nature. Well this newly awakened weather, lashing out at anything that displeased it,

185

certainly qualified as trouble. Even with Billy's ineffectual attempts to help the Weathermakers, there seemed no controlling it now.

Then Billy thought about the never-ending flow of new groves, birthing new sylvans. The old man working himself down to a nub to service the wood. Had he and the sylvans been preparing for this all along?

SIXTEEN

"What do you want me to do?" Para looked up at last from the research documents spread out across the lavish carpet of her living room. She had been poring over them for hours in the hope of coming up with a miracle to help the Weathermakers face another extraordinary meeting of families later that afternoon. In the quicksilvering light that gloomed in through the window she looked drawn.

Billy had been telling her but she refused to listen. "Get him out of there."

"You know it's not that simple..." She'd already told him there would be a bidding war to indenture Kim, and the Weathermakers had far less achievement capital now than they'd had when they bought out Billy's sentence. "Even if we had a chance of securing him, what would it benefit us? Would all those sylvans respond to him any more than they have you? Would the clouds?"

"I don't know." Billy slumped down on the embroidered sofa and stared into the fire. Though the continuing battle in the Institute square was ostensibly between the clouds and the sylvans, there were reports of collateral damage coming out of the lowtown now too, tales of victims of fire and building collapse as the hostility raged on. Para's blithe reassurances did nothing to ease the feeling that Billy ought to be doing something. The guilt was twisting him up inside.

He sighed. He'd never asked to be responsible for anything but right now, who was at fault if not him? For Kim's incarceration, for Rabbit being subjected to who knew what *investigations*, and for the arrival of all these sylvans in this city which had never seen a solitary one until a month ago. If only he had obeyed his first instinct and sent Smout packing... Well, there was no taking back what had happened. As to what he could do? Rabbit was deep in Radlett Hall and, despite repeated attempts to hail Chop in the Institute square, the old sylvan might as well have been no more than a stockade post for all the response it gave, so his concern now had to be for the old man.

"I just want to make sure he's well," he said.

"Those Institute buildings are strong." Para glanced at the window as hail rattled the glass. "He's as safe there as anywhere."

"You're probably right," he said, but found no comfort in it. He didn't like the idea of the old man in that place. He couldn't shake the fear of him getting stuck in there for good.

It wasn't as if he hadn't tried to do something. On leaving the square, followed by a trio of black-bellied clouds like watchdogs that left him wondering about the possibility of his *own* thoughts placing him on the weather's shit list too, he had gone up to the Exchange. There, he'd not been allowed to see the master, but he'd been instructed at length about his alleged transgressions. It seemed that, as a youth, Kim had been one of a group working in secret with Tatsuko Oshi on a variety of outlandish experiments into the properties of motes, including those that produced constructed intelligence. When they were, inevitably, discovered, Oshi had been sent to the Institute and her three acolytes had disappeared. Since Kim was apparently the only one whose identity was known, it was little surprise that the authorities had jumped on him the second he'd surfaced again. It didn't matter that they were wrong, that the sylvans' intelligence was natural. Billy had tried to explain but no one had listened.

"About the indentureship," he said. "You can have Crane's cash. All of it. It's all unearned riches anyway."

Para sighed, pushing the books and charts away from her. "Thank you, but it wouldn't be nearly enough."

More frustrated than ever, Billy glared at her. Although the look she returned him lacked her characteristic cocksureness she still managed to hold his stare with ease. The stand-off was interrupted by a chittering rattle on the window pane that Billy assumed to be another bout of hail until he caught sight of the steel-bright hooks of Tocka's beak. He hurried over to open the window and a squall blasted the bird-thing over the sill, tumbling it to the floor.

"Hey!" Even as she clutched at her papers, Para's exclamation of annoyance changed to one of disgust. "What the hell is *that*?"

The ragged bundle sprawled on the carpet was not an attractive sight. Tocka had never been a lovely creation, but it was a ruined thing now. As the bird attempted to straighten itself out, Billy saw that the canvas wings were tattered and that the creature's movement was hobbled because its wirebush legs were buckled.

"This is Tocka," Billy said. "And it looks as if it's had a hard time of it out in your weather."

As Para came over, the ersatz crow gave its wings a feeble shake. A flap of canvas fell off. "Your master made this? Was he drunk?"

"He was in a hurry."

Tocka managed a sort of mechanical cackle, then it spoke. *Sky*, it said. *Sky… is wild.*

"We'd noticed." Billy smiled in relief.

"You're not telling me that this thing talks as well?" Para's frustration that her sensitivity was strong enough to understand the words came across as peevish.

He ignored her. "And you've been in the worst of it, haven't you." Faithful Tocka, still doing its duty. "What about the master? Have you seen him?"

The crow managed to convey sorrow in its clatter of beak parts. *Bad skies over prison place. Master nowhere under Tocka's eye.*

Billy felt a fresh clawing of disquiet in his belly. The crow had been unerring in finding him when it needed to, the old man should not have been any more of a challenge. "It says Kim isn't at the Institute."

"He must be. The Judiciary won't run the auction until after the families have met." Para frowned. "And even in the vanishingly unlikely possibility he's not, try to stop worrying. There's only been a handful of accidental casualties."

She neglected to say: *thanks to the sylvans.* Billy went back to examining the state of the sylvan bird. It was a wonder it had made it all the way up here. He tried to straighten a wing but felt something in it close to giving. *Stop worrying?* She said it as if it was easy, and by *hardly any casualties* she meant human ones of course, but what about Tocka here? What about Seldom and Rabbit? What about the dozens of beautiful sylvans broken and burnt, putting themselves in harm's way, for what reason he didn't understand, but at least perhaps distracting these wild clouds from seeking out other minds that might make voice thoughts. Like his own and Para's? Who knew, maybe everyone had the ability of motal speech, deep down that they were wholly unaware of? Maybe everyone was on the verge of being awakened? Maybe Kim could be targeted too if it took their fancy. He knew Para was preoccupied, but her offhand disregard of the sylvans annoyed him.

"You should have tried harder to persuade Moraine Otterbree to give Seldom up," he said abruptly. The subject almost felt an irrelevance now but he was sore enough to use it as barb. To get her to listen. "Or maybe you could have asked your special friend, Stillworth?"

"What's that supposed to mean?" She peered at him, hands on hips. "I told you, she wasn't giving that sylvan up to anyone. There's certainly no reason to believe the Constructors have been given access —"

"Well they don't need it, they have Rabbit now. They can just roast a few fingers to afford the Sisters' asking price for altering someone's mind."

"Oh, do shut up." She turned away so he wouldn't see her face. "We don't know what the Cranes went to those two for. It was probably something minor."

"Oh, come on," he said. "No one goes to those women for something *minor*. He's a changed man. One minute he's glacier ice, the next minute he's melting all over your kidskin boots."

"How would you know exactly?" She picked up a page and pretended to stare at it. "You've known Still for what, a week? I've known him since childhood."

"Oh, so it's *mutual* admiration?"

Para whirled back around, now rigid with anger. "What is this?" she scorned. "Is it jealousy, Billy?"

Billy was struck silent for a second. *Jealousy?* He would have laughed if he wasn't so angry at her. People like him didn't get to have the luxury of emotions like jealousy. "Now it's you being stupid. Why does everyone in this place assume that I think you walk on the clouds? First the newspaper, then Roach, and now you too?"

"Oh, how wonderful it must be to be such a free spirit —" She was interrupted by an impatient rap on the apartment door, and whoever it was didn't wait for an answer before opening it. Wide-eyed, Para threw a damasked cushion to Billy who bundled it on top of Tocka.

A colossal arrangement of flowers entered the room. A study in shades of red, composed of blooms that Billy would have said were lilies and roses and orchids, except the specimens that grew naturally in the mountains never grew as tall or as straight or as perfectly petalled. Or as red. The Horticulturists of Karpentine had excelled themselves. The flowers rustled, and Stillworth Crane peered around them, smiling broadly. "Paraphernalia," he said without preamble. "I think that it's time…" His smile died when he spotted Billy. "What's *he* doing here?"

Para was still bristling from her exchange with Billy and this presumption did nothing to quell her. "Mister Braid is an employee of this family, Still. He needs no more reason —"

Stillworth grimaced. "He's a convicted criminal."

190

"He's being improved."

"And you think your own rooms are the proper place to entertain an *improvee?*"

"Stillworth Crane." If Billy had begun to feel aggrieved at being talked about as if he wasn't there, any notions of weighing in to this argument vanished when he heard the steel with which she enunciated those two words. "Who I choose to invite into my personal apartments – for whatever reason – is my business. And I do not appreciate people coming in here uninvited and presuming to tell me otherwise." In the face of Para's rebuke, Stillworth was struck silent. Billy guessed that this was not a man who was used to being rejected. "Oh, Still." Pushing her anger aside, Para crossed the room and spoke with Crane in a gentle hush. Embarrassed, Billy looked away. Shortly, he heard the door open and close again.

"He doesn't remember, does he?" Billy said. "Going to the Sisters. Being made to love you."

"I don't know. I don't think so."

"So are you going to marry him? Instead of Killick Roach?"

"I don't know."

"You don't know?"

"Fine, yes, maybe. Marriage… ugh." She balled her fists. "The family should be strong enough to ride this out without having to resort something so… *basic*, but it appears we're not. It's so unnecessarily old fashioned! Aunt Jelena thinks reintroducing ink into the family blood will buy us favours from Moraine but… there's no way I can marry Killick. I just can't. If I have to marry someone, I want to present a better alternative, a stronger alliance." She rubbed her eyes with the heels of her hands. "But I didn't expect this. Why would he do it, Billy? Why would he go to them?"

"Did it occur to you that his father must want that alliance pretty badly too? And with Roach announcing your match…"

"And you…" There was contrition in her glance. "Okay, I admit I used you, just a little bit, to stir up the situation. I'm sorry. It still doesn't make sense, though. The family stock is tanking."

Billy shrugged. He'd already guessed as much and it wasn't the first time he'd been used as a pawn in someone's attempt to secure – or get out of – a match. Although that didn't mean it didn't hurt. "I can't believe Merit Crane wants an alliance with the Weathermakers," he said as gently as he could. From her confused expression he could tell she still

191

didn't see it. "But anyone would want their most valuable asset... you. And Stillworth? Politics aside, he's genuinely infatuated."

For once, Paraphernalia Loess was lost for words.

The couch cushions rolled to the floor as Tocka jerked. The flick of Para's eyes betrayed her distaste. "I promised Stillworth I'd meet him at the Exchange before the meeting," she said. "I'll call for you afterwards and tell you what happened, but for now you'd better go." Another flick towards the crow, as if it were the source of all the city's problems. "And take your friend with you."

They found a shop bag illustrated, ironically, with birds, and the crow's protests at being placed inside were worryingly feeble. At the door Para kissed Billy on the cheek, and whispered her thanks. For what, he wasn't exactly sure.

Billy spent the following hour attempting to repair the crow, but his skills were inadequate. He splinted the broken bits, straightened the bent, but he could do nothing about the ruined charring or the pieces that were missing altogether. He soothed Tocka but, although the beak sometimes moved, there was no reply now. The thing lay on the table. It twitched occasionally but, the longer Billy looked, the more it resembled nothing more than a jumble of wood, canvas, wire and steel. Then the poor thing ceased moving altogether and, sorrowfully, Billy put away his tools.

After a little trial and error he found a stair that led to the top of the Loess mansion and a door that opened onto the pitched roof. To his left it rose sharply, water gushing down the tiles, frothing like a weir where they were newly broken and streaming between the pillars of a parapet too low to make him feel safe. In the queasy light, he edged along and found a sheltered spot among the chimney breasts. Rain wicked off the shoulders of the old man's coat. Still there for him after all this time, and making him feel like an imposter for how he had failed to do the same for Seldom and Tocka. His fingers fumbled the matches, but eventually the newspaper he'd stuffed in with Tocka took the flame and then the bag was alight too. Billy watched blackened curls of paper rise towards the clouds as the flames finished what the weather's brattish behaviour had begun. When nothing remained but hot ash and a few pieces of metal, he kicked the mess off the roof and went back inside.

Tocka may not have been much of a sylvan, but its short life deserved better recognition. Though Billy had done the best he could do under the circumstances, it didn't bring him an iota of peace. He tried to read the afternoon's paper, but it told him nothing he didn't already know. The news of the freefalling fortunes of the Weathermakers was now reported with something akin to scorn. The alarm over the weather was almost as hysterical as the scandalised fright affected by the arrival of the sylvans. Learning from the Bellos, Billy barely let his eyes scan the blazing headlines and opening paragraphs, but it was still enough to infect him with a jittery fearfulness. It wasn't only the ink. There was good reason for Karpentinians to be nervous. What would happen if the clouds did start getting upset over human thoughts and then really let loose?

At least he was spared having to attend the meeting. After his very public failure to control the clouds – which the newspaper, while scorning his failure, also managed to use to hint that the destruction of refugee camp may have been a deliberate act – he would only have been a convenient stick to beat the Loesses with. And it wasn't as if there weren't enough of those already.

More than ever, he felt no loyalty to the Weathermakers – not even to Para really, no matter how close to the mark he suspected she may have been with her accusation of jealousy – but he still couldn't shake the yolk of responsibility either. He'd allowed himself to be distracted by money, that fistful of unearned achievement waved under his nose by Bully Smout. There would have been other visits, of course, and not just from blowhards and unnatural animals, but he and the old man and the sylvans would have seen each one off and, eventually, been left alone with their trees and their sky to just get on with getting on. He shook his head. That last bit was wishful thinking. One of these bastard families would have found a way, somehow, to steal a sylvan away to the city. The weather would still have grown monstrous. The Judiciary would have come calling for Kim sooner or later. No, they wouldn't have stayed out of it forever. But sylvans wouldn't have had to die, and for that at least Billy accepted the blame.

He imagined them all at the meeting, taking a turn around the big table to shout out his crimes, each count knocking the Weathermakers' achievement down another few points. Everyone perhaps, except Moraine Otterbree. He could visualise her sitting back and letting it all play out. The *spider*, she was called, and with good reason.

Thinking about the people around that table reminded him of something. With everything that had happened over the last couple of days, he realised he'd completely forgotten about the paper helicopter that had hit him as he was leaving the last meeting. He grabbed his coat, and searched the pockets until he found it, now so crumpled that he could not imagine how it had ever been capable of flight. As he smoothed it on the table, the paper flattened out like silk. It was the softest thing he'd ever felt, so luxuriant that he had to force himself to stop stroking it even after the wrinkles were reduced almost to nothing. He held it to his nose. It smelled of vanilla and spice, a delicate sensual aroma that warmed him somewhere deep. While he recognised this instantly as manipulation, it was not like what Sister Skin had done. Both feelings had been unasked for, but this was an invitation, not an assault.

The last thing Billy did with this exquisite example of the Papermakers' art was very tentatively read what the sender had written there. He was no expert in poetry but, well, the ink was a nice shade of lavender, and the penmanship was exquisite. The words themselves were doggerel, extolling the author's many virtues in ill-matched couplets. He suspected that he was supposed to be bowled over but, familiar now with the sly tricks of ink, he could have laughed at how little effect they had. Now that Miss Creasey had his attention, however, he did remember her as a strong, capable person. And not unattractive, in a certain way. If no one else could be bothered to help him find the old man, it wouldn't hurt to pay her a visit.

Billy sneaked out beneath the bruised overcast, pulling his hat down over his ears and hunching shoulders against the bitter bluster. In the distance, the sky rolled like the contents of an overturned coal scuttle, interspersed even now with detonations and silvering spears. He'd have to head in that direction to get to the Exchange. But why assume Alicia Creasey would be there? Wasn't this extra session supposed to be an exclusive gathering? The more he thought about it now, the harder he was gripped by the conviction that Alicia, like himself, would be considered non-essential to the proceedings, a *distraction*. Instead of heading for Trades Hall then, he turned up the hill and headed for the very highest mansions in the city.

As Billy climbed the upper reach of Prospect Avenue, the buildings became even grander, the avenue wider and more gilded with decoration before it ended at the base of an ornate staircase. On one side the steps were white marble, on the other basalt black. They swept upwards towards the two greatest houses in Karpentine society.

The private houses of the Otterbrees and the Creaseys faced each other across a plaza, but they could not have been more different in character. The home of the grand dame of the Inksmiths was surprisingly subtle in its ostentation. The façade was sheeted in polished basalt, with only the occasional fleck of gold adding extra lustre to the dark perfection. The simple, straight pillars supporting the portico under which a row of soft golden lamps burned were made of the same material. The windows were all dark.

To reach the house of the Papermakers, Billy had to go around the fountain, a curious thing fashioned to resemble a shallow scroll of white paper, rolled around the rim. In the middle of it sat a copper inkwell and a fan of arcing quill pens discoloured by dark drips – when the fountain was in operation he could imagine that they would spray black water into the air. He supposed the monstrosity was some sort of attempt at a show of partnership.

The Creasey residence had once been as impressive as the Otterbrees', but the yellow-white marble showed signs of neglect. It was greened with mildew and many of the scrolled ornamentations around the windows were chipped. Billy approached the peeling front door and used a heavy brass knocker shaped like a sealing stamp. He was surprised that the door of the dilapidated house opened so quickly. Doubly so that it was answered by Alicia Creasey herself.

"Oh, it's you." She was dressed neither as glamorously as she had been at the ball nor as smartly as she had been while she scribbled gauche poetry in the Trades Hall. Her copper hair was messily gathered and the blue of her eyes watery. She still had something about her, though.

"You're surprised?" As Billy pulled the letter from his pocket he couldn't help rubbing it. "Didn't you send me this?"

Alicia's sniffed haughtily. "Well of course I did, but responses to my summons are usually immediate. What took you so long?"

Billy recognised that he was being scolded. "I was busy."

Alicia laughed raggedly. "Oh, I've been hearing all about that. I suppose you'd better come in. Close the door behind you."

Billy did as he was asked, only realising as the door latched that the hallway was all but in darkness. A fringe of light emanated from somewhere ahead, but its source was obscured. What should have been a grand vestibule – looking up he could just about make out the sweeping shadows of a vaulted ceiling – was choked to a narrow passage by what he discovered mostly by feel to be stacks of paper. Towers of books. Walls of newspapers, magazines, and other sorts of printed material he

195

couldn't immediately guess at. Many of these remained vertical only because they leaned on their neighbours, but others had succumbed to gravity. Alicia had vanished. "Where are you?" he said. "How do I get through?"

"Sorry." Her voice was a distance ahead. "This family doesn't have the achievement to squander on instantaneous lighting. And, for reasons that should be obvious, we never use candles."

Billy felt his way around a bank of paper that, from the evidence of the dimly perceived dots and scratches covering a loose-hanging sheet, contained music scores. Ducking under an overhang of song sheets, he tripped on the corner of a leather-bound album and stumbled, toppled the pile in a slithering slippage.

"Careful, you oaf. Those were all sorted." From somewhere, Alicia's voice dripped with exasperation. Shortly afterwards, Billy heard a lamp dynamo being wound and an additional source of light appeared, sending dancing shadows chasing around the ceiling as it moved towards him. When she arrived, the swinging lamp amply illuminated Alicia's displeasure. "Come on then," she snapped, scowling. "Before you cause any more havoc."

Beyond the hall they entered a kitchen as large as Kim's cabin. In more prosperous times, teams of chefs and servers would have bustled in and out, preparing grand meals for the Creasey family and their guests. Hard to imagine in this strange grotto where every surface and much of the tiled floor, was ceded to stacks of paper. Into the stacks were jammed kitchen utensils, and from these makeshift brackets hung more lanterns, ticking softly as they dimmed.

Alicia dangled her lantern from the handle of a ladle. It overhung a washtub across which a mesh frame had been placed. She gave this a gentle shake, making the pulp that covered the screen shift gelatinously. On the counter next to the tub Billy spotted the screw of a hand-press. On the floor were baskets of what had been clothes, ripped to rags and sorted into silks, cottons, linens. And, next to them, a long box held faggots of a dozen types of wood. The floor was a mess of splinters and sawdust and dried splodges. Throughout all this, at a height that made Billy constantly have to duck, were washing lines hung with paper sheets like stiffening shrouds. The old master would have blown his top to see a workspace in this state.

On the kitchen table sat a stack of beautiful books. The gilt pages of the one propped open were exquisitely illustrated with recipes and diagrams. The table itself was ink-stained and littered with numbered paper scraps, on each of which was scrawled a sentence in soft pencil.

"You're making your own paper." Billy said.

"What, in the house of Karpentine's principal family of Papermakers?" Alicia flicked pulp from her fingers. "They all said you were a sharp one."

"*New* paper, I mean. I was told your family hadn't made new paper in years." Billy lifted the top sheet from a stack. It was creamy, smartly trimmed and had a watermark that bore not her own family colophon, but a simple letter I.

"Don't touch that." Alicia snatched the page back and replaced it. "It's for a customer." She sagged a little then, lacking the heart for more snide remarks. "Don't look so surprised. Moraine might mass-produce her poisons, but we're still craftspeople over on this side of the summit. Sometimes I do bespoke work for private clients. Work that they don't need to know about down at the Mill." She cast her eyes around the chaos with something like despair. "Mostly, though, I'm trying to find a way to free my father from the spider." She levelled a stare at him, scoured him for a response.

Billy remembered Para's opinion of Alicia: *She's always been a bit strange.* Now he'd got to meet her, he thought that might have been unfair. Intense, perhaps obsessive, but if he understood her, she had reason. "She trapped your father into marriage? With *ink*?"

"No, of course not." She stared at him like he was stupid. "Even she couldn't get away with that. But after my mother's death, when my father's wits started to wander, you can be sure that she took full advantage. Got him to the matchmakers, got him to sign away our business, our family's secrets, our *heritage*. She doesn't love him... she can barely abide having him near her." Alicia nodded towards a corner where an ornate, brocaded and rather tatty throne of a chair nestled inside an arbour of piled paper. It held a blanket and pillows. A plate containing sloppy half-finished food sat on the floor beside it. "He lives here, and she only rolls him out for show when it's absolutely required. I look after him the rest of the time."

And when she wasn't looking after him... Billy looked again at all the paper. So many different types, textures, consistencies of sheet. Soft, crisp, ragged, trimmed. Experimenting, blindly and without success. "How long have you been doing this?" he asked.

"*Years.*" The doubt behind her defensive defiance made her voice shake, and she filled the silence where his next impertinent question ought to have been. "At first I thought I could find a paper on which I could write words that would bring father back. But his illness..." She expressed a shuddering sigh. "No, the only way I can break her hold on him is to break *her.* Her standing, her achievement, her name. I'm researching paper that is resistant to the effects of all her clever inks."

Billy looked closer at what she had been doing. There was a trimming knife on the table and those scraps of paper all said the same thing: *cut yourself.* Alicia saw him looking and tugged the sleeves of her cardigan down, but not before he glimpsed the nest of scars on her inner arms like a litter of pin needles, white, pink and raw red. And he glimpsed something else on her white skin too.

"Why did you ask me here?" Pieces of something were falling into place in his mind, but... did he just imagine a soft noise out in the hall?

Alicia's face tightened into a screwed-down little smile. "Well, isn't it obvious? I want your help."

This time Billy definitely heard it, a somehow-familiar tap-tapping, a snuffling of breath. The beast emerged into the kitchen like a ghost. The white of the antlers first, the symmetrical stripes on the black hide. He recognised the buck as it tripped over to Alicia. When she scratched its head, its ears twitched agreeably. Both of them watched for Billy's reaction, Alicia smirking now.

"Has he worked it out yet?" The buck's voice was deep and it elongated the vowels into soft lows. It reminded Billy now of the Sisters' cats more than the dumb animals in the animeaux emporium.

"The buck is yours?" He felt sideswiped by this, stupid. Just as he'd been on the verge of understanding something important too, but he'd lost the thread.

"Guilty," said Alicia. "As soon as I heard the first whisper about what your master had been doing out in your mountains I saw the opportunity. Working wonders with wood, they said. I had to know."

"So you sent this creature to spy on us? But it's *intelligent.* Such a thing..." The buck stomped a hoof on the tiles and Billy caught himself on the verge of the kind of piety he loathed. "What if you'd been caught?"

Alicia's reply was scornful. "My family has nothing left to lose."

"So you went to the Sisters?"

She nodded. "I went to the Sisters. For an intelligent animax to do my spying for me."

"From what I know of those two, there would have been a price. And yet you say you are poor?"

"There was a price all right, and I don't regret paying it one bit."

And that was it. Finally. "That?" Billy indicated her arm where, above the scarification, he had seen a tattoo. A rudimentary cat with wings on *nice white canvas*.

Alicia grasped her arm as if to prevent him seeing through her sleeve. "You don't understand. Before, I was meek. I did what I was told. I made my own desires secondary to the family name. Terrified of upsetting my step-mother, the great Moraine Otterbree, for fear of how it would reflect on us. But now I do not give a flying blue fuck about opinion. Not my father's, not yours, and certainly not that inky spider bitch's. I'm *free*. I'm going to take back what's rightfully mine and I don't care what I have to do to achieve it." Her cheeks were pink, her eyes afire. "And, right now, I need the secrets of your sylvan wood. The Sisters gift to me was made from the ash from bird bones. Such liberation! Imagine what I could create with pulp from your free-spirited friends!"

A tattoo that gave you *freedom*, that allowed you to break the rules. Billy remembered that his Institute neighbour had vanished the night he had been tattooed. Had he just got out of bed and walked out, his sentence broken by the ink on his skin. And now Alicia wanted to make paper that did similar.

But much though he could see value in such an exercise, Billy couldn't even consider aiding her. Not after what had happened to Seldom, what might befall Rabbit, what the host of the sylvans were even at this minute engaged in outside the Institute. He couldn't, shouldn't, but it took an effort to shake his head to her. Alicia gripped his arm. Her breath in his face was sugar and smoke.

"Come on, man," she wheedled. "What do you owe these people? This city? If you can help the Weathermakers with their clouds –"

"But I couldn't," he said. "Nothing I've done has helped them at all." Actually, he doubted that the clouds would ever heed his voice again.

Alicia's fingers dug deeper. "If you have so little ability, how did you resist my note for so long? Any other man would have come running and begged me for a chance to please me. You took *days*."

Billy shrugged. "In truth, I forgot about it."

199

Alicia looked confused. "Then why did you come if not summoned by my paper?"

"Because I wanted *your* help." As the words came out of his mouth, he realised. What had he expected from her? It *had* been the paper all along. He dug it out of his pocket. Even now its silkiness made him want to please her all over again. Not overwhelmingly, but enough to confuse his thinking. "What did you send me?" he breathed, dropping the note on the floor.

Alicia's eyes widened mockingly. The buck snorted. "Just a little poem on standard seduction stock, fat good that it did. I apologise for trying to trick you. But forget that." Now she was earnest. "I do have some influence, Billy. You want to find your master, don't you?" She nodded as she saw the undisguisable confirmation in his face. "I'll help you if you help me first. The square by the Institute must be littered with dead wood by now. I only need a little for the moment and, believe me, if your sylvans had entertained my company we would not be having this conversation. Get me some of that wood. Do that, then we'll talk."

SEVENTEEN

From the sporadic flashes persisting over the Institute of Improvement, the battle of attrition between the weather and the sylvans wasn't yet over, but the intensity had diminished. Instead, the clouds, giving every impression of having become bored with that particular game's ability to satisfy their new taste for destruction, had started to discover there was a whole city to play with. Looking down from the apex of the hill, Billy saw fires across the rooftops, billows of black smoke. He buttoned his coat against the freezing rain as he descended to the lowtown and tried not to contemplate how he was going to do what Alicia had asked of him. His last visit to the square had been a dismal failure.

Assuming he'd manage to get that far. Winds bullied him from different directions at once, mugged him from gusting alley mouths. Precipitation pelted down in unpredictable bouts: fat rain that shocked him with its coldness one second, then rattles of hail that lashed his exposed skin the next. Billy's boots skidded on the cobbles, sloshed through the gutter streams, stumbled over smashed slates and chimney pots. As he approached the Exchange, he narrowly avoided a flailing red and gold assailant that he recognised as a family banner torn from its rooftop mooring. On its final swipe he saw almost too late that the flag still trailed half a flag pole, the splintered wood slashing inches from his face. He caught his breath, then hunched his shoulders and pressed on.

Between the High Town and the docks road he hardly saw another soul, but as he neared the turn-off for the Institute he encountered a flow of people, coughing and weeping. They all had the same beseeching eyes, the same black smudges around their noses and mouths, the same stink of smoke. Within another fifty yards he smelled the smoke itself, and then saw the fires close up. Flames licked from sundered roofs. Billows gouted from windows. Fire engines had been brought bearing huge tanks from which people filled sloshing buckets that were passed from hand to frantic hand into doorways choked with people passing empty buckets the other way, but also bringing their possessions out onto the street. Clothes and clocks, bedsteads and books, armoires and artworks – lifetimes of mundane achievement – were all dragged out of the burning buildings and piled up in neat corrals for the rain to ruin at its leisure. Billy watched a bucket chain forced to pause while a father and three daughters attempted to negotiate a dressing table out of the entrance. The imprecations of consternation at the scene reached his ears over the churn of the wind, but he they should have been nothing compared to the voices of the combatants in the square around the corner. He strained his mind's ear, listening for the patient determination of the sylvans, the bellows of the clouds.

That he heard neither made him break into a run.

The Institute square was a scene of destruction. The ironwood staves were now in bad way; many a good deal shorter and most charred and smoking. Of the sylvans who had attended them, though, there was no sign. Billy was still no wiser why they had come in the first place, but where they could have gone was equally confounding. They couldn't just have left, could they?

In his urgency he'd come all the way into the square, but he felt the dreadful post-release inertia now. It crawled like a sickness in his belly, but wasn't quite as immobilising as the last time. And since he was here, he had work to do.

It was just a few pieces, he told himself. Skelfs and splinters. The sweepings of the workroom floor. Billy slipped through the uncanny, denuded forest, crouching to retrieve the most intact and unburned pieces of wood he could find. Putting the things in the canvas sack Alicia had given him and trying not to look too closely. Trying not to feel like a grave robber. Trying not to think about the peace of the old groves where these sylvans should have gone at the natural end of their lives many years in from now.

He thought about Kim instead, keeping the old man paramount in his mind as he searched, so it was perhaps no surprise that sooner rather than later he ended up outside the Institute gates. As soon as he realised where he was, his legs wanted to propel him away but he stood his ground. The facility appeared remarkably undamaged. There was a finial missing from the gatepost, some blast marks on the pathways and the gatehouse wall, and the smoking remnants of one small fire which the rain itself had doused. Safest place in Karpentine, Para had said, but Tocka hadn't been able to find him. Billy couldn't take the uncertainty. He had to know that Kim was all right.

There was no sign of guards out in the downpour. The Institute didn't normally require patrols, although under the circumstances it wouldn't have been out of place tonight. But, no, the guards would all be cosied up inside. It would be the perfect opportunity if he hadn't been frozen with dread.

"You thinking of going in there, Mister B?" The boy emerged from the shadows of the sentry post where he must have found some sort of shelter from the elements, although not much judging from his thin, sodden clothes.

"Vern? What the hell are you doing out here?"

The boy stiffened at the unintentional scold in Billy's tone, but at the touch of the white hand that appeared on his shoulder he relaxed again. Clymie's face drifted out of the shadow to join her brother's. Only a shawl covering her head protected her from the elements. "We was worried, Mister Braid," she said. "About all this lightning so close to the Institute."

Of course, their mother. Then Billy saw the bag she was trying to hide behind her. "What have you got there?" He might have managed to rationalise his own actions in making capital out of the sylvan's bravery, but to see someone else doing so brought on a flash of rage. "You little *vultures.*"

Clymie flinched as if he'd slapped her. "There's a high demand for these bits and pieces, Mister Braid," she said, stung. "We know it's not respeckful but we'll do anything for our mam. And it's not like there's much pickings left. Just tiny bits." Billy screwed his eyes shut and swallowed the anger down. The girl was right. They both had reason to be here, and he couldn't blame them trying to scrape a coin or two out of the situation. And she was right about something else. Given the damage that the sylvans had taken, there should have been much more lying around here than just splinters. Someone had cleaned up. He hoped it had been the sylvans themselves. Again he puzzled at where they had vanished to.

"I'm sorry" he said, then nodded at the Institute. "I share your fears. My master is in there too." As he spoke, a belt of rain rattled through the grounds, and a fork of lightning speared over the dockside streets beyond the promontory wall, followed by a gleeful clap of thunder. With the sylvans gone, no part of the low town was safe now. Billy had to do something. Not just go into the Institute, but try and get the old man out too. So why not the kids' mother at the same time? "What does she look like, your mam?" He handed his sack to Vern and edged closer to the entrance. Even those scant inches made him feel sick. The brief description Clymie provided could have been of herself so Billy didn't

203

think he'd have much trouble identifying the woman if he came across her. Another inch. He was shaking now. "I'll be as quick as I can."

"Good luck." Vern's voice was hoarse, but whether it cracked out of hope or fear it was impossible to say.

The first step proved the hardest and he almost couldn't do it; the fear instilled by his release, the physical admonishment to avoid returning to the Institute, was so strong. But it was only one step, and it had only been one sentence. Feeling like he wanted to vomit, Billy pictured the words, imprinted into his mind with bright black ink. Made himself think instead of the blank whiteness of the paper around them. The slip had been smooth and officiously edged and designed to support the words it carried. But what was paper in the end? Just pulped cloth and wood. It was only one step, and he made it. The inertia faded, and he was able to walk through the gates. The dread, however, remained. Billy didn't want to be in here any longer than he needed to be. He focussed on the job in hand.

While he remembered snatches of certain things from his month inside the Institute, he had to think hard about where he might find the old man at this time of night. It would be after most of the work shifts and the evening meal, so the best bet had to be the dormitories. The ones on this side, he thought, housed the male inmates.

Deserted though the grounds were, Billy went cautiously, and his caution was soon repaid. Halfway to the first dormitory block he heard voices well ahead of the guard patrol coming into sight and, heart hammering, he hid behind a tree, holding his breath while they passed. From the bitterness of their griping he doubted if they'd have noticed him anyway, but the jitters instilled in him by his release wouldn't let him take any chances.

"What gets me is how unnecessary it is," one said, rain drumming on the flat of her uniform cap. "It's not as if they're going anywhere."

"Some of them have," replied her companion.

"It's shoddy sentencing, isn't it?" said the first. "I've been saying for ages that the ink in't what it used to be. But still that's no reason for us to be out in this madness. We could just as easily have watched the gate from the window of the hut."

"I told you before, it's no achievement to —"

"And I already told *you* that I don't need your hand-picked quotes from the Book. Tonight's going to be long enough…"

Billy waited a little longer, then crept to the door of the long dormitory building. When he slipped inside, he found it in total darkness. Swallowing hard, he retrieved a torch borrowed from Alicia from his coat pocket and ground the handle briskly. The beam picked out the pineboard stairs leading to the upper stories, the white tiles of the washroom and the door to the ground floor sleeping quarters which he entered. At first he thought that he had come too early after all, with the inmates still eating their meal or working, but then he heard a huffing of breath, a soft cough, a low murmur of someone talking to no one in particular.

The torch beam was a sharp-edged cone, slicing the darkness open as it roved across the beds, and that nudged a memory. *The beam sliding across his blankets, pausing, considering. Dark eyes observing him before moving on to the next bed. A whisper, a question, the pulling back of covers, the patient application of ink to skin. A glistening winged cat. The next day, an empty bed.*

His light made a cheese-coloured moon out of the face of the man in the first bed. The eyes blinked slowly.

It wasn't Master Kim.

Billy shook himself to stamp out the jitters. If he didn't get on, this was going to take all night and he'd end up back in one of these beds himself. He strode the length of the room and then back down the opposite side, playing the light across the faces of the inmates. Some looked back, as empty-eyed as cows. Some slept. A few, covered by the blankets, demanded closer inspection. None were Kim. By the time he had completed all three floors in the first block, Billy was worried. By the time he had completed the second he felt panic threading his veins. And, as he neared the end of the third block, the feeling had turned to icy fatalism.

Outside, he sheltered in the shadow of the partially constructed new dormitory block. The impassive grey façade had grown quickly and, although still roofless and uninhabitable, it dwarfed those around it. What had the newspaper called the place? A bold statement of the city's stance against the rising numbers of citizens who chose to disregard the Law? Billy wondered briefly whether there was any chance that the lower stories had already been pressed into use. He found a window and peered through, but his first impression was correct. The building was only a shell. And from the deep, grinding groan that issued just then from within, he wondered nervously how sound the structure might be.

205

If, for instance, it really was strong enough to withstand the weather's excesses.

Another noise made him start, but it was only the chitter of a glory beetle that had alighted on the sill. Billy watched the insect meander along the undressed stone looking for food. It wasn't the iridescent green of the creatures he'd seen elsewhere in the city, but ink black, wings stretching now and then with a flash of silver. Antennae twitching, the creature's mandibles tested the corner of a dressed block and rather impressively chewed off a piece. Billy withdrew his hand from its reach. He was wasting time here anyway, putting off the inevitable. He tried to convince himself it wasn't possible because there hadn't been nearly enough time, but there was only one place left to look. The Institutionalised.

Across the landscaped garden in the centre of the compound, a low building nestled among the trees. It was plain and sturdy, which suggested that it was a good sight older than the rest of the complex. Perhaps even the original prison block left over from the time before ink, when walls and locks were necessary to keep miscreants in their place. As he watched, the doors of the building opened and a snake of men and women shambled out. Billy crept across the lawn and quickly ascertained that the old man was not among them either. The queue shuffled towards the refectory block where they would sit with their soup for an hour before returning to confinement. As if on cue, the doors of that building also opened and an identical cadre of Institutionalised shuffled forth. If any of this new group even saw him as they passed within feet of where he stood not one of them betrayed any sign. Again, his master was not among them, but one face was familiar. In the short time since Billy had last seen Ralston Maundy, the dapper little trickster had greyed to a shade. His skin was doughy, his eyes lifeless, his features overgrown by a patchy beard. He must have been ripe for this, but even so, for him to fall so far in, what, a matter of days…? Again, Billy tried to convince himself the same couldn't have happened to Kim, unless…? How severe *had* his sentence been exactly? Maundy shuffled past him without even so much as a flicker.

As the group filed into the old block, Billy slipped in behind them, then stopped in confusion. He had expected dormitories. What he found were steel stairs, leading downwards. Maundy's group of Institutionalised were tramping down rusting steps that went down not just one level, but dozens. He watched them trudge off onto a landing, then heard the squeal of door hinges, which came again a minute later as the same door was closed. The implications took his breath away. The Institutionalised was not a single group of lifeless wraiths, ruined by overexposure to incarceration, too apathetic to feed themselves, too grey and faceless to be any longer recognisable one from the other. There weren't even just two or three groups, either. There were who knew how many? And the thought that Kim might be amongst them already chilled his heart.

Laughter bounced up the stairwell. An exchange of conversation, which meant there were at least two guards on duty in this block, maybe more. And they were climbing the staircase. A bell began to clamour somewhere outside, and it was followed quickly by an equally urgent alarm within the building. In response, the guards' laughter ceased and was replaced by a clatter of feet on stairs. The fear surged then and Billy panicked, blundering through the doors and throwing himself over the top of a decorative hedge. He stifled a cry of pain from landing on a rock, and held his breath while the guards charged past his hiding place. Only then did he dare to raise his head.

The guards from the Institutionalised block were rushing to join a phalanx already clustered at the gate house. And the reason for the alarm was the ghostly figure, all wild, blonde hair and flapping nightdress, bearing down on them from the female dormitories on the opposite side of the compound. Billy knew who she must be, though much resemblance to Clymie was all but subsumed by the dynamism and effort that contorted the running woman's features, but it was not the woman herself that convinced him. It was the two despairing faces just visible on the other side of the gate. The two thin voices pleading, despairing as she burst through the cordon and disappeared into the city. Some of the guards gave chase. The rest cast confused recriminations among themselves, then – still arguing – drifted back to their duties. Even if Billy found Kim now, the chances of getting him out of here were zero.

He had to get out himself. Get out now.

The fear jangling through his body, Billy got ready to sprint for it but as he rose someone grabbed him and dragged him down again, pressing his face into the soil. Snorting earth out of his nose, he found a face inches from own. Mischief darkled the eyes of Sister Skin. When he opened his mouth, she brought something to her lips: not a finger, but something bone white. The carved design he could now see was of cats chasing each other's tails up to the tip where the needle had been lashed with a tight spiral of twine. Needle and twine were stained black, their work done. A prisoner, suddenly gaining her freedom. It didn't take much to work out who Vern and Clymie had been collecting sylvan debris for.

The sounds of boots and orders came from the other side of the wall. Billy and Skin lay listening to them receding and then lay still for a few seconds more. Then Skin winked at him and sprang up and was gone. Billy followed more cautiously. It took him several more nerve-jangling minutes to creep, ducking and hiding, to the gate. He'd almost reached safety when he heard a shout.

"*You*. Stop where you are." The instruction was unnecessary. The residual inertia froze him from the first word. To his left, figures re-emerged from the guard block, weapons drawn. Their captain marched forward. Her face was a snarl. "So, we've got you at last. That's the last sentence you're going to break for sure. I don't know how you've done it, but you're going to tell us…"

She might have gone on longer if it hadn't been for the noise. A crack, like thunder, but not really. All heads turned towards the far end of the compound where the new dormitory block stood. Another crack, then another, and then came a great fluttering thrum and a cloud of glittering darkness that swallowed the meagre light of the Institute's lamps. From beyond the din, Billy heard a tiny voice. "Mr B… run!"

Billy bolted. The sudden storm passing overhead lent him the cover he needed to cross the square and identify Vern's white face at the mouth of an alley. Looking back, he saw only the maelstrom. It filled the square and, he realised, was not after all some new manifestation of the petulant weather, but a great host of beetles.

"Look at them glories!" Something like pride infused Vern's exclamation as the swarm rose and wheeled up over the rooftops. As the air cleared, Vern pointed again. "See what it says?" In the Institute compound, the face of the unfinished building now had a different contour. Billy thought of the creaking groan he had heard while he stood in its shadow earlier, unaware that something had been reshaping the building from within. Thousands of tiny jaws ready to burst out and reveal their design.

Now the walls had crumbled away leaving only storey-high letters that read: THE LAW FOR ALL.

EIGHTEEN

Another alley, barely wider than Billy's shoulders. It was strewn with obstacles and, where Vern skipped nimbly over rubble and around puddles, Billy stumbled, bumping against flaking brick, splashing through the gutterwash. Their flight had been a series of alleys and switchbacks and stairs, and he had lost any sense of where they were. Somewhere in the dockside warren from the brine in the air, but that was as far he could tell.

"She just ran straight off like she didn't even know who we was." Vern couldn't stop talking about what had happened to his mother. He had his usual brave face on, but fear riddled him like an infestation. "D'you think she's all right?"

"I'm sure she's fine," Billy said, although he was only half listening. So much had changed in the last couple of hours that he really wasn't sure of anything any more. "She's free, isn't she?"

"But she din't even know who we *was*."

"That's just the Institute." He tried to weight his words with confidence. "Waking up from it is a disorienting experience. Your sister will be taking care of her by now. And when she sees you she'll give you a big hug." When Clymie had hared off after their mother, she'd taken both their and Billy's collections of Sylvan pieces. He didn't expect to see his again but at least it had bought someone's freedom. As for Kim, if he *was* among the Institutionalised, Billy didn't think Alicia Creasey had anything like the influence to help get him out of there.

A conflict of hope and scepticism waged in Vern's open expression. "But d'you really think she'll be all right?"

"Of course."

The boy carried on to the alley's end where he looked left, right and, as Billy also now found himself in the habit of doing, up. The street was empty and the clouds had retreated to a remote height, dispensing only a sullen drizzle. At the sound of someone approaching, Vern ducked back into the alley, but it was only his sister. Clymie's cheeks bore flushed roses and her eyes betrayed that she was close to panic. On seeing her, Vern lost his remaining composure. "Where's Mam?"

"I don't know. I tried to follow but the guards was too close."

"Din't she go home?"

"No, she just kept on running! They'll catch her for sure. What are we going to do, Vern?" She turned to Billy. "You have to help us."

"Me?" Their distress was heart-breaking, but what could he do?

Even in his panic, Vern's blunt practicality rose to the fore again. "He doesn't know nothing, Cly. She was spooked bad by our glories. We'll have to ask the boss."

Their glories? The ones who chewed out The Law For All?

After the revelations the day had brought so far, learning that Vern and Clymie might have had another reason for being in the square tonight, one that involved the people the newspaper called seditionists and rogues, was probably the least surprising. If the Law favoured anyone in Karpentine, it wasn't these two. Billy found himself increasingly in sympathy with these Refacers, whoever they were. "If you're going to meet the Refacers, I'm coming too," he said.

Clymie shot a terrified look at Billy but quickly realised there was nothing they could do to dissuade him. "If anyone asks, you followed us, right? You seen them anyway, so I suppose you could have worked it out." Her eyes said she doubted anyone would believe it. "Come on," she said to Vern. "Let's go home."

She took them to a boarded-up tenement a few streets away. Halfway along the wall was a gap not even wide enough to be called an alley. Billy pulled out his lantern and ground it into illumination. The bricks glistened with running dampness. It wasn't inviting, but Vern and Clymie slipped lithely inside and Billy was left with no option but to join them. Soon they came to a ladder bracketed to the brick. It rattled under the youngsters' ascent.

The climb took longer than Billy would have liked, and given the degree to which the ladder shook in its brackets he considered it a small miracle that the three of them made it at all. He'd tried not to look down, and any attempt to gauge his progress by looking up rewarded him only with a face-full of dislodged rust flakes and moss. By degrees, the ladder stopped shaking, and then there were no more rungs and Billy flopped onto the flat roof.

Clymie and Vern had already opened a door and descended a stairwell. Billy caught them up on the floor below in a candle-lit hallway, its wallpaper, patterned with green flowers and shadowed with damp, looking bruised in the unsteady light. The nearest door had a rim of light beneath it. From inside came the resonance of voices.

"Political? Of course, it's *political*. That's what this is all about."

"Not like this, Giteau." The response was strained with frustration.

Finlay Giteau.

That had been the name of Billy's bed neighbour in the dormitory, the one who had been tattooed by Sister Skin and vanished just like Vern and Clymie's mam. And, with the name, came a memory of something Maundy had said. Giteau, the seditionist, whose slogan was: *The Law For All*. Billy didn't recognise the voice especially, but he did know the one arguing with him. He knew it very well.

Vern opened the door and the occupants of the room instantly ceased their argument. Billy recognised the angular profile of Giteau straight away. Next to him was Marcus Golspie, the man who'd come to the Trades Hall meeting with a grievance about the increasing number of people being sent to the Institute, but he didn't know the third man or the anxious looking woman by the window.

The fifth occupant of the room was Paraphernalia Loess. Both she and Giteau spoke at once, and said the same thing: "What the hell are you doing here?"

"Well, Vernon?" Giteau hunkered by a set, but as yet unlit, fireplace. His hands were black and he had smuts smeared across his cheek and between the lapels of his shirt. Except the latter wasn't soot. Billy had witnessed its inking, after all. Even if Giteau had failed to get the fire going, his anger burned hotly enough. "Your mother was a good friend to us and your family's aid in allowing us to meet in your home is appreciated, as are your services as a Messenger, but you've been expressly forbidden from coming here when we're meeting. Be quick with your explanation, and make it utterly compelling."

Vern set his diminutive stature pugnaciously. "It's our mam, in't it? We got her out but the glories messed it up and now we don't know where she is." He glanced at the woman near the window, her coat still dripping rain onto the floorboards.

The woman growled a retort but Giteau silenced her. "Be glad she's out of there, boy," he said, "but she didn't come back here."

"And what about you? Were you at the Institute too?" Leaning forward on a threadbare settee, it was Para's turn to play the interrogator.

The question caught Billy off guard. "I was worried about Kim."

"So you decided to act on your own." The look she gave him was as stony as Molspur scree. "And did you satisfy your anxiety?"

"I couldn't find him."

211

Her eyebrows arched in mocking surprise. "Oh, couldn't you?"

In that moment she sounded like the epitome of High Town superiority and Billy could have hated her. "I *think* he's become institutionalised."

Para tilted her head, a minute movement that dislodged the antagonism from her like a skin of ice. "It's only been a day, Billy," she said wearily. "No one can become institutionalised that quickly."

Billy couldn't match her restraint. "Doesn't that depend on their sentence?"

"Sentences are a matter of public record, and are never so severe."

"Sentences can be changed."

Giteau chose that moment to intervene. "What do you mean?"

Billy didn't know *what* he meant. Not really, there were too many pieces and he couldn't make them fit. "I mean that there are *hundreds* in there. That has to be happening somehow."

Giteau barked a laugh. "You're accusing us? You're making no sense, you fool. We're trying to bring about equality in Karpentine."

"If you truly believed that you'd be *doing* something about people's sentences. Not just talking about them." Billy glanced pointedly at Marcus Golspie who looked at the floorboards, then he turned back to Giteau. "Just as well *someone* is helping people to get out of there, isn't it?"

Giteau blanched, but he didn't reply.

Para appeared to have missed the significance of that last exchange. "Billy's right," she said. "We should have stuck to action instead of political posturing." She balled her fists. "All it does is threaten our work."

"And we could go on changing the city by removing one over-entitled, eye-sore at a time." Giteau dragged his anger from Billy with difficulty.

"What's wrong with that?" Para replied. "Using Llodra's animax glories to demolish those buildings at least creates work for those willing to get their hands dirty." The rain-damp woman looked uncomfortably from Para to Giteau. "And having Golspie on the committee that awards civic construction contracts has allowed us to influence the creation of affordable housing to help the likes of these two out of these fucking dockside slums. Isn't that enough?"

"No, Paraphernalia." Giteau was seething now. "It is not enough. Not for me, and not for the majority of lowtowners. The wider our cause is reported the better."

Para sucked her teeth. "Do you really think that Moraine Otterbree will print any more about our activities than she has to? Do you think she'll fan your little flame, or snuff it out?"

Giteau shrugged. "If we build the fire high enough, she'll have to."

"If you build the fire high enough, the whole city will piss on us until we are irrevocably dowsed." Para rubbed the bridge of her nose. "Giteau, if we carry on as we started out, we can do so without fear of discovery.

"Discovery." His smile was nasty. "And loss of privilege."

"What do you mean by that?"

"I mean…" Giteau seemed to deflate as if the last of his anger was spent. "That it seems our association has come to an end." With no more to say, he left the room. The other people mumbled embarrassed farewells and followed.

Para put her head in her hands. Billy looked from her to the siblings. Clymie stared at the floor, but Vern was ever hopeful.

"I shouldn't have made the kids bring me here," Billy said. "I'm sorry." He meant it. Not long ago he'd been sarcastic at the idea of someone as High Town as Para being a philanthropist. Now he found out that she really was, and an active one at that.

"It doesn't matter." Para got up from settee. "You didn't cause this and you couldn't have prevented it. Giteau was already set on taking his own path. He's changed since –"

"Since he got out of the Institute?"

"Actually, yes." Para pinned him with a look. "He told me the printer he works for bought out his sentence. What do you know, Billy?"

Billy went to the window and eased the mouldy curtain open a crack. The sidestreet below was deserted. They should be on their way too while it was quiet. "He doesn't even recognise me," he said. "We were bed neighbours for weeks and he doesn't remember. He was the one I told you about. The one Skin tattooed in the night." He nodded at Vern and Clymie. "The same thing that happened to Giteau happened to their mam tonight. Nothing was holding her back. She raced out of there like a wild thing. And Skin was there. I saw her."

"Fine, I believe you." Para rubbed her eyes. "If anyone could come up with an ink to combat another ink it would be those witches, I suppose. But why?"

"I doubt it's for the public good. Skin would have to be in there all night, every night to even start to redress the number of inmates." He let the curtain fall closed. "I really am worried about the old man."

"Don't be." Para rolled her neck as if doing so would rattle all of this new information into some sort of order in her head. "He's not institutionalised, I promise."

"But if the Judiciary know people are escaping it makes sense that they'd make the sentences harder to break…"

"Maybe, but not in his case. I just learned that Benoit Kim was indentured by the Artisans before he even made it to the Institute."

"The *Artisans?*" That stopped him cold. It was the last thing he expected to hear. "How?"

"He's hot property, Billy. I didn't know about it until tonight or I would have told you, I'm sorry. Sky knows where they got the kudos from, but they won the bidding fair and square."

"Oh." Billy didn't know whether the thudding in his chest was relief that the old man was safe or anger at knowing who now had him.

"As to the other thing," Para went on. "Yes, there's been speculation for a while about the increase in sentence severity. Folk are ending up in the Institute for the slightest of misdemeanours now, and staying longer."

Clymie piped up then. "Our mam never done nothing. And they din't tell us nothing at the Exchange neither, even though we queued every day."

Para smiled sympathetically. "You're not alone. Golspie tried to obtain records for Institute admissions. It proved impossible." She flicked her gaze shyly away. "Even when you have connections." Para stood and went to the window as Billy had done earlier, hugging herself as she looked out.

"It's a tangle," Vern said solemnly.

"No, it's a web," Para muttered.

Billy stared at her. "You think Moraine Otterbree has some involvement?"

"No. Perhaps." Para sighed. "I don't know. Moraine makes credit from the supply of paper and ink for legal use but the recipe for the obeisant used for sentences is a matter of public record. If she were to tamper with that, *someone* at the Judiciary would know. It'd be too much of a risk to her position."

"At the top of the tower." Billy didn't keep the scorn out of his voice. "Which she attained by profiting from the misfortunes of others."

"True, although in a way you've got to admire her. It takes formidable tenacity to stay on top, to keep everything balanced, with new factors coming into play all the time. And she is a master at it."

"I thought you said ink and paper had always been the heart of this city?"

Para's laugh lacked humour. "Oh, indeed. But it wasn't always the Otterbrees who ran the vats. Back when inksmithing was a craft, not an industry, there were plenty of changes at the top. Even now there are other families waiting in the wings should her achievement crash, so the spider balances everything in this city beneath her, setting family against family, cause against need and, through the printed word, weaving truth and lies to manipulate public opinion into that tower on top of which she perches and watches, making inky little adjustments here and there in her newspaper so that nothing threatens the integrity of the whole. Not the underachieved, not the Kinster refugees, not our weather, not the *Refacers*…" she pronounced the word with bitter irony, then smiled sadly. "Not even you and your sylvans. As far as Moraine is concerned, more improvees just means fewer lowtowners complaining and an upswing in approval from High Towners that the Law is being adhered to. She's not directly responsible for it, but she'll make damn sure she takes advantage. You saw how she brushed off Golspie at the last public meeting?"

Billy recalled the end of the meeting. How Golspie had come fired up to deliver his demands, but then had lost his way "He read something," he remembered. "It totally derailed him."

"I missed it at the time because I was still fuming over Aunt Jelena's dressing down, " she said, "but I remembered afterwards when I saw how strangely Golspie was behaving… If I didn't know better, I'd say she hit him with an ink trap. It'd be quite an innocuous thing, but it must have been potent to throw him off his stride to that degree. No doubt she made sure the evidence was disposed of, but to do that so publicly? That was a hell of a risk by her standards."

"Something about this Institute business is shaking her tower harder than she'd like people to know?" Billy said.

Para raised her eyebrows but said nothing.

"So what about the Institutionalised?" Billy said.

215

She shrugged. "If there so many more improvees, it stands to reason that more will become habituated…"

"Not *that* many," he said. "Why couldn't someone be upgrading inmates' sentences? If not via the Judiciary, then some other way."

"You said that before." She frowned. "But for what purpose?"

Billy looked at her levelly. "Someone's maximising the cheapest source of labour." he said. "Growing a disposable workforce. The Institutionalised are what's left over."

Para paled as she considered that. "I can't deny your logic," she said. "But I find it hard to believe, even of them…"

"The Cranes?"

She spread her hands as if to say, *who else?* "But we're trying to catch zephyrs here. We can't go about making accusations about this until we have some sort of evidence. Unfortunately, my relationship with my contact in the Exchange is somewhat frosty at present." She smiled wanly. "Even if we were talking, while Killick's become something of a rising star lately, he takes his duty seriously. Getting information out of him is like getting rain out of a stone." She rubbed her temple. "But all of that is by the by. I'm afraid I have more pressing priorities at the moment. I wouldn't even have come tonight if Giteau hadn't been behaving so belligerently."

"What do you mean, priorities? Billy said. "Look at these two and tell them about priorities." Vern and Clymie's faces were masks of dismay.

Taking them in Para sighed. "I'm not saying it's not important," she said. "In normal circumstances…"

"If you didn't have your family's achievement to think of first?"

Her face pinched and she took an obviously calming breath. "I'm trying to tell you that this is not a trivial thing. You want to try and find out what's going on in the Institute? Well, right now I can only think of one way of doing that."

It took Billy a moment to catch on, and when he did he wished now he hadn't pushed. It was the last thing he wanted to contemplate. "Go back in?"

Para seemed oblivious to his horror. "It'd be under a false sentence, of course. It couldn't be me, unfortunately," she said. "And not just because of all the other stuff. It would draw too much attention."

"So you're saying it has to be *me*?"

She couldn't have missed the dread this time but pressed on regardless. "It'd be the only way," she said, matter-of-factly. "I suppose we could release you from your indentureship, say you've outlived your usefulness –"

"You really think they'll believe that?" He scrambled to think of reasons, excuses. It shamed him but he couldn't help himself. The edict in his release was still too strong. "I'm only slightly less newsworthy than you are. And what's to stop anyone else from buying me out again straight away?"

"I didn't say it was a perfectly plan."

"I'll go." The small voice was Clymie's. There was rigid defiance in her round face. "When they catch our mam and put her back in there with a new sentence she'll get institutionalised for sure," she said. "We want to help, and Vern's too young. So it's got to be me, dun't it?"

"You can't be expected –" Billy began, but Para cut him off.

"No, she's right," she said, a note of admiration in her voice. "She's a lowtowner. No one will look twice at her. It's the perfect solution."

Billy despised himself for the relief he felt.

NINETEEN

Billy and Para left the kids in the rotten tenement that they called home, with a promise to return once Para had thought about how to proceed. Guiltily, with their little hearts full of worry for their mother, Billy asked Vern to put the word around his Messengers to see if anyone had seen the sylvans departing Karpentine. To his credit, the lad vowed to do so.

On the way back to the Loess residence, Para avoided the thoroughfares Billy was familiar with in favour of poorly lit alleys and winding stairs that connected parts of the city in surprising ways. Had he taken this route on his own, he would have been wary but Para navigated the passages with confidence. Their route offered them shelter at least from the weather's unpredictable squalls which had now turned wintry, the temperature having dropped markedly while they were inside.

Not for the first time, he chewed over the enigma of Paraphernalia Loess. Born with a golden kudo in her pocket and showered with credits because of her family name, she should have had nothing more to worry about in life than what to spend them on. He had learned that she had a kind heart, but it shamed him to admit that until now he had never suspected her of actually earning her place.

"How did you get involved with Giteau and his lot?" he asked.

"Oh." His question had jolted her out of her thoughts. "When I first started hearing the clouds in my teens, I didn't attribute the emotions I was picking up to them initially," she said. "I thought they came from people. And was callow enough to believe I was sensitive to the anguish of city. Even the knowledge that the city *had* anguish opened my eyes to a lot of things and I decided I wanted to help. Several years of doing shifts in soup kitchens followed, then I met someone who knew someone, who knew someone who asked if I *really* wanted to help. And there we were." A few steps behind her on a covered stair, Billy could only smile. With the adrenaline generated by the evening's exertions finally draining away, he was too tired to do any more.

They entered the mansion via the garages. Avoiding anyone that might start asking questions suited him fine because the only thing on his mind now was that small but welcoming bed that he had come to think of as his own. At the bottom of the stair that led to his floor he mumbled good night and turned away.

Para touched his arm. "Billy, can I…" Her face was a sketch of uncertainty. "Can I come up?"

He stared at her dumbly, unsure why she suddenly felt the need to ask. She interpreted his hesitation as something else, however.

"Not for sex," she breathed. "Just… to be with someone."

"Someone?" Should he feel privileged? It wasn't like she didn't have plenty of options, but this time he didn't voice that thought.

Para's attempted smile was weak. "Someone I trust."

Billy shrugged and began to climb the stairs. "All right," he mumbled. "But no sex."

In his room, they discarded only their outer layers before tumbling into bed. They spooned on their sides, close enough for warmth, although the light weight of Para's forearm at his hip was their only contact. Billy lay listening to the even slough of her breathing.

"You're not sleeping," she said at length.

He didn't turn round. "I'm still worried about the old man," he said into the darkness.

"I told you before…"

"He's safe with the Artisans?"

He felt her soft chuckle. "They'll have wrapped him up snugger than the Tower Diamond. No expense spared, believe me."

"Meanwhile I get the attic room in your servants' wing? You really know how to make someone feel his worth."

"Falsehoods are no achievement…" she chimed softly.

"Shut up, eh?" Then in the quiet that followed, he asked: "Can I at least see him?"

"I'm sorry," she said. "Can't you just be content that he's safe?"

Billy slipped into a drowse after that. When he drifted awake again, he said: "So, which is it to be then?"

"Huh?" Her voice was small, smothered by sleep. "What do you mean?"

"Stillworth or Roach? Which one's to be the lucky man? Have you worked out a plan for that or do you intend to play them both off against each other for as long as you can get away with it?"

"Are you telling me you care?" He felt her sigh on his neck. "No, don't answer that," she said. "It wouldn't make any difference."

*

When Billy woke again the room was washed with grey light. That he was alone was unsurprising, and he refused to acknowledge the pang of disappointment he felt. He'd been dreaming of sylvans being tossed into the back of a truck like firewood. He stared at the ceiling and convinced himself it wasn't real. He hoped he'd hear from Vern's Messengers today. Hoped harder that their news would be that the sylvans had left the city entirely. Karpentine was no place for their kind.

When he threw back the blankets, he was thankful that he'd been too exhausted to undress. The room was colder than his own back home got in midwinter. His first instinct was to light a fire, but this was the city where the sun always shone, and it was still supposed to be summer so the grate was spotless and there was nothing to burn. Billy pulled his boots on, and then Kim's travelling coat which he buttoned all the way up to the neck. Not for the first time, he was grateful for the gift. It wasn't just a hard-wearing piece of leather, Billy realised now. When the old man had started him down the long road to Karpentine he'd wanted him to have a symbol of both his care and his trust. Thinking of the sylvans and the Tailor children, Billy couldn't help feeling something of a sham wearing it.

In the servants' mess, the only tables that were occupied were the ones nearest the kitchen. Billy gratefully accepted tea and porridge, and felt better the moment he started consuming them. The same couldn't be said for his companions. Most of the mansion's employees were swaddled in what looked like all of the clothes they owned, hats, gloves and all. And still they appeared unable to bear the temperature.

"It's nothing short of a scandal," said a woman seated along the table. He thought he recognised her as one of the household staff, but with her woollen scarf pulled so high around her chin it was difficult to tell. She hadn't been addressing anyone in particular, but when she saw she'd got his attention she waved a cereal-caked spoon at him. "We knock our pans out for this lot, don't we? An honest day's work ought to be rewarded, oughtn't it? And a body ought to be able to do her work under reasonable conditions, ought she not?" Billy nodded non-committally. "Yes, she ought. And, let me tell you, do you know what my neighbour, Mrs Hooper, said to me yesterday." Billy shrugged, but the woman paid him no heed. "She said to me, Geraldine, she said. What are you people going to do about this rain? She said that to *me*. *You people*. I told her, I'm not one of them people. I only cleans for them. I haven't got any business with their business, I said. I'm on your side in this matter."

Somehow amid all of that talking the woman had managed to polish off the last of her breakfast and lick clean the spoon and she was now pointing it at him again. "You see how things are? Tarnishing all our good names, this lot are. I tell you, if this goes on, I shall have to consider my position."

"That's... understandable." Somehow he didn't think his reply was sufficient, but the woman humphed one more time then rose from the table and bustled out.

He reached for his tea but someone sat down next to him, jostling his arm and spilling it. Turning to protest, he found himself confronted by the grin of Erudite Bello.

"I wondered how long it would be until one of you showed up again." Billy extracted his sleeve from the milky spillage expanding towards the edge of the table.

Erudite withdrew the meticulous houndstooth arm of his own coat too. "Expecting a visit, were you?" He lowered his voice. "Well it can't be because you've suddenly decided to tell us everything you know, because I know you're aware that Mr Crane's offer was rescinded. Perhaps you're feeling guilty about something?"

Billy's laugh echoed like a crow's call around the room, causing a peak in the communal grumble. "Not at all," he said, hoping he sounded as confident as he wanted to. "It was Mister Roach's proposal I was thinking of. I'm expecting to be paid at some point. Why else would you come and see me?"

He felt Erudite shake softly with laughter. "I think not, little Billy." He patted Billy's shoulder. "You've not kept your side of the bargain, you naughty boy. You've not kept your hands to yourself." His fingers found Billy's scapula, dug in. "As *in-struct-ed.*" Each syllable was punctuated by a taloned squeeze.

Billy squirmed. "I haven't touched her."

"No? You've been seen in her company an awful lot lately."

Billy shook himself free from the loathsome man's grip. "Well, she owns me, doesn't she?" He realised it had been a while since he felt that was actually true, but Erudite didn't need to know that.

"Your indentureship has limitations. Where, for instance, was she last night?"

Billy wondered which of the staff in the family wing had been bribed to tattle when Para's bed hadn't been slept in. "How should I know?" he said. "We got back late and I went straight to bed. What Miss Loess did

221

is her own business. Besides..." He stood and gave his sleeve another shake, flicking the spray in Erudite's direction. "Your employer has far more serious competition than me."

Bello stood as well. "Indeed he does, Billy," he said. "And that is very likely the reason that Mr Roach has not thus far ordered retribution. But believe me, if he finds proof and can avoid paying you, he will. He's a man who treasures his kudos."

"Fine." Billy smiled as amiably as he was able. "I get the message. Tell Baby Cock that my warning is duly renewed." He turned and stalked out of the mess. His anger put fire in his legs, and he was almost at a run when Erudite caught up with him.

"I'm sorry, Billy. You've misunderstood me. All of that was by the by. I actually came here to do you a favour."

"A favour? Right."

Erudite's lips twisted with disapproval. "Please. Scepticism is natural, but a gentleman of worth would at least try to disguise it."

"All right then." He slowed down. "What kind of favour?"

"Mister Shankhill has invited you to the Lodge of the Artisans. There's someone there who very much wants to talk to you."

Billy stared at him. "Master Kim?"

"Well, obviously. I've even gone to the trouble of procuring a car. It's well known how you hate to walk."

The vehicle idling in the mansion courtyard was the most impressive that Billy had yet seen. More complex than Para's car and, at the same time, more harmonious in design than Bullivant Smout's ostentatious affair, this was a thing of genuine beauty. The bodywork of the roofless cabin was a sweeping celebration of the art of marquetry. Billy ran his finger over the bonnet and counted the thin strips of wood that had been expertly laid and pressed to form whorls and teardrops of light and shade and colour before being finished and stained and lacquered and polished until it was nearly impossible to tell one constituent timber from the other. It reminded him so strongly of the sylvans that his heart swelled, although the work here surpassed even the old man's abilities. To top it all, six pipes of burnished ironwood protruded from the plunging rear of the vehicle, each of them trailing a finger of steam from the idling engine.

There was no mistaking that this was an Artisan's car.

"What is it?" asked Erudite in response to Billy's surprised laugh.

Shaking his head, Billy climbed into the back. "They've used ironwood instead of iron."

Erudite climbed in after him and closed the door. "So what? It works, doesn't it?"

"I wouldn't be surprised," said Billy as the driver in the fussy fawn Artisan livery eased the car into gear, "if there wasn't a scrap of metal in this whole thing." Proving him right, the immediate indications from the suspension were that this wasn't going to be a smooth ride.

While the streets still couldn't be described as busy, there were at least people out and about now. Huddled figures scurried through the dank, frigid mist, attempting to resume their lives, open up their businesses, stock up on essentials because who knew what the weather had in store next? The sparseness was a fortunate thing because the car skittered on the icy cobbles and, once, almost lost traction entirely while cornering.

Billy hardly minded. He was surrounded by beautiful wood and the solution to the one thing that had worried him more than anything else had been handed to him in the most unexpected manner. "The master is well, then?" The car had slowed to descend the grand curving avenue that Billy remembered from his last visit to the Lodge. As the mist lifted, the view across the rooftops to the fields and far forest beyond the city wall was breathtaking. The only thing that marred it was the scatter of churlish clouds. Even as Billy noticed them, more appeared, sloping into view with latent menace that reminded him of the bullies that at one time had waited for him outside the school gates. His fear that the weather might move on to targeting awakened people was becoming an uncomfortable conviction. "You can just piss off," he murmured in their direction, and immediately regretted taunting them, even quietly.

"Well enough, but unwilling." The Courier, slouched into the collar of his coat, was watching the buildings they passed on the inside of the road without interest. "Your master understands the obligations of his indentureship, but he has refused to perform them until he has talked to you."

Billy kept a wary eye on the darkening sky. "Did he say why?"

Erudite only grunted in answer. On his side, the white, mica-clad pillars of an ornate portico swept past and were replaced by a remarkable wall of textured iridescence. As they passed, the knurled knobs of colour swam: purple to blue to green and Billy realised that they were beetle shells. The effect was incredible, but was cut short as the scintillating

223

carapaces were suddenly shadowed. And then so was the car. Billy looked up again to see that those bullying clouds had made a move, and they'd done so with quiet purpose. Gone were the sizzling, churning tantrums of previous days. Now they were serious and grey and filled with a brooding determination that he was certain now was centred on him.

"Can we get a move on?" he asked.

Erudite rewarded him with a patronising grin. "In a hurry for the family reunion, are we?" Then he saw the direction of Billy's gaze and the smile fell away. As he tapped the driver on his shoulder the skies opened.

It started with crystals so fine that it was impossible to tell whether they had drifted all the way down from the clouds or simply crystallised out of the air. The specks were tiny but they stung Billy's skin and, of course, they were only the beginning. In seconds, the crystals became pea-sized hailstones. First one nestled in the folds of Erudite's coat sleeve; then two, three, four snicking against the windscreen; then, even as the vehicle accelerated and pulled at last out of the bend, an instantaneous, hissing downpour that pelted the occupants of the car and flooded the road with ice marbles. Billy and Erudite ducked down inside of the car, crossing their arms over their heads. Billy felt the driver gun the engine and the car respond uncertainly on the treacherous surface. The wheels skidded and the rear of the vehicle swung out before the driver managed to right it. Amid the tumult, Billy heard Erudite shouting at the driver. He hoped that, if it was an order to speed up, he would ignore it.

The tone of the downpour deepened into a rattling roar. The first of the hailstones, as big as an egg, fractured the windscreen glass and frightened the driver so much that he almost lost control. The onslaught doubled in ferocity. The stones thundered down like rocks, crazed the window glass further and raised splinters from the beautiful wood and howls of pain from the occupants.

Billy's hands and arms grew raw from protecting his head. He felt ice water and hot blood trickling down his face. He heard Erudite shouting again, *faster*, and felt the driver reacting in the opposite manner. The momentum of the car dropped, but it was too late. As it approached the open gate of the Artisans' Lodge, it spun sideways. To Billy it seemed that the car revolved slowly, graceful as a sycamore seed. And then they hit the ornate granite gate post, and with a great sound of rending and splitting the fabulous car folded in half.

TWENTY

Billy felt arms around him, dragging him through the hail, up a step and through a door, and then everything stopped apart from the ringing in his ears.

Erudite was already on his feet. His face looked like a well-kicked football and he dabbed at it with a soft towel. Sitting up, Billy accepted one too from a fawn-clad servant who immediately turned her attention to helping a colleague with the motionless driver. The towel was in the Artisans' colour, embroidered with a chasing design of interweaving branches and leaves and pretty much the softest piece of cloth Billy had ever felt. It pained him to ruin it.

Erudite tossed his own bloodied towel onto that wondrous mosaic floor. "Hurry up," he said.

Easing to his feet, Billy discovered that virtually every part of him hurt, although nothing appeared to be broken. The leather of Kim's old coat was scuffed in several new places, but it had undoubtedly saved him from worse damage. Wiping the blood from his face, he found that mostly his cuts were minor, although there was a seeping welt on his cheek. He kept the towel pressed to it as he took in the artistic wonderments of the vestibule.

"I said, hurry up." Erudite dealt him an unkind shove and, reluctantly, Billy followed him to one of the staircases. Where Erudite's boots scuffed the tiles, Billy trod reverently.

The upper hallway was as different in design from the ground floor as it was possible for Billy to imagine. In place of the mosaic, the floor was carpeted in what looked and felt like moss. And the walls and ceiling, stripped of the magnificent complexity of the plasterwork, were given over solely to wood. Long panels, each composed of a single sheet of timber and framed by a simple border. Everything – the preparation and presentation, the choice of cut and the lightest of lacquer – focussed the eye on the wood itself. Billy could quite happily have spent hours attempting to identify the timbers he knew from Kim's teachings and marvelling at the more exotic ones that he didn't recognise. There could be no doubt that this was the world his master had come from, and it was a world Billy had known next to nothing about. He wondered how long he'd have with the old man here. He suddenly had so many questions.

Billy got lost in his thoughts. When he next looked, Erudite had disappeared through one of the doors. Putting the towel reluctantly aside, Billy entered a large office. The walls here were lined with paintings, tapestries, sculptures on plinths. Every one of them was exquisite, but the main feature of the room, behind an impressive desk and chair, was the window that spanned the entire rear wall. The window was not only curious because of its size, however. Unless Billy had lost his sense of direction, the glass wall faced into the centre of the Lodge. So, how to explain the daylight streaming into the room?

He suspected that the man silhouetted in front of the glass would be happy to tell all, given the chance. Though *happy* might not be the correct word. It seemed that circumstances had changed since Billy's last visit here. Gone was Lemuel Shankhill's unctuous simper. When he turned to greet his visitors, the Grandhandmaster's face was contorted by fury.

"What took you so bloody long? You were supposed to be here an hour ago. You bloody upstarts have no sense of *application*."

As the tirade began, Erudite slipped out of the room, closing the door behind him and leaving no question that it was Billy who was the subject of the diatribe. He opened his mouth to reply, but Shankhill was still in full flow.

"Come here and see what you so-called *weather people* are responsible for now."

Billy joined the man at the window. He found that he was looking out over a vast courtyard which served as a communal workshop space for the Lodge's artists. Right now tutors and apprentices were standing talking while youths had been pressed into service with brooms. Frequently they looked upwards. Because above it all, equally as grand as that above the Loess family's ballroom, was a glass ceiling that provided the workers the daylight that Billy had puzzled over. The sky currently looked less violent than it had been on Billy's arrival, but it had certainly left its mark. The panes were cracked and holed in many places.

"The hail..." Billy said.

"*The hail*, "Shankhill mimicked. "Well what else would it be? Seagulls? I tell you, your shiftless lot have much to answer for, Braid."

"They're not my lot," Billy said through habit. "I'm only –"

"You're only *indentured* to them. Of course, silly me. Do you really think I care?"

Billy wondered if Shankhill had learned yet what had happened to his car. He decided not to bring it up. "Your servant said you wanted to see me." He tried to keep his voice as neutral as possible.

Shankhill appeared to have blown himself out anyway. "Not me, you ignoramus, I couldn't care less if I ever clapped eyes on you again."

There was a timely knock at the door as Erudite returned with the master. Kim looked older but he drew himself tall, puffed himself out. "Grandhandmaster?" the old man said.

"Say what you have to say," Shankhill stalked towards the door. "And be done quickly." He pulled it closed as he left."

The master joined Billy at the window and then broke into a tired smile. "I thought I told you to go straight home?"

"Never was the best at doing what I was told. But I understand you're being quite the rebel yourself. Is what they want to do so terrible?"

"Terrible?" Kim turned to the window. The youths had finished and the students were being coaxed back to work. "Do you know how long artisan apprentices spend down on the floor?"

Billy shook his head, finding it hard not to be irked by the irrelevance of the question. How could he know that? He'd never been told anything.

"Eleven years." Was that pride? Was he *happy* to be back here? "You think I worked you too hard and taught you too slowly? Son, your education was a skim of the surface compared to what you should have had. Eleven years of learning your skills, eleven years of finding a material that speaks to you, of dreaming about how to make it speak back. An artisan apprenticeship feels like it takes a lifetime, but when you look back it is gone in a flash. When you leave here you believe you are capable of great achievements and terrified that you will create nothing at all because, even after eleven years, you feel as if you have learned nothing of any significance. Suddenly you have no one but yourself to rely on. You don't even know how to have an idea of your own, so you look for help, advice, inspiration, guidance."

Perhaps it hadn't been pride after all. Perhaps it had been more of a yearning regret. "Are you talking about Oshi?" Billy asked.

The master's face cracked that smile again. "Yes, I'm talking about Tatsuko Oshi." He wheezed out a sigh that sounded as if it had been trapped under the weight of years. "There were three of us. All newly qualified. All fizzing with creative energy and no direction to expend it on. Nothing suited. Everything had been done before. When Oshi approached us with her crazy ideas at first we laughed, then we scorned, and then finally we took the opportunity she was offering."

Whatever Billy might have expected from Kim, it hadn't been a… *confession*, he supposed you could call it. "Which was?" he prompted, eager from him to go on.

"Oshi was a Constructor…" the old man continued. "Ach, no, she wasn't. She never built anything in her life, not with her hands. But in her head? That was a different story. She was a thinker, and she was convinced that the motes left behind after the Turning – which everyone had always maintained to be inert – retained some properties from the damnable machine intelligences which we purged from our world. And she believed that – under the right circumstances – these properties could be reawakened in some form."

"Under what circumstances?"

"She didn't know. There would be no way, thankfully, to reawaken them to function as they had once been used, but Oshi thought that since they had been part of the world for centuries there might be some resonance that could be awakened by natural means. So she sought to enlist the skills of experts in the manipulation of natural materials." Kim laughed, a breathless sound. "Of course, no *experts* would have risked their reputation on such a venture, so what she ended up with was us. Fry, the stonemason who was charged with trying to awaken the motes in the rocks. Myself, the woodworker. And Mackie Loess who, before he became obsessed by the air, was a metalsmith of considerable ability."

"Mackie Loess? You mean Jelena Loess's father?"

Kim nodded. "The very same. We all performed our work in secret. We had to. Our investigations in themselves wouldn't necessarily have contravened the Law, but the association with poor old Oshi would have clouded the rest of our careers."

"As long as you didn't succeed?"

Kim grinned ruefully. "Ah, that would have been a different matter. But we couldn't dream what form success might take, could we? We were looking for tiny effects, glimmers of something that might support Oshi's theories and might one day be developed into something of use."

The old man placed his fingers against the glass and his gaze was directed at something further away than the artisan school below them.

"So what happened?" Billy said. "When you succeeded."

Kim let his hand fall to his side, looked at Billy sidelong. "My discovery was purely accidental. I had been growing trees together, not by design but because there was only a limited plot of ground that I could use, and I had been combining the woods in various ways. I could have chosen any form, of course, but it became my habit to bind them into little articulated manikins. It was patient work, growing, crafting, observing and, while my expectations were low, Oshi's pockets seemed deep enough. No one was more surprised when that first manikin stood up and tottered across my work bench… and, well, you know what that led to.

"I told you that the three of us rarely got together, but on this occasion I had to share my news. We chose a quiet barroom deep in the warrens on the low side of Radlett Hall. We sat in a back corner, and even so I whispered my news. Their reactions could not have been more different. Fry was bubbling over, and he also admitted to having had success, although he was reticent about the details and he shut up entirely in the face of Loess's flat dismissal. Mackie told us he'd discovered nothing and didn't believe that we had either." Kim winked slyly. "Of course, the world knows now that he was lying. He must have discovered by accident how to influence the atmospheric conditions, but decided he would do better keeping it to himself instead of sharing it with Oshi, who would have treated the knowledge in merely academic terms anyway."

"So what happened?"

"Someone talked," the old man said. "It must have been Fry. He was never the best choice, to be honest. Gifted, yes, but too easily cowed with two young daughters to take care of. I arranged to meet him again to talk without Loess present, but he failed to appear. In fact he never showed up again."

"You didn't think that…?"

"He was sent to the Institute? Or worse?" The master shrugged. "No, I didn't think that. Rumour has it that the Constructors made him an offer he couldn't walk away from and he was absorbed deep into their family to spill the secrets of whatever he'd found. You know they started rebuilding Radlett Hall the following year? It was the start of their rise and the Artisans' end. Anyway, when Lem Shankhill found out that one of his own was working for the enemy he brought the weight of the Judiciary down on anyone working with motes at that time. It was too blunt a tool to trap the Constructors of course, but Oshi did end up before them, and Mackie Loess too. That sly bugger must have talked convincingly to persuade them that, whatever tangential relationship he and Oshi had, it had come to nothing. Tatsuko didn't have Loess's guile. At the time, the newspaper played up her maverick reputation, made her sound crazy. No one was surprised that she went to the Institute for a long time."

"And you?"

"Well, they came for me too of course, but I was so engrossed in the work that I'd been sleeping in my workshop and hadn't been back to my rooms for some days. When I finally heard about the others, I realised that my future lay down one of those paths: to be squeezed by some family like Fry, to renounce my discoveries like Loess or to be incarcerated like poor Oshi. So, I chose my own path."

"You left the city."

Kim nodded. "It broke my heart to do so, but I gathered a few tools and other belongings, then I set fire to the workshop, to the saplings, to the manikins." He sighed at the bitter memory. "And while everyone's attention was on the blaze I got myself as far from Karpentine as I could."

Billy shook his head in disbelief as the story reached the bit he knew about. He'd always thought the old man *hated* this place. "And you carried on the work."

"And I carried on the work. In my new home in the Molspurs. As best I could, anyway." Billy was surprised to detect a note of disparagement. "Certainly, I no longer had limited resources of raw materials but..." Kim screwed his face up trying to find the right word, "...We are sorely limited up there in our resources." He sighed sadly. "I admit there were times in the early years before you happened my way when I thought of returning to the city. A short stretch of improvement might have been a small enough price to pay to spend the rest of my days perfecting what I knew would be my life's work. Which is why, when you ask me if what they want me to do is *so terrible*, I can only answer, no. Not terrible, *wonderful*."

Billy could see it in his eyes now, like a shining light. Benoit Kim was an Artisan to his bones. He had never hated this place, not really. It had birthed him and given him the skills to do what he loved. That characteristic taciturn anger that surfaced every time he had turned his face eastwards had been no more than resentment at his estrangement. A deep pain, distilled over decades. And now he was home, and *so happy*.

230

But there was a chip of black ice in the corner of the old man's bright eyes that said this still wasn't the whole story.

"Is this why you *really* came back?" Billy asked bitterly. "You brought all the sylvans here to, what? Show off?"

Kim went silent for a moment, then murmured, "I didn't bring them, son." He looked Billy directly in the eye for the first time since he'd arrived in this room. "But I knew they were coming. And I couldn't let them come alone."

"What do you mean you *knew* –?" Billy began, but the old man shushed him with a glare that told him that the Artisans would not have left the two of them alone without a means to eavesdrop. That, indeed, everything Kim had said up to now had been for their benefit as well as his. In a furious whisper Billy said: "*What are they doing? And why did they leave again?*"

"As to the first, I don't know." The master put a frail hand on his shoulder. "You're the only one who can ask them that, but you've already seen that whatever is happening can't be good. As to the second, I don't believe they have left. This thing isn't over, not nearly. They'll still be here somewhere, biding their time until they're needed again. But if you want my advice, don't hang around to find out. Go back to the mountains, or go somewhere else entirely. Travel as far as you can. Go across the sea to another country if you can find a way."

"What? Why? Do you think they mean to arrest me again?"

"No, son." Kim patted a seam in Billy's coat, is if he wished there were more to it than leather. "I'm pretty certain they mean to kill you."

Billy stared at him, dumfounded. It was ridiculous. He might not be popular here but what would anyone have to gain by seeing him dead? "What are you talking about? I'm no threat to anyone."

"Oh, but you are," Kim said, gently. "And you know why."

And Billy realised he did. "Because I'm awakened?"

"You're proof that man is *not* 'Rightly Bound by the Limits of his Humanity'. You're a living contradiction of the Law of Man. They have no idea what you can do, and it doesn't matter how much or little that turns out to be. If one family can't find a use for you, do you think they'll wait around to see if another one can? Promise me you'll go."

Billy nodded dumbly. All his life he'd been treated poorly, after all. An outsider, a freak. He'd never thought that he could be seen as a danger, though.

Anything else Kim might have said was forestalled by the return of Lemuel Shankhill and a page. "I think you'll agree you've had more than enough time," the Grandhandmaster said. "So there will be no further delays to your starting the work we require of you?"

Master Kim managed to effect a smile. "None at all. I just wanted to impart a few last instructions to the boy." He joined the page and turned one last time to face Billy. "Remember what I said." The tone was the perfect impression of the long-suffering master. "Be diligent. Work hard. And take care of yourself." Then Kim and the page were gone.

"Thank you, Mister Braid." Shankhill could not have been more dismissive. "Bello will show you out."

Given what the master had just told him, this was the last thing Billy wanted to hear. "That's all right," he said, "I'll find my own way." When he left Shankhill's office, he found Erudite waiting along the corridor with the wood on display, so he went in the other direction, walking quickly in his quest to find another route back to the staircases.

"Oh, now, don't be like that." Erudite's laughter followed him down the hall. "I'm only going to show you to the door. Although, after that, I'm afraid you're on your own out there." He meant the weather. Despite its new maturity, Billy still thought he could handle the weather as long as he didn't do anything to call attention to himself.

Billy lost his bearings. One too many turnings at the junctions of near identical corridors brought him not to the main staircases but a sloping passage that zigged and then zagged down the inside of an exterior wall. Through windows coloured like gemstones, Billy made out a series of yards bordered by a lane that wound in one direction towards the front of the building and in the other to a precarious staircase that ascended the blind side of the hill. That would do him nicely. He broke into a run.

When he reached the bottom, sure enough he found the door he'd been hoping for. And Erudite, waiting next to it.

"Watch yourself out there." Flashing his teeth, Erudite slid back a long bolt. "Those clouds certainly made a mess of your manikins, didn't they?"

Keeping his distance, Billy remembered the dearth of sylvans in the Institute square and, as the implication of the gloat hit home, his stomach felt like a boulder. "You were up there?"

"Let's just say our client has more than enough of her special carbonblack supplies for now." He opened the door and stood back to allow Billy to leave. "As for you? You have nothing to worry about in here. Your master extracted a promise, albeit a reluctant one, from the Grandhandmaster, that you will suffer no harm from the Artisans."

A frigid gust blew in from the high walled yard beyond the threshold, disturbing a litter of shavings. The walls were over twice Billy's height and there was a plain but sturdy gate at the far end. Standing beside it was a familiar figure who tipped him a wave.

Erudite leaned close. "My brother on the other hand has no such restrictions. We'd rather like to send a message to your Weathermakers, you see and, at the same time, we're hoping to interest our client in something that we hope will prove rather unique in the boneblack line. Goodbye, *Billy Braid*."

The shove sent Billy stumbling out into the yard. He heard the bolt dogging home even before Erudite's shouted final sentence finished reverberating off the walls. The echo was chased by the wind, which stirred like a dog showing interest in the scent of a rat. The light shifted as the clouds above the Lodge stirred in response.

At the other end of the empty yard, Innocent Bello had eased open the heavy gate. Not much, just enough for a man to slip through in a hurry. "Hello, *Billy Braid*," he shouted. "Nice to see you again, *Billy Braid*." He risked a glance at the already gathering sky, and as the yard darkened and the temperature dropped Billy saw him smile. He'd been set up.

Even as the first of the hail crystals ticked the ground, they were superseded by larger stones. Billy ran for the gate, but he was miles too late. Innocent had already slipped through and pulled it shut. Over the rising stutter of the hail on the brick floor Billy heard the chink of a chain, the snap of a stout padlock. When he reached the gate he pulled at it anyway but it was shut fast. As the hail became chunks that clattered and splintered and rolled around his feet, he cast around him but there was no scrap of shelter, and no prospect of climbing his way out. The pine planking used for the walls may have been too poorly grained and too heavy with knots to use for aesthetic purposes but it was stout and expertly jointed enough to be impregnable.

The first of the serious chunks of ice landed several feet behind Billy, but he felt its force, felt the shrapnel of ice chips and pieces of broken brick rain against his back and legs. That first chunk was followed by more rocks of ice raining down into the yard, clattering across the slabs and knocking with hollow sarcasm off the fence.

Billy moved, ducked, dodged away from the gate, headed back towards the lodge. The hail changed direction and followed him. The door took a pounding, and the tessellated brickwork around it too. One of the windows smashed and rained red glass down on him as well as everything else. Yelling, Billy pummelled his fists against the door, but even if anyone inside was of a mind to help him he doubted they could even have heard him above the noise of the hail. A rock of ice splintered the door where his fingers had just been and ricocheted painfully into his shoulder. Billy spun away, back towards the far end of the yard once more.

"Stop!" Billy shouted. He risked a look up into the sky, just a snatch, just enough to see that the icy ejecta arrowing down at him out of the roiling black was aimed straight into this narrow yard and nowhere else. He even spotted a taunting rim of blue sky. Something hit him above the eye and he thrust his arm up to protect his face. "You don't have to do this!"

He listened to the roaring in the weather. The first time in Para's dirigible, he'd heard amid the wind and thunder, the inchoate tantrumming of a nascent mind. Up on the Weathermakers' tower and then with Rabbit, there had been coherent words. A fearful consensus that lashed out at what it didn't understand. Now, there was nothing. He thought for a glimmer that he detected jealousy, seething envy, but it was impossible to say if he was imagining it. That the clouds had learned to keep their sulky, scheming counsel.

"Please," he tried again. "I mean you no harm."

There was a fractional pause in the downpour, and he thought for an instant that the onslaught might be abating, but then it resumed with double the ferocity. Rocks of ice pummelled his shoulders, found gaps between his arms to crack his skull. Dizzy, he stumbled into the corner of the yard and cowered against the unforgiving walls.

At least if he were to die, he would do so with good plain wood for company. He felt the coarse grain under his fingers, traced the whorls of a rough knot, imagined them as the trunk and branch they had once been, imagined the tree that had once stood tall in a forest far distant from this place. Heard the gentle sloughing as the wind stirred its branches, the pattering scamper of squirrels up its trunk, the occasional snap and lonely *tunk* that marked the loss and separation of a pine cone falling to the bed of browning needles on the forest floor. He felt the energy of its slow growth, its season on season patience, its lack of any ambition other than to be.

As the falling ice bloodied and bruised him, Billy buried his head further into the corner, his temple pressed against the roughness of a knot. More than a roughness in fact. A protuberance. He felt with his fingers. Where previously there had been a flat plane, now there was a definite lump. He risked raising his head for long enough to look and sure enough there was the stump of a branch, green new growth joining the cauterised dead end that had been the knot in the plank. It was already an inch long and it was still growing.

He looked higher and saw that, impossibly, other knots had also begun to sprout new growth. Billy placed his ear to the plank and above the rattle of the hail he felt rather than heard the creak and course of life. This long-dead board had sap and purpose. There were now four slender knobs. Not much, but enough to loop two fingers around, enough to wedge a boot against. Enough to make a ladder.

As if sensing it, the clatter on the paving became deeper and the ice fell in chunks as large as footballs that tore up the slabs as if they were paper and shook the entire length of the fence. Even as Billy rose, one of the rocks ricocheted off the angle of the fence and caught him on the knee. He almost went down, but retained his balance. He gripped the highest of the miraculous new branches that he could reach and then searched for the lowest with his boot. One good heave and he was able to haul himself up. He stretched up again, looking for the next hand hold, making it. One more step up and the top of the fence itself would be in reach. His knee shrieking, he grimaced as he stretched for the next stump. An impact below him and to his left jarred the fence again and it was all he could do to retain his grip. Billy swung himself up, cried out when his injured leg took his weight, reached for the top of the fence as two further impacts shook the fence, and he was jolted free, falling back in a cloud of ice chips. Then something closed round his wrist and pulled him up. Billy flopped over the top of the fence, his relief immediately seesawing into the fear that he was going to plummet over the other side, but the same strength that had hauled him over, lowered him to the ground.

The hand released him, four graceful ironwood fingers. Billy had never in his life been so relieved to see anyone as he was to see Chop right then. The sylvan's careworn pebble eyes stared down at him. In his mind, over the incessant raging of the storm, Billy heard a fluster of wings, the shiver of a vacated branch. The sylvan's meaning was clear: *Flee.*

Billy tried to rise, but his knee betrayed him. When Chop reached out to catch him again, he saw something that sickened him. While the hand that had pulled Billy out of the yard was as beautifully formed as the day it had been sculpted, the sylvan's other hand was reduced to a stump, no more than a palm and a thumb that flexed stupidly against it. He did not have to look far to see what had happened. The reverse side of the plank he had climbed had four fingers jammed into the places where the knots had been.

A missile hit the top of the fence so hard that the boards cracked, and the next volley cleared the fence entirely, blasting clods out of the grassy slope across the lane.

Chop shook Billy's shoulder, and repeated its urging. *Flee.*

This time Billy managed to get to his feet and urge his body along the lane towards the foot of the staircase. The rise was a series of flights slashed into the hillside. There was nothing fancy about it, not even a hand rail. From here it looked close to vertical, and worse still, completely open to the elements.

"Chop, I'm not sure I can…"

Climb.

Billy climbed. The risers were high. Every step hurt his knee and he stumbled frequently, but Chop was constantly at his back, urging him on and sheltering him from the worst of the pursuing weather. The frozen missiles careened off the rocks either side of the stair, throwing loose stones and earth into the air and rolling down the steps like a mountain landslide. Those that did not miss the target found Chop's broad back. The regular thud of ice on wood was like a feared visitor knocking persistently on your door. The sylvan bore the onslaught stoically and drove him on.

Billy had never been so grateful to enter one of Karpentine's ubiquitous alleys. Chop urged him on again when he stopped running, but his beaten body needed to rest and he saw that Chop was in even worse shape. The torso was bashed all over and splinters rose from the shoulders like thorns. The sylvan's movements were awkward and stiff. Billy placed a hand on it, felt the pitting the hail had made, tried to will it to knit but the damage was too severe. Grateful though he was for the rescue, he didn't know whether to be relieved that, whatever it had amused Erudite Bello to imply, the entire sylvan gathering had not ended up in the Inksmiths' incinerators, or anguished that they had not, as he had hoped, left the city. He had so many questions, but he collapsed them into one. "Chop, what's happening?"

Chop raised its head and gazed up the brick alley walls to the ribbon of quicksilvering sky above and the impression that came to Billy's mind was of a purposeful planting of seeds into unyielding earth. *Preparing*, was the word that resolved out of it. And that was followed by the sense of a forest, an entirety.

"All of you?" Billy asked. "Preparing for what? Where are the rest of you?"

The sylvan merely repeated the planting thought. There weren't many seeds and they were too far apart. *All of us*, it repeated. *All but one*. In Billy's mind he heard the scurry of paws in leaf litter and understood. Whatever the sylvans were doing it needed every last one. And Rabbit was locked up in the Radlett Hall. With everything that had happened he had to hope it was possible that Stillworth Crane hadn't got round to starting his analysis yet. "I'll talk to Para," he said. "We'll get Rabbit back. Where can I find you?" A skitter of hail pattered into the alley. "Chop, where…?"

Chop lowered its head and, with a final push, urged Billy back into motion: *Flee*.

Waiting in the market square at the alley's end was a familiar car. The dark clouds, shifting in reflection across its black paintwork were just a foretaste of the mood of its owner. On spotting their arrival, the door opened and Paraphernalia Loess raged out.

"What have you been up to, Billy? I mean seriously, what in a month of shitting sleet was going through your mind?" Billy started to speak, but on seeing his injuries and then glancing at the sky she cut him off with a furious gesture. "Just get in, will you? I don't want my paintwork scratched on top of everything else." The ride back to the Loess mansion passed in stony silence as Para focussed on driving. The black clouds rolled after them, but were not quick enough to rain down their fury on the vehicle before it was safely garaged.

On entering Billy's bedroom Para aimed a kick at the morning's newspaper which had been pushed under the door. It fluttered across the room like a crippled bird.

"Thank you," Billy said, trying to defuse her mood, "for rescuing me."

Para laid the paper on the room's little table and began smoothing the pages out. Her face was ashen, but she said nothing.

"Look," Billy tried again. "I'm sorry, but I had to see him."

Para shot him a sideways look. "And so you just went with one of the Bellos when the invitation mat was rolled out?"

He stiffened at the rebuke but tried not to rise to it. "In my position you'd have done the same."

She didn't deny that. Instead, her fingers continued working the paper. "So, how was he, your old handmaster? Chained up in an Artisan dungeon? Starved at all? Tortured?"

"You don't have to worry. I didn't tell them anything. I just... needed to see him. That's all." He couldn't work out what was making her so angry. "And, thank you. He's fine."

"Oh, he's *fine*," she snarled. "What a relief. Their *prize asset* is in good spirits and ready to start work." She slapped the newspaper shut. "Don't you ever stop to think how what you want affects anyone else? There could have been advantage in keeping the two of you apart, but of course that's all gone now because you *wanted* something."

Of course, he saw it now, and felt stupid and angry at the same time. "Well how did I know it was intentional? You never tell me anything."

"You don't need to know what my intentions are, Billy. If you value your safety and your master's, in future just do as I ask."

"As you *tell me* more like."

"Yes, very well, as I tell you."

"You can't control everything, Para."

"No?" Her eyes were blazing now. The words came out like steam. "Well someone has to try." She looked at his face, surveyed the bruises. "At least you didn't suffer any real damage."

It hurt Billy to shrug but he attempted it anyway. "You're not telling me you care?"

Para looked ready to spit. Her fingers grasped the newspaper she had just smoothed out, scrunched it in her fist. "I only care about myself." She thrust the bundle at him. "Read all about it."

TWENTY-ONE

The newspaper had plenty of news. The headline announced another extraordinary meeting to demand answers of the Weathermakers on behalf of those who had suffered personal, property or financial injury as a result of what the writer called *professional negligence*. There were pictures of flood and ice damage, and of the ruined and now-deserted refugee camp outside the city walls, whose existence had until recently been so abstract to most Karpentiners that the Kinsterites may as well have stayed in their drought-ravaged homeland. There were many reports of injuries and a death toll, low but mounting.

Negligence? Billy supposed it could be called that. Although perhaps it couldn't really be laid at the door of the current members of the Loess family and their ignorant engineers who found themselves in a hopeless position attempting to control a powerful force that they were now finding not only impossible to manipulate, but actually wilful. No, if anyone was really responsible for the disastrous position that the Weathermakers found themselves in, it was their founder, Mackie Loess who had leapt too quickly into assembling wealth and status on the basis of a technology about which he knew practically nothing. According to the old man, he'd been a metal worker by trade. What had he known about the motes in the air?

The paper had also now forgone any pretence of editorial impartiality in favour of laying into the Loesses at every opportunity. The tone of the main article was scathing. The front page prominence of the weekly table of achievement, off the bottom of which the Weathermakers had fallen entirely, far from coincidental.

A fuse of frustration had fizzed in him since Para left. Thanks to her dramatics he hadn't got to tell her that some of the sylvans had escaped or to ask about Rabbit. Still, Billy felt increasing sympathy for the family. Not for old Jelena, perhaps, but for the decent people that worked for her. And especially for Para. She was stretching herself in all directions, and was in danger of breaking herself apart.

It should have been just a short announcement, and might ordinarily have been nestled in among the other social notices and family

239

intimations, but the newspaper's editors had not missed the opportunity to cast appropriate light on it.

In happier news for the beleaguered Family Loess, prominent socialite and Weather Engineer First Class, Paraphernalia Jane Loess has announced her betrothal to be allied to Stillworth Crane, only son of the Governor of the Guild of Constructors. The betrothal follows a whirlwind romance. While not an officially sanctioned match, when consulted, the Matchmakers predicted a better than average achievement yield for the Weathermaker family.

"We are thrilled to cement this alliance between two great families," said Jelena Loess in a prepared statement. "The opportunities born of such a match, not only to the benefit of both families but the whole of Karpentine, are secondary only to the obvious happiness of two young people in love."

At the time of going to press, Merit Crane was unavailable for comment.

Billy had no difficulty imagining what Merit Crane's response would have been. Only a couple of days ago, the Constructors were so far behind the Weathermakers that he had dragged his unwilling son to the Sisters to make him desire Para. With the Weathermakers' current fortunes as low as they were now, it looked like his guild had saddled itself with a very public millstone.

Billy tossed the paper aside. The marriage was a desperate last resort but, if it meant turning one of the Weathermakers' most vocal critics into the allies they so urgently needed now, he was in no doubt Para would see it through. Only by pooling their motal knowledge might they actually have a chance of working out what to do about the weather. He realised that he admired her now, more than ever.

And what about him? Was he going to sit here stewing? Weren't there things he could do to help? If he was useless to aid Para, then couldn't he do something for the sylvans? Wherever Chop was now, even the master would not able to restore its beauty. The fingers, though? Yes, there was something he could do there. He grabbed his toolkit and shrugged painfully into his coat. It felt stiff. He knew it was because of the cold and the rain it had endured recently, but he couldn't escape the resurgent notion that it had never really fitted him. As he forced the buttons through the holes and went out, he wished the old man had taken it back.

The journey back to the Artisans' lodge was uneventful. Billy found a bicycle in the garages and guided it through the backstreets, keeping to the lee of buildings and the shelter of eaves where he could. In the short time that he had been inside, the clouds which so recently threatened his life had dispersed, the chill had lifted and the air had taken on a sweaty, close feel. Distrustful of the respite, Billy hurried.

He left the bicycle in the alley at the top of the staircase and crept down towards the fence. There he found that the barred gate had been opened and a river of icemelt trickled down the lane. Billy's heart tightened until he ascertained that there was no one in the yard. The miraculous branches on the inside of the fence had withered, but the four slender stumps of Chop's fingers still protruded from the outside and they were fixed fast. Billy tried to prise them out with a bradawl, widen the knotholes with chisels, extract them with pliers like obstinate teeth, but it was no use. There was no dislodging the digits from the plank. It was as if they had always been one single piece of living wood.

He glared at the now whittled joints, spat with frustration. It was no longer a matter of being able to restore Chop's hand, there was no way he was leaving here with one scrap of his friend still remaining on Artisan property. Delicacy thrust aside, four applications of chisel and mallet and he had what remained of Chop's fingers in his coat pocket.

That in itself, though, did nothing to ease his frustration. Instead, his anger bubbled. Billy stalked along the lane, chisel swinging like a pendulum at the end of his arm. If either of the Bello brothers had appeared at that moment, there might have been an unpleasant end to things. As it was, the lane remained empty and the chisel had to be content with the bite of pine planking as he passed yard after yard. The last one was a dump for apprentice work. Billy hated to imagine what cruel criteria would relegate some young person's work to this forgotten corner, but the best of the artisans who had created these chests and armoires, cabinets and sideboards had been mediocre. There was no chance any of these students would rise to having their work proudly displayed inside the Lodge itself. Billy ran his fingers over the surface of a clock casing. The lacquer was so thick that it was impossible to identify the wood, the lines were rudimentary, and the corners had begun to soften and grey from their exposure to the elements. This courtyard was a lesson: great art lasts, inferior work fades.

Even on his worst days, Master Kim had never treated Billy's efforts with such disrespect. And *effort* was the appropriate word. People with ability that came easily never appreciated the amount of effort those less gifted than themselves could put into their work while never coming close to achieving greatness. Someone ought to teach these Artisans a more instructive lesson. If Para's friend, Giteau, were here, no doubt he would use that woman, Llodra's, hungry glories to chew out the requisite message... but all Billy had were his hands and his tools.

It took a long time to carve his message. He thought at first to make the letters rough-hewn, exposing the raw wood beneath, but his pride in his own modest abilities took over and he attempted instead to bring some element of grace to these lifeless pieces. He made the letters tall and sweeping, he flourished them with serifs and curls, he smoothed the lines. He became so absorbed that a crowd could have formed and he wouldn't have noticed, but when he finally stepped away and looked around the neglected little courtyard was as empty as it had been when he stumbled across it. He wondered if anyone would ever even notice his rendition of *The Law For All*. Billy attempted to wipe the perspiration from his face with his coat sleeve but only succeeded in smearing his flushed skin with shavings. It wasn't just the work, he realised as he skulked away; the day really was getting hot.

There were no hailstones on the staircase now. Even the rivulets of meltwater were drying up. At the top of his climb, Billy stared at the sun, trying to remember when he had last seen it. It burned white and hazy, more like a memory of the sun than the real thing. It made him nervous, but he swallowed the nerves down because he wasn't done yet.

At the top of the Artisan district, he found a Messenger and sent her to pass word through the network of urchins for Vern to meet him at Radlett Hall. As he made his own way there, people were venturing back onto the streets, eyeing the sky with the universal mistrust. He rode the bicycle quickly but with caution. He felt certain that he would spot either of the Bellos before they saw him, but who knew who else they might have looking for him on the promise of a kudo or two?

Billy chose a route of splashy lanes and passages to the Hall's lowtown gate. There he waited and watched the Constructors' yard. It was as busy as ever with industrious workers coming and going, although perhaps there were more guards in evidence than there had been on his last visit.

"Probably best ditch the bicycle, Mr B." Vern had appeared at Billy's side without him even noticing. "It's a dead giveaway."

As Billy leant it against the wall of a nearby pub he asked, "How are things?"

"Peachy!" Beneath his cockiness the lad was white as milk.

"Your mam?"

Vern sniffed. "Back in the pokey. Had to treble her sentence to get her to stay put, though." He said this with something approaching pride.

"And your sister?" Billy asked quietly.

"Well now, she has a job to do." If anything, Vern's chest swelled further. "She went to meet your Maestra Paraphernalia."

Billy nodded, though he hated to think of the girl entering the Institute in his place. "I wish she hadn't."

"She made a promise, din't she?"

"I know." Billy sighed and returned his attention to the Constructors' complex. "You remember I asked you to find out what happened to all the sylvans?"

"There's been rumours, boss, that's all," Vern said earnestly. "Striding through the streets in the night, they say, but no one agrees where."

"That's okay," Billy said. "Ask them to keep looking. But I know where one is at least… and I intend to get it back."

"From in there, Mr B?" Smart boy. He nodded through the gates at the hall.

"The very heart of it, I think."

Vern sniffed again. "Then it's a good thing I'm here, isn't it?"

"Seriously? There are a lot of guards."

"Yeah, but who do you think cleans that bloody thing? C'mon." Vern led him confidently through the gates and across the courtyard towards the mechanical wonder at its centre. The kinetic business of the Hall's exterior was even more purposeful than last time. The cams pumped like a lumberjack's saw arm, the races rattled, the signal boards clatter-cascaded and the chimneys billowed smoke as if to rival the clouds themselves. "Don't gawp, Mr B. Not if you want it to look like we belong here."

Billy dragged his eyes away. "It's still impressive though," he murmured, then realised that the lad was leading him away from the main entrance.

"It's all for show, in't it? Them Constructors is always busy and whenever there's something going on this place gets busier than the Tower Summer Fair. You can set your watch by it." Vern frowned. "If you're High Town enough to own one of them things." As if it had been listening to their conversation, the Hall gave out a cascading peal of bells. Vern looked around. "Noon shift change. Hurry up."

Around the corner, the hall's outer layer was a nest of cogs that ranged from the size of a fingernail to three times Billy's height. The cogs meshed in complicated arrangements, some revolving quickly, some slowly, some just rocking in place. Vern stopped before two of the largest and stared at the place where they met. These cogs' great teeth interlocked, stilled and then heaved on. Beyond them was glinting darkness.

Vern grinned. "I'll go first, Mr B. You wait for the next revolution."

That was when Billy spotted that both cogs were missing one tooth, and that shortly they would line up, creating an aperture. "You can't be serious…" he began, but Vern tensed and when the space manifested he wasted no time in dashing through. Two seconds later it was as if he had never been there. "Are you all right?" Billy peered through the metal.

"Shush," came the reply from the darkness. "Try and act natural until it's your turn. And don't forget to duck."

The cogs seemed to take an age to come round again. Billy moved a few yards down the wall and pretended to take an interest in a clacking display board just in time to avoid the suspicion of a pair of engineers who rounded the corner a moment later. "That's the old sewer flow board," one of the women said as they passed him. "We don't keep that one up to date. If it's flooding you're worried about check the integrated sanitation and water information round the other side."

"Oh, thanks," Billy muttered and got a strange look from the women when he didn't scurry off immediately, but they wandered off nonetheless just as the gaps in the cogs began to align for the second time. Billy looked around to make sure he wasn't being observed, then went for it. As he squeezed himself through the gap he was aware of the thickness and solidity of the colossal cast iron wheels, felt the building's energy thrumming through them. He just made it through, the descending teeth brushing his hair and chunking closed at his back.

"Vern?" he whispered, and for a second thought the lad had abandoned him there, but then his face ghosted out of the darkness.

"Not a word, Mr B," the boy whispered back. "We're inside the skin of the Hall now. Come on, this way."

Radlett Hall did not have conventional walls. There was a framework, a cage of pillars that supported everything, but the space between them was filled with the machinery of computation. The Constructors claimed it to be an engineering marvel. They might even be right.

Somehow, Vern managed to find a route from the outside of the building to the centre. It meant ducking and squeezing and stepping over and climbing. It meant getting oil in their hair and sludgy grease on their clothes. It meant Billy banging his head frequently and being surrounded by the constant purr of moving parts. A building without walls might have seemed something of a security risk, but it would take someone who really knew what they were doing to thread their way through like this. And even he had occasion to retrace his steps from time to time.

"So you've worked here a lot?" Billy whispered.

"Used to." The boy had clambered onto a beam wider than he was. When it shot forward and up, he jumped for a ledge and hauled himself onto it. "All this has to be cleaned and greased so it runs smooth, dun't it?" The boy waved Billy to follow. "Hop up."

When the beam came back down again, Billy took his turn. He barely had time to get his balance before it swept him upwards. He stretched for the ledge.

"Mind your head."

"Ow." Billy didn't know what he hit this time, but luckily his fingers managed to find the ledge without his brain's involvement. Ears ringing, he pulled himself into some sort of duct. Vern was already crawling ahead. Billy just had enough shoulder room to follow.

"You're right about them using a lot of them from the Institute here at the Hall, Mr B." Vern's whisper echoed flatly in the duct's confines. "Whole teams of them out there in the foundries and works, and breaking their backs too making all this go around, but you won't find them in the workings here. Like as not they'd not miss a finger or two, but in here you need nimble little hands, dontcha? One of the last places a little un can earn their day's kudo."

The confinement of the duct was brief, but the relief Billy felt when he flopped out at the other end was palpable. Vern put his finger to his lips. "Now, serious like. Hush." His words were barely audible above a deep, grinding vibration. He pointed through the steel grid above their heads and, even as Billy considered Vern's caution to be overstated, he recognised where they were. Through the grating he made out the nearest of the great capstans, saw the shuffling shoes of the Institutionalised who heaved it around. In his imagination he turned the space upside down, remembering it as he had last seen it, from above. The Hall's central chamber.

"Which way now?" Vern whispered into his ear. For all his swagger he was nervous.

Billy remembered them hauling Rabbit away, up a flight of stairs. He pointed through the gridwork. "Up, I think."

Vern began to edge in that direction but then froze, and with a widening of the eyes indicated to Billy to do the same. Out of the incessant vibration of the motive wheels came footsteps. It soon became clear who they belonged to.

"...see that upstart family finished for good and be done with their notions of marrying into the Cranes at the same stroke," said Merit Crane. Two pairs of finely tooled leather soles crossed the gridwork.

"And what if I *want* the marriage to go through?" Stillworth's voice replied, less deference to his old man than Billy had heard before. He wondered at that.

The elder Crane stopped and confronted his son. Their shadows fell on Billy's face. "Don't be so bloody stupid."

"Stupid is it?" Stillworth's laugh was dry. "Come, father, you wanted me like this. Why so surprised that I now find the notion agreeable."

"I thought she would be an asset, but this catastrophe has tainted her. No, Stillworth, any association with the Weathermakers is a risk to our name that cannot be countenanced." Merit's next words were stinging. "If you'd not been so bloody obstinate in the first place, none of this would have been necessary."

"You know my research comes first." Stillworth sounded unperturbed.

"Your research –" His father's voice oozed with contempt.

"My *research*," Stillworth repeated, "has yielded a method of ridding us of the Weathermakers' influence. For good."

His father's reply was edged with a meagre hint of interest. "Is that so? Well it took you long enough. We'll discuss your idea after the meeting. But even if it was a *miracle* it would not gain my assent for you to marry that Loess sloven. Leave her to the Roach boy. He's more than she deserves."

Stillworth laughed then. "Oh, we'll see about that, old man." And it was the younger Crane who led the way up the steel staircase.

Billy was momentarily torn between continuing to look for Rabbit and getting to the Exchange to warn Para of the trouble in store from her intended husband. But the Loesses already knew they were up against it today. And there would never be a better time to steal something from the heart of Radlett Hall.

He listened in the hope that he could hear the Rabbit's skittish thoughts, but there was nothing. Vern cocked his head in a *come-on* gesture, indicating a hatch in the meshwork not far from the stairs that the sylvan had been taken up. Billy strained in that direction. No, still nothing.

But there was something, muddled and faint, coming from below. Just for an instant. A mind impression, like a sylvan voice, but not quite. And... echoey. Almost as if there were more than one of them. Billy had fretted that the sylvans from the square had been abducted and it had been a relief, from meeting Chop and hearing Vern's rumours, to know that at least some were at liberty. But what if the Constructors had captured the remainder? What if there was not just one sylvan trapped here but many? Stillworth Crane, he was sure, wouldn't think twice about using up such resources as he carried out his *research*.

"Down," he murmured.

"Down?" Vern whispered back. "But you said..."

"And now I'm changing my mind."

They emerged from the workings of the Hall by squeezing through the supports of a ramp that down from the central room.

"What's down here?" Billy whispered, edging along the corridor. There was a corner ahead.

"Never been here, boss." Vern shrugged. "But I think this is where Stillworth Crane does his sums"

Around the corner, the corridor continued for a short distance and ended at a double door. There was a notice on the door and, by the time they were close enough to read it, it was too late. Two words, simply printed. Compellingly inked.

Keep Out.

Billy and Vern stood side by side, unable to move an inch closer to the door, unable even to contemplate pushing it open and entering the room beyond.

"I might not be able to read so well, but I know them words," Vern said. "I s'pose that's that, then. We should just go home."

There was no arguing with the boy's logic, but Billy couldn't just leave. Not if there were sylvans in there. He could hear them again now. Definitely multiple voices. Questioning, as if realising that someone was close at hand. Whatever the reason they had come to Karpentine – whatever they were *preparing* for – they absolutely did not deserve to end up in this place, lined up to be disassembled at a Constructor's whim.

Billy glared at the notice. It was so insultingly dismissive. The authoritarian words made with expensive ink were an affront to even the cheap signweight paper they were stamped on. Billy regretted not having been able to deliver those sylvan pieces to Alicia Creasey after all. It wouldn't be a bad thing to lessen the abominable imperiousness of ink in this city. Paper was such a simple thing by comparison. Wood and rag and water. Water and rag… and *wood.*

Billy refused to let wood be used against him.

He stretched towards the notice but couldn't quite reach. Even leaning almost to the point of falling over he was inches from touching it. He made himself unbalance and staggered forward a step. He heard Vern gasp as if he'd just turned the moon green. Billy placed his hand on the note, felt the paper. Not as smooth as it might have been, slightly fibrous in fact. He thought about the soft filaments that had been tainted by the compellant ink, and thought he felt an imperceptible relaxation in the sign's imperative. He focused and felt the relationship between ink and paper weaken further. And that was all he needed. Billy squeezed his fingers into a fist, ripping the notice from the door and bunching it into an ineffectual ball. Then he pushed the door open and beckoned the astonished boy through.

Stillworth Crane's workroom – with its shelves of neatly stowed tools and devices, it could not be anything else – was smaller than Billy would have expected for a self-proclaimed genius. More like a playroom… and of course that's what it was: a room for an exceptionally bright young man to experiment to his heart's content, only dragging out those things into the light that his father might deem to have commercial potential. An octagonal worktable stood in the centre of the room. It had a padded stool and an array of lamps and magnifiers on retractable arms. Its sides held a hundred drawers, each of which according to typed index cards contained some type of screw or washer, clamp or lens. Billy checked a few at random. The contents matched the descriptions without fail. No component was out of place. The obeisance to order made his scalp itch.

On the desk stood a rack that held six receptacles. Five of them held egg shaped devices made of some polished metal, their surfaces textured like layered leaves. The last was empty. On the desk before them lay a flat, lobed key.

"There's a big one over there." Vern was pointing to the other side of the room. This one was the size of a pig. When Billy ran his hand over it, he felt like he might be able to pry the layers up, but the edges were too tight to get his fingernails under. The thing sat in a cradle, the cradle on a stand. Actually, more like a pedestal than a stand. Stillworth was obviously proud of this. He was proud of the whole room. It was a place of order and understanding, of thought applied like an obsession.

What the room lacked was evidence of even one sylvan. Billy listened but now heard nothing. Next to the plinth there was a boxlike shape with a tarpaulin over it. It looked innocuous enough, but for some reason it gave him a feeling of foreboding. He reached out to tug the hanging folds of the cover but a noise behind him stayed his hand. The precise, tensioning *crrrick* of someone winding clockwork. He whirled. "What are you doing?"

Vern held one of the small egg-shaped devices and was turning the key in it. "I want to see what it does, don't I? Must be nice to have so much achievement that you've the spare time to make toys."

"We're here for *Rabbit*," Billy snapped. "In and out without getting caught. Put it down."

Undaunted, Vern wound the key another one, two, three times, and before Billy could admonish him further, the thing stirred. The silver leaves peeled up from the surface and became blades, and then the blades began to rotate, slicing the air faster and faster. With a yelp, Vern jumped back, dropping the device... but instead of clattering to the floor, it hovered and then began to rise.

Billy and Vern retreated to the room's perimeter as the delicate machine, humming sweetly, began to circle the air above Stillworth Crane's desk. The blades spun faster and the pitch of the hum rose to a whine, and the whine took on a keening edge. Then, abruptly, it ceased its travel, and hovered, vibrating, shaking, juddering. Billy and Vern ducked instinctively at the moment the device exploded.

"Not much of a toy, is it?" Disappointed, Vern bent to examine a casing shard that had landed near his feet but Billy hardly heard him because he was stunned by the cries of terror that filled his mind. He ripped the sheet off the covered box, and stared in horror at what he saw in the glass cabinet underneath. The floor was littered with more pieces of casing. There were impact marks on the thick panes that showed the force of the contained explosion, and an opaqueness as if some fine liquid had misted the inside. There were marks on Rabbit too. Gouges and dents in its arms and legs and torso, fresh wood exposed through gashes in the exterior stain. One foot was missing entirely and its head had been covered with a burlap bag whose material had what looked like fine copper wire running through it. Those were the extent of the sylvan's obvious injuries. At first glance it might have appeared to have

249

got off lightly in comparison to Seldom and those among its kin whose end had come in the Institute square, but Billy knew that an awful fate had befallen it. He was not looking at a sylvan here, he was looking at an inert thing, a statue, beautiful wood and no more. There was nothing there of Rabbit. No voice, no personality, no life. Stillworth Crane had created something that had killed the sylvan's *self.* Something that had been contained within that case when the clockwork bomb went off. He was suddenly very grateful that the one Vern had wound up had been empty.

What had Stillworth said to his father about having a solution to the Weathermakers' hold over Karpentine? If a small bomb was capable of snuffing the life in one sylvan...? Billy looked at the device on the cradle. "He's actually crazy," he breathed and ran his fingers down the edges of the cabinet, looking for a way to open it, trying to shove it over, but finding it impregnable.

"Who's crazy?" But Vern's small voice was drowned out in Billy's mind by the clamour of agreement.

Crazy, insane, a monster!

Clear to him now, the voices weren't impressions like the sylvans, they were clear human words. And they weren't coming from the dead sylvan either. Billy looked frantically around the room again but there was still nothing...

Who is it? Is it Fry? It doesn't feel like Fry. The other one then? No, we know him. *Who is it, then? Who is it?*

The voices pulled his attention towards the floor, where he saw that the edge of one of the plates was scraped. Using a jemmy he found on a shelf nearby, he levered the plate up to reveal a ladder leading down into the space below the floor of the workroom. Jumping down, Billy discovered that the space was tiny. Even stooping, his hair brushed against the ceiling. There was barely room for the folding table and stool that sat there let alone anyone or anything that might be responsible for the voices. Most of the rest of the space was taken up by neat stacks of paper that brought Alicia Creasey to mind. A lamp stood on the table. Billy found the switch and was rewarded with a splash of brownish light that barely illuminated the papers. He picked up a sheet. It was all figures.

"What is this place, Mr B?" He heard Vern drop lightly to join him in the hidden space.

Billy shook the paper at him. "This must be where Stillworth interprets the Hall's calculations," he said. "But why bring them down here instead of to the control room upstairs? Why would he hide himself away to do sums in the dark?"

Because their machine is a sham.

Billy whirled. The cacophony had resolved into a single voice but where was it coming from? "What?" he said.

A sham. A mockery. The place you call Radlett Hall, that machine, *is nothing but purposeless moving parts. It's all for show.*

"Who are you?" Billy said, only peripherally aware of Vern's gawp of disbelief. "*Where* are you?" He scanned the room again, but there was nothing. Just the papers, the lamp, the stool, the table. Wait... He looked closer at the table and saw something that in the poor light he had missed. An oil-dark cube the size of a sugar lump.

Talk to us, the voice said.

Billy touched the cube and was blinded by light. He squeezed his eyes shut, but it made no difference. It took several moments before his vision adjusted and he realised that he was looking at... the *sun.* The sun riding high in a clearer sky than even Karpentine had ever seen. The precise blue stretched wide in every direction, and beneath it was a rolling land of wild grasses that swayed even though Billy could feel no breeze. "What...?" he whispered. The grasses in front of him whipped in the non-existent wind. Whipped and wound, and grew. Twisted into cords, corded into ropes that became legs and trunk and arms, that became the knotted bolus of a head, with emptyhead seed cases for eyes and billowing barley hair.

A whorl in the head became a hole the size of a mouse's nest. *You're not Fry.* The stems that lined the hole vibrated when the thing spoke. *And you're not the other one, Crane. So who are you to come into our world uninvited?*

"My name is Billy Braid," Billy replied. "And I don't know where I am. I didn't mean to come here."

And yet here you are. The grass man tilted its head. *And that is a new thing. Fry could only talk to us. Crane is barely able to make himself heard enough for his threats to be understood.*

"Threats? What *are* you?"

We are the ones who moved on. A peaceful, private people living our long lives the way that we see fit.

"You're the ones who turned away?" Billy wasn't even sure that his whisper was audible, but the grass man acknowledged it. "The ones that

251

chose idleness over honest toil." It was one of the more pious quotes from the Book, but faced with the person he was talking to he couldn't help himself spouting his mother's rote.

We are the ones who chose a world of equality over a world where one man always has advantage over another.

Behind the figure, the grasses hissed as they writhed and surged, as they knotted and braided and rose in a rush, forming a tower that thrust into the air and in no time rivalled both the Weathermakers' edifice in height and the Artisans' Lodge for craft and beauty, because the grasses that formed the walls did so in intricate weaves, deep layered geometries that only got more complex the longer Billy looked because the grasses were still growing, still weaving, creating ever more beautiful patterns.

"What an achievement," Billy whispered. The tower was in every way superior to the Tower of Hands, not only in scale and design but because it had risen in seconds compared to the centuries of lumpen manual accretion that had built Karpentine's great edifice. He looked back at the grass man, now looking more substantial in the tower's shade, almost human. "But it is no achievement at all, is it?"

In our world, any of us can make anything irrespective of skill or strength. We are limited only by our ability to imagine.

An aperture opened in the tower then and other figures emerged: a spry man made of twisted wicker, a woman spun from grey dew-dropped cobwebs, spiders scuttling through her skeins, a lumbering dog-like creature of thorny briar. The grass man's companions kept coming, and soon there were hundreds of them.

In our world, any of us can be anyone or anything.

"It's too easy…"

Easy makes it universal. The voice snapped like twigs. *Easy makes it fair. We do not require your approval, and we did not invite your presence. So, we ask again, how do you come to be here?*

"I don't know," Billy said again. "I just picked up the cube thing." The grass man began to shake gently, soundlessly. It took a moment to realise that with a mercurial change of mood he was laughing.

You have skills you haven't the first idea how to comprehend. Your world is waking up. Whether you want it to or not. It is slipping from your control and you people can do nothing about it.

The *world* was awakening. "The motes are waking up in the earth and in the wood," Billy mused. People had been saying that since he got here.

And in the people too. Some people more than others, for now. The grass man threw his head back in another laugh, this time shaking so hard that a mouse peeked its head out of the mouth hole and twitched its whiskers. The creature vanished in a flash when he spoke again. *Fry and his friend were the first. They delved deep into our mountain following the silver and the ores of iron for their experiments, but they found us instead.*

"And they went running to the Constructors?" Billy asked. This was the part of the Oshi story that the old man hadn't known. Fry's *friend* must have been Mackie Loess, but that didn't make sense. If they had worked together, why had Loess scorned Fry's claims of success? Then he remembered that Kim had said about Loess had being a metalsmith at the time. A Constructor or at least an ally. "Loess sold Fry out didn't he?"

When the grass man nodded, the barley shook. *Fry was too trusting. His friend couldn't hear us. He didn't even know what we were. He couldn't use the cube, so he sold it and his friend along with it.*

"And that is how you fell into Stillworth Crane's possession?" Billy said.

Something soft touched his hand. The cobweb woman had sidled up to him and was scrutinising him with dead fly eyes. *You're not here*, she whispered.

The grass man spoke over her. *Stillworth Crane, yes. Although it was a while before he became known to us. First they forced Fry to persuade us to perform their trivial tasks. Stillworth was only a boy then, but he grew up handling the cube and eventually he was able to make his voice heard to us too.*

Billy saw now why these people called Radlett Hall a sham. And hadn't Para said something about when they were children... that Stillworth had claimed the hall worked by *magic?* Merit Crane had given the order for the Hall to be built around the cube and transformed the advantages that came from it into a fortune. All he had to do was keep Fry out of sight and claim that his son was a genius. No one else would have to know. "So *you* perform Stillworth's calculations?"

Calculations, yes. Paltry and pointless numbers. Endless engineering, atmospheric, financial irrelevancies.

"But the Constructors gain the credit for them."

Credit is unimportant. We only want to live without intrusion and threat. At the beginning we only acceded because Fry and his daughters were our friends.

That rang a bell. Kim had mentioned Fry had a family, and that had made him vulnerable. And then they had all disappeared. Certainly no family he had met in Karpentine boasted anyone of that name.

Then Fry was replaced by Stillworth who inundated us with first more demands, and then increasingly dire threats. It was only then that we realised we had been careless. We hadn't paid enough attention to the tasks he set us. We hadn't realised until it was too late what knowledge he was assembling.

"How to destroy motes?"

Exactly so.

"Sadly," Billy said. "I believe he has perfected such a device."

For all of his life the popular conception of the Turners had been that by giving themselves over to their machines they had betrayed their humanity, but in reality all they had really done was chosen a different life. Now they were left vulnerable, helpless to defend themselves or to escape.

Then his threats are real and we are yoked into his service forever.

"What can I do to help you?"

The denizens of the world within the cube caught their breath, and then they spoke as one. *Find us a mountain and bury us deep. Find us an ocean and sink us to the depths. Lose us and let us live in peace.*

This was something Billy could do. "You can count on me," he said.

Thank you. The grass man put his arm on Billy's shoulder. *Although as your world wakes, I do not think there is anywhere that will keep us safe from you forever.* The scratchy grass stalks that formed the fingers traced a line down Billy's sleeve and came to rest on his left fist which he realised now had been clenched all this time. *Open your hand, Billy Braid.*

Billy opened his hand and let the cube roll onto the table.

"Mr B!" Vern was shaking his arm. He was white as snow. "Are you all right?"

Billy pulled his handkerchief out and carefully wrapped the cube in it. He opened an outer pocket of his coat but his fingers brushed Chop's ruined fingers there, so he slipped the bundle into an inner pocket instead. He felt it there, a tiny thing over his heart that nevertheless possessed the weight of a world. In fact, two: the one inside and the one outside, whose great achievers, all of them, had built their fortunes on lies. "I'm fine," he replied, already making for the ladder.

"Where are we going now?" Vern said.

"The Exchange," Billy said. "I'm going to give those bastards what they deserve."

TWENTY-TWO

The streets thronged with bewildered crowds. Many who had dressed for the cold now had sweat pearling down their florid faces. Those that were shopkeepers inspected their windows and awnings for damage. Those who were customers darted from door to door. A Courier on a recently bashed bicycle rolled warily past a gaggle of Messengers loitering around a lamppost, alert as rabbits. The street conversation was peppered with anger. Like a brush fire it sparked from shopkeeper to customer, crackled in street corner chats, caught and flared in the cafés. Billy didn't catch many of the words, but from the frequent resentful glances first to the heavens and then to High Town, it wasn't difficult to work out what they might be.

Billy strode on, towing Vern in his wake. The closer they got to the Exchange, the denser the crowds became and the louder their grumble, but it was only when they emerged into the plaza that he realised that many of the crowds were heading there too. At the Judiciary they had to push through a massive queue waiting to lodge formal complaints about the weather. The faces that scowled his way as he ducked into the quiet vehicle compound that led to Para's favoured entrance were dispirited and bedraggled.

At the door, he turned to Vern. He wasn't certain exactly what he was going to do in there, but whatever that turned out to be it would not benefit the boy and his sister to be associated with him. Not when he produced the cube. He'd known immediately that he needed to break his promise to the Turners and promised himself that he'd find a way to keep it later, but for now they were the only proof of the Cranes' monumental hypocrisy. And those bastards had to be stopped. After what he'd heard in the Hall, Para's marriage to Stillworth couldn't go ahead. It wouldn't result in the union of knowledge and resources that would magically provide the answer to the bloody weather. It would mean the end of her, and her family. And then there was Stillworth's ghastly device too.

"Vern," Billy said. "I'm going in there, but it's really important now that you find the sylvans, wherever they are in the city, and tell them to go home."

The lad's face screwed up in indignation. "But I want to help…"

"I promise by doing this, you're helping. Tell the sylvans to leave Karpentine. Tell them from me. Now go!" Without waiting for another word of argument he went through the door and then wedged it with a gilded chair. The handle shook as the boy tried to disobey him, but Billy was already making his way towards the Trades Hall. Before he even got close, however, the clamour rumbling down the corridor suggested that wasn't going to be easy to do. Cracking open the door that led to the foyer, he found it jammed with bodies, the hot crush already angry and only agitated further by the slowness with which the crowd edged towards the gallery doors.

As Billy retreated to look for another entrance, something slunk through the gap. He recognised the artfully blemished skin. The cat turned its head and bared its teeth. "Follow," it said and scampered off.

Giving chase, Billy barely managing to keep the animal in sight as it took first one junction then another through corridors that were ever more opulently furnished. Finally, the animal paused before a tapestry. A masterly depiction of a wildcat, all tufted ears and grey-striped fur, snarling and twisting in the act of trying to snare a white dove. The bird had panic in its eye as it attempted to rise, spread-winged, out of the predator's reach. White feathers rained down. The artist had left it uncertain which would emerge victorious.

The tattooed cat slid under the hanging and disappeared. Peeling the material back, Billy found a slender twist of staircase and climbed it for what seemed an age. Beyond a curtain at the top, he found a narrow and steeply-raked box recessed between the ornamented pillars that supported the roof of the hall. It afforded a perfect view of the chamber, the families seated around the table and the noisy galleries filled to bursting above them. Billy liked to think that he had a head for heights, but the view brought him a wave of vertigo. He focused instead on what was in front of him. The Sisters. Turning, Sister Skin smiled that taunting smile of hers and patted the seat next to her, but it was Sin who spoke. "Come and join the outsiders, wild one." Her voice was thin, the cough that followed, a dry hack.

Billy took the seat offered to him. As soon as he was settled, the cat, Bastipol, leapt into his lap. Normally, he would have stroked an animal that did that but the bony thing's feather-sketched skin repulsed him. The cat didn't look like it cared either way.

Billy peered over the ledge. Down in the hall below, he saw the circle of families. From this distance, he realised how few people actually held the power in this place and that thought chimed with the question that had been running through his mind since his conversation with the Turners. Who else, knowingly or not, had taken advantage of the awakening of motes? The Constructors had immediately built unassailable capital from it. And whatever discovery Mackie Loess had lucked into had come shortly after. Kim, of course had discovered the sylvans, and hadn't he said that the barroom they met in was close to the Hall? There was one other person that would have benefited, and not only indirectly, as awakened motes were churned out by the manufactory chimneys and found their way into the trees and animals, became present in the soot and the wood, and in bones. Billy would bet his life that the Inksmiths laboratories had been incepted around that time too. With her arsenal of inks, with her newspaper and sly notes, Moraine Otterbree could control everything. And now it all threatened to collapse beneath them. No wonder they were so desperate, returning repeatedly to this place to savage each other under the pretence of the highest civility. Billy despised them all.

He watched the inner circle, their various allies around them. Merit Crane and his son looked impatient. Lem Shankhill had an air of satisfaction that did not suit him. Alicia Creasey fussed around her doted father, and Otterbree, ever vigilant of the balance of things below her eerie, stared unflinchingly at the final grouping in the circle. The Weathermakers were positioned directly below Billy's vantage so that he could only see the tops of their heads. Jelena sat stiffly, tapping the flagstones with her cane in a frustrated rhythm. Her niece was a head bowed over papers. Even at this remove, Billy could see the tension in Para's shoulders, the agitated bounce of her hair as she shook her head at something. Someone approached her then, and when she turned to greet them Billy recognised the gleam of pate through that pouf of hair. Para accepted the document folder that Killick had brought. Her smile of thanks gave him an excuse to linger. She smiled again then, opening the folder, turned away. The distance did not disguise the speed at which the smile slid off her face. Nor the involuntary glance at the Constructors' seats to see if Stillworth was watching. He was. His eyes had not strayed from Para for an instant.

Billy was surprised that the proceedings hadn't started yet, and guessed that it was due to the crowds still filtering into the galleries.

Indeed, down in the Hall some of the second and third tier families, caught up in the crush, were still taking their places too. He scanned the galleries. Now that the occupants had settled, the mood had changed a little. Some of the anger had dissipated and many of the assembly were looking around and whispering to their neighbours, visibly impressed by their surroundings. It was very likely that, although these family meets were open to all citizens, most of these people had never bothered to come and see what the high ups talked about before. Billy leaned further forward to get a better view, but Bastipol squirmed around on his lap and put its paws on his chest. "Careful, now," it said. "Don't want to give ourselves away."

Billy slumped back. "I need to get closer."

Skin shot him a look and placed two fingers over her lips but her eyes were laughing. Her sister smiled too. "You're welcome to try and find somewhere," she murmured. "But over the years we have found this to be quite adequate."

Billy frowned. "We're miles away. How will we hear anything?"

Skin's mouth was at his ear. Her breath a hot whisper. "Patience." There were delicate black vines inked around her eyes. She blinked and their leaves unfurled. She kissed him, her tongue strong like a tap root, probing, searching. She retreated with a sly smile.

"Aw," she said. "You were right."

Billy stared at her, overwhelmed by a surge of lust so powerful it made him momentarily dizzy.

"Told you," Sin murmured. Then, as Billy regained his faculties, she sat up straight. "Here we are, then," she said.

The crack of a brass-heeled staff silenced the chamber. "Who here calls this assembly?" It was one of the Ore Masters who had taken on the neutral role of getting things under way. The elderly woman leant on the staff for support. She looked neither strong enough to bang it so loudly, nor hale enough to make her voice heard this high up, but both had carried with perfect clarity. Billy nodded an apology to the Sisters. The hall had been designed by grandhandmasters. Of course the acoustics were impeccable. As good as this observation spot was, however, he still felt detached from the proceedings, and it fretted him. He inched forward again until the cat flexed another warning claw.

The Ore Master drew herself up, banged the gleaming heel of the staff once more. "I said, who here –"

"It was me." Merit Crane rose unhurriedly and even managed a laugh. "Well, someone had to, didn't they?" The laugh fell away, leaving behind something that felt like regret, but Billy knew Crane better than that. "I wish that onerous duty did not fall on my family. Not in the wake of the news of our joyous alliance with our meteorological colleagues." He smiled at Para then Stillworth, but he may as well have spoken the last two words through gritted teeth. "Some might consider it ill-advised to be making such lasting bonds under such difficult circumstances, but love pays little mind to business. As a measure of our esteem for the happiness of these two young people, I can assure the assembly that the Crane family would not dream of reneging on the agreed match. And equally, as a measure of our esteem for our new partners, the Weathermakers, I can also assure them that the Constructors will stand with them and render every support possible until this unfortunate hiccup in their affairs is resolved." Crane finished this with the slightest bow in Jelena Loess's direction. She nodded in return, but that was all the reaction she gave. The Governor's opening statements, however, created a hubbub of surprise that rippled through the seated families and around both levels of the gallery.

"Oh, bravo." Sin and her sister mimed applause, evidently enjoying themselves.

Billy scowled. "Lying toad."

"However..." Crane's voice hushed the room again. He let the word echo up to the rafters.

"Here it comes," whispered Skin.

"However," Crane repeated. "Matters have arisen. Citizens will remember the quality control lapse that was the cause of our last, all too recent, extraordinary gathering here. At the time, Madame Loess assured us that a number of strategies were in train to correct the problem, although she declined to elaborate on them as I recall."

Loess's cane stilled its tapping, but even at this remove Billy could see the spark dancing at its tip.

"Some of those strategies appeared frivolous at the time," Crane went on, and Billy had the uncomfortable impression that the Governor was referring to him, "but who am I to denounce a novel approach to an engineering problem?" This earned a roll of laughter from certain sections of the floor. "And while you have Karpentine's gratitude at least for resolving our little refugee problem, that somewhat sweeping solution hardly addressed the root cause. We were assured that more was being done to regain control over the damned weather, and instead it is allowed to go on a rampage. As we have all borne witness to over the last forty-eight hours. Madame Loess," here he appealed directly to Jelena, "this has gone beyond malpractice. Good hands have been lost; people have *died*. Please tell me you have good news." Crane relinquished the floor.

"Such false pride, Merit," Sin murmured bitterly. Skin nodded agreement.

Jelena Loess sat rock still for a moment then, at last, rose. She looked diminished, Billy thought, by her recent travails. But she was not yet spent.

"Thank you, Governor Crane." Jelena's voice fizzed. "These continue to be testing times for our family. Very likely, in fact, the most challenging since my father first forced the other families to accept meteorological engineering as among the major contributors to our society."

"Her father," Skin sneered. "Always her sainted *father*."

Below, a rumble broke out but was quickly hushed. Madame Loess ignored it. "Those engineering skills have not been lost, Governor. In the generation since our founding, our techniques have been honed, our understanding broadened. Who here has not benefited from our work? None of you can deny that you are only too happy to use the electricity provided by our collectors, and continue to do so even now. And who has not eaten food from fields watered to exactly the right degree by our rain? Which of you Cooks and Caterers or you Lumber Masters has not profited from that?" Some among the groups she indicated nodded. "And how long has it been since Karpentine was christened the Sunshine City? Who here has not enjoyed our fine weather, day in, day out?" She punctuated her words with cracks of her cane. "And a Sunshine City it will be once more. You have my word on that."

"That's what you said last time." The shout came from the floor, but it was impossible to see who had spoken. One of the Artisans, Billy thought.

Again Jelena Loess refused to rise to it. "However, the scale of the troubles we now face is unprecedented. New factors have come into play whose influence on the motal equilibrium, I confess, we have yet to fully understand." Heads nodded all around the Hall now. Everyone knew what the *new factors* were. It didn't seem to matter that the sylvans had arrived after the clouds had started to behave strangely, it was easy enough to give them as a reason.

"And though it pains me to do so," Jelena went on, "Family pride can have no place in a discussion of the safety, the *lives*, of Karpentine's citizenry. I therefore declare myself grateful for the generous offer of aid from our colleagues in the other families. This is a city-wide problem and we must put personal achievement aside and face it together." This statement produced a gasp from the galleries. No one could fail to appreciate what it must cost the head of one of the great families to make such a concession.

"Oh, well played." Sin mimed applause again. "Jelena knows if she gives him a confrontation and it goes to a show of hands, she has lost. Let's see how he deals with this."

From the stoniness of his expression, Loess's acquiescence was the last thing Crane had expected. He got to his feet and reiterated the offer of aid that he could not now publicly retract. He tried to lace it with warning and censure, but he had chosen to grandstand in public and Loess had grasped the situation and turned it around. The Weathermakers would lose some achievement in the standings but they had already lost far more. At least they still clung on to control of their own affairs.

"Interesting to see what the son does now." Skin was watching Stillworth. He slouched over the table, fiddling with his cufflinks, as if the goings on around him were of no consequence. Even from this distance, however, his sneer was apparent.

"What did you do to him exactly?" Billy said.

Skin winked. "Only what he asked us."

"Forced him to love Para?"

"Oh no, wild one," Sin whispered. "That was what his *father* asked us. Stillworth's aims are much more straightforward, and he was able to come up with the asking price all by himself."

"Which was...?" But Billy knew. He remembered what had been missing from Rabbit's carcase.

"Not very much. Only a foot or so," Skin said slyly. "But it was enough for an experiment."

Merit Crane was still waffling on, but his son dispensed with his distraction and slowly got to his feet.

"What kind of an experiment?" Billy said.

"Oh, that boy," Sin purred weakly, "has served a lifelong sentence under his father's eye. A sentence more severe and more difficult to escape than most ever see going into the Institute. Something that required a little extra wildness to break. So what if he has to love the girl? He always did. Being able to pursue her is just one avenue open to him now that he doesn't have to obey his father."

Billy knew then without question that if he were to examine Stillworth's skin he would find a winged cat, freshly stippled with ink made from sylvan ash. "You've made him dangerous," he said.

"Nonsense," Skin spat. "He was already dangerous. Anyone with control over that box would be. We've made him free."

Below, Stillworth tapped his father on the shoulder, murmured into his ear.

"You know about the box?" Billy froze, as if even mentioning it would draw attention to what nestled in his pocket.

Sin's expression gave nothing away. "I've been inside the man's head, just as I was inside yours, wild one. He has no secrets from me." She raised an eyebrow, quizzical, but for some reason of her own elected not to pursue the question of how *Billy* knew about it.

"But we knew about the box before it ever fell into the Constructors' clutches," her sister chimed. "Our father, you see, brought the finds from his field trips home. We regularly had Auntie Tatsuko and Uncle Mackie," she said the Weathermaker's name as if it tasted of shit, "round for dinner and he used to let us sit in his workshop as he bubbled his ores and teased his wires. It was us that discovered the cube, you see. Such a curious stone in his bag of rocks. He took it off us almost right away, but by then we'd had communion with the Turners."

"We'd been awakened," Sin said.

Billy's heart tripped as he looked from sister to sister. *Communion with the Turners?* They had to know, but still they said nothing. "You're Fry's daughters?" he said.

Skin nodded. "Father was an awfully trusting man. Mackie talked him into showing the cube to the Constructors, and they gave him a job that kept him at the Hall for long hours. He slept over. He stayed away for days. And then he never returned."

"I'm sorry," Billy said.

Sin shrugged stiffly. "Change is growth. It made us who we are."

Below them Stillworth had replaced his father opposite Jelena Loess.

"If you know about Stillworth's relationship with the Turners," Billy said, deciding there was nothing to be gained from pretending. "If you know the danger, why on earth have you given him free will?"

Both sisters grinned.

"Change is growth," repeated Sin.

"And this city needs to grow so very badly," said Skin.

"Not the way he's got in mind," Billy muttered. "He intends to destroy the motes."

"That might be interesting," murmured Sin.

"Not just in the weather. In the wood and the ink... in *people.*"

"And that would certainly level the playing field, wouldn't it?" Skin replied.

Billy wanted to make them understand the threat, but Stillworth had started to speak. His volume was little more than conversational level but the words still carried to the hidden balcony. "My father has generously extended the offer of aid to our meteorological colleagues," he said. "But if it please the assembly, I would like to propose an alternative solution. I have at my disposal a simple method for quelling our weather immediately."

The statement brought a round of gasps from both the floor and the gallery. When they died down, Jelena Loess spoke. "That is not possible."

"I assure you, Madam Loess, that it is."

"You do not have that knowledge. No one has that knowledge."

Stillworth ducked his head condescendingly. Billy thought he might have winked too. "I have more resources at my disposal than you can dream of," he said. "Beg me to deploy them."

"*What?*"

"Beg me. When your niece and I are wed, we will control the most powerful alliance in Karpentine." He smoothly forestalled objections from both Jelena and his father. "My father will retire in due course, and you, Madam Loess, will also presently step down. This catastrophe happened on your watch. It is the honourable thing to do. I will save what is left of your family's reputation and, in time, I will build it up again as I deem appropriate. But first you will beg."

Billy spilled Bastipol from his legs and leaned out over the balustrade. "Beg him not to instead," he bellowed and was gratified to see all of the heads in the hall jerk up, trying to see where this new voice was coming from. He felt one of the Sisters tug his coat, but shook her off,

263

simultaneously ignoring the cat clawing at his ankles. "The solution he speaks of is a bomb. A *bomb*, Lady Loess, that will kill every mote in the sky, and very probably everywhere else as well." Fingers pointed in his direction. Guards moved for the doors. "Stillworth Crane is a charlatan," he yelled. "His lies give achievement to the few and none to the many. His family exploit the poor and the Institutionalised." Billy didn't need to turn around to know that the Sisters had already deserted the eyrie. "And the deceptions of the Constructors are nothing compared to those of the Inksmiths," he went on and was gratified by further gasps from the galleries. "They all need to be brought before the Law. The Law For All," he shouted. "The Law For All." Surprisingly, his cry was taken up by the packed galleries. At first a handful of voices, then more and more. "The Law For All." He wanted to say more, to tell them about the Hall and the cube, but the place was already in utter uproar.

Down in the inner circles, the families were packing up their papers and making ready to leave. Jelena and Para were already gone. The only point of stillness in the whole room was the tiny figure of Moraine Otterbree. She was staring up at him, long and steady and unblinking.

TWENTY-THREE

If most of Billy's life been one of being shunned, over the next few hours he discovered what it was to be hunted. He waited for an age behind the tapestry until the sounds of running feet had died away, but on emerging he still managed to blunder into a cohort of guardsmen around the first corner he crept up to. They chased him through the corridors of the Exchange as far as a goods elevator which carried Billy down and out of their reach at a terrifyingly leisurely pace. Not that the elevator led to safety. It opened on to the loading bay at the rear of the Inksmiths enclave. There he found a dark spot in the storage racks to hide in until the pursuit died down and the shift bell trilled and he was able to creep out. The streets and alleys he chose were miraculously empty, but that only heightened his nerves as he crept from one to the next. It took him hours and it was getting dark by the time he made it back to the Loess mansion, although the evening remained as stuffy and sticky as the day had been and he was sweating profusely.

Inside, Billy took additional care, wary not only of guardsmen but the Bello twins too. He slunk through the house towards the residential quarters, peering around the corners and treading lightly on the stairs, but the only other person he encountered was a bedroom attendant delivering a glass of milk to one of the family. The liveried servitor barely spared Billy a glance, but he hurried on nonetheless until he was safe inside his own room with the door firmly shut and locked.

He didn't know what he was going to do now. He'd not only denounced the Cranes as frauds, but he'd taken away the very source of their success too. Which meant, even if they *were* to stand by their offer to help the Weathermakers, they wouldn't be able to do so. So there was no reason for the Loesses to protect him from the consequences of his outburst. And if the old man hadn't warned him, if the Bello brothers hadn't already tried to actually kill him once, the look Moraine Otterbree had given him had been unequivocal. He was done here. He wished he could have achieved more, but every effort he'd made to help in some way had come to nothing. Well, there was one promise he could keep now. He could take the Turners' cube back home and bury it in the Molspurs.

As he reached for the light switch, the low glow of the bedside lamp came on instead. Para sat on his bed. She wore an outdoor coat and, perched with her hands between her knees, she looked like an exhausted and frightened child.

"What's happened?" he said. She flinched and he went to her. "What is it?" Wordlessly, she handed him a freshly printed newspaper.

EXPOSED!

Beneath the headline was an entirely unflattering sketch of herself followed by a histrionic diatribe against her character. There were any number of slanders on that front page alone, but the principal one linked her explicitly with the Refacers, and their slogan: the Law For All. Billy's rabble rousing outburst came up several times as evidence. Although it had all been for nothing, as the rabble, the newspaper went on to reassure the reader, had most assuredly not been roused… Billy forced himself to stop reading.

"I'm sorry…" It was all he had.

She sniffed. "It's all right. They really don't credit you with that much autonomy. You're just a handy hook to hang me by."

"How did they know?"

"My guess? Finlay Giteau."

"But doesn't this shoot his movement down in flames?"

"Maybe, but it also spreads the message far and wide and has the added bonus of a convenient martyr." She took the paper off him and carefully folded it inside out so that the story was hidden. "Otterbree is playing a dangerous game with this. She might even have overreached herself."

"Wait, you're saying this is a good thing? They'll want to arrest you!"

"You think?" Para picked up something that lay beside her on the bedcover. "Have you seen this?" She unrolled it. It was a bill poster.

Keep calm and obey the Law of Man.

Instantly, Billy felt an icy deadening descend upon him.

"They were up all over the city within an hour of your little party piece." Para didn't glance at the paper herself, but continued to hold it out for him to look at. "People are shambling around like they're drugged. Oh, this was something she's long had up her sleeve in case the underachieved started to get demanding." She watched for Billy's reaction.

"You expected better of Moraine Otterbree?" His words sounded like dulled bells. He felt bound, and hated it. The effect was stronger than the sign outside Stillworth's laboratory, but not irresistible. Once again, he shifted the focus of his thoughts from the words to the paper they were printed on. Then he reached out and snatched the poster from her grasp, balled it and tossed it into the fireplace.

Para ghosted a smile. "You never stop surprising us, do you, Billy Braid?"

He felt his limbs loosen. "That was a test?"

"Just curiosity. I wanted to be sure. You remembered things from your sentence. No one does that. *And* you overcame your release. Are you so impervious to ink?"

His tongue felt like it was his own again. "No, but I can affect the paper somehow. I think it's something to do with the wood."

"Ha. That makes sense I suppose. You should talk to Alicia Creasey. Perhaps between us we might find a use for you at last."

"What makes you think I haven't?" he said, but that provoked another sharp glance, so he changed the subject. "This isn't something Otterbree's had ready for ages. This is very recent."

"How could you know that?"

"Have you ever seen a compellant so forceful as this?" Para shook her head. "This has to be the effect of sylvan carbonblack. She must have been experimenting since Seldom but the Bellos took her the fallen sylvans too. She's been stockpiling, but only since the sylvans arrived."

Para frowned. "I don't understand. The Sisters wanted the sylvan wood too. I assumed that was for their tattoos that set people free..."

"It must have a powerful effect whichever application it is set to," Billy said, although he was grasping for the logic, trying to make sense out of it even as he said it. "And the Sisters have a supply too. They used bird bones to begin with. On Giteau and," mentioning Alicia Creasey's name again would raise awkward questions, "...others. But the stuff they used on the Tailor kids' mother had a much stronger effect." He shrugged. "Look, I'm sorry if I caused your family trouble, but I had to stop Stillworth from talking your Aunt into agreeing to his use of the bomb."

"*Bomb.*" Despite the heat, Para shivered. "The very idea – *destroy not one brick or stroke of the works of others*, and all that?"

"I promise you, it's true." Billy took a deep breath, and related what he had learned in Stillworth's workshop. About Rabbit and the devices, about the Turners' world in the cube, about the Constructors' big lie and about her great uncle's part in things. Again, though, he didn't tell her everything. Like the Sisters, it was best if Para believed the Turners were still at the Hall, and not here in his pocket. He watched for her reaction. If she'd thought the idea of building a bomb was ridiculous, what must she make of this? But she listened with a serious face.

When she said: "But Still's always been so *straight*. Why all this showoffery now?" Billy told her about the Sisters' extension of their experiments with skin and ink and about Stillworth's liberation to follow his own desires that went beyond the service they performed on him for his father.

"You can't go through with the wedding now," he said.

"Can't I?" Her eyes were shining. "And miss out on the chance to ask these Turners for help? If they're really so powerful…"

"No," Billy cut in. He knew how it would go. She would ask for help with taming the weather. They would refuse. And she could not afford to take no for an answer. Even if her intentions were the purest, giving her access to the cube would no less be slavery than what Stillworth had done. "Stillworth had to force them. Blackmail them with extinction. Would you do that too?"

She held his gaze as if he personally were denying her the Weathermakers' last chance at redemption, then cast her eyes to the floor.

"The game's over," Billy said gently. "The weather is going to do whatever it's going to do." He didn't mention the sylvans because he hardly dared hope that they really had a plan, wherever they were. "But you're a good person, Para. You want to help people, you *can* help people, and there's plenty that need it right now. Just go out into the city and do it."

"Without my family behind me I'd be just one person," she said morosely. What can one person do?"

"We all have two hands. We can all do the same."

She looked up from the floor. "You make it sound so straightforward."

"What's complicated about it?"

"Well, I'm *me* for a start…"

"Could you just let go of your High Town vanity for one moment?"

"Is that what you think it is, Billy? It's not vanity. It's sacrifice. You're right. The Weathermakers are out of solutions. We're fucked. But my only chance of helping *everyone* is by staying in a position of achievement and using what little influence I have left. And my best hope of *that*, even if the Turners refuse to help – and I sure as anything would *not* force them against their will, but I'd certainly try my damnedest at persuasion – remains an alliance with the Constructors." She moved from the bed to the little window and peeked out. "That's assuming the weather lets us survive that long."

Billy couldn't help sliding his hand over his pocket, feeling the hard shape knotted up tight inside the cotton of his handkerchief. Inside that, he felt the Turners' attentiveness and heard in his mind a soft: *Shhh!*

Para furrowed her brow and glanced towards the door. "Did you hear something?"

Billy swallowed. "You're just jumpy."

"Bloody right, I'm jumpy. Merit is after your head for slandering his family back there. He's not going to let that lie." She came back to the bed and laid her hand on his. Her skin was clammy. "I can't protect you now, Billy. You need to leave here tonight. Find somewhere safe and hide out until morning, then... just leave and never come back."

How could he tell her that he'd planned to do exactly that? Or that her persistence in trying to do the right thing even now shamed him so deeply that he just... couldn't. Not yet. "I'll be all right," he said. "But what about the old man? What about those two kids and their mam? What the Institutionalised? What about...?" He didn't say *the Turners* for fear that they suspected his change of heart. He most certainly would fulfil his promise to them, but it would need to wait until he had done all he could to help the people that lived here who didn't have the luxury of living in a world where inequality was a thing of the distant past.

"You can't do anything to help them, Billy." She smiled sadly. "Your master is out of your reach now, and if you get caught sneaking back to the Institute you'll only make things worse."

"I've got two of these." He showed her his hands again. "I can do what one person can do, or at least try. Together, we could do even more..."

"No, Billy." Gently she pushed his hands down. "I have to –"

"Marry Stillworth?" He gripped her hot fingers. "Merit Crane would rather see you dead!"

Para stared at him for a long time, then her mouth tightened and she nodded resignedly. "You're right," she said. "I'm fooling myself. And you were right to call me out on my vanity. I have lived a very privileged life. The Book of the Law may tell us that there is no worth in self-reflected achievement, but that doesn't stop it feeling good when your

269

face opens doors, your name alone is enough to make things happen." She looked on the verge of tears. "This name, this face? They're worthless now. Less than worthless. Dangerous to me and those around me."

"So what are you going to do?" he said.

"I'm going to disappear."

Before Billy could ask what she meant, something hit the bedroom door hard enough shake it in its frame.

"Little pig-wrestler?" The voice, cruel and gleeful, belonged to one of the Bellos. The door banged a second, then a third time.

"We know you're in there." It was both of the Bellos.

Para's eyes widened. She put a finger to her lips then, sliding off the bed, went to the window and deftly opened it. The door banged again, this time loud enough to wake the whole wing. "Come on, Billy, don't be tiresome," Innocent or Erudite moaned through the wood. Para stretched nimbly up onto the sill and swung her legs out and, motioning with her eyes for Billy to follow, dropped out of sight. "Oh, very well." The Bello brother's voice had lost its playfulness. "If you won't come out…" The banging was replaced by a scraping and scratching. The door key was ejected from the lock, tumbling onto the rug and the scraping sounds resumed. Billy wasted no more time, climbing out of the window. As he dropped to the ledge below he saw the bedroom door swing open. The faces of the Bello brothers contorted as they took in the empty room, the window and Billy's vanishing face.

He ignored their roars of rage, concentrating instead on his balance as his feet found the ledge and trying not to think about the drop to the courtyard below. This had seemed a lot simpler when he'd plotted his escape after he'd first got out of the Institute. He looked left and then right but couldn't see Para. Then her head popped up a little way along and he spotted the anchoring loops of a ladder. "Hurry up," she hissed.

Billy scuttled along and looked over the edge. The ladder was short and Para was already stepping off the bottom onto a pitched roof. He quickly followed her, jumping down the last six feet, his boots skidding on the mossy tiles. It was only flailing at a rung that prevented him pitching down into darkness. He heard the Bellos bellowing his name. Two faces peered down, two sharkish grins.

"Billy, Billy, Billy," Innocent said. "Not great at this 'running away' thing, are you?"

"Your mouthy bint seems to have a better idea of the game," said Erudite, indicating Para who was backing away along the roof ridge. He raised his voice. "Don't worry, Miss Loess, we'll get to you too. Young Mr Roach is really rather put out, you see."

"Although," Innocent added, "we reckon now that he might consider that he's had a rather fortunate escape."

Para shook her head and mouthed something that might have been *I'm sorry*. Then she turned and ran. After a further second's thought, Billy did the same. He felt tiles crack and moss slip under his boots. A chimney breast loomed out of the dark and, unable to trust his footing if he should leave the ridge to go around, he pulled himself up and squeezed between the chimney pots. They had been carved into a choir of children, mouths open to praise the sky, some Artisan's greatest work that no one would ever see. On the other side of the chimney breast was another stretch of ridge, and then another similar arrangement of chimneys which Para was already negotiating. From the excited whooping, the Bellos weren't far behind.

On the far side of the second chimney breast, the roof stepped down to a complex arrangement of abutments where several wings of the mansion met. Para had already dropped down and chosen one. She turned for one last unspoken goodbye and disappeared down a flight of steps. Billy counted one, two, three heartbeats and then dropped down to the junction and chose a ridge that ran in the opposite direction.

He realised his mistake almost immediately. What he'd thought to be a kink between two levels of the roof he quickly saw was a yawning gap that went all the way down to the shadowed flagstones, and it was too late to turn back. The Bellos had already cut him off. When they realised, they slowed to a saunter.

"Oops," said Innocent. "Well, it's not your first mistake since you came to Karpentine, Bill. But it's probably your most fatal."

"Let's face it," said his brother from behind him. "We've got you."

Billy edged away. "You may have me," he cast a backward glance to gauge whether the amount of roof left would be enough for him to try and leap the gap, "but you don't have her."

"Her?" Both brothers laughed, but Erudite replied. "You think someone with a face as famous as Paraphernalia Loess's is going to be hard to find in this city? It's only regrettable that we may not find her first. Mr Roach is keen that you both be brought to justice to the point of embarrassing largesse."

271

"Very generous," said Innocent, stopping because Billy had stopped. "Oh, if you want to try for it, be our guest. You'll never make it, but it'll be hilarious watching you try."

Billy gauged the gap again. It wasn't *that* far. The opposite side had crows steps on the gable end and that meant something to hang on to. He could make it, though it would be tight. There wasn't much of an alternative.

Turning back he saw that Innocent now held a sharp blade. "Please," he said. "We insist."

Billy didn't wait for him to finish. He turned and sprinted along the ridge, pounding his legs for all he was worth as if he was jumping a stream for fun at home, all the time hoping his footing stayed sure and nothing broke or slipped and caused him to lose momentum. At the end of the roof, he launched himself, arms pinwheeling, across the black void that all too apparently now was much wider than any stream. Failing to reach the other side was not going to result in a soaking. And he *was* going to fail. Billy stretched for the crenelated edge, but he fell just short. Instead, a stone wall rushed to meet him. He met it with forehead and knees, with fingers that scrabbled and found nothing to grip. *Someone save me*, he thought. Then he bounced and fell backwards, and heard laughter from above... laughter that ended abruptly at the same instant that he realised that he was falling *into* something. The slap of twigs, the bowing bend of branches that slowed his fall, cradled him.

A *tree?* Opening his eyes, sure enough he was caught between branches and trunk of a tree. How could he have missed seeing it before he jumped? Regardless, he was grateful for its presence. Billy's entire body pulsed with the pain of the fall as he looked up to see the Bellos glaring down at him, but he managed a grin of relief nonetheless.

Then he realised that he wasn't out of danger after all. The brothers were preparing to follow him down. He needed to work out how to reach the ground through the tangle of limbs. It would be slow going. He shifted into a more or less vertical position and was preparing to lower his foot to a likely looking branch when an impact shook the tree. It was all Billy could do to hang on.

"Don't go anywhere, you lucky fucker." Innocent's voice came from somewhere close. "You are not slipping away this time."

Billy scrambled down to the lower branch, and then held on tight as Erudite landed amid the branches too. He heard the man groan. "There has got to be an easier way of earning a kudo, brother."

"But few so satisfying in the end." Innocent's voice was even closer.

As Billy looked down, unable to decide which way to go, the tree shook again as both brothers began their descent. And then, in his mind: an image of acorns dropping to a softly carpeted forest floor. A sylvan voice that simply said: *fall*. Billy had never trusted a voice more. He let go of his branch.

The drop was painful, but after the initial few moments of terror he realised that whichever direction he bounced in there was always a net of springy branches to slow his fall. And then, in a state of surprise, he found himself standing on the ground.

He laid his hand on trunk. He couldn't tell what species the tree was, but it was solid as ironwood, dark barked as black willow. Standing close to it, the air smelled so reminiscent of the Molspurs that could have wept. "Thank you," he said to the tree and looked around for the sylvan he had heard but there was no one there.

"Braid!" Above the Bellos were attempting to follow him, but rather than aiding their progress, the branches snared them. "We will have you, Braid."

"We will fucking eviscerate you." Then their threats changed then to agonised yelps.

Billy snatched his hand back because he now realised that needle thorns sprouted out of the tree's bark. Not only had he been lucky to survive the drop, but missing those thorns had been a miracle.

"Thank you," he told the tree again, and anyone who may also have been listening.

TWENTY-FOUR

Billy went back to the lowtown tenement. It was the only place he could think to look for Para. No one was there, but it was as good a place as any for him to hole up for the night. There would be more chance of finding her during the daylight, he told himself.

He explored the apartment that the Tailor family called home. In addition to the main room there was a closet kitchen, a narrow bedroom and a bathroom. Assiduous attempts had been made to keep the place clean, but the bathroom especially smelled so strongly of damp that he shut the door and blocked the gap underneath with a wedge of carpet. In the bedroom he found three piles of threadbare clothes. All the occupants owned in the world. The bed was a mattress covered by a much-darned sheet. It would do. It was too warm for blankets anyway. He took his coat off and rolled it into a pillow. The mattress was too soft for the bruises his body had endured lately, but he slept all the same.

He was wakened by a noise. Not a voice, not a knock or a thump. The sound of someone creeping. His first thought was that it might be Para or the boy, his second that it was the Bellos. His body felt like the Tower of Hands had fallen on it and he cinched his lips as he rolled off the mattress. He looked around the bedroom for a weapon. His eye settled on the fireplace decorated with blue and white tiles, some plain, some depicting soot-obscured dolphins. The fire had not been used in years, and neither had the rack of dull blackened irons next to the grate. He lifted the poker from its hook, hefted it.

Billy felt his way along the hall to the door of the main room. The sounds of someone moving around were clearer now. Someone moving with intent. He raised his poker, counted silently to three and then with a bellow opened the door and barged through.

Vern stood at the window, peering through the mouldy curtains. His face was washed by an odd light. "Din't want to wake you, boss" he said.

"What time is it?" Billy put the poker down.

"Nearly night." The boy let the curtain drop. "I was looking for your Miss Paraphernalia," he said. "Figured she wouldn't be stopping in the High Town after what happened." He craned his neck to peer into the darkened hallway. "Not in there too, by any chance, is she?"

274

Nearly evening? Billy winced. He'd slept through almost a whole day. "No, she's not. Is it the sylvans? Did you talk to them?"

The boy shook his head. "A kid up in the Praiseworthy estates is s'posed to have seen some, but he ain't a Messenger so you can't take it as noteworth, can you? I went up there to look but…"

"That's all right," Billy said. "We'll need to keep looking. So why did you want Para?"

Vern brightened. "I got a message from my sister." He reached inside the waistband of his trousers and handed a neatly folded square of paper to Billy. The paper was unbelievably fine, the writing on it contrastingly clumsy. Billy imagined a sheaf of gossamer pages and a pencil stub secreted somewhere about Clymie's person when she'd entered the Institute, her rabbit-like nerves as she'd deftly substituted the sentence the she was given with one provided by Para, her fear as she effected the pretence of dull calm coached into her. She was a brave soul right enough.

Despite the awkwardness of the tools, the note was surprisingly legible.

Dear Maestra. I have found something. The work they make us do is mostly the common stuff that a person would be glad to take a kudo for. It's easy enough to do and still keep my eyes open, like you said. The women in my detail is of all stages of their sentence. Some are new in like me, but you can tell them that's been there a while. They get quiet and soft. I didn't see Mam yet.

Last night I stayed awake and one of the guards came in. He went round the beds and woke up two inmates that's been here a while. He made them read something then they went back to sleep. This morning one of them was quieter than ever. The other one was gone. Reckon as she's a lifer now.

Our work today was here. They took us down into the bit where they keep the lifers. Eerie quiet that place is, and the stairs they go down forever. You can hear them shuffling about at the top levels, but the further you go down, it gets real quiet. It is like the dead. Our work was to carry sacks from outside the big door at the very bottom up to the front gate. One of the men's details took them away, I don't know where.

Maestra, I'm afraid, but I will stay here and try and find out more, and also look for my mam. Please, I hope she is not in that place.

Tell Vern be good.

C

"She's done okay, hasn't she, Mr B?" Vern's eyes glistened.

"Very good. Maybe too good." He was shocked by the revelation that the guards were the ones who were extending inmates' sentences, but at least they knew where Moraine Otterbree's stash of sylvan ash was being kept now. Was she using the whole Institute for her private gain? "And I don't think it's safe for her in there."

Vern clearly shared his reservations. "We need to find Miss Paraphernalia, don't we?"

Billy didn't know what Para had meant by *disappear*, but if she wasn't here they might spend all night looking for her, and that would keep Clymie in danger for too long. His mouth went drier than the Scour at what he was about to say next. "I'll go back in there tonight and get Clymie out." Pushing down the wave of Institute dread that came with those words he found a pocket in his coat for Clymie's note. A different one from the one that held Chop's fingers and the one where the Turners nestled. So many unfulfilled promises. He sighed, but wasn't that why he'd stayed in Karpentine? "I'll take a proper look at that place where they keep the Institutionalised while I'm at it. We need to know what's down there. We need evidence of what's in those sacks. So there's no mistake." Billy took Vern's place at the curtain. Outside there was an odd sort of twilight. The blanket of cloud directly over the city had dropped low and was the colour of bruises. In the distance, brooding thunderheads curdled with menace. His insides matched them as he said: "I'm going to go in once it's fully night."

"Me too."

Billy looked at Vern. Who was he to stop the boy trying to help his family? He nodded. "I suppose two witnesses are better than one."

Gloomy as it was out, Billy reckoned there to be still two more hours before nightfall. Shortly afterwards, the distant pealing of the Constructors bells told him that it was three. He sent Vern out with some money to get food and set about building the fire. It might still be far too warm to need one but this was what Kim had always done back home on stormy nights. It was a cheerful sight and made the apartment feel slightly less desolate.

Vern returned with a canvas bag stuffed with food. Billy decided not to ask how he had managed to squeeze all of this out of a single credit, but Vern's first words as he unpacked his booty were: "I didn't steal none of it."

Billy speared sardines on forks, held them over fire, using his coat to damp the heat conducted through the utensils. "No one suggested you did."

Vern tore open some rolls. "It was all freely given. All I did was point at the posters and say I was collecting for the guard out doing the city's business in these troubled times. Never hurts to chance your arm, our mam says."

Carefully, Billy turned his forks, bringing the charred sides up, and exposing the uncooked ones to the flames. "What posters? The ones about keeping calm?"

"I don't like them. They make me feel stupid even if I can't read all the words."

"Me too, Vern. They're there to make everyone docile… stupid."

"Didn't work on everyone, then." Vern handed Billy a roll to put the blackened fish on. The oils barely had time to start soaking into the fluffy bread when the boy slapped the top shut and took a huge bite. Who knew when he'd last eaten? Billy wasn't entirely sure when he had either. "Anyway," Vern continued through a mouthful of hot fish, "it weren't them posters. It were the other ones. I said I was helping the guards that was hunting them villains whose faces was on the posters. The man in the shop called me a liar. Said the guard don't need scruffs begging for them. And asked who I was really collecting food for." The boy's face went tight. "And I couldn't help it. I couldn't help looking at the posters again."

"Whose faces, Vern? Whose faces are on those posters?"

"Yours. And the Maestra's."

So it wasn't just the guard and the Bellos now. The whole city would be looking out for them, and would be compelled to act if they were spotted. He hoped Para was good at disappearing.

The boy was trembling. "It's okay," Billy said. "But I need you to tell me, Vern. What did you tell the man? Did you mention this place?"

Vern shook his head. "He never even asked. He just laughed, and then winked and muttered, 'the law for all, son'... and then gave me all this stuff."

"What? He wasn't acting docile? He didn't ask you any more questions than that?" A thought struck. "Wait... did you notice anything about him, Vern? About his skin, perhaps?"

The boy thought, and then nodded. "He had this picture. Under his vest. Here." Vern patted just beneath his own collar bone.

"A cat, with wings?" he asked although, thank the Sisters, he was fairly certain what the answer would be.

Vern nodded again. "Mr B?"

"What?"

"Can I have another fish?"

They cooked and ate all of the sardines and much of the bread which, when the fish had gone, they had with cheese and a pot of fruity chutney. There were tomatoes too and pastries, although both showed their age. There probably hadn't been too many produce deliveries in recent days. There were some bottles of beer too, and some sort of cordial which the boy turned his nose up at, so Billy shared his beer with him. Afterwards, Vern fell asleep, so Billy carried him through and laid him on the bed. Returning to the main room, he pulled a chair over to the window where he could escape the direct heat of the fire and watch the darkening of the day.

He waited until the peal of eleven, then slipped quietly into his coat. After all its adventures it was as stiff now as bark.

"I told you I was coming too." Vern stood at the door, his face pale but determined.

"You looked like you needed to sleep," Billy said. "All right then. Come on."

There were guard patrols on the streets, knocking on doors and asking questions, but Vern's knowledge of the alleys allowed them to reach the Institute without confrontation. Billy bit his lip, a spike of pain to puncture the familiar dread. There were guards at the gate too but Vern knew another way in. The Refacers' destruction of the new dormitory block had caused some damage to the sea-facing wall of the complex. It required some nerve to edge along the buttressed cliff edge that rose above the harbour and twice Billy froze with fear, but Vern tugged him on and, with the lad here, it was easier this time to cross the threshold and enter the Institute grounds.

"No need to thank me, Mr B," Vern chirped with brittle bravado as they cowered behind the shell of the now almost entirely demolished building. "I know you're glad you brought me along." By way of answer, Billy ruffled the boy's hair. To have tried to speak, he was certain, would have resulted in him screaming. Nevertheless, they were in now.

Once he had gathered himself, he began picking his way around the rubble. The front of the building had fallen in completely, although he was doubtful that it had done so of its own accord. Those enormous words would have been erased from public sight at the earliest opportunity. "Come on then," he whispered and, heart hammering, led Vern to the Institutionalised building and pushed the door open.

"Do we have to?" Now they were here, Vern's bravery was wavering. He sounded exactly as scared as Billy felt.

"I do," Billy said. "You can hide up here and wait if you want."

The boy shook his head. "My mam might be in here."

"Okay then, but not another word once we're in here."

When the boy agreed, Billy pushed through the doors, going to the banister and peering down the stairwell. The building was tomb silent. *Quickly*, he mouthed.

Billy and Vern slipped down the stairs. At the first landing, a door-lined square that ran around the stairwell's spiral, they stopped to listen and were rewarded by a muffled murmur, the odd cough, a sigh. Before Billy could stop him, Vern had opened the nearest door and started scanning the lethargic occupants. The immediate disappointment in his face was replaced by a pugnaciousness that said he meant to check every one of these rooms. Billy nodded and patted him on the shoulder and, with a glance back up to the doors at the top, left Vern to his search and continued downwards.

There were five cells per side of each square landing. If they were all occupied by two or three people there had to be several hundred inmates down here. Around halfway down Billy opened a door and saw maybe thirty bodies, stick thin and lying like sardines on pallets on the floor. The collective whisper of their breathing was all that told him they were still alive. Those guards had been busy. As he'd suspected, this building housed a workforce ready-made to do the worst jobs without complaint. He cursed the Cranes and didn't open any more doors after that.

When Billy ran out of stairs he was confronted by a stout steel door. On the door was a sign similar to the one outside Stillworth Crane's workroom. Billy read the words *Keep Out* and then, below them, an

279

additional word: *Forget.* He turned around and climbed the stairs and soon was standing on the landing above, confused. There was a level below this. Had he checked it already? The sign turned him back three times before he was able to concentrate enough to try and deal with it. It was much harder to disentangle the paper and ink than before but eventually he managed to tear the notice down. The door itself wasn't locked. There wasn't any need for it to be.

Inside, Billy found a hellish scene. Assaulted by the heat and the stink of roasting, he peered around the basement and tried not to choke on his rising gorge. By the orange glow emanating from the toothy furnace grates he saw Institutionalised shuffling around. They were all thin enough to have been resident here for a while but they retained enough strength in their wasted muscles to stoke the furnaces, to lug the things from the pile on the floor onto the steel tables, to wield the cleavers and flensing knives like sleepwalking butchers, to cart barrowsful of glistening white from the tables to one furnace and toss them inside, to scrape out the cooling furnace next door and to sieve soft grit into sacks. He stared in horror as a skeletal man dragged a full sack towards him and left it lined up with others by the door. The old fellow's complexion was like the skin on old milk, his eyes were sunken and lifeless. Billy shied away, trying everything he could not to acknowledge that the nightmarish figure was Ralston Maundy, and failing. The once lively little man showed no sign of recognition. He just shuffled away to get the next sack.

Billy had been wrong. This was not a workforce. It was a tower of production. The more able residents from higher up the tower butchered and burned those below who had faded to nothing at all and been allowed to die. Normal inmates came to get the ash, others ported it away. Everyone shuffled down a level. And none of them remembered a thing about it.

They were making nothing less than *Institutionalised boneblack.* A circular production line: inmate to Institutionalised to ink. The ultimate means of control. Distilled obeisance of fearsome strength that had already been put to use in posters all around the city.

It was incredible to comprehend. Had Moraine Otterbree become *so* paranoid about losing her precious status that she'd risk all her achievements on something as abhorrent as this, though? He couldn't quite see that. Someone else had to be involved.

Billy teased open one of the sacks and scooped a small handful of the gritty contents into the remaining empty pocket of his coat. The feel of the powder made his skin crawl. Dusting his hands off, he slipped back out and made his way upstairs. He tried not to think of what lay beyond the doors he passed. The inmates who were being allowed to die. The inmates who, sentence after sentence, were weeks or days away from joining them. Like poor Ralston Maundy.

He was three floors from the top when he heard the noise of a door opening. He reckoned that it must be Vern, but in then he heard adult voices, the ring of boots on the stairs. He pushed himself to the outside of the stair spiral.

"Mr B." Vern's face appeared at the railing of the landing opposite and above. "In here," he whispered.

Quickly, Billy joined the boy, slipping through an open door and closing it silently as the footsteps rang louder. The room was the same as the one he had peeked into earlier. Pallets on the floor, a toilet bucket in the corner. There were fewer occupants here and each had their own pallet and blankets. Most were sitting up. A few were talking in distracted murmurs, though Billy couldn't make out actual words. Vern had gone over to one of the pallets and now held the hand of the woman who sat cross-legged there, combing her blonde hair with the fingers of her free hand. Billy could hardly believe this placid woman to be the same as the one he'd last seen making that dramatic bid for freedom. The edge of a tattooed wing emerged from the neck of her cotton shirt.

"There's no hiding place in here," Billy said. "If they come in, we're trapped."

"There." Vern pointed behind the door.

"What about you...?" Billy started to say, but the voices were suddenly right outside their door.

"We don't *have* to check on them, you know," said a man's voice.

"Sorrow." The voice that replied was shockingly familiar. "I do agree, but the ones on this level are so prone to catatonia. I just like to check they're all right." The door opened and two figures entered. From behind the door Billy saw that they were both wearing the uniform of the Institute guard, but sure enough, one of them had the distinctive, chinless profile of Killick Roach. The two men surveyed the room, the occupants staring disinterestedly back. Vern was nowhere to be seen. "Well, everyone here seems perfectly perky." Roach jotted something down in a notebook.

281

"You new?" The first guard said as they went out. "I don't remember seeing you on the roster before?"

"Oh, everyone here forgets me pretty quickly," Roach said as the next door along opened. "I've got one of those faces." There was something about the way he said it that made Billy certain that he was covering his tracks using the kind of methods only available to those connected to the Inksmiths.

Killick Roach, the lowly Judiciary clerk who recently always seemed to have plenty of unexplained credits to bandy around. Who had risen so fast in achievement, and didn't care who he trampled to do so. It was all making horrible sense now, but the knowledge would be useless if Billy didn't escape this place. "Vern?" he whispered. "Where are you?" The blanket covering the man behind the boy's mother shivered and fell away and the lad's face appeared. "We have to go."

"But my mam…"

"We can't help her by dragging her bodily out of here. Only by telling everyone what we know."

But not before Killick Roach got a taste of what was coming to him.

TWENTY-FIVE

"No, no!" Almost as soon as they had negotiated their way out of the Institute, Vern had a change of heart. He squirmed around and tried to go back in. "We can't leave her in there."

Billy dragged him into the shadows. "You saw your mam," he whispered. "Nothing is going to happen to her." He tried to keep the words *for now* from showing on his face. It was hard enough disguising his terror at discovering the sheer lengths to which people would go to gain status. A production line of human ash that could subdue the will of the entire city? The whole thing was monstrous beyond belief. And for the one profiting from it to turn out to be someone as ineffectual as Killick Roach was staggering. It was a monumental achievement... if *achievement* could ever be the right word.

Vern stopped struggling. Sweat sheened his cheeks. "What about Clymie?" For all his stoicism, there was a child's whine to his voice. He right of course, but this news was too important to risk capture while looking for his sister. Roach, Otterbree, this whole enterprise needed to be stopped.

"She'll be safe in there for another night too," Billy said. "We'll come back and get them both out, I promise." He wondered whether Roach ever crossed paths in there with Sister Skin, his natural adversary, freeing people from their sentences even as he doubled down on those of their neighbours. What a place this was. "Vern, listen," he gripped the lad's shoulder to get his attention. "You remember that kid in the High Town who claimed to have seen the sylvans? I need you to go and talk to him again. Find out everything he knows." By now he didn't expect much, but had to give the boy something to do to distract him from his panic.

Vern swallowed, then nodded. "Meet you back home, boss." He melted into the shadows. In seconds Billy couldn't even hear the sound of the boy's feet. Once he was alone, he found a spot against the Institute wall where he could watch the gate, and waited.

It wasn't long before he heard voices approaching.

"Honestly, in my view, they're overreacting," said the first. It was the other guard, the one who had accompanied Roach. "No one's escaping from here with all of these extra patrols."

"Quite so, quite so." At the sound of Roach's voice, Billy risked a peek. The two uniformed figures stood in front of the guard hut.

"Not that I mind the overtime," said the first with a laugh that became a dry cough. "And I'm really looking forward to a cuppa. I'm parched."

As the guard turned to enter the hut, Roach tapped him on the shoulder. "Just one moment," he said. "What do you make of this?"

The guard looked at the slip of paper. "Oh, right," he said and then, forgetting about Roach entirely, entered the guard hut on his own. As Roach smiled and sauntered towards the gate, Billy withdrew only to find that the odious man seemed partial to the shadows too. Ducking into a spot not far from where Billy hid, he rummaged behind a bush and removed the hat and jacket of the uniform in preparation for changing back into his normal clothes. Billy waited just a little longer before making his move.

"Never a good idea to be caught with your pants down, Killick."

Roach attempted to freeze, trousers around one ankle, the other leg raised in the act of removal. He wobbled, hopped, and with a snapping of twigs fell into the bush. "Braid?" He looked around as if expecting aid from guards, but of course he'd chosen a time to be here when he knew the square would be deserted.

"There's no one here, Killick. Not at this time of night." Billy stood over Roach as he struggled to kick off the trousers that still bound his ankles in the most undignified manner. There were sweat patches on Roach's shirt too, the cotton soaked to a degree that even accounting for the temperature suggested that he was not as relaxed during his imposture as he had appeared.

Roach righted himself, regained his composure and rediscovered his sneer. "I only have to raise my voice, Billy. You're a wanted man."

"Really? And how would you explain that uniform you're... almost wearing?" Billy slipped his hand into his coat. "How would explain that little note of forgetfulness in your pocket? How, especially, would you explain this?" Extracting his hand, he blew grey dust into Roach's face.

There were several admonishing passages in the Book that could have been applied to the amount of enjoyment Billy got from the resulting coughing fit and the blotchy patchwork of Roach's reddening skin, but he really didn't care. It was abundantly clear now that, in Karpentine, the Law was considered to be something you got extra achievement for finding a way to circumvent rather than live your life by.

Roach, however, was far from contrite. "You think anyone will take your word?" His lips were grey from the ash. "Against mine? You think you've got evidence? They won't even get as far as asking for your *evidence*. Not when it's the word of a High Towner versus that of a most wanted criminal."

"Maybe not, but they'll believe Paraphernalia."

Roach smiled so widely that he almost choked on his own teeth. "I'm afraid you're mistaken. That jumped-up underachiever is more sought after than you are and, now that her double life has been revealed and who knows what other deceits wait to be uncovered, her word is worthless. Ha! To think I almost married the bitch."

Billy didn't let the man's venom shake him from his purpose. "Then maybe I should be the one to call out, while you still have it about your person."

He saw the quiver of uncertainty in Roach's eyes, but the resolve didn't break. "I dare you." Roach laughed, then reached for the bag hidden in the bush and extracted his own clothes, which he proceeded to put on. He looked up from fastening his shirt. "What? No dramatic sacrificial gesture? Go away, Billy. You think I'm cruel? *Boo hoo*. You can't change a thing without achievement. Go, get lost. You're certain to end up back in the Institute sooner or later, and you can be sure I'll make a point of paying you a visit." This time his smile was sickly. "Unless the Bellos catch up with you first and save us all the bother."

"Maybe..." Billy seethed, but Roach was right. It didn't matter what evidence he claimed to have, if he tried to present it in person no one would take any notice. Roach was shrugging into his coat now, confident that Billy couldn't touch him.

Well, he was wrong about that.

Billy's first punch burst Killick Roach's fat nose. His second split his eyebrow and put him down. Billy stood over him, punching and kicking in a blind rage. Roach barely even defended himself. He just cowered among the bushes, whimpering, pleading, but Billy didn't stop. All he could think were the words: *Who's the high up now? Who's the high up now?*

"Who's the high up now, eh? Who's –?"

He made himself stop when he realised that he was bellowing. From within the Institute there came the clamour of an alarm. Breathless, Billy staggered back and took one more look at Roach. That he was still moving made Billy want to finish the job, but his desire not to be returned to the Institute was stronger.

285

He ran.

It wasn't Roach's words that had set him off, Billy thought as he trudged through the lowtown lanes. It wasn't even what he'd done. It was the prick's swagger. That was the thing that made the already monstrous a thousand times worse. It encapsulated this place to the ground, its obsession with achievement, that even the least fortunate child in a peer group, as Roach undoubtedly had been, seized on an opportunity to maltreat and bully those they perceived as less than they were. He hadn't even seen in Billy enough of a threat to deny his atrocities. Billy's aching hands testified as to how much of a mistake that had been. He took pride in each throb.

Billy kept to the lanes. Even so, he was frequently forced to double back, to duck and sprint and hide, because on every corner were the green uniforms of the civil guard. On every wall, door and lamppost, those posters with Para and Billy's faces. The sketched likenesses were remarkably faithful but it was the Keep Calm ones that were the danger. Even an unguarded glance made Billy want to lie down in the street and wait for it all to be over. Each time, he managed to focus on the paper and tear it off the wall, but it got increasingly difficult to do so, even using the activities of Roach and Stillworth to goad himself into action.

All wasn't lost, he told himself. He could still do something but he had no weight here alone. He needed help.

Billy stopped at the corner of an alley that emerged onto Prospect Avenue, not far from its junction with the graceful road that led down to the Lodge of the Artisans. He flapped his coat to give his body some air. Accidentally, his fingers brushed the breast pocket. He felt a stirring of consciousness. In seconds it had become a barrage of voices.

Not safe. We are not safe. You said. You would take us to safety. You said. You would bury us. Make us safe. Make us safe. You said. You said. You said.

Billy braced himself against a wall of rough, warm bricks. "I know," he whispered. "I'm sorry. But there's no place in this city that you will be safe."

The mountains, the voices shouted. *The sea! Why are you still here?*

"Quiet," he hissed, looking instinctively upwards. Already the pressing blanket of cloud immediately above where he stood was swirling. "I'm doing what I can, and I will leave as soon as is possible. But there are others who need my help first." He had a thought. "Look, you did calculations for Stillworth. How about you do something for me?"

Why would we do anything to help you? You're repairing a wrong done to us by your people. We owe you nothing.

"If you help me find my sylvans, I can publicly denounce the Cranes for their crimes –"

And have your entire city of despisers know of us? This was shrieked, fear and indignation.

Great fat drops of rain spattered the ground. When they hit the flagstones they sizzled. When they hit Billy's skin, they scalded.

"All right!" Billy whispered. "Keep it down or you'll put us all in danger." The voices fell silent and Billy took the opportunity to dodge out of the alley in search of shelter. The rain followed him as he dashed across the avenue, but when he found a doorway, heavily-lintelled around red-glossed oak, it seemed to lose interest and petered out as if content that a reminder had been delivered. This heavy heat, Billy thought, must be leading up to something.

"That was some strange squall, eh?"

Billy started. He hadn't spotted the other person already sheltering in the shadows. The fellow was well attired and the reeked of booze the finer type of brandy. His voice was slurred, but the sluggish monotone was not only the result of the drink.

"You're not kidding," Billy muttered, edging away.

A fist grabbed his lapel. "Wait." The man squinted. "It's you, isn't it? *Wanted.*"

Billy prised the fingers off him. "You're drunk," he said.

"Oh." The man's face fell. "Sorry to have troubled you then."

"It's all right." Billy stepped out of the doorway into the brightly lit High Town street, tried to get his bearings and hoped that the citizens in his pocket would keep their counsel now.

"No, it *is.*" The man peered at him again. "You're *him.* You're Billy Braid. You're *wanted.* Come here." He lurched, and Billy ran.

The drunkard gave chase as far as the next junction then fell away, but his shouts of alarm dogged Billy. He could still hear the fellow's blare several streets away, getting hoarse now. It didn't look like anyone else had taken up the call, but Billy took extra care in making sure he wasn't observed slipping into the park.

The air was fresher among the trees, freer of the pungent taint that he realised now imperceptibly pervaded the baking streets. Billy skirted the islands of lamplight, preferring the shadows and the closeness of the boles. He laid his hand on their barks as he passed, enjoyed the calming whisper of the leaves.

The Sisters' street was silent. Every scuff and footfall that Billy made, every crunch of gravel under his boots, resounded off the tenement walls. In their close, the candles were cold and he was overwhelmed with the notion that the place had been abandoned. He made himself climb anyway. The paltry beam of his windup light skittering around the walls like a glory beetle.

He was hot when he entered the Sisters' apartment. Out of breath. The walls sweated too, the carpet scraps squelching. No cats came to meet him as he followed the dark corridor to the door at the end and entered Sister Skin's room. It smelled foetid. In the lantern light, the muslins hung like swathes of cobweb.

There was no one here. Billy turned to back out of the room when he felt something slink against his legs. The dwindling lamp revealed a ghostly feline face.

"Bastipol?" The voice was feeble, muffled, and came from the nest of cobwebs. "Is it him?"

"Follow," the cat said to Billy.

Billy followed it into the centre of the hanging folds, and was surprised to find not Skin, but her sister. Sin lay in the swaddles of fabric with the rest of the cats. Big eyes watching him with suspicion.

"Where's your sister," he asked. "Out sowing havoc as usual?"

Sin's response was a dreamy smile. "My sister does what she needs to. We told you we favoured change. You don't think this place can do with a few more minds thinking independently of the law?" She rolled in her nest, winding more of the grubby material around herself. The cats stretched grumpily and then settled again. "The *bastard law* is responsible for too much closed-in thinking, wild one. I'd have thought you of all people in this city would have understood that. Everybody cheats, you know. You wouldn't believe, Billy Braid, the thoughts they bring to me. The fancies and predilections they all feel so guilty about. Everyone has an inner sin. How you deal with it is what makes you human. Our bastard Law of Man compels people to self-torture. The ones who are in the know and can afford it come and dump their unwanted business on me. And let me tell you, Billy Braid, the sins of those ones are the nastiest of all." Sin coughed, a whispering hack. "My sister can't help the effect they have on me, but she feels she can help other Karpentiners, especially the ones who find themselves incarcerated. You know what goes on at the Institute by now?"

Billy nodded. "I know how they're making their awful obeisant ink, and I know who is doing it. I've proof…"

Sin's laugh was surprisingly musical. "You're a sweet boy, Billy." She patted the floor beside her. "Sit with me, I'm getting a crick. Bastipol, give the boy some room."

All of the cats perked their heads up and several of them slunk away. "They're all called Bastipol?" Billy dusted a patch of floor clear of bone detritus, and sat.

"Why shouldn't they be?" Sin settled back into her nest and watched him with shy eyes. "It was our father's name, Bastipol Fry. Now sit closer. I would beg some of your warmth, but I still have my pride." When he hesitated, she said, "Don't worry, I don't have my sister's appetites. But even I relish human contact from time to time. Please?"

Billy shuffled over and put his arm around her and she put her head on his lap. Her brown skin was clammy. "Thank you," she whispered.

"Did Para come here?" he said.

He didn't think Sin was going to respond at first. The answer was a sleepy murmur. "That would be her business and not for me to divulge."

"It's important," he said. "We have…"

"Do you really think anything you can do will change anything? In this city? You think if you expose who is making this *ink* you will right all the wrongs? It's not just the ink. Ink is nothing on its own. It needs a compliant canvas. You bring one person down, a whole family even, there are ten more waiting to take their place at the top table. Otterbree makes sure of that. It's in no one's interest to make a fuss."

Billy swallowed down another protest. She was right. They were all right. But he couldn't – *wouldn't* – accept it…

"Don't look so sad, wild one," Sin said. "All is not lost. I will tell you this much. Paraphernalia Loess is doing what she can, and it involves considerable personal sacrifice for which she will never get a jot of credit. Who knew she had such selflessness in her?"

Billy tilted Sin's head, made her look up at him. "What are you saying? What has she done?"

Sin smiled her dreamy smile, and said. "Disappeared."

Then she reached up, touched his face. Despite the swelter, her fingers were ice. He pulled her hand away. "What do you mean, disappeared? What do you mean *sacrifice*? What have you done to her?"

289

"You're asking the wrong sister about that, Billy. It wasn't her heart needed changing."

She'd come to Skin, the sister of the flesh? And Skin had made her invisible. How?

Billy tried to get up but Sin clutched his lapel. "It's too late. It's done." Then her fingers brushed his chest and Sin's eyes widened. "What's this?" she whispered, and she was quick about slipping into his coat, coming back out holding the cube, his discarded handkerchief dropped to the ground. "What are you doing with *this*?" Her wide eyes stretched further then because the voices had begun.

Who is it? Is it Fry? It feels like Fry. No…

"I took them from the Cranes. I'm trying to deliver them to safety." Billy grabbed at the cube and then both he and Sin were in the grassland at the foot of what had been the tower. It had grown since his last visit. Now it was a woven city, an impossible structure of interweaved boles, towers tall and slender whose tops waved against the blue sky like grass stalks on an unimaginable scale. The whole edifice creaked and knocked and boomed.

Sin turned to him. "What have you done? Where have you taken me?"

"You don't know?" Already figures emerged from the city. "These are the people you and your sister talked to as children. This is the world of the Turners."

And with a rustle and rush, the grass man was beside them. *What kind of ally do you profess to be, Billy Braid? We asked you to keep our secret, not conduct sightseeing tours.*

"And I will do as I promised," Billy said. "But I'm not only an ally for you. There are others who need my help before I can leave the city and find somewhere…"

A general purpose saviour, are you?

"I've kept you out of the Cranes' hands, haven't I?" The grass man said nothing. "Then trust me to continue to do so, and deliver you to a safe place when I can."

We wonder if we can trust you. But we do not seem to have a choice. The rustling head whipped around then with a sound of snakes. *And who is this danger you have brought us?*

"You don't know her? She knows you. She is Bastipol Fry's daughter."

The grass man cocked his head. *We do not remember…"*

We remember. The words came from above as a soft shape drifted down out of the sky. The cobweb woman alighted nearby. *Before the Cranes, before Fry. Caran and Joi. They were the girls with such prodigious gifts.* The woman reached out and caressed Sin's cheek. *We remember.* Neither the web woman nor the sister said another word but Sin nodded as if an entire conversation passed between them unspoken and, in the next instant, both she and Billy were back in the tenement with the cats. He watched her throat working as she swallowed something down.

"They're safer with me." Sin wheezed the words, tapped her chest. "When I die no one will come to sift my bones."

"But I promised them…"

"Does it matter, as long as they are safe?"

Again, there was no denying that she was right. Billy would have ended up blundering around until he was caught with the thing in his possession, but still he felt its absence from his coat. An empty pocket, a failure. Like his promises to Clymie and her mam, to the Institutionalised, to the sylvans. Like all the ways he had failed to help Para, who had now vanished beyond his help. "But I promised," he said.

Sin wrapped herself in the nest of muslin. Her skin streamed with sweat. "I'm so cold," she said, her teeth chattering. "Give me your coat."

He wanted to, but he'd made so many promises.

"It never really suited you, did it?"

When Billy removed his coat, the relief was indescribable. As he tucked it under her chin she was already asleep.

TWENTY-SIX

Disappeared? How could anyone with a profile like Para's disappear in Karpentine? Billy imagined Skin working some arcane pattern magic with her needles and ink, but to what end? Disguise? Disfigurement? Maybe a tattoo that made people forget her face? No, that would be outlandish, even for Sister Skin. He hoped whatever the method, it was worth it.

Right now he could only envy the ability to simply vanish. It was well after midnight but the streets still crawled with guardsmen. From the shadow of an alley he watched two of them knock on a door, the lenses of the filtering spectacles they all wore now swimming with reflected street light as they showed the dazed inhabitants first one piece of paper, then another. Even though the residents shook their heads, Billy had no doubt whose faces they were memorising, what obeisant-inked instructions were even now sinking in.

Now he was truly on his own, he didn't know what to do. It was too risky to try and get to the city gate, and probably just as bad to attempt to go back to the tenement room. He had no idea where Vern was, and there was no chance of getting close to the old man, cosseted happily now in the clutches of the Artisans.

He still needed an ally, though. Who did he know that was no friend to the Inksmiths? Well, there was always Alicia Creasey. She might not be best pleased that he'd failed to provide her with sylvan ash, but she had been desperate to find a way to create an impervious paper. Perhaps now that he understood his ability better he could offer to work together. It was a long shot, but he had nothing else.

The climb to the apex of the High Town exhausted him. The air had become tainted something foul and by the time he reached the twin residences he wore a skin of sweat inside his shirt. It streamed down his spine and the backs of his legs. His arms were heavy, his boots felt like stumps of ironwood. He was glad at least to be rid of his coat, the weight of it. Sin had been right. It had never fitted him.

Finding the door of the Creasey mansion ajar, he pushed it all the way open to find the lights blazing and that the hallway a mess of tumbled paper. Caution stilled his tongue from calling out. Indeed, his first thought was that the city guard had been here looking for him and might still be on the premises.

"Come here." The buck appeared beside him. Its hooves muffled by the fallen paper.

"Where is she?" Billy said.

The animal cocked its head with something like amusement. "Not her," it said. "Someone you've been looking for." Without waiting for a response, it turned and began to ascend a carpeted staircase that had been hidden in the shadows on his last visit. He followed the white scut up into the darkness.

"What's going on?" Billy asked when they reached a turn in the stairs. The hush of the house forcing him to whisper. The buck continued to climb. When it reached the first floor it trotted along a landing lined with doors that looked like they had not been opened for years. Only… one stood ajar and a fan of light spilled out, illuminating the pattern of reams and scrolls on the carpet and the fur of dust on the ornate banister. It wasn't the light that gave him pause though. It was the voices. He recognised Alicia's clearly enough. The other belonged to the despicable, and apparently resilient, Killick Roach.

Billy stood there stunned for moment, then pieces clicked into place. Sin saying ink was nothing on its own. The stack of commissioned sheets that Alicia had been working on. It was a *partnership*. Yes, the new ink itself was horribly effective but Killick had done what no one else had done for a long time: matched it with a paper specifically devised to enhance its properties. Almost no one could resist that combination.

He pressed against the wall and listened.

"Yes, of course, I want our relationship to continue," Roach wheedled, his voice clotted and nasal. Billy hoped he'd broken that nose at least.

"Then, I must press you to do what you promised, Killick, darling." Alicia's tone was a raspy purr. "You said you would use your family connections to leverage the witch, but I've yet to see a shred of evidence. I want my birth right."

"Sorrow, Alicia." Roach's said thickly. "But it's not simple, going up against Auntie Moraine. It takes time to build a network without her knowledge…"

"Then you would imagine, with her eye on destroying the Weathermakers, that this would be the perfect time. What use is that exquisitely habituating paper I make for you if you're not going to take advantage of it? It's working isn't it? You're putting the awful underachievers to good use?"

"Working?" Roach managed a phlemy chuckle. "You wouldn't believe how well. And my aunt has no clue as to the real source of the new boneblack…"

Alicia's laugh was humourless. "Oh, Killick. Do you honestly believe that?" Roach began to bluster in response but Alicia did something that shushed him. A rustle of paper that was as seductive as silk.

Along the landing, the buck huffed, tossed its head, urging Billy to move on. Billy nodded but lingered. Alicia might not have been his first choice of ally, but at least they'd shared a common enemy in the ink witch. To find that she'd teamed up with Roach was a shock, but then he already knew that anyone who bore Sister Skin's stamp of liberation could not be depended upon have scruples.

"You men," Alicia mused, "Why must you always disappoint? I mean look at the state of you." Roach tried to say something, but it came out as a moan. The paper rustled again. "I wrote you a love poem," Alicia went on. "Don't just fondle it, do me the service of actually reading the thing…" obediently, Roach started to mumble… "while I explain why your dear Auntie Moraine – although, to be fair, Killick, she's not technically your Auntie, is she? More like ninth cousin or something? – has finally agreed to divorce my father and officially re-establish something approaching proper terms of trade for the Papermakers' services…" Again Roach mumbled. "What's that, dear?"

"I love you, Alicia."

"Of course you do. You were kind enough to give me a sample of your devastating new ink after all, and I have produced an even more perfect paper to match it… as you are right at this minute discovering. So it should come as no surprise that *our* arrangement has also changed. Otterbree knows where that special boneblack comes from. I told her. And I told her that I will ensure its supply will continue. Essentially, my love, you work for me now. You will continue your night time escapades, won't you?"

"Yes, but…"

"But what?"

"She might not keep her word."

Alicia's laugh was bright and piercing. "Oh, Moraine Otterbree's word has the least value of any in this entire city, Killick." She tittered, sighed. "So, it's just as well that I have a contingency plan, isn't it?"

The buck huffed again, and this time Billy had heard enough. Leaving Alicia to continue her enslavement of Roach, he crept away from the door. He followed the animal up the next flight of stairs, and then another after that, soon having to wind his lantern to see the way. The top floor of the mansion was more poorly furnished than the lower ones, but it was just as packed with stuff. Here, under the sloping eaves, the play of his beam revealed reams of paper tightly bound with yellow string, knots cinched solid. Some of the pages were even organised into catalogue books, and there were shelves along the hallway with labelled compartments identifying samples of scabby wood and rotten rag.

The buck led him to a door between the shelves. There it reared up and applied its hoof to the handle. As the door swung open, Billy knew exactly what he would find inside.

The attic room was not deep but it was long, like a gallery. A crowded lumber room, he thought at first, only the contents of this space were not the family's old furniture and bric-a-brac. The room was occupied by sylvans. Kneeling, standing, packed together in the dimness, many bearing the chars and scars of the battle with the clouds. Heads bowed and motionless.

Billy approached one, recognising the pattern of the grain on its chest, a teardrop-shaped whorl over where, on a human, the heart would be. "Freshet?" He stroked the curve of the sylvan's chin and saw that half of its face was charred and it had lost a polished pebble eye. Its lifelessness reminded him of poor Rabbit.

"Fucking Stillworth Crane..." Billy seethed.

"Master Crane has not been here," the buck said calmly at his back.

Billy turned. "Then how did they get like this."

The animal snuffled. "They went to sleep."

"Sleep? Why would they...?" Looking at the crowd of still sylvans again, these weren't bodies piled on top of each other, they had fitted themselves into this space. A deliberate act of hiding. There were only perhaps a dozen of them. That meant there had to be other caches, places of safety sprinkled throughout the city. He wondered if Vern's lead had uncovered those others yet.

"Wait..." Given Alicia Creasey's demand for sylvan ash, this should have been far from a place of safety for them. "Alicia doesn't know they're here?"

The buck regarded him with its soft brown eyes. "She rarely ventures further than the lower floors," it said. "I believe however that they feel

295

safe where wood is respected, and I am showing you this because you will need to know where they are when they wake up. Although, as you have seen, the mistress's position has changed. It is dangerous for you to be here now too."

Billy joined the animal outside. "When will they waken?"

"Only they know that." The buck bowed its striped head, then backed out onto the landing. "Go quickly, go quietly. And be ready."

Billy didn't need a second invitation, but he had taken no more than three steps towards the head of the stairs when he heard someone coming up.

Beside him the buck startled. "This way." It trotted to the far end of the hallway. Around the corner there was another set of stairs. "This leads to the kitchen. You know your way from there." It trotted back along the hallway.

Billy was wary of the stairs. The carpeted treads were soiled and ripped, and they delved down into complete darkness. On the other hand he could hear Alicia's voice in the corridor. He snapped his lantern off.

"There you are," he heard her say. "What are you doing all the way up here? I was looking for you. Why is this door ajar?"

"I thought I heard someone up here," the buck replied and there was a knock of hoof on wood, then the door latching. "I was wrong, but there have been too many visitors recently." The voices moved away, and Billy wasted no more time. He descended as quickly as he dared in the darkness, feeling his way down an entire flight before he dared wind his lantern again to guide him the rest of his way.

When he reached the bottom, he emerged at the threshold of the Creaseys' cavernous kitchen. The stalagmitic columns of sheets here had not suffered the same catastrophe as the ones in the hall, so he could see little of the room beyond the back of Augustin's chair and the corner of Alicia's work table. He could hear nothing beyond the steady drip of the pulp suspended over the sink, and a gentle riffling which he quickly attributed to the pages pinned to the drying lines fluttering in some draft. *Ah.* Someone had opened a door or a window, a means of escape. He hoped that right now the buck might be delaying Alicia's descent from the upper floors.

Creeping a little further into the kitchen Billy saw, sure enough, that it was empty and that the edges of the pages that comprised two ceiling-high stacks near the sink were visibly fluttering. He could feel the breeze on his skin now and there was a man's-width gap between them. Wasting no more time, he darted around the old man's high-backed armchair. Then he stopped, because there was someone there.

Vern

The boy looked tiny in the once-lavish chair. Like a doll perhaps, its shoes up on the sagging footstool, legs straight and arranged neatly together, arms at rest by its sides. "Vern?" Billy crouched beside the chair. Even the lad's face was porcelain pale, his eyes glassy. "Vern?" He was so still.

The blow came out of nowhere. A punch, no – something harder than a punch, something with an edge – impacting his jaw and wrenching his head around and sending him to the floor. When he gathered himself enough to look he saw two pairs of immaculate shoes. "Up you get, Billy." Innocent – or perhaps Erudite – bent down and grabbed his shirt front, heaved him into a sitting position, propped him against the base of the chair. "Let's have you and your little friend together. It makes a lovely tableau."

Holding his aching face, Billy looked up at them. Today the dandies were dressed in linen suits, creased and coloured like tobacco leaf. Creamy cotton shirts. Yellow silk ties. Identical brass-rimmed spectacles with so many lenses in place they looked opaque. They both held something in their hands.

"Let the boy go." His jaw was agony. "He doesn't deserve this."

"Oh, you know, you're quite right. Your poor little rat here has been very helpful, hasn't he, Innocent?"

"Oh, most helpful. We'd never have thought to look for you here." Innocent made a sad face. "Unfortunately, it's too late."

"What have you done?" Billy spat, there was dark blood in his saliva.

"Well," Erudite crouched so that he could see him better. "First we showed him this." The Courier was quick about holding up the paper. Billy barely even registered the word: *Watch*, but suddenly his eyes were wide, staring, taking in everything. Erudite stood up and was replaced by his brother, who slowly unfurled a second paper, smoothed it flat on the floor. "And then," his murmur, like a cat's purr, "we showed him this."

The paper was plain and the ink was the blackest Billy had ever seen. The three letters of the single word written there glittered. They said: *DIE*.

It was like suddenly realising that you are tired. A bone-deep weariness. A leadenness of the limbs, a sluggishness of the blood, a reluctance of the lungs.

A heavy heart.

This must be what it felt like to be institutionalised. Sentence upon sentence delivered with the ink of Roach, the paper of Creasey. It was capitulation to utter despair.

Somewhere in the kitchen there was laughter and then receding footsteps, but he paid them no attention. All he could see was the sign that told him to die. Slumped against the chair, Billy stared at the word and felt his body obey.

He tried to resist. He didn't have to give in to this. Alicia may have used all her skills to create this paper, but it was still made from wood. He tried to shift his attention from the black to the white. But it was too hard, they were inseparable.

Then there wasn't just the sign. There was a person sitting on the floor beyond it. Even as he continued to stare at the word in front of him he was aware of them, legs crossed, making a lap of work-spoiled corduroy in which nimble fingers caressed a pristine sheet. The fingers were attached to hands, to lightly scarred forearms extending from brazenly rolled-up shirt sleeves. A hint of ink. A face right at the periphery of his awareness. Billy became aware that Alicia Creasey was talking to him, although he could not say how long she had been talking for.

"...such a shame," she was saying. "But then you have proved so disappointing, so perhaps it is no loss. I'll leave it there I think. The Bellos want you dead, and you are no use to me."

As she talked, her fingers worked. The paper's edges were precise, the corners sharp. Under her painstaking foldings and scorings, the page took on a new geometry.

"I'm following your example, you see, Mr Braid." Her brow showed strata of concentration. "You've set a trend. Self-determination is the new vogue in Karpentine. Doing what you..." She put a lot of force into scoring first one long diagonal and then another, "...*like.*"

Billy felt about as far from being able to do what he liked as he could imagine. He couldn't hear his own pulse in his ears. He couldn't feel his breath.

"Of course," for a moment she appeared to be talking to herself, "free will brings its own challenges, and responsibilities. I wasn't expecting to have to make *another* of these today, and bladeweight is *so* expensive." Alicia looked up, smiled, then shuffled closer, holding up what she'd made of the paper. A long thing, a sharp thing. A knife. "What a thing it is, though, to be unbound by stricture. See, if I *liked*, Billy..." she pointed the tip at his face "...I could kill you. Right now." The paper knife slashed the air. "Or free you." Alicia leant forward and applied the edge of her blade to the deathly note. Paper parted paper. If he had been capable he might have felt hope, but in any case Alicia sliced off just the corner. The text that was killing him and Vern remained intact. She let the scrap tumble to the floorboards in front of where Billy sat and now he could see the grey-pencilled digits written on it.

"My research into ink-resistance never did work out. Maybe if I'd been able to get my hands on one of your sylvans, even just a piece, but... Alicia does not get those sorts of favours, does she?" She effected a sarcastic moue. "Time for a more direct approach. What I am going to do... what I *like*... is go down to that Exchange and take back what is rightfully mine."

In an eyeblink, she was gone. There was just the killing paper lying on the ancient floorboards, the sound of dripping water from the sink. And Vern. He didn't even know if the boy was still... Well, it didn't matter now. There was nothing he could do, and he didn't expect anyone to come and rescue them. Not even Alicia's beautiful animax.

The light changed. Dimmer, darker. He felt a surprising twist of panic at the thought that his sight was failing, but reason told him it was merely the lanterns in the room winding down. Time was passing.

He stared at the paper's sundered corner. The pencilled number had three digits. Hundreds of attempts to produce paper whose compliance enhanced the deadly obeisant ink. And it had paid off. He wondered how many attempts Alicia had gone through in her desperation to find a paper that resisted compellant before she turned to this. More or less? How many times she had cut herself, her failure hurting more than the physical pain. Would sylvan motes have made a difference? They might have done, but Moraine Otterbree had foreseen that possibility and had stockpiled the sylvan remains to pre-empt anyone using their motes against her.

Again, a glimmer of emotion. This time it *was* hope. How much mastery did Alicia Creasey really have over paper? She was gifted, but an amateur. Wasn't it possible that there might be some flaw, some weakness there? He needed to keep trying. Once more, Billy made himself stare at the paper not the ink, the white not the black. Fought to think about the fibres not their stain. Willed them to dissolve, or catch fire. Or, simply, for the words to fade. He concentrated so hard that his brain hurt and his body shook. He passed out.

The light had dimmed again, but nothing else had changed. The paper was there, and he was still compelled to stare. His world, what remained of it, was the paper and those ancient, uncared-for floorboards. Mountain oak, he recognised. Once they had been stained and varnished. In more prosperous times the kitchen staff would have danced an industrious ballet on this floor, a weaving of heels and trolley wheels, and at the end of the day every corner of it would have been mopped until it gleamed. Now it was beyond dirty. A landscape of hardened pulp and splinters, the boards peeling and soft, dust and spoiled food gumming the cracks that had once been invisible joins. *This wood is dead*, he thought. *Like a sylvan, long returned to its old grove.* He could almost smell the must of slow reclamation. He wondered if that was to be his fate too. If anyone would find him and Vern before they too had softened and become cloaked in a furze of black and blue and livid green.

The light changed again. The dregs of the lantern glow replaced by an insipid illumination from somewhere else. The window, perhaps. Billy found that he could breathe out, a shallow exhalation that nevertheless emptied his lungs. Then he took a shuddering gasp in and coughed, choking on the very pungent reality of air clogged with spores.

The killing paper had become patterned with a thin fur, the moulder extending to, or perhaps originating from, the rotten boards beneath and the words all but obliterated. Billy stretched out his leg and kicked, and the note crumbled to bits.

Billy laughed with relief. It hurt his lungs and made the blood in his head pound, but he laughed anyway. Whatever gift his motes bestowed on him may never have been of much use to others, but he was grateful nevertheless.

"Vern!" Billy twisted around and saw the lad in the chair, but the physical alertness that had made him sit up stiff and straight and stare at the paper had departed his body. Now he was slumped to one side, his chin resting on his chest, his eyes open and seeing nothing at all.

A raw, animal sound emanated from Billy's mouth. It would up and up, voicing the despair of his failures. He raged and he roared. He rioted around the Creaseys' kitchen, tumbling paper everywhere he went. When he was spent, he sagged down beside the boy, and touched his limp hair.

Had there ever been a chance for him and his family in this awful place? He picked up Augustin Creasey's old blanket from the floor and tucked it around the boy in the chair. From the look, he might only have been sleeping but he was most certainly dead.

And he wasn't the only one. In the entry hall, Billy found the buck kneeling on a drift of paper. Its throat had been opened and it had bled out. The sticky red of the pages beneath it already drying, resembling winter leaves on snow.

Then a voice echoed in Billy's head, an image of a plump apple, russet on the branch and ripe as could be. He looked up and saw the dormant sylvans gathered at the foot of the staircase. Two dozen slender shapes. They must have been packed even tighter into that attic room than he'd thought. The voice thought came again. The ripe apple, ready to fall.

It is time, the sylvans said.

TWENTY-SEVEN

At first Billy put it down to his ordeal in the Creaseys' kitchen. The lightheadedness, the shortness of breath. The guilt of Vern's death. But that notion dispersed when he and his new companions stepped outside the mansion. A cloudmass the colour of rotten apples now blanketed the city so low that it all but touched the chimneys of the two highest homes. Skeins of yellow mist trailed like dewy gauze and the air tasted so foetid out here that Billy gagged. As he passed the fountain, he spat bitter saliva into its bowl.

A shivering fracture of lightning and an accompanying thunder crash snapped his attention away from his immediate surroundings. Looking down over the High Town, the lowtown rooftops beyond almost lost in settling fog, he saw that the perimeter of the blanket was a besieging ring of thunderheads. The clouds hadn't run out of ideas after all.

The lightning came again. It flashed close to the city gate, the only egress from the city's beautiful walls, built to keep the underachieved out but now just as effectively keeping the populace in. Two more strikes erupted on the opposite side of the hill. Down in the bay, boats attempting to gain open water were foundering and aflame. Billy couldn't discern distinct thoughts from the clouds but there was an air of entrenchment about it all.

The first clue as to what the clouds had in mind came as he and the sylvans descended the great staircase. An animax hound, its fur sleek as honeyed silk, its features refined characteristically just beyond nature, lay on one polished step. The dog's head lolled and its ribs shivered. As Billy approached, it whimpered and licked its frothed lips.

Billy would have stopped, but the sylvans didn't break stride. *Down,* they said.

The second clue came in the High Town where a mustardish mist hung, cloying in the streets. The few people out this early were dazed, pale and sweating. Their faces, masks of docility. Those that even noticed Billy and the sylvans managed only to stare, slack-jawed, as they passed. Once, as they hurried down a residential street, Billy thought he heard a voice thought amid the echoing knock of wooden feet. But it was not a sylvan whisper. He looked around and found himself facing an agitated man framed in a window. First he pointed at Billy, and then he yelled and banged on the pane. Billy rushed on.

At the Exchange, the mist thickened to a bilious soup. And the sylvans' arrival was greeted by sounds of an altercation echoing across the great plaza. Peering through the fog, Billy made out a clot of people shouting and jostling with guards. A *lot* of guards, he thought, although the figures were indistinct and formless. There couldn't be anyone of any import in the Exchange itself to protest to so early in the day, but the complex was an obvious place to vent for those that were free-minded enough to do so.

"Wait." Billy ducked into an alley. "We need to be cautious." Apparently in agreement, the sylvans did so. The rough alley walls had sported a row of posters, but they had either been torn down or painted over with *The Law For All* in rushed red letters. Another indication that not everyone had been rendered docile by Otterbree's ink. Not for the first time, Billy gave silent thanks to the Sisters, even though there surely couldn't be nearly enough liberated souls in the city to make any kind of stand against this assault – there was no other word for it – on the liberty of Karpentine's people. Giteau, he realised, had been right all along.

"Where now?" His whisper sounded loud in the blanketed air, and he thought he heard the words echoed back to him, rendered sullen and mocking. If it was a voice thought, his companions did not acknowledge it. They edged back out onto the plaza. Grouped close together, he supposed they might pass for people blundering around in the fog in search of clean air. Nevertheless, he hoped that the guardsmen remained occupied by the protestors until they had passed into the lowtown.

The final clue was the starling that fell like a stone out of the stinking sky. Seconds later, another hit the mosaicked bricks and then there followed a horrible downpour, an entire gyre of stricken feathered corpses plummeting to the ground, scattering the citizens and guards alike in search of shelter.

That was when the kudo dropped all the way. Only days ago the clouds would have tittered or brayed when they did something destructive like this. Now they remained silent, but there was an undeniable air of grim pleasure. It filled the plaza as completely as the fog… No, it *came from the fog*. And the source of the pleasure was a clear and single-minded determination to kill every living thing within the city walls. Withholding the air until all were dead. Because that was the surest way to destroy every creature with awakened motes.

"This is what you meant?" Billy whispered to Freshet, the sylvan with the missing eye and the teardrop mark on its heartwood. "This is what you were preparing for."

It was always coming, the sylvan replied. *This and what follows.*

"But what can we do?"

We do what we can.

After the birds finished falling there was a moment of shocked silence before the shouting resumed. As the original protestors reassembled and renewed their attempts to access the Exchange, a cohort of the defending guardsmen peeled off to form a cordon across one of the main routes out of the lowtown. An additional group had appeared from that direction. The closest ones resolved from outlines to individuals and Billy recognised their leader's sharp features. Finlay Giteau.

As the sylvans continued their stealthy traverse, Billy saw that the guards wore those reflecting lenses over their eyes and bandanas across their mouths, and that they carried rifles. They looked like an army of toymaker's automata.

"...such treatment of your fellow man is not only contrary to the Law, it is *inhuman.*" Giteau's invective was punctuated by a hack of phlegm onto the stones. "People are suffocating down there. You *have* allow us to bring them up to the High Town, to air they can actually breathe." Of the people with him, some were disorientated. Some were sickly and needed support from heartier comrades. The guard cordon remained eerily silent and gave not an inch of ground, making Billy wonder grimly how their orders had been conveyed.

Giteau snarled: "Please... the aged and infirm at least." When he attempted to pass, the nearest guardsman shoved him back. Giteau bellowed with frustration and charged his opponent. Still silent, the uniformed figure swung his rifle butt and cracked him across the cheek. Giteau went down, blood pouring from a gash under his eye. His followers yelled, but unless they dropped their sickly comrades they could do nothing. It didn't matter anyway, because the scuffle had attracted the attention of the free-willed protestors over at the Exchange and the situation was about to become even more complicated.

Throughout all of this, the sylvans didn't so much as pause, their tall outlines disappearing into the fog. Billy followed. There was nothing else he could do.

*

Alone, Billy would have taken hours to find the Institute of Improvement. In the fog every street, every cross, every corner was identical, but the sylvans navigated without error. With every step, the presence in the fog became stronger. Every time he spun around, he expected to see… *something*, dogging their footsteps. And every time it was just the coils and billows of tobacco-spit vapour. But he knew it was there.

As Giteau had described, the sweltering air was chokingly thick down here, the sulphurous taint seasoned further by the tang of the harbour. It made Billy's lungs tight and his breath shallow, made his head both swim and throb. He began to glimpse forms lying motionless in the streets but, again, the sylvans strode on without pause. They'd said they were going to do what they could. He'd assumed that meant to help people. Bewildered, he followed on.

Just before the Institute square, they finally came to a halt. "What now?" Billy whispered, feeling the now familiar dread of proximity to the place, but instead of entering the square the sylvans found a corner and then stopped there. "Well?" They were still as trees. Devoid of thought or life, just as they had been in Alicia's attic room. "Freshet!" He shook the sylvan's arm, but it stood firm and didn't reply.

What was he supposed to do now?

The swirling fog cleared momentarily, and Billy was able to see properly into the square. It was packed. Erstwhile inmates in sweat-soiled uniforms were slumped on the ground all over the square, but other people passed among them, aiding and organising. More of Giteau's free-minded, he guessed. Inside the Institute grounds, more of them were leading prisoners out of the dormitories and coaxing shuffling Institutionalised up from their hellish silo. There were no guards here to stop them. It was obviously considered more important now to deploy manpower to protect the High Town air from the undeserving lungs of the underachieved. As far as those up the hill were concerned, those below could all survive together or die together.

Para wouldn't have stood for that if she'd been in any position to influence things. Billy wondered what she was doing now. If she was here. He began looking, but quickly gave up because all the eyes of helper and needy alike were red and streaming, all the mouths covered by cloth. In the fog, everyone looked the same.

"You there."

He whirled because the tone was so like her. The speaker, taking a moment to rest a handcart piled with boxes labelled IoI STORES, even had something of Para's poise too, but she was older, her expression sour and her scraped back blonde-grey hair a million miles from the bounce of Para's curls.

"What?" The word felt like it was sucked out of him, his lungs shrinking around its absence lest he breathe in any more of the fog than was absolutely necessary.

The woman wore a sweat-patched vest, shorts, boots and a loop of wet shirt sleeve around her neck that she'd been using as a mask. She shook out her muscles. Then in a lowtown accent, the strain in her voice from overuse or simply breathing the fog now evident, she said, "Have you come to help or what?"

"Sorry," Billy wheezed. In truth he didn't know why the sylvans had brought him here. "My track record of helping people isn't so great."

With unexpected compassion she held her hands up, fingers splayed. "You've got two of these, haven't you?" Her lips turned out something like a smile. "Come on. We'll have a lot more chance of persuading them up top to allow us to breathe their air if we arrive with our own food and water. You can do that, can't you? Be a Porter?" She tapped the handles of the cart. "We're using a masons' warehouse in Helpmeet Street. You know where that is?"

Billy nodded, but he didn't move to take the cart from her. The things she was saying... His heart raced.

"What is it, Mister Braid?" He started at hearing his name. "Oh, we know your face. It's not like we don't see it everywhere." Then her expression hardened again. "Bit of a celebrity, are you? Too special to do the same work as everyone else?"

"Of course not." Billy couldn't help reaching out. "But when did you see her?"

The woman eased away from his hand. "See who?"

Billy hesitated, but he hadn't imagined those phrases. *You've got two of these... You can be a Porter...* "You must have seen her."

When he reached for her again, the woman batted him away. "Oh, you've *lost* someone?" She waved to indicate the listless crowd, which Billy was certain had grown even larger over the course of this short conversation. Their collective breathing was like a sigh, but not as big a one as there should have been for so many people. "You're not the only one. And many more are going to be lost unless those of us who can do

306

something about it. They're relying on us." She heaved up the handles of the handcart, the muscles in her arms taut as cords. With a last look, she said: "You want my advice? Stop looking for someone you can't help and offer aid to someone you can."

Billy watched her weave through the crowd. He could almost believe that somehow… But that was just wishful thinking, which was the last thing he could afford right now. He was in no doubt, though, even if she hadn't admitted as much, that she'd been in Para's company at some point, been infected by her bullish attitude. In the face of all this, knowing that Para was around after all helped.

The gathering in the square was not only comprised of former inmates. Regular lowtowners had found their way here too, although their attire was the only way to tell them apart. They all shared the same vacant demeanour, the same feeble retention of the breath in their lungs. And that was the ones who, Billy knew without looking too closely at the stiller forms, hadn't surrendered even that to the noxious air. The free-minded toiled among them, harrying and cajoling, organising and shepherding and physically carrying the worst cases, but they were too few. Even if they managed to talk their way into the High Town, there would never be enough time to save all of these lives. This was a futile endeavour.

It was the pallid gold hair Billy recognised. Vern's sister sat propped against a wall, her mother's head in her lap. The only signs that the pair were still alive was their breathing, rapid as baby birds, the froth bubbling on the recumbent woman's grey lips and the mechanical motion of the girl's fingers as they combed her mother's hair. Both of them bore marks on their throats that looked for all the world like fingers had pressed there. Their own, perhaps, as they struggled to keep breathing.

"Clymie?" Billy crouched beside her, but he had to say her name again before she raised her head. Her crusted eyes took a moment to focus and then she smiled the meagrest of smiles.

"Mister Braid." Her voice was a whisper. "I'm happy to see that you are well and I'm sorry I couldn't find out any more." Every word pained her.

Billy made his face do something he hoped looked like a smile. "You found out more than we could have hoped for," he told her. "And the person who did this to your mam won't be doing it any more."

It seemed to take his words time to penetrate because Clymie nodded absently for a few moments before a smile widened and lit up her face. "I am glad." She raised her hand then as if to touch Billy's cheek but, her smile collapsing into a moue of distress, she grabbed a fistful of his shirt instead. "Where is Vern?" She cast around. "He's not here?"

Billy squeezed her hand gently because he had no words, no way of telling her that her brother was murdered and that he was to blame. All he could do was shake his head.

Clymie took that as an answer. "He's in the High Town then? He is safe?"

"He's in the High Town." That wasn't a lie and neither was what followed, but they gave her hope, and hope might help her survive a little longer. There would be time for the truth later. "He's in the High Town, and he has all the good air he needs."

Clymie beamed. "Well that's a piece of luck, isn't it?" She choked on the last two words. Hacked convulsively. If her mam was disturbed, she gave no sign. Clymie spat on the ground. "You still got the luck I gave you, then?" she said. "I know what you think of it, but you can't deny that it brought good fortune to you and Vern at least."

Billy only nodded, because what choked his own throat now was not the fog. He found his wallet in his pocket and extracted the scrap of embroidered cloth. The white cotton had become dingy but the brown of the tree trunk and branches was still strong, the green of its leaves vivid. "Here it is," he said. "It'll bring us all luck." It felt like the emptiest promise he had ever made.

He sat with them, mother and daughter. Sitting on the ground with his back to the brick. Here, they were a distance from the Institute gate and the other avenues of activity. Here, there were people just trying to breathe. The whispering sound of it was thin and insufficient. It softened the spirit. Billy felt the fight drain out of him like the wine from those poor abused clouds in the Weathermakers' ballroom. His body felt heavy and his head light. It was in many ways similar to how he had felt when he had been trapped by the Bello brothers' killing note. For all the good he was, it might have been better if the note had completed its work… No, while he still had breath and his two hands, there were still things he could do. In a minute, he'd get up and find something to carry up to Helpmeet Street. In a minute.

He stared across the square. The fog swirled over the recumbent forms, hiding and then revealing one person then another, as if by capricious whim. As if choosing who to kill next.

It should have been an impossible surprise when a billow of mist, coalescing over one of the Institutionalised formed into something that roughly resembled human shoulders, a swirling bolus of a head on top and two arms reaching for the man's pasty face, closing over his nose and mouth and holding them there for the mere seconds it took for the feeble convulsions to stop. It *should* have been, but Billy heard the quiet satisfaction that went with it, even as the fog coiled away from the dead man.

No, it was no surprise at all.

TWENTY-EIGHT

Once Billy became attuned to the notion that the weather was able to manifest vapour into something approximating human form, he saw it happening all over the square. Forms materialised out of the fog, suffocated the weakest and then dispersed.

"No, no, no," he whispered to himself and sprang to his feet, ready to tackle the next one that appeared. Poised, he started to doubt himself. They couldn't be real. No one else reacted to them in any way. Oh, the intent and the outcome were all too real, but rather than the weather somehow manifesting in a way that only he would see was it not more likely that his oxygen-starved brain was inventing them? They were near enough parodies of his beloved but absolutely useless sylvans after all. He just couldn't accept that people were dying all around him, and there was nothing he could do to prevent it.

Billy left Clymie and her mam and looked around to see if the woman in the vest had returned. He couldn't see her, but he did spot a commotion on the other side of the square so he went to find out what was going on.

A group of newcomers had arrived, carrying or dragging limp forms and placing them in a sheltered spot being used as a makeshift infirmary. It was populated already by several unfortunates bearing evidence of flash burns that suggested they had tried to escape the city. These new casualties had battered faces, broken limbs; one, a gunshot wound to the head. A shrewish lass had him propped up and was using a cloth to staunch the blood seeping from where his ear had been. It took Billy a second to recognise him. Marcus Golspie merely stared ahead. It was impossible to tell if he was ink-subdued or all but dead.

"There are too many of them and the bastards don't care who they kill." Finlay Giteau was slumped against the tenement bricks. He had escaped being shot, but his face was livid with blood and bruises. "We'd need an army."

"They've torched the supplies too." A circle of free-minded had quickly gathered. This speaker was a stout woman. There were a number of grim faces at her back, among them after all the woman that Billy had conversed with earlier.

"Not the Masons," the uncertain looking lass who had been treating Golspie piped up, Billy guessed out of some lingering family loyalty. "They wouldn't..."

"Someone has," the older woman cut back. She was exhausted. "Helpmeet Street is ablaze. It doesn't matter who did it. They're all the same."

"No, the Masons are a fair family. Always been evenly high and low..." The loyalist had a mouse-like nose that twitched as if it didn't believe the words coming out of her own mouth.

Giteau growled. His eye had swollen shut. "Yet, they have air, don't they? And not one of them has come down here to help."

"We still have air..." The Mason apologist was pitiful, as if begging everyone to disbelieve the evidence of their own lungs.

"Fucking High Towners." This was a lad barely out of his teens, his callow bravado already eroded sufficiently to reveal the childish fear that underlay it. "How can they get away with this?"

"The same way as they get away with everything else," Giteau replied grimly. "The right words, the right ink. Tell the story whatever way suits them – oh, *such* a tragedy, who on earth can be to blame? The High Towners will wring their hands dutifully and hang the Weathermakers from their own fucking tower."

The group seemed as deflated by this outburst as Billy already felt. No one in their hearts could deny it.

"Look." The mousy woman had collected herself a little. "Okay, so the High Towners are panicking. This fog is one of the worst things in memory, and someone will answer for it in due course, but... it's only *weather*. When the wind changes it'll clear away. If we just keep calm and wait it out..."

Billy watched half of the assembly nodding their heads. He could understand them wanting to believe it but they were horribly wrong. Even as they nodded, a billow of fog swirled into the infirmary behind them, shaped itself into arms that reached for the supine form of Golspie.

He made himself look away. "This fog isn't going to clear," he said.

All heads turned, someone spoke Billy's name like they were reading it off a wall poster and before he could react he was seized by the arms. "Oh, come on." He wriggled and wrenched, but the men who held him were strong. "I'm trying to help."

"The inglorious Billy Braid? Trying to *help*?" Giteau's sneer was lopsided. "You Weathermakers are the ones to blame for all this. I'd be amazed at you showing your face in the lowtown at all if your stupidity wasn't the greater part of your fame... oh, but of course." Giteau mimed slapping the side of his head as if he'd just remembered something. "Your family won't protect you now, will they? Not when you and your gobshite mistress are sought the city over."

"I'm not a Weathermaker," Billy protested. "I've never..."

"Shut him up." A hand came out of nowhere and gripped Billy's jaw like a vice. "We don't need to hear a word from you. But it is very good to see you, Billy. Very good indeed. Because now we have something they want. Thank you for volunteering."

"That's not going to work." The new speaker was the woman in the vest. Her face and hands were smudged with soot. "This laggard? Seriously? They don't care about him." She looked him over. Her eyes engaged his for an instant and then flicked dismissively away. "Look at him. They have no use for yokels like this. They might want him *dead* – and if you take him up there you'll certainly give them the perfect opportunity – but..."

"Wrong." Giteau shook his head. "If we give them Braid, we give them a chance of luring out Paraphernalia Loess."

The woman laughed at that. "You really think she cares about him? If that was the case why is he here, fending for himself? And you can see how good a job he's made of that."

Billy shook his jaw free of the fingers that held it. "She's right," he said. "Para won't come out of hiding for me."

"I told you to shut him up..."

"However," the woman said. "You *might* want to listen to him. If there's any truth at all to the rumours I've heard from the delivery lines."

"Oh, really, Anya?" Giteau stared at Billy but didn't repeat the order to silence him. "What can this idler possibly know?"

Anya's smile was enigmatic. "He worked with the Weathermakers and he studied under Benoit Kim, so he knows about motes. Isn't that right, *Porter*?"

Those same words again. Now Billy stared at this Anya. The way she delivered them... if he closed his eyes it was exactly like talking to Para. It couldn't be, but... *She had gone to the Sisters and they had done something disappear to, something to change her in body. And it couldn't be a small thing to disguise Paraphernalia Loess. It had to be...*

312

Everything.

And now he suddenly knew, because... *Porter, again...* she wanted him, and only him, to know that this person *was her.* Hiding in plain sight and doing – as she'd promised – all that one pair of hands could do. It must be killing her to remain anonymous but to announce herself would be to give herself up as Giteau's hostage, so she was trying to tell Billy something. And he knew what that was, and it chilled him.

"I am not a Weathermaker," he began, "but, as this lady says, I have worked with them." He almost lost his nerve then. What could he say? How could he expect people to take him seriously if he told them that the clouds had thoughts, let alone a murderous will? He couldn't help but glance at Golspie. The clot of fog had cleared and he was very still. How could he tell these people that even now the clouds were calmly squeezing the life out of every person in the lowtown, and after that would move on to the High Town too. No, talk of intelligence would make him sound crazy. He had to make it sound like it was all about the motes.

"I can tell you that the Weathermakers are screwed," he went on. "They don't understand these motes a hundredth as well as they thought they did and they've completely lost control now. The Weathermakers can no more put a stop to this fog than I could bring a smile to Moraine Otterbree's face." The gathering muttered in growing consternation. "But someone can."

Giteau didn't look like he believed one word. "And who might that be?"

"Stillworth Crane."

"And exactly how would the Constructors acquire the knowledge to control the weather?" Giteau scoffed.

"Not the Constructors. Just Stillworth." Billy felt the hands that gripped him loosen a little and shook his arms free. "As to how he came by the knowledge, believe me that is quite a story and I look forward very much to the world hearing it when this is all over. However, the knowledge he possesses is not how to control it but how to stop it. He has built..." He could hardly force the words past his lips, "...a bomb that has the power to kill motes." It chilled him because using it meant destroying the sylvans. And who knew what would happen to people like himself, the Sisters, and the Turners who now lived within Sister Sin?

"And what will this bomb accomplish?"

"I believe it will make the weather behave more naturally. Once the motes are deactivated, the fog, the clouds, all of it should I think disperse in time. But…"

"You can vouch for this, Anya?" Giteau glanced at the woman who was Para. "He could be making all of this up to save his skin. Is that what you want, Braid? To be sent up there to sneak back to your masters. How do we know you'd even come back?"

A grim smile came to Anya's lips. "The bomb exists. It was ported from Radlett Hall to the Exchange last night and I happened to be present at a demonstration of a much smaller prototype for the high ups." A genuine shudder gripped her and involuntarily she touched her temple. "It is very effective."

So, Para had lost her own motal awareness. Whether through what the Sisters had done to her or by being too close to Stillworth's demonstration, she was now as deaf to the voices of the weather as everyone else. But she still knew the danger.

"Fine then," Giteau said. "There's no time to lose." He turned to the stout woman and the angry youth. "Kirsten, Hassim. Go with Anya up to the Exchange. Tell the guards we'll swap Billy Braid for an audience with Stillworth Crane."

"No, wait…" Billy said. "The bomb will kill *all* the motes. We have to allow the sylvans to leave first…" *And the Sisters*, he wanted to say. And everyone who had a little something special in them because they had been awakened, whether they knew the reason or not. But it was impossible to save everyone.

Giteau scoffed again. "People are dying. Do you expect more do so for the sake of toys?"

"Master Giteau is right, son." Everyone turned to see who had joined the conversation and none were more surprised than Billy to see that it was Benoit Kim. And that, behind him, stood a host of sylvans. Dozens of them. There were clearly many more survivors from the first battle than Billy had imagined and they must have squirreled themselves away in pockets all over the city. They all bore scars and damage to their beautiful forms. "The sylvans did not come all the way to Karpentine merely to walk home again."

"Then why *did* they come?" Desperation made him shout it.

In response to this, the sylvans at the front of the group, among them Freshet and Chop, all spoke together. Impressions of ripe fruit filled Billy's mind. *It is time.* And almost as the chorus of sylvan speech had begun, he sensed a growling, snarling backwash and the fog in the square thickened and swirled. The stink intensified unbearably and the square's population started gasping and coughing in distress.

Kim's eyes and nose were streaming. "Your people will not last much longer in this," he told Giteau. "I suggest you go about your plan now."

"Are you still here?" Giteau gave Kirsten and the lad a shove to get them on their way. Anya, however, had already made herself scarce. Billy wondered what plan she had.

"As for him." Giteau choked around the words, spat and wiped his mouth with his hand. "Make sure he goes nowhere." The burly men who had held him earlier moved in on him again, but this time their way was blocked by Chop and Freshet.

"Billy won't go anywhere." Kim's voice was barely a croak. "He has work to do."

Billy stared at the old man. "What are you talking about?" Very little air seemed to be getting to his lungs now. Each word came in an aching pant. The fog swirled and thickened and everyone but the master beside him vanished. Billy felt the vapour on his skin like the gentle but repellent touch of someone he loathed. His vision swam and an arm appeared around the old man's neck, forced itself under his chin in a choke hold. Kim's eyes went wide.

"Hurry," he gasped.

"What?" The word squeaked out of him as a crushing weight pressed on both his chest and back at the same time. It felt like knuckles thrust against him. "Tell me…"

You already know. A face materialised out of the fog. Dark and oval, eyes of milky opaline. Chop's battered face seemed to be growing a leprous patina, something that softened and mouldered the wood even as Billy noticed it. So, the fog was as destructive to sylvans as it was to humans. There would be little left of any of them if something wasn't done soon. But what? The sylvans kept saying that it was time. *Time for what?*

Then Billy felt the sylvan's good hand close around his own and place it on the ruined stump of the other. And in his mind he was shown an image that was also a memory. A sapling planted in snow and grown with slow patience over the years; a sapling that was also a boy who was given a long dead twig and asked: *what would you do with this? Plant it,* had been his answer. *Make it grow.* And yes he could do that. It was his one paltry ability, after all. He could heal living wood and make the dead

315

wood grow, bring forth branches and leaves. And... *of course*, leaves might turn at least a little of the bad air into good. And he realised now that he must have done exactly this before – because where else had the tree come from that had saved him from the Bellos? He had heard a sylvan voice, and the sylvan had answered his need even as he fell. Changed to save him. At his will. Yes, he could give these people the gift of good air, if only for a limited time. And it might be enough to keep them alive until the High Towers could be persuaded to explode Stillworth's bomb. But it would still mean the end of the sylvans.

"No," Billy told Chop. "They're not worth it."

None of them?

Billy had already started shaking his head, but Chop cut in.

This day was inevitable and we made this decision long ago. It is our nature. As it in is yours, and the nature of all the world. Chop repeated the image of the slow growing sapling. *We prepared you for this*, it said. *For now and for what comes after.*

The logic was, as ever, without guile or complication. Billy closed his eyes and gripped Chop's stump tighter and imagined the sylvan when it had been whole. Imagined it when it had been newly assembled. Imagined the healthy copse of trees that had produced its wood. The ironwood, the teak, the ash. The willow, beech and birch. The wirebush all around. The comingled profusion of their leaves. The sweet and spicy, vital nectar of the air around them. He imagined breathing it now, that sweet air swelling his chest instead of the sickening mist. He imagined it so hard that he could taste it.

Around him he heard gasps. Opening his eyes, he found that Chop had grown branches, a thicket of new wood. They jutted up and outward from its chest and shoulders and arms, and each branch sprouted twigs and on each of those, vibrant green leaves unfolded. As the sylvan raised its arms, twigs and leaves continued to burgeon.

Billy breathed out, and in again. The air was notably clearer. The fog too had cleared enough for him to see that Kim was recovering. "Now do the rest, son," the old man wheezed. "Quickly."

Billy focussed and, with the sylvans' acquiescence, made it happen. In a way it was like watching a forest fire spread. In the rustle and creak of growth, and in the brightness of the greenery that caught and flared and jumped from sylvan to sylvan. As soon as the foliage began to sprout, each sylvan walked off to find somewhere to dispel the fog a little, bring respite to the people wherever they were to be found.

316

It took a long while and, by the time the last sylvan had been transformed, Billy was exhausted. He watched the nearest one, more tree than figure now, but so dignified in its sacrifice. Utterly different and yet no less beautiful.

He felt the old man's hand on his shoulder. "Well done, son."

Billy squinted into Kim's face. "It's not good enough," he said.

"Don't be so hard on yourself," Kim replied, although he could not disguise his concern as he observed the sylvan. The soft grey patches of scummy patina, the browning curl of the edge of its leaves. "It buys us some time."

"I don't mean for us." Billy pulled himself to his feet. "I mean for them."

Entranced by the miracle of the walking trees, no one tried to stop him leaving for the High Town.

TWENTY-NINE

Even Kim. That was the thought that smouldered like kindling as he stomped and stumbled up the network of steps and thoroughfares towards the Exchange. Even the old man, whose hands had birthed each and every one, hadn't paused for a second when it came to the notion of whether it was *right* to explode the bomb. When weighed against the lives of humans, those of the sylvans were of no value. After all, they were not people. They were merely things.

He came across one at a junction, now twice as tall as it had been in the square and so thick with shimmering foliage that it had become too unstable to go further.

Such a sacrifice. And they were all very grateful, the lowtowners, but if they could have the bomb too, please, that would be perfect. Kill off those pesky clouds, erase the Weathermakers' mistakes and start again, and if the sylvans had to die too, well... they were *very* grateful.

It was no different to the attitude the city dwellers had shown to the Kinster refugees. Or that the High Towners were even now displaying with extreme cruelty to the low. Where was the Book's sacred *every hand the same* in all of that?

As Billy began the final climb towards the Exchange, he readied himself for a fight, but he found the plaza in disarray. When he had passed this way with the sylvans, there had been perhaps a few dozen free-minded citizens remonstrating against the compelled guards. Now there were hundreds here, enough to have overpowered the guard cordon and started attacking the doors of the Trades Hall with a makeshift battering ram whose impacts rang out across the plaza.

He couldn't work out at first how Skin had managed to free so many minds. It was only when he saw that many of them were around his age or younger that he realised. Like him and Para and the Sisters, they were naturally awakened. Enough to resist being compelled, at least, and who knew what other talents and advantages they might secretly possess but rarely dared to use?

In the lee of the labour exchange lay a number of unconscious uniformed figures. Their jackets had been removed, shirts ripped, and on every scrap of exposed flesh Billy saw angry marks, blood and ink.

Hastily stippled winged cats. Now that he was closer to the crowd he spotted that there were guard uniforms among those that toted the ram too. Their faces were set with cold determination. Billy imagined that if he'd just been awakened to find that he'd been forced to shoot at his friends and neighbours, he might also have a taste for retribution. He scanned the faces for Anya, Kirsten and Hassim, but couldn't see them. They must have sought another entrance.

The protestors ran the ram one more time at the doors, and there was an audible crack, followed by a sort of breathless cheer that collapsed into a fit of coughing. Billy felt it too, sticking in his throat, the stench of it plugging up his nostrils. The fog had returned to the plaza and there were shapes moving in it. Figures, only superficially human, that matched the free-minded for every ounce of their determination.

Billy ran. First he went to the car compound, but the door there was locked. As he toured the complex, he found with increasing frustration every door the same. It was so stupid. If the families were in there, they wouldn't simply barricade themselves in. They would have a plan.

The spider would have a plan… and Para would certainly have guessed what it was.

The ramp down into the Inksmiths' and Papermakers' enclave was eerily silent. The vats were still and the gangways deserted. Billy found the freight elevator at the back of the bottling area. The grind of the mechanism and the chatter of its chains put his heart in his mouth as the caged platform rose slowly. When it came to a clanking rest, however, there were no guards with rifles waiting for him. Just some empty trollies in the open area from which several grimy service passages radiated. He let out a shuddering breath and pressed on.

The passages had signs he had been too busy running to notice the last time he was here: *Judiciary, Labour Ex, Civic Records,* and the like. Billy followed the one for the Trades Hall. After the first couple of corners, the dirty brick was replaced by flagstones and plaster. After another, and a slight incline, the passage had doors. None of this was familiar. He couldn't visualise how close he might be to his destination, so he had to check each one. Sure enough, at the first door on the next stretch of corridor he heard voices. Not the belligerent shouting match he expected from the hall itself although, while quietly spoken, the tenor of the exchange didn't lack for invective. Inching the door open, he peered into a store room. Cartons of paper filled the ceiling-high shelves on one side. Gallon jars of darkling ink were racked on their sides along the other.

Between them, two women faced each other. A tall one and a tiny one. Both rigid with fury.

"Say that again." Alicia Creasey paced like a restless lion. She pointed a white finger at her adversary like a weapon. "I dare you."

Moraine Otterbree's lips curled into a vicious smile. "Oh, you heard me perfectly well, my dear. The one silver lining around this accursed fog is the hope that it'll finish the old fool off for good. I don't need him, and I certainly don't need you. And as for that neglected pile of rubble you call a home? Let's just say I'm looking forward to improving my view."

"Oh, you don't need me?" Alicia snarled. "Really? You're not at all interested in developing new papers to actually compliment your inks? And you're not remotely interested in retaining the supply of that extraordinary new boneblack..."

"I *most certainly* am not." Otterbree snapped.

Alicia squawked a disbelieving laugh. "You can't be serious. Not after seeing its power. It controls *everybody*."

"I am deadly serious. Have you *seen* what's happening out there? Right now there are hundreds of very angry people trying to enter this building to demand answers. That's very fucking far from *everybody*. They know that someone tried to control them against their will and they want answers."

"So? Do it again, make it stronger. Or are you afraid now? Is the great Moraine Otterbree actually scared of wielding the power afforded to her by her station?" Alicia snorted. "Move aside and let someone with some balls take over."

Otterbree had stilled. "How long do you think you would last trying to rule this city, using enforced obeisance on that scale? Hmm? They'd string you up from the Tower Of Hands." She steepled her fingers. "Here's how this whole unfortunate event is going to be reported: in the midst of the recent high state of emergency, the justiciary regrettably felt it necessary to order the placement around the city of posters to impose civic control. So large was the order that the Inksmiths were forced to make a new batch of the rarely used obeisant ink. And, while the recipe was the same as always, the boneblack used – which had been bought in good faith from a new vendor and had not yet been tested – turned out to be horribly potent. It was a terrible misfortune and steps have been taken to make sure it is never repeated."

Alicia stood beside the ink racks with her back to Billy. "You're a fool." She produced something from her coat. Something angular and white. With a flick of the wrist, a cork fell to the floor and the nearest jar began to empty itself in dark arterial pulses. She dipped the tip of the bladeweight knife into the stream, watched it change from white to black. "You're seriously going to give this up? What's to stop me walking out of here and finding another buyer?"

"You are welcome to try, Alicia." Otterbree's smile looked weary now. "But you should know that, in the days to come, the provenance of that boneblack will be thoroughly investigated, and its source revealed. These monstrous, undeserved acts inflicted on our citizens. The identity of the monster who perpetrated them..."

"You can't do that." Alicia flicked her weapon accusingly at Otterbree. Black drops flew from it, sparkled in the air. The bladeweight did not appear remotely diminished by the liquid it had taken on. "Think of what you're giving up!"

"Giving up?" Otterbree neatly stepped away from the growing puddle. "I already have everything I want. I'm not giving it up, I'm keeping it. Heed this lesson, girly. This is how you stay in power."

"By making a scapegoat of your own family?"

"Killick is as guilty as a liar's purse. He deserves everything that's coming to him. As will anyone who appears to be closely associated with him." She raised her eyebrows airily. "That's why you won't find a buyer for your dirty boneblack. Now, if you'll excuse me, I need to instruct some men about a bomb..."

Billy shrank back from the door, but the dainty clip of Otterbree's shoes receded. The storeroom must have another exit, one that led to the Trades Hall. Through the crack, he only saw in fragments what happened next. He heard Alicia say: "You are inexcusable." Then there was a sudden movement, a flash of black and white, a sound like the parting of silk. A soft sigh. He let the door ease shut again when he heard the sound of something slumping to the floor.

Billy stood in the corridor, paralysed by what he had witnessed. He couldn't tell if the ragged breathing he heard was Alicia's or his own. He waited until he heard another door opening and closing. Then he waited a few minutes longer, and finally steeled himself to look inside.

Moraine Otterbree's body lay curled like a petite question mark. Her eyes and mouth were open in an expression of sad surprise similar to the one Billy had seen on his mother's face many times when he'd chosen to disregard some entry or other in the Book that no one else ever even questioned. The paper knife jutted from her neck. The pool of blood spreading from around her head met the ink spill. Red and black, swirling together.

Now that he was inside the storeroom, Billy could see the door that he guessed led to the main hall. When he stepped around the spider's body he saw that he even had a trail to follow. Inky paw prints. He hadn't been the only witness to Alicia's crime, then. There was a Bastipol around.

He followed the cat's trail through a maze of turns and junctions. Easily at first, but they faded quickly and ran out entirely halfway along a corridor. He followed it anyway until he recognised where he was. This was the one that was decorated with wall hangings. At the end were the doors that led to the Trades Hall lobby. They had been jammed shut with an iron bar and from the edge of desperation in the hoarse shouts coming from the other side, it was clear that the free-minded mob had finally gained entry to the building.

Finding the hanging with the cat and the bird, he pulled it back to reveal the stairs and climbed up to greet the Sisters. Sin lay along the row of seats. Skin sat beside her. Where Skin's palm rested on her sister's cheek, the flesh looked healthy but the rest of her was ashen. Her breath rattled and she shivered in jagged fits, despite the cloak of cats that had arranged themselves around her for warmth and solace. And despite his master's old coat. She looked lost inside it, as if she was shrinking. The garment reminded him of the responsibilities he had shucked off. He looked away. Skin stared grimly down into the hall, the predictable sounds of whine and bicker rising up. Only the Bastipols acknowledged Billy's approach.

"Is this what you planned?" he asked Skin. "When you said you wanted to shake things up."

The Sister's voice was a hoarse murmur. "The details? Of course not. Who could have predicted all this?" She nodded to herself. "But the outcome? The destruction of all that pointless pontification, that artifice? Oh, yes. Very much so. All foundations crumble. All towers fall."

"*Is* it destroyed?"

"Listen to them. They can't even agree on how to save themselves."

Billy leaned out and saw the great table, the people around it, very much as he'd seen them before, except most of the second circle and the functionaries were absent, as was the gallery. In their place stood a phalanx of stiff guardsmen. Stillworth Crane's bomb sat on a trolley in front of the thrones of the Papermakers and the Inksmiths. From this distance it didn't look so dangerous, resembling not much more than a prize-winning pumpkin on display at the harvest fair in Canza, but his heart clenched all the same. Not least because the closest person to it at that moment was Alicia Creasey. She took no part in the toing and froing, as if where this bomb might be exploded barely mattered. She had what she wanted, after all. For now, she lounged, stretched out between her father's chair and that of his erstwhile wife. In the seat behind that had traditionally been hers, Killick Roach sat meekly, smiling happily to himself despite the satisfying mess that was his face.

After listening for a minute, it became clear that a gloating Stillworth, supported by his father and the lumber and ore masters, advocated detonating his device at the top of the hill to be closer to the clouds. It was all arranged, he claimed. Billy wondered that, given the freedom of his tattoo, he hadn't just gone ahead and done so. For all his bold words to his father, perhaps some filial responsibility remained in him. On second thought, it was more likely that he wanted this opportunity to grandstand and be publicly lauded for his achievement. If so, he had clearly been disappointed. The younger Crane became increasingly agitated as the remainder of the assembly, positing the fog as the primary threat, took laborious pains to put the case for exploding the device in the heart of the lowtown. At no point did any of them mention the risk to life, human or otherwise, of either plan. And no one asked Jelena Loess for her opinion. She sat stone-faced in her chair, apparently forgotten. Kirsten and Hassim loitered uncomfortably behind where Para would have sat. They looked even edgier than Stillworth, whom they watched like people who had just entrusted their life savings to a gambler.

There was still no sign of Anya. Could he have been wrong? Had Para made no attempt to influence these proceedings after all? He found that disappointing.

"Wild one..." Behind him, the whispered words blew from Sin's dry lips like dust from a derelict house. It was a whisper with echoes. When Billy knelt beside her and held her cold hand, he felt the stirrings of the Turners within her. Their fear. "You shouldn't be here," he told her, but was unsure if she heard him. Her eyes were open but she was looking at something over his shoulder. "You need to find a way to leave. I'm going to try and delay the explosion. I can give you maybe a couple of hours. The sylvans bought us enough time but you need to go now. Find a way out and..."

"And go where?" Skin, to the side, snapped.

"There is only one sky in this world, wild one." Sin's eyes widened as if she were looking at it right then.

"But the Turners..."

"They have their own sky, and it is beautiful and welcoming to all who would venture there."

Billy sighed, exasperated that her illness had detached her so far from reality. "But the motes in their box that make their world possible... *they* are in *this* world, and they are very close to a bomb that will destroy them."

He felt Skin's hand clasp his. "Then it is up to us to protect them."

Before he could ask her what she meant by that, there came a crash below that boomed around the ancient hall. It was quickly followed by a squawk of protest from one of the High Town speakers, that in turn was swamped by the roar of the incoming crowd.

Billy scrambled up and, together, he and Skin watched what was happening. The space, which seconds ago had been a place of stultified inaction, was now frantic. Free-minded were pouring through the broken doors, and with them came the fog. Even from this height he felt the onrushing animosity as it poured into the hall like an army, forming body shapes that overcame the guards before they even had time to set themselves in defence of their betters.

Those betters were in a state of utter panic. Billy saw the Ore Master go down under the boots of the free-minded and the Lumber Master purple in the face, throttled by the fog. He saw Merit Crane standing stiff as an iron post in disbelief, Alicia Creasey bellowing orders that no one paid any heed to, the blissfully oblivious Killick Roach disappearing under the scrum, and Lemuel Shankhill and Cecily Roach scuttling away from it all. He saw Stillworth run awkwardly to his creation and wheel the trolley towards the rear of the hall.

If Billy wanted to get his hands on that bomb it had to be now. He ran for the stairs, the Bastipols preceding him in a lithe scamper.

Together they thundered down the stairs and then turned left into the corridor and left again, and barrelled straight into the fleeing Crane. Billy flung himself at the man's splinted arms, breaking his hold on the trolley handle. While the contraption continued for a distance, Billy and Stillworth went down in a heap.

"Braid?" Stillworth's voice was a squeak of outrage. "Get off me, you feckless layabout. You're endangering the entire city."

Billy manoeuvred himself to sit across Stillworth's chest, pinning one of his arms with his knee. "And you're in too much of a hurry to show off your cleverness. I can't let you explode this until some of the ones that it endangers can get to a safe distance."

Stillworth sneered. "You mean your precious puppets?"

"Them, and a few others. Like the ones you used as slaves to enable you to build that bloody thing."

"The Turners?" Stillworth looked genuinely surprised at the mention of the cube. "It was *you*? Where is it? What did you do with it?"

Billy drew back his fist. "They're nowhere you'll ever find them." He put everything he had into the punch, and didn't see what Stillworth did until it was too late. At first he thought he was raising his free arm to defend himself, but then he heard the solid click of a mechanism, saw a blade extending from the wrist-strapping. Felt the punch of pain in his arm. He still connected with Stillworth's jaw, but the blow was now no more than a glancing one.

Billy bellowed and rolled away, clutching his forearm. His shirt sleeve was instantly wet and red but, although the pain was a burning spike of silver, it didn't seem to be gushing. He heard Stillworth laugh and start to get up. Then he heard a massed hiss and yowl, and the Constructor went down again under the clawing fury of the cats.

Billy got up and seized the trolley handle and shoved. The metal egg wasn't as heavy as he expected, but his arm still throbbed. He gritted his teeth and rolled the contraption away. They were close to the car compound entrance here, and that was undoubtedly where Stillworth had been heading. Which didn't make sense. Stillworth couldn't have been oblivious to the Exchange's lockdown... So, there must have been a plan. At the next junction Billy slowed down and peeked around the corner. Sure enough the outside door now stood ajar. When he nudged it open with his boot, he knew immediately that someone was waiting.

A figure huddled in the yellow fog. They were standing in front of what could only be a vehicle. Not a car, something larger that, in the billows, seemed to shift and drift. It took him a second to realise that it wasn't the fog that gave that effect. He was looking at a dirigible.

On hearing the door open, the vehicle's operator looked up. "You took your time. It's bloody desperate out here." Anya's muffled voice was thin and pained, as if her windpipe had been throttled. Then she saw him, and dragged her makeshift mask off. "*Billy?*"

"You were expecting someone else with a bomb?"

Her face twisted. "You know what it's like down there. They're all *dying*. Someone had to do something."

"How long have you been working with him? Does he know who you are?"

"No." She peered through the open door behind him, then shook her head. "No, he doesn't. That's why I needed Giteau's deputy. After boasting about his bloody bomb, Stillworth was in no hurry to use it. So I had to present him with a reason that would appeal to his starved ego. A way of making himself a hero in the eyes of the lowtowners. Even then he needed to go before the families and have it formally ratified to make sure that everyone bloody knew. And even after *all that*, he didn't have a clue what he was going to do with it. But it has to be the clouds. It all starts and ends with the clouds. So I told him I could get him a dirigible." It was weird to see her inside someone else's skin now she had dropped the character of Anya, but the longer the conversation went on, the more of Para's personality he saw. She looked over his shoulder again, nervous. "He's not with you, is he?"

Billy shook his head. "The dirigible is a great idea, we can get it right away from here, out of anyone's reach."

"What are you talking about? We have to destroy the motes in those clouds. People are…"

"I know, dying. But not immediately. They have a little more time, thanks to the sylvans. And because of that I want to allow my friends time to get out of here before we use the bomb. Them…" he swallowed "…and the Turners."

She didn't reply to that but he saw the tell-tale pucker of anger between her eyebrows. All she said was, "Help me get it in the basket."

"Para…"

"No time, Billy. For whatever reason, we need to get it out of here. We can argue about what to do with it once we have it up in the air."

Of course she was right. She always was. He could sense the weather's intelligence. The temperature of its vengeful mood had shifted from determined murder to building fury. Something was coming, something bent on absolute destruction. Even now, the fog in this little square was thickening again and the clouds directly above had become heavy and black. He could feel the prickle of static in the air, the familiar smell of an incipient storm.

"All right," he said.

The trolley proved too large for the door frame, so they had to lift the bomb off its cradle. Even then, it barely squeezed through. The device itself was awkward to carry, slick under their sweaty hands. Twice they nearly dropped it before they got it as far the dirigible's basket. The balloon swayed and nosed above them, the mooring rope straining against its cleat like a horse eager to escape a burning barn.

"You're bleeding," she noticed, climbing inside while he took the weight.

"Stillworth had a surprise up his sleeve," Billy grunted, bracing the bomb against his chest and feeling power vibrating through the casing. "This has already been wound up," he panted, rolling the device over the basket's rim and helping Para lower it to the floor. When he let go of the dirigible it rode closer to the ground than before. He hoped that it would fly.

Finishing her preparations in the tiny space permitted by her bulky cargo, Para looked up, but it was another voice that replied. One laden with gleeful sarcasm. "Oh, indeed, it's all ready to blow." If Stillworth Crane felt pain from the many lacerations that had been inflicted on his face, he didn't show it. If anything his smile was breezy. "And thank you for doing all the hard work, Mister Braid – credit where it is due, after all – but I believe we can take it from here." Stillworth hardly even seemed to be limping as he crossed the courtyard to join them. Billy hadn't given him much of a chance with the Bastipols and he actually found that he was quite impressed at his resilience. Then Innocent and Erudite Bello appeared in the doorway, with blood on their shoes and trouser cuffs, and the Constructor's survival made sense.

They grinned, as ever, in tandem.

"So he's not dead after all," said Innocent as they came over.

"Such a pity," Erudite leaned close to Billy's face, "but at least we can look forward to killing him all over again."

Stillworth leaned into the dirigible. "Are you ready to take this thing up?" he said, inclining his head.

Para followed his gaze into the churning cloudmass. "Me, sir?" The response gritty, businesslike. All Anya.

"Yes, *you*. You offered…"

But his tone, the assumption that he outranked her, broke her pretence. Her next words were pure Para. "I offered, *Stillworth Crane*, to procure you a dirigible so that you could explode this abhorrent creation in the place that it would have maximum effect. I did not offer to fly it for you."

Stillworth flinched as if she had slapped him, but he couldn't quite make his eyes believe his ears. "Well, here's the thing," he said. "Someone has to."

"Don't…" Billy began but that single word was all that made it out of his mouth before Erudite rabbit punched him and the breath was ejected from his lungs.

"See, this bomb is ready." Stillworth patted the casing. Then in a single fluid movement he swept open a hidden flap and did something internally. Immediately, there was an audible whine. "And now it is arming itself to detonate. Ideally, what has to happen over the next few minutes is that you fly it right up into the heart of the clouds until that whine becomes almost unbearable, then tip it over the side and get to safety. I warn you that the wings will engage fifteen seconds before detonation, so you're going to have to time it just right… but I'm sure even a person of your meagre achievements can manage it. Just think of the glory when you return."

"If I return." Para glowered at him. "You're sure you don't want the glory for yourself. It seems only fitting. It is your bomb after all, and the dirigible really is very easy to fly."

"Oh, I would." There was something in Stillworth's eyes that said that he *knew* he was talking to Para. "But I'm not nearly so expendable. If I were you I'd hurry."

Innocent shoved Billy towards the basket. "Stick him in there too," he can give her a hand.

Stillworth shook his head. "And risk our noble Mister Braid heroically crashing the whole thing into the sea to save his wooden toys? I hardly think so." With a flick, the blade extended from his wrist brace again. When he tried to use it, a swirling gust of angry wind whipped out of nowhere, yanking the dirigible to the side, dragging the basket with it and pulling the mooring rope tight.

"Billy?" In times of stress Para's face had always been unreadable, but he understood her now. Innocent was closest, so he punched him first. It landed true on the side of his immaculate jaw and put him down with a look of beatific surprise on his face. Billy landed another blow before turning to meet the oncoming inevitability of his brother. And he was far too slow. Erudite smacked him about the ear so hard his vision blurred and his knees went, and in the next instant the dapper oaf was on top of him, spittle flying as he snarled words that were snatched away by the now howling wind. Billy managed to get a hand up to his face to defend himself from further blows. He used it to try and push his assailant away from him, and then the other one regained his feet and joined in. Somewhere he heard Para, shouting but there was nothing he could do to help her. Not under the weight of both of the brothers.

The wind had risen to a shriek now. Even at the bottom of the pile, it found ways to buffet him almost as hard as the Bellos' blows. Within it, he heard Para's voice again, and then another joined it. A full throated scream, the wildest sound he had ever heard made by a human throat. Whoever was making it threw themselves on top of the Bellos. Billy couldn't breathe. He was going to pass out.

And then the weight was lifted. All of it.

He raised his head to see the oddest tableau. The Bellos were kneeling on the ground side by side. Sister Skin stood behind them and had them both in a headlock. The muscles on her forearms strained like hawsers. Her expression was filled with such fury that Billy knew that the Sisters must have found what remained of the Bastipols. The brothers struggled, but Skin was implacable. From behind them came Sin. Kim's old coat hung off her, dragged on the ground and billowed in the wind so that Billy worried she might get blown away, but she had enough presence left to stand in front of the pair. To lay a hand on each captive head and grab a fistful of hair, and speak soft words that first widened the brothers' eyes, then made them wrench their heads around to look at each other with mounting and utter hatred. Sin stopped speaking and stepped away, and the instant that Skin released them the pair flew at each other in a swinging, kicking, screaming rage.

"What did you do to them?" Billy shouted, getting painfully to his feet.

"Nothing that wasn't already in their minds." Skin reached down to pull him up. "They won't stop until one of them is dead. They're well matched, so probably both."

"Billy!"

This time he made out Para's words. He turned to help her out of the basket, but all he saw was Stillworth Crane, staring upwards with a victorious smile. The basket was twenty feet above their heads, the unsevered rope dangling down, swinging the cleat that had moored it. Para leant over the rim, calmly winding the rope with as unhurried and practised a motion as undoubtedly she had yanked the cleat out of the ground.

"No," he shouted back. "You don't have to…"

But she was grinning. "Anonymous service is admirable, but it's not my style. Tell them it was me. Make sure everybody knows that Paraphernalia Loess saved Karpentine."

And then she was too high to be heard any more. Billy watched the dirigible bounce and swerve and then, purposefully nose around and up in a wide, ever-rising spiral. "And killed the rest," he said, under his breath.

"Paraphernalia…?" Stillworth had lost his smile. "But *I* built the bomb. It was *me*. The achievement is *mine*."

"On the subject of undeserved acclaim." Sin and Skin stood on either side of him now. "There are some people who have a grievance with you."

Sin embraced the Constructors' heir for a few seconds, and when she released him the body of Stillworth Crane collapsed to the ground. The expression on its face was quite empty.

Sin herself looked to on the verge of collapse. Billy and Skin reached her at the same time. "We might have a chance," said Billy. "If we can bury ourselves beneath a mountain."

"Or the closest thing at hand," Skin growled.

They were making a nest out of the Papermakers' colossal rolls of newsprint when they felt the concussion. They dived inside and threw themselves on top of Sin, and were still lying that way when they felt the strangeness, like a wave of death, rippling through them.

They didn't move from their refuge until the first of the flood waters came gushing down the ramp.

THIRTY

It rained, and it rained, and it rained. Not in droplets, but in sheets. Then in an endless outpouring that did not slacken or stint. Not on that first day. Not in that first week. Not in the months that came after. The sky was all cloud. The world was rain.

The water sluiced down the High Town gutters, made rivers of the lowtown streets. Within a week, a lake had formed around the Exchange. Within two, the sea had broached the harbour. After the first month, much of the lowtown was uninhabitable. And still it rained.

The fog dispersed immediately, but the first thing Billy and Skin did was move uphill anyway. Billy led the way while Skin carried her sister on her back. In the weeks to come, many more citizens would follow them, those that survived, but on that first day it was just them, bent under the force of the downpour. If there was any vindictiveness in the assault, he couldn't detect it. But he was unsure if that was because there was no longer any motal awareness in the weather… or in himself.

They went to the Weathermakers' tower and found the complex deserted, so tainted was the Loess family name. The only residents of the place were a cadre of transformed sylvans that for some reason had settled and grown tall in a ring around the tower. It reminded Billy of the buildings the Turners had made.

And just as he was unable to detect awareness in the clouds, the same was true of the sylvans. They seemed to grow well enough, but they could as easily have just been trees. As for the Turners, Billy sat with Sin often, held her hand and talked to her, but he never once felt a glimmer from the people that lived in the box that was inside her.

For Sin's part, she breathed. She swallowed a little water or food when helped to do so, and sometimes she whispered nonsense to herself, but there was no indication that she was aware of her companions, and that made Skin sick with anxiety. So Billy took it on himself to be the one that foraged for food. In the mountains they preserved fruits and cured meat so they would not go hungry in the winter. Here in the Sunshine City, they had always had so much plenty that even the lowest had fresh bread to eat every day. Now the flour in the stores lay ruined. For almost a week he managed to line up and take a ration from the mess at the Weathermakers' mansion before someone recognised him. After that he was reduced to taking what he could find. Whether that would be called stealing seemed a moot point.

Often his sodden excursions took him into the lowtown and on his first visit he found the Institute square under two feet of water. He looked for the old man everywhere he went, without success. During the early weeks, before the harbour was gone, he sometimes saw the dark outlines of boats out on the sea, heading away from Karpentine. Taking their chances that they would reach somewhere more hospitable before their supplies ran out. After all of the boats had departed, he mostly hoped that Kim had been on one. That he found somewhere else to be than here.

Billy didn't ever look for Anya's face. When he thought about her it was as Para. And on those occasions he imagined that she had somehow escaped the blast and landed the dirigible somewhere outside this flooded nightmare of a city. He made himself see her walking off to somewhere where it wasn't too late for her vivacity and kindness. Pretty childish thoughts, but without them he would have been unable to leave the tower every morning.

By the third month the waters had rendered Karpentine an island. From the tower Billy saw the waves lapping at the doors of the Exchange. The lowtown tenements, the Institute of Improvement, all of that, gone. The city's survivors now crammed into the High Town and squabbled over whose achievement outranked whose for the right to eat and stay dry and live a little longer as they all, whether they knew it or not, waited for what would come next.

The trees around the tower burst into blossom. Flowers of pale pink and peach that were ripped off their stems by the rain, petals littering the cobbles. They left behind buds that swelled quickly into velvety pods the size of Billy's fist. Every day he stroked them reverentially. He became so fixated on the fruits that, at first, he didn't notice what was happening to the trees themselves. On the first day that he twigged, he thought he was imagining it. On the second day, however, there was no question. They had reached taller up the tower... now they were shrinking, drawing in on themselves. When he went out on the morning of the third day, they had clenched down into fists, dense knots of wood.

Scattered across the cobbles were the pods, many split open to reveal what they contained. Billy collected as many as he could find.

"What are these? Skin looked thin now. As did Billy. They'd been giving most of the food to her sister.

"Seeds," he replied. "Sylvan seeds."

She picked one up, turned the hard sphere in her hand. In the grey rain light, Billy observed the reluctant admiration in her face. The swirling patterns, the deep burnish. It was like something a master craftsman would make.

"It's time, isn't it?" She was crying.

Billy nodded, and then he went down and waded out to the sheds.

He had been building the boat from almost the first days of the flood. On one of his early trips he had found a sylvan tree that had succumbed to the fog's scum. Before it died, it had grown a straight, stout trunk. He and Skin had lopped it down, dragged it up to the tower and lifted it off the ground to dry out. Stripping off the poisoned bark, Billy had discovered that the rest of the wood was in fine condition, so he notched out the heart with tools he found in the sheds. He had steamed and smoothed and shaped the log into a dugout. And then he had dressed and seasoned it until it was as seaworthy as he could make it. He made paddles too. The boat was a far cry from artisanship, but it was the best thing his hands had ever made.

They waited until just before dawn so that they could carry everything down to the small natural harbour that had been the Exchange plaza unhindered. They laid Sin in the boat first, and then the few other things they had brought. Only once Skin had settled herself to row did Billy jump in too.

And that was how they left Karpentine.

"Where shall we go?" Even starved as she was, Skin's stroke was strong and even.

Billy stopped bailing the rain water and looked out across the sea. "There's only one place we can go." He reached into the bag at his feet and pulled out a sylvan seed. He enjoyed it, for its beauty now and for the potential of what it could become, perhaps, when the waters receded, and then dropped it overboard. "Onward."

Skin nodded and kept on rowing. Billy nodded and kept on bailing. Every now and then he would stop and drop another seed. They rowed until the bag of seeds was empty and Skin and Billy both could no longer lift their arms.

"You think this is far enough?" the sister asked.

Billy looked over the side of the dugout. "I think it is deep enough."

333

"Very well then." Skin tossed her paddles overboard. "We have arrived."

Billy nodded back and dropped his bucket into the water. It sank instantly.

He helped Skin lie down on the floor of the boat beside Sin. There was already an inch of water in there and, now Billy had stopped emptying out the rain, it was rising quickly. When she was settled, he lay down with her, and then he took the rope that ran under the boat over the top of the three of them and knotted it hard. After that it was just a case of waiting till the boat filled full enough of rain that it sank, and they all went down to the bottom of the sea. It wouldn't take long.

Someone slipped their hand into his.

Someone whispered.

Come.

A blue sky.

A rolling land of wild grasses.

A woven city.

Sin and Skin and himself, lying naked in the grass. Stretched out, all of their brown skins warming in the sun.

"All of us are grateful." The straw man stood over him. The hand he extended to help Billy up was dewy and smelled faintly of manure. "Most won't tell you that in case it makes you think you are special. No one is special here. We're all equal."

"Except one." The cobweb woman was hugging the Sisters. "For now."

"Aye, except one."

And then they were inside the city, in a neglected corner that the sun did not touch. Here the city's weave was coarse and it formed a space roughly the shape of a cube. Inside the dark space was a blob of deeper darkness, a bloated, glistening thing.

"Who's there," the thing said in a familiar voice. "I demand to know who's there. What have you done to me?"

As Billy and the straw man watched, a rippling skein of spiders slipped out of the shadows. They nipped and teased at the thing of darkness, and in response it screamed.

"He does that a lot." They had rejoined the cobweb woman and the Sisters, but now they were in a vast woven hall so intricate that Billy couldn't take it all in.

"Stillworth?" he whispered. "How long will you keep him like that?"

The straw man shrugged. "Until he has given back what he took. He is a resource, as we all are. And in our world resources are shared equally." There were spiders on the floor, a carpet of them. They swarmed around the cobweb woman and up the Sisters' legs.

"What's to become of us?" Billy said.

And the straw man's laugh was like the wind in the wheat fields of the Canza valley. "Anything you can dream of."

Skin changed first. Transformation was her skill, after all. As the spiders receded from her, she stretched as if she'd woken from a long comfortable sleep. And as she stretched, she flowed, and where there had been a naked woman, there was now a beast. The cat was a patchwork of fur tufts and hedge wool, but it had bright eyes and a twitch of mischief in its ears.

The form Sin took was of a bird. It was a motley thing, as if assembled from the discarded feathers Billy used to find in the forest litter. The feathers were dove white, gull grey, raven black. They were spotted like a thrush's, striped like a falcon's. All together they were indescribable. As soon as her transformation was complete, Sin beat her wings and flew high into the hall's rafters.

Then the spiders came to Billy. "I don't want to change," he told the straw man.

"No one is asking you to. Just be what you are."

The wave of spiders tickled up his legs, swarmed up his torso. Their bites were painful, but only at first. Billy didn't make any kind of conscious choice but he knew he had changed nevertheless. He brought his hand up to his face, flexed the fingers. They were exquisitely turned and jointed. The staining and polishing, a work of art.

Billy lifted his heavy head and regarded the straw man through eyes of pebble glass.

"How can I help?" he said.

335

ABOUT THE AUTHOR

Neil wrote *Queen of Clouds* as a thematic prequel to his previous novel, *The Moon King*, which was shortlisted for British Science Fiction Association and British Fantasy awards.

His short fiction has been nominated for the BSFA and British Fantasy awards and, with Andrew J Wilson, he edited *Nova Scotia: New Scottish Speculative Fiction*, which was nominated for the World Fantasy Award.

Neil lives and works in Glasgow, Scotland. Find out more at: neilwilliamson.blog.

Lightning Source UK Ltd.
Milton Keynes UK
UKHW011138020322
399453UK00002B/82